MW00528049

Dangerous to Know & Love

To Renee,

with love from Wilson.

Jane Harvey-Berrick

Jane Harvey-Berrick

♡
2.5.15

HARVEY
BERRICK
PUBLISHING

First published in Great Britain in 2013
ISBN 9780957496163

Harvey Berrick Publishing
www.janeharveyberrick.com

Cover design by Hang Le / byhangle.com
Cover photograph by Yuriy Zhuravov, with permission from
Shutterstock

Permission for *Fall At Your Feet* by Neil Finn (Meniscus Media)

DEDICATION

**This book is dedicated to the special women in my
life, friends without measure**
Lisa, Kirsten, Ana, Dorota, Libby, Nicky and Judith.

ACKNOWLEDGMENTS

This story was inspired by my father who had his own battle with hearing loss. But there are many other people who've been with me on this journey, too. So I'd like to thank all these lovely people...

Special thanks to Jane Goodfellow who checked all the details on cochlear implants and for her wonderful blog deafbecomesher.blogspot.co.uk; Brett Robertson, General Manager at the Ear Science Institute, Australia; Ear Sciences Centre, School of Surgery, University of Western Australia; Gemma Upson, Manager, Cochlear Implant Centre; Benjamin Von Schuch, Attorney, for explaining the Georgia speeding laws.

The Book Bloggers
Smitten's Book Blog; Totally Booked—Jenny, Gitte and Trish; Rose, The Book List Reviews; Angie, The Smut Club; Lindsay, Madison Says; Lisa, The Indie Bookshelf; Emily and the Girls, The Sub Club Books; Lori's Book Blog; Crystal's Random Thoughts; Marie, Book Crush; Bookish Temptations; CBL Book Reviews; Fifty Shades of Tribute; Liezel's Book Blog; Live Love Laugh & Read; Once Upon a Twilight; Read This—Hear That; Read-Love-Blog; Romantic Book Affairs; Scandaliciious Book Reviews; Selena Lost in Thought; The Autumn Review; The Book Hookers; The Boyfriend Bookmark; The Drunken Pervy Creepers; The Forbidden Book Affair; Twilight—the Missing Pieces (PA Lassiter); Waves of Fiction.

The Readers
RRR—where it all started (you know who you are); FanFiction; FB friends; Goodreads; readers of *The Education of* series Lara Davis Mattox; Laura McCarthy Benson (even though she was moving house and state at the time); Kirsty Lander; Kirsten Papajik (honey, your name just pops up everywhere in my thanks—you know why); Trina Miciotta. And to Fred LeBaron, for your kind and patient ways of answering all questions.

The Advance Readers
Who are important in soothing our nerves and telling us, 'it'll be all right!'
Vikki; Lise *the deleted gif gal*; Becka; It's just me Shelly B; KatLynne; Baba; April; Jen; Elizabeth; Sleepy; Reese Call (research queen); Wendy LeGrand; Audrey Orielle (bonkers in a good way); Dina Fardon Eidinger (for instituting Sebastian Sunday and excellent research on pictures of hot guys); Dorota Wrobel and pB (always wild, always wonderful); Cori Pitts (whose name I shamelessly stole) and her mum Shirley Wilkinson; Christopher Lindsay (so strong); Sasha Cameron (a friend I've never met); Ana Alfano (whose scary brightness is matched only by her wonderfully bizarre humour); Ellen Totten (always a lady); Jacqueline Tria (for helping me make the dialogue hip, daddy-o); and a special thank you to Lara (again).

And More...
Rebecca Slater for legal support; Phyllis Davies for proofreading; front cover graphic artist, Hang Le; additional graphic art, Sarah Hansen, Okay Creation.

Thank you all.
jhb x

PROLOGUE

Beneath his window cars were driving, bikes pedaling, people jogging, dogs walking—the world passing by. Each activity with its own unique set of actions, an orchestra of noises: tires, brakes, talking, barking. None of the sounds penetrated.

He felt a presence behind, and turned to see his brother's concerned eyes watching him.

"Today's the day, College Boy."

Daniel grinned and shrugged. "I guess."

Zef held out his hand and they shook quickly, before he pulled Daniel into a tight hug.

"I'm proud of you, bro," he whispered. "Mom and Dad would have been proud, too."

Then he pulled away and thumped his brother on the shoulder.

"Don't fuck up."

Daniel grinned.

"Not making any promises."

CHAPTER 1

When Lisanne stumbled into the lecture hall with Kirsty clinging to her arm, there were already a number of students spread out across the room. It was too early in the semester for many cliques to have been formed, but a few girls were sitting in groups for comfort, giggling nervously. The boys were too cool for that, and sat in glorious isolation.

Lisanne cast an eye over the assorted examples of humanity. Most looked average, like her, dressed in jeans and t-shirts, but there was one guy who was wearing a button down shirt and a tie. Good grief! Lisanne made a bet with herself that he had a copy of the *Wall Street Journal* in his backpack. She was only surprised he wasn't carrying a briefcase. Why on earth had she agreed to take 'Introduction to Business 101'? Oh yeah, because her parents didn't think majoring in music was going to lead to any great career opportunities.

The response from her new roommate had been to look on the bright side.

"That sucks," said Kirsty. "But, you never know, you might meet some cute guy who'll turn out to be the next Mark Zuckerberg."

"What, short, with bad taste in clothes?"

Kirsty laughed. "No, dummy: brilliant and filthy rich!"

Lisanne sighed.

"Hey, Lis! Get your head in the game!"

Her head snapped up, away from Mr. Big Time, then her expression cleared as Kirsty winked at her and kicked off her shoes.

"I'm surprised you can even walk in those—oh right, you can't."

Kirsty raised her eyebrows.

"Hello! They're Manolos! They're meant to be seen—not walked in."

"Of course. Silly me."

Kirsty sniggered. "Yeah, whatever. Okay, seriously—which of these guys would you hook up with?" and her arms swept out to indicate everyone in the lecture hall.

Lisanne laughed. "None of them for *any* of *that*."

"No? You don't think the guy with the red t-shirt is cute?"

Lisanne craned her neck. "He's okay, I guess. Not really my type."

"What *is* your type?" asked Kirsty, curiously. *All cute guys were Kirsty's type.*

Lisanne shrugged. The truth was, she hadn't dated much in high school. Okay, make that *never*, unless she counted her junior prom and the non-date fiasco. How a non-date could be a complete disaster remained a mystery to her, but it had been one of the worst, most humiliating nights of her life, involving vomit—someone else's—and ... no, she didn't want to think about that. It definitely didn't count.

"Come on, Lis," said Kirsty, encouragingly. "What about that guy you were chatting with on Facebook last night?"

"Rodney? No, he's just a friend from high school."

"So he's not...?"

"Ugh, no! I've known him since kindergarten—that would just be ... weird."

"So you're available?"

Lisanne was *very* available. She just hadn't seen anyone she liked that way.

"Well, tell me what you're looking for—in case, you know."

"Oh, I don't know: somebody *different*. Somebody..."

"Like *him*?" said Kirsty, nodding her head at the guy who'd just walked in.

He was *different* all right. In fact, Lisanne was pretty sure that

3

he'd wandered into the wrong classroom by mistake. No way someone like *him* was taking the Introduction to Business class.

All eyes, male and female, swiveled in his direction as he sauntered into the lecture hall looking like he owned it. He slumped into a seat in the second row, oozing arrogance, pulling off his Ray Bans as he did so. He was tall and slim with short, spiky black hair. He shrugged out of his leather jacket, and even from that distance Lisanne could see that he had a broad back and strong, muscular arms with swirls of red, gold and black tattoos drifting down them. He turned to scan the hall behind him, and Lisanne couldn't help noticing a small silver ring piercing his left eyebrow.

Without speaking to a soul or making eye contact with anyone, he tossed his jacket onto one seat and his backpack onto the other side. Surely there was a law that all the cool kids sat in the back row? But no, not him.

Lisanne felt her eyebrows pull together in a frown.

"Ugh, no, I can't stand guys like that," she said. "All emo, and thinking they're better than everyone else."

"Yeah, but he's *cute*," said Kirsty, licking her lips. "That boy is fine. I'm going to find out who he is."

"Definitely not my type," said Lisanne, with a note of finality.

Professor Walden marched into the room and immediately the light chatter quieted, and everyone started pulling out paper and laptops, ready to take notes. Everyone except the guy with the eyebrow ring. He didn't move. He didn't even get out a notepad to doodle on.

Lisanne felt unreasonably irritated with him. Her parents had paid good money for her to attend college, and losers like that guy were just there for the ride. Lisanne couldn't stand people like that—people who were fake.

She realized that she'd already spent entirely too much time staring at 'Eyebrow Ring guy' and that the lecture had started.

But every now and then, her eyes were drawn back to him. She'd half expected him to fall asleep, or play with his iPod, but his eyes were trained on Professor Walden, hardly blinking during the entire 50 minutes. It was weird. Maybe he was stoned? Even though it was only nine o'clock in the morning, it seemed the most likely answer.

At the end of the lecture, Mr. Big Time asked several questions, and even pulled out his copy of the *Wall Street Journal* to illustrate his point. Lisanne gave herself an internal fist pump: she prided herself on reading people well.

As the lecture hall started emptying, she couldn't help noticing that Eyebrow Ring guy didn't speak to anyone, still not making eye contact with any of the people who shared his class. And he was wearing his sunglasses again. Indoors. What a jerk.

But she had to admit that Kirsty was right about one thing: he was a *cute* jerk. His hair was so black it was almost blue, and his clear skin carried a golden tan. From what she'd seen of his eyes, they were a light hazel color, framed by long lashes over perfect cheekbones and full, kissable lips. *Kissable?* Where was the real Lisanne Maclaine, and who the hell was having these thoughts?

With a huff, aimed at the unfairness of the world where beautiful people could get away with being jerks, Lisanne went straight to the practice rooms for her one-on-one with her violin professor.

As she hurried across the quad, she couldn't help wondering why such a beautiful boy would want to desecrate what God had given him by covering his body with tattoos, and pushing a piece of metal through his eyebrow. True, she had pierced ears, but that was different. Obviously. She didn't really get why the girls at school were so into tatted up guys. Lisanne just didn't see the point, and she certainly had no intention of getting one herself. It was only going to look weird when she was forty.

She sighed, wondering why she'd been born so damn sensible.

The morning went quickly after that, and Lisanne forgot all about Eyebrow Ring guy. Her violin tutor, Professor Crawford, turned out to be amazing, and Lisanne thought they'd really hit it off. He'd given her some tips on how she could improve her bowing, and it had helped immediately. So she was in a good mood when she bumped into Kirsty again in the cafeteria.

"Hey roomy!" came the loud voice. "Sit your ass over here."

Kirsty was slumped in her seat at a table with three girls Lisanne didn't know. She was amused to see that Kirsty's feet were bare and propped up on the seat next to her.

"What happened to the Manolos?" Lisanne asked, with a knowing smile.

"Let's just say I'll save them for an evening out where I'm going by limousine," snorted Kirsty.

Lisanne raised an eyebrow. "I was impressed you even tried to wear them. I'd have broken my neck."

Kirsty laughed loudly, and several guys glanced her way, checking her out. From the looks on their faces, they obviously approved. Well, there wasn't anything to disapprove: Kirsty had wheat colored hair that curled in ringlets almost to her waist, with perfect curves, a pixie doll face and huge blue eyes. If she'd been taller, she could have been a model.

Lisanne was plain by comparison although, to be fair, most girls were when compared to Kirsty. Her own face was too square, her jaw too heavy, gray eyes ordinary, straight brown hair featureless, and even though her figure was decent, it was nothing special. Nothing special at all.

Part of Lisanne, the bitchy part that she wasn't very proud of, would have really liked to dislike Kirsty—but the girl was just too damn *nice*. Ugh.

Kirsty introduced her to the other girls at the table: Trudy, Shawna and Holly. They were all fashion majors like Kirsty. Not that Lisanne would have needed the introduction to figure that out—their clothes screamed 'designer' from half a mile.

"How were your other classes this morning?" said Kirsty.

"Yeah, pretty good. My violin professor is awesome."

"Violin?" sneered Shawna. "That sounds majorly lame."

Kirsty laughed, but said briskly, "Not the way Lisanne plays it." She smiled and winked at her roommate, but then her attention was distracted and her eyes flicked across the room.

"Check out Mr. Tall Dark and Deliciously Dangerous!" said Shawna, licking her lips, as she followed the direction of Kirsty's gaze.

Lisanne saw Eyebrow Ring guy making his way through the cafeteria. He was still wearing his sunglasses. He was still alone.

"Oh, him," she snorted. "He's in our Introduction to Business class. He's a real jerk."

Even as she said the words, they felt awkward in her mouth. Rationally, she knew he hadn't done anything specifically to annoy her. It was just the way he'd sat there, without taking any notes, like he was above it all.

Shawna smiled in a superior way. "For your information, his name's Daniel Colton. He's a local, and he's got a rep—that's what I heard."

"What sort of rep?" said Kirsty, eagerly.

"He's gotten into two fights already this week," said Shawna, pleased to be the one to deliver the news. "Went postal on some grad student for no reason." Then she dropped her voice. "They say he's the go-to guy if you want anything extracurricular. You know, weed, booze, coke, speed—the guy's got it. I wouldn't mind spending some extracurricular time with him, if you know what I mean. I heard he's a freak between the sheets."

Lisanne's lips curled down in disgust, and not just at the glazed expression on Shawna's face. How on earth could that guy get away with being so blatant as to sell drugs on campus? It fit in with her low opinion of him, which had taken a further nosedive. But then again, if people knew about him in the first week, it wouldn't be long before the college authorities heard about it, too. In all likelihood, he wouldn't even make it to the end of the first semester.

"He's certainly got the bad boy vibe going for him," agreed Kirsty.

"Mmmhmm," murmured Shawna. "Hot, definitely hot."

"Mad, bad and dangerous to know," said Kirsty, smiling. "What do you think, Lisanne? Got a thing for bad boys?"

Lisanne shook her head so hard she could have sworn her brain rattled.

Kirsty laughed, and started to talk about plans for the weekend.

Irritated with herself, Lisanne put all thoughts of Eyebrow Ring guy out of her head. Some people just didn't know their luck.

Lisanne's first week away from home had been hard, to say the least. She missed her family. She missed being able to talk to her mom, who was also her best friend. Sure, they talked on the phone every night, but it wasn't the same. She missed her dad's bad jokes and his strong, quiet presence—the feeling that whatever problem she had, he'd sort it out. Lisanne even missed her little brother Harry who, at 13, was not so little, and a real pain in the butt. Still, she missed them all.

And college was so different. For a start, she was sharing a room for the first time in her life, which meant there was little privacy, even though Kirsty turned out to be pretty nice. *There was that word again.* She had to get used to the communal bathrooms, and wearing flip-flops in the shower, irritated that she'd have to wait until her sophomore year for the women's dorms to be renovated with private bathrooms. She missed being able to cook for herself, and instead having to eat all of her meals in the cafeteria. And the amount of work her professors were piling on had been overwhelming. She felt a little panicky when she realized how heavy her schedule was going to be, and the fact that, by the end of week one, she was already behind in two classes—especially business, which could have been in Ancient Greek for all she'd understood of it.

But it was Friday night, and Kirsty persuaded her to go downtown for a pizza with some of the girls. Despite the fact that Shawna was there, it was more fun than Lisanne had expected. They spent Saturday morning studying and in the afternoon hit the outlets and, at Kirsty's insistence, Lisanne spent more than she ought to on a new pair of jeans to wear clubbing that night.

By Sunday, Lisanne was so worried about her homework that she was determined to spend the afternoon and evening at the library. *Jeez, how sad was that?*

Not surprisingly, the library was almost empty, the main study area echoing loudly as she scraped her chair along the floor. Three guys who appeared to be pre-med seniors, hunched over anatomy textbooks, threw her irritated looks, surprised by her intrusion, and a couple of people wandered aimlessly through the stacks. She turned off her iPod with a sigh, letting the last notes of Love and Theft's *Runnin' out of Air* die away, then Lisanne's surprised eyes fell on the last person she expected to see in a library, let alone on a weekend—Eyebrow Ring guy.

He was sitting at a table by himself, with his business studies textbook propped open in front of him. Every now and then he'd type some notes into his laptop.

Lisanne flopped down at a table that just happened to have him in view. She'd decided he was most likely there to meet one of his druggie contacts, and if he was, she'd tell the on duty librarian. Probably. Maybe.

But she found herself mesmerized as his long fingers intermittently swept through his hair, or tugged at his eyebrow ring.

After half an hour, she had to admit that he was doing nothing more sinister than studying, even though he seemed the type of guy who would be recovering from partying hard on a Saturday night. Eventually, she turned her eyes to her own pile of homework, that hadn't lessened during her 30 minutes of mindless gawking.

After nearly four hours of actual studying, Lisanne's eyes felt tired and gritty—as if the pages of her books had been covered with sandpaper as she'd read them, and she wanted nothing more than to go back to her room and sleep. She really hoped Kirsty wasn't going to come back hyper and noisy, although the odds were against her. She rubbed her face and looked up— straight into the hazel eyes of Eyebrow Ring guy.

She expected him to glance away, but he didn't. He held her gaze, his face impassive. Much to her annoyance, Lisanne felt her skin heating with a blush. *No, no, no! Not in front of him!*

But her blush was badly behaved and didn't pay any attention to her whatsoever.

She was saved by the librarian, who announced that the library was closing. By the time Lisanne looked back, Eyebrow Ring guy had already shoved his laptop and books into a black canvas messenger bag, and was on his way out.

Hastily, Lisanne grabbed her books and hurried after him, telling herself she didn't want to be alone in the creepy old building. He was twenty feet ahead of her when Lisanne tripped over the library's threshold, and went sprawling across the cold steps.

She cried out as she grazed her hands and landed painfully on her knees. Eyebrow Ring guy didn't even break pace, let alone turn around to help her. Although he must have heard her yell, he ignored her completely, striding off into the darkness.

Hurt and humiliated, Lisanne gathered her books, quietly cursing the black haired boy who had distracted her so disastrously.

The next morning, Lisanne crawled out of bed far too early for someone who'd been woken, as predicted, at 1 AM. The palms of her hands were scraped raw and her knees were black and blue. But, worse than that, she felt bruised inside. How could he just ignore her when she'd hurt herself like that? Lisanne knew that *she* wouldn't let a stranger lie sprawled on the ground without trying to help. What kind of person behaved like that?

She *definitely* didn't want to find out.

"It's too early," moaned Kirsty. "And who the hell allows a construction crew to do roadwork on a Monday morning outside a dorm room?"

Lisanne glanced outside. Nope, no road crew. The pounding was all in Kirsty's head.

10

Lisanne rolled her eyes, but couldn't help a sympathetic smile slipping out as she watched her roommate nurse a grade-A hangover.

"You look like you had a good night?"

Kirsty pulled herself up to lean against the headboard, bunching the duvet around her.

"You should have been there, Lisanne, it was awesome. Our fake IDs were totally cool. Shawna was drinking tequila shots—she was a mess."

Lisanne couldn't help a small, superior smile, and Kirsty looked at her curiously.

"What did you do?"

"Not much. Studied."

Lisanne couldn't bring herself to tell Kirsty about her misadventure in the library, or rather, on the library steps. And she certainly wasn't going to mention Eyebrow Ring guy's part in it. Well, that was a giant non story anyway.

Kirsty groaned and Lisanne couldn't help wincing, too. She'd been drunk once, and she hadn't enjoyed the sensation. It had been at her cousin's wedding and it was not a feeling she wanted to remember. Ever. Especially the part where she'd vomited down the front of her new dress.

She grabbed a bottle of water from their tiny fridge, and placed it with two Advil on Kirsty's bedside table.

"You are a lifesaver," moaned Kirsty, her fingers scrabbling for the pills.

She looked up as Lisanne started to open the door.

"Where are you going?"

"Classes!" said Lisanne, raising her eyebrows.

"Okay, see you later? We're going Italian tonight."

"Um, no thanks. I've got some stuff to do," said Lisanne, evasively. "See you."

Kirsty moaned, and gave a small wave.

It didn't seem such a good idea, now Lisanne was standing outside the building. She bit her lip and checked the flyer again.

Yes, this was definitely the address, but it didn't look like the kind of place she wanted to enter without an armed guard. Scuzzy: that was the word. Rundown: that was another. Disreputable. Scary. A dive. Even standing outside, she could smell stale beer, and the sidewalk was littered with cigarette butts. At least it was broad daylight. Not that anyone inside would have known that fact—the windows on the street side had been painted black.

She felt slightly nauseous, and realized her palms were sweating as she rubbed them against her new jeans. This was a bad idea. She should go back to the dorms before she made an even bigger fool of herself.

Lisanne had just convinced herself to turn around and leave when the steel door swung open. The biggest man she had ever seen stared down at her. Jeez, he was enormous. He looked like he could have crushed her ribs with one hand if he wanted to. His head was either bald or shaved, and his arms and neck were entirely covered in tattoos.

He smiled at Lisanne, and she automatically took a pace backward.

"Hey, girly, you here for the audition?"

"Um, yes?" said Lisanne, hesitantly.

"Come on in, honey."

Lisanne wanted to say no. She wanted to turn and run, but somehow her feet wouldn't obey her body. The man was still staring at her, so she took a deep breath and stepped inside. She really wished she'd left a message with someone to say where she was going—so they'd know where to find her mangled corpse. Maybe her cell phone had satellite tracking. Maybe she should hide it somewhere in the club before...

"This way, honey."

Giganator led her into the bowels of the building, the dark walls saturated with the scent of sweat and hard liquor, or possibly liquor that had been sweated out from dancing, heaving bodies every weekend.

The lighting was dim, and no daylight had been permitted to

enter the crypt like web of rooms. Lisanne tried hard to tell herself that the staining on the floor couldn't possibly be blood.

Then she heard the echoing sound of someone laughing. It was such a happy, carefree laugh—not at all how she'd imagine a serial killer would sound. Unexpectedly, she felt her body relax.

Peering through the gloom, she saw a group of men standing on a small stage. As one, they turned to look at her, and the laughter died away.

"Another lamb to the slaughter," came a low voice, and several of them snickered quietly.

Lisanne swallowed, then straightened her shoulders and walked forward with a determined air, belied by the way her stomach rolled and lurched.

They watched her with amusement but despite their scary appearance, their behavior wasn't threatening. She ground to a halt when she saw one of them was Eyebrow Ring guy. Why did *he* have to be here to witness her further humiliation? He gazed back at her without recognition, and Lisanne felt ridiculous for thinking that he'd know her—or even remember her.

He was leaning against the piano, one foot propped up behind him, his knee bent, his stance relaxed and at ease. As Lisanne approached, he jumped down from the stage.

"I'm outta here—fucking auditions," he said, in a bored voice.

"Sure, Dan." One of the men spoke quietly. "Don't be a stranger," but Eyebrow Ring guy ignored him, pushed past her, and carried on walking, swinging a motorcycle helmet in one hand.

Lisanne felt incensed by his rude behavior. He was such a jerk.

Daniel was irritated with himself for going to the club. He knew it would just stir up a shit storm of memories, and he really didn't need the aggravation his brother would give him when he found out: but somehow he hadn't been able to stay away either. Even so, there was no way on earth he was going to hang around for another lame audition. He had his limits.

He'd been surprised when the latest victim had turned up. She didn't look anything like the kind of girl who would go to their club. He loved the place but he had to be honest: it was a shit awful pit. She looked too young, for a start, and too *fresh*.

But Daniel knew that appearances could deceive. He was all too well aware how people judged him the moment they saw him. The reactions were predictable. Mostly, he didn't care what people thought. No, that wasn't true. He didn't care what people thought about the way he *looked*. He knew that his tats, his piercings, the way he was dressed, gave people a giant fuck off message, and that suited him just fine. That shit was deliberate. He'd learned to be wary of people in general, and starting at the college was a big deal for him. He'd already had to lay out a couple of assholes, and Zef had given him hell when he'd come home with bruised knuckles two days running. Which was pretty fucking funny when you thought about it. Maybe 'ironic' was the word.

He was used to the way people reacted to him: girls checked him out, even some older chicks, which was cool; guys either avoided him or tried to prove that they were harder than he was. They rarely were. Most adults just pigeonholed him as a delinquent and passed by on the other side. His professors didn't seem bothered, for which Daniel was grateful: tats, piercings, weird clothes and hairstyles—they'd seen it all before. But Daniel wanted to avoid trouble as much as possible at college. Unfortunately, that looked like it was going to mean avoiding people, too.

He was aware that his so-called rep was already following him around. It infuriated him, but when you were Zef Colton's brother, there wasn't a lot you could do about a bad rep. Which was why he'd pounded on those two dickwads last week: they'd made the painful assumption that Daniel and his brother were the same—painful for them, anyway.

That girl had looked at him the way everyone else did: she checked him out but thought he was trash, too. Bitch.

It was only when he'd pushed past her on his way out of the club, and saw the flash of anger in her eyes, that he recognized her: Library Girl. He'd seen her there on Sunday evening. In fact, he was pretty certain that she'd been staring at him for at least 20 minutes. It had started to freak him out, and he'd just about decided to say something when she'd finally started concentrating on her own work, and he was able to relax.

She'd been reading the same business studies textbook as him, which meant they must share at least one class. But she'd also been surrounded by orchestral scores, which made her a music major.

What a fucking waste of time. Daniel didn't have any room in his world for people like her.

Despite his insistence that he had no interest in Library Girl whatsoever, he found himself wondering how her audition had gone. He couldn't imagine that she'd have what the guys were looking for, but he wasn't in a position to judge either. And that thought pissed him the hell off.

He'd text Roy later to find out.

Daniel would have liked to just go home and chill once he left the club, but Zef had told him to get lost for the whole evening, having some business to take care of at the house. Daniel was used to that and it didn't really bother him. Zef was pretty cool most of the time.

So instead of going home and to his books, Daniel rode to the campus fitness center. He parked his motorcycle, locked away the helmet, and strolled inside. Throwing some weights around and running ten miles on the treadmill would burn off some of his ever present nervous energy.

In the locker room, Daniel changed into sweat pants and a tank top, and carried his towel and a bottle of water into the weight room.

Two guys from the football team were already in there, but they ignored him and continued with their bench presses.

After nearly an hour, he headed to the training room where the treadmill, rowing machines, and fitness bikes were arranged

in rows. There was a small group of girls already there, all
wearing tiny boy shorts and crop tops. They eyed Daniel
hungrily, and he automatically checked them out. The one with
red hair was hot and *definitely* interested in him.

Daniel sighed and looked away. She wouldn't be interested if
she knew the real him. Besides, he preferred anonymous
hookups to coeds. It was easier.

He focused on the treadmill and began pounding away,
adding up the miles. He'd been in the zone for 25 minutes when
he felt someone touch his arm, and he jumped.

It was the redhead.

"Oh, wow, sorry!" she giggled. "I said 'hi' like three times!
You must have been really concentrating."

Daniel smiled awkwardly, slowing the machine and springing
down. "Yeah, something like that."

"So, I was wondering: do you want to get a coffee? My
friends have to go and I hate drinking coffee all alone."

Daniel was internally assessing how to answer.

"I have to be somewhere right now," he replied, thinking
quickly.

He found he didn't want to blow her off entirely, but he
needed time to think about how to play it.

"How about we meet up tomorrow night instead? The Blue
Note on West River Street, you know it? Bring your girlfriends."

"Um, isn't that place, like, dangerous?"

Daniel smiled.

"No, it's cool. My friend works there."

The girl's face brightened.

"Well, okay, that sounds great. I'm Terri."

"Daniel."

She giggled. "I know."

He frowned slightly, wondering if it wasn't him she wanted
to hook up with, but what his brother could offer. Well, if she
was after anything else, she'd be disappointed.

"So, um, Daniel, what time will I see you there?"

"I'll be there after 9 PM." *Your move, beautiful.*

"Cool! I'll see you there."

She walked away, her hips swaying, and Daniel licked his lips.

As a general rule he didn't date. Which wasn't to say he didn't have women, because that would be a fat ass lie. But maybe it was time to turn over a new leaf and try that dating shit. Maybe. It felt like he was taking a huge risk, what with everything he wanted to keep hidden. But this year was all about new beginnings. Right?

The relaxation he'd found during his workout evaporated as his uncertainty grew. Irritated with himself, he hit the showers and let the hot water heat his skin, calming him.

When he'd finished, he draped a towel around his slim waist and headed back to his locker.

"Hey, man."

Daniel eyed the two jocks warily, mentally assessing how much room he'd have to swing a punch if they started something. They weren't any taller than him, but they were both heavier by about 20 pounds.

The expression on Daniel's face had the jock backing up and raising his hands.

"Whoa, easy, man! I just, um, wanted to ask you something."

Daniel took a breath. "What?"

"Well, um, just wondering if, um … we heard girls really get off on that."

He gestured toward Daniel's chest.

"Some, yeah," said Daniel, holding back a smirk, knowing exactly what the guy was going to ask him next.

"Dude, it must have really hurt!" said the other jock.

Daniel shrugged. "It was worth it," and this time he couldn't help a huge grin slipping out.

The football players raised their eyebrows and grinned back.

"You get that done in town?"

"Sure. TJ's tattoo parlor will do it for you. They'll do any type of piercings."

The bigger guy went white, and Daniel wondered if he was going to faint.

"Seriously, dude?"

Daniel laughed. "Yeah, nipple rings are normal stuff for TJ's. They'll pierce pretty much anything if you ask them. Anywhere."

"Man, I gotta sit down," said the big guy, crashing onto one of the benches.

Daniel shook his head and smiled to himself. *Pussy.*

Pulling on clothes over his still damp body, Daniel checked his cell phone. Zef had texted the all-clear—he could go home.

He strolled into the parking lot and couldn't help smiling at the sight of his motorcycle. She was a 1969 Harley Davidson that he'd bought as scrap and restored. It had taken him two years of saving up money from working weekends and summers at a garage, but he'd done it.

As he mounted the sleek machine, he saw Terri giggling with her girlfriends. She waved and he nodded back at her, feeling a shiver of anticipation mixed with anxiety.

When he drove up to his home, the road outside was lined with bikes and cars—looked like it was open house at Zef Colton's. Again.

It was a well known secret that you could get pretty much anything you wanted at one of Zef's parties. And Daniel had done a lot of partying over the summer. Luckily, the brain cells he had left after all the pot he'd smoked and all the booze he'd drunk, seemed to be in good working order. His college classes hadn't presented him with any problems.

He looked enviously at the joint that was being passed around, but stuck by the promise he'd made himself not to get high or wasted on a school night. College cost good money, and he wasn't about to piss away his future.

He felt someone tugging on his arm.

A pretty blonde girl was leaning against him to keep her balance. She looked like she was about the same age as him and Daniel wondered if she was a student. He hoped they didn't go to the same college—he was trying to keep home life, such as it was, separate from school.

"Hey, handsome! You want to party?"

Several other female students threw her angry looks, but Lisanne didn't even notice. Much.

Hesitantly, she walked down the steps toward him.

"Hi," she said shyly, feeling lightheaded.

He held out his hand toward her and she shook it quickly. His skin felt warm and dry, the palm slightly rough.

"You're Lisanne," he said. "Roy's friend. I'm Daniel."

"Um, yeah," was her genius reply.

They stood staring at each other. Lisanne couldn't help noticing that he had incredibly long eyelashes, and his irises were a light hazel, flecked with green and gold.

"So," he said quietly, looking her in the eye, "can I have my hand back? I might be needing it."

"Oh, sorry!" she gasped, dropping his hand as if she'd been electrocuted.

She could tell he was trying to hold back a smile, but she didn't think it was possible she could blush any redder. He raised an eyebrow and she waited for him to make a smart comment, but he didn't.

"How do you want to do this?"

"What?" she stuttered.

"The assignment. Do you want to work at the library?"

"Um, yeah, sure. Whatever."

"Okay, what's good for you? Sunday evenings?"

She looked up to meet his eyes, and this time she saw a definite smirk.

"So you did see me there," she shot back.

He shrugged.

"But you didn't see fit to stop and help me up when I was sprawled all over the library steps!"

He frowned. "I don't know what you're talking about. I saw you studying—that's all."

"Oh sure! I was only a few feet behind you when I fell over. You *must* have heard me yell."

A look of sheer rage washed over him and Lisanne instinctively took an anxious step backward.

"Well, I didn't," he snapped.

There was no answer to that. Lisanne simply added 'liar' to his list of failings. She had the feeling it was going to be quite a long list.

"Anyway, I'm busy on Sunday evening," she said, trying to sound disdainful. Just because he was beautiful didn't mean he could get away with being an asshole. Not with her.

He continued to stare at her, his face tight with anger.

"What?" she said, irritated.

"So when *do* you want to work? I don't want to start dropping grades because of you."

Lisanne's jaw snapped shut with a loud click.

"I'm free Sunday afternoon," she spit out.

"Two o'clock," he said. "Don't be late."

Then he picked up his leather jacket and messenger bag, and walked away.

"What a jerk!" she muttered, mostly to herself.

She glanced over to see that Kirsty was still enjoying the attentions of Red T-shirt guy.

Lisanne sighed and rubbed her forehead tiredly.

At 1:55 PM on Sunday afternoon, Lisanne was hurrying across the campus toward the library, determined not to be late. She didn't want to give *Daniel* any excuse to be even more of a jerk.

She'd just got to the library's large revolving door, when she saw him jogging across the quad. He took the steps to the library two at a time, a serious look on his face.

"Afraid you were going to be late?" she said waspishly, when she caught up with him.

"No."

His tone was brusque.

Lisanne blinked. Perhaps she'd deserved that.

"Look, I'm sorry," she said. "We need to work on this together, so … let's just try and get along, okay?"

He shrugged. "Whatever."

Lisanne snatched back the olive branch, and marched into the library, steam coming out of her ears at his rudeness.

She picked a table toward the back of the room and flung herself into a chair. Daniel was still standing, shifting from foot to foot.

"Um, do you mind if I sit there?" he said, pointing toward Lisanne's seat.

"Excuse me?" she snorted.

"I … um, I like to sit with my back to the wall, so I can … see everything…"

"Suit yourself," she said, in a clipped tone, "but I'm not moving."

He scowled at her and finally pulled out a chair opposite Lisanne, which left him with his back to the rest of the room.

From the way he twitched, jerked his legs up and down, and kept tugging on his eyebrow ring, Lisanne didn't need to guess that he was feeling uncomfortable. She smiled smugly to herself—she liked having him on the back foot; it made her feel like she might have a chance of holding her own.

He scratched at the fine stubble covering his cheeks and chin, and slumped back in his chair.

"Where do you want to start?" he challenged her.

Lisanne had one good idea, which she proudly lay before him.

"That's a bit basic," he scoffed.

She blushed, mortified that her idea was so obviously lame.

He let out a long breath and Lisanne risked a glance at him. Even when he was pissed and irritated, she still couldn't help wanting to look at him.

To her surprise, his expression was sympathetic.

"You're not really into this, are you?"

She shook her head, her cheeks still flushed.

"Roy said you're majoring in music?"

"Um, yeah."

She was surprised to hear that he'd spoken about her to Roy.

"So you're taking Introduction to Business because…"

35

"My parents. They thought … I should have something to fall back on."

Daniel nodded slowly.

"They're right. Your parents. Nothing's guaranteed. It's good to have a backup plan."

Those weren't the sentiments she'd expected to hear from someone like him—he had such a devil-may-care, *couldn't give a shit* attitude.

"Look, it's quite straightforward if you think about it like this," he said, pointing toward the second chapter in the textbook.

To her surprise, he'd come prepared and had some really good ideas. Even more surprisingly, he'd been able to explain some of the concepts she'd been struggling with—industrial inertia, production flow—in clear, non-patronizing language.

It seemed so simple! Lisanne couldn't help laughing out loud, and Daniel grinned back at her.

"Yeah, I'm a funny guy."

"Actually I thought you were an ass."

"Fuck you very much," he said, solemnly.

Lisanne sniggered.

"You're welcome."

She decided that she much preferred his smile to his scowl. Both were hot, but his eyes were soft and happy when he smiled. Then she realized that the laugh she'd heard at her audition had been his. She hoped she'd get to hear it again. A lot.

He stretched his back out, pulling his arms over his head. Lisanne couldn't help but stare at the sliver of stomach that she glimpsed above his waistband, and the taut muscles of his chest that she could see shadowed beneath his t-shirt.

She tore her eyes away when she realized that being caught checking him out would not be cool, and might unleash his inner jerk.

"There's a book I used in high school that might help you," he said, distracting her from her ogling. "I could see if they've got a copy here, if you like."

Lisanne narrowed her eyes, wondering if he was suggesting that she wasn't up to the current course level, but she saw nothing except sincerity on his face. She felt ashamed of her shrewish thoughts.

"No, that's okay, thanks. I'll find it in the stacks. What's the title and author?"

He wrote down the details for her, and carried on flicking through the textbook for more ideas.

Lisanne wandered past the rows of tall stacks until she found the right shelf. She pulled the book out and flipped through the pages. He was right: it would really help her.

Suddenly a loud, blaring alarm rang throughout the library, making Lisanne jump. Everywhere, students were throwing books into bags and heading for the fire exits.

She ran back to their table and was amazed to see Daniel still sitting calmly, his head bent over his books.

"Daniel!" she yelled. "The fire alarm!"

He didn't move.

"Daniel!"

Nothing.

"Daniel!"

Still no reaction. Jeez, he must be listening to his iPod.

Annoyed and worried, she hurried over, slamming her books into her bag.

"What's up?" he said, clearly confused by her actions.

"The alarm!"

For a moment, blank incomprehension washed across his face, then he glanced behind and saw the other students departing rapidly.

Muttering to himself and cursing under his breath, he swept the books into his bag and followed Lisanne out of the library.

Students were milling around in front of the building, and spilling onto the quad. Everyone was wondering if it was a real fire, or just a drill. Was there any smoke? Had the fire department been called?

"Should we go wait on the grass?" Daniel said, casually.

"Sure."

They found themselves a free space, while Lisanne tried to ignore the incredulous stares from other students because *the* Daniel Colton was hanging out with a nerd. One was the redhead that she'd seen him with at the club. She was scowling at Lisanne and muttering something to her friend.

"Um, your girlfriend is over there," said Lisanne, pointing quickly over Daniel's shoulder.

He frowned and looked around, then gave a small smirk.

"She's not my girlfriend."

"But … I saw you with her at the club."

Daniel shrugged.

"We just hooked up."

"Oh."

Lisanne wasn't used to people talking so casually about, well, sex.

"She doesn't look very happy."

"Not my problem," he replied, frowning again. "She got what she wanted."

Lisanne didn't know how to answer *that*.

He lay back on the grass, propping himself on his elbows and stretching his long legs out in front of him. Then he pulled a squashed cigarette packet out of his pants' pocket and lit one, sucking in the smoke appreciatively.

"Smoking's really bad for you," said Lisanne, disapprovingly.

Daniel looked amused.

"Yeah? I don't think anyone ever mentioned that to me before."

Lisanne rolled her eyes and he winked at her, then took another drag.

Lazily, he blew smoke out of his nostrils, and Lisanne watched the plumes swirl around before the light breeze tugged them away.

And then she noticed something. "You're not listening to your iPod."

He looked puzzled.

"Um, no."

"You weren't wearing earphones in the library."

"No," he said, suddenly looking tense—defensive, even.

"The alarm…"

"What about it?" he snapped.

Lisanne was taken aback by the anger in his tone. She hesitated.

"Nothing," she mumbled.

His eyes narrowed, but then looked away from her.

"Whatever. I have to go now."

"But we haven't finished studying…"

He didn't answer; just stubbed out his butt on the grass and flicked it away with his fingers.

"Hey! No littering! Birds could try to eat that."

He didn't even look at her as he stood up and strode away.

Lisanne was left wondering what the hell had just happened.

No, he wasn't getting away with this crap—not after they'd been getting along so well. She scrambled up and chased after him.

"Daniel!"

He didn't break stride.

"Daniel!"

No reaction.

Her pace slowed until she was walking behind him, and calling his name, but he didn't turn; he didn't look at her.

She grabbed his arm and he swiveled so fast, his fists raised, that Lisanne jumped back. He relaxed a fraction when he saw her, but only a fraction.

"Daniel?"

"What?" he spat at her.

"I was calling your name. You didn't hear me."

He shrugged. "I was thinking about something else."

"No. I mean you didn't *hear* me."

His temper exploded; his eyes dark and furious.

"What do you want from me?"

"You didn't *hear* me, did you?"

39

He tried to shrug her off but she wouldn't let go, gripping her fingers around his arm tightly.

"You didn't *hear* me!"

"Get off!" he snarled, pushing her away roughly.

Her hands dropped to her sides and she felt like she was gasping for air.

"You *can't* hear me!" she whispered.

He turned away, but not before Lisanne saw the desperate pain on his face.

"You can't hear at all."

CHAPTER 3

Daniel felt his blood freeze as he stood staring at Lisanne's bewildered face.

"Don't … please don't tell anyone," he said, flicking his eyes away from her toward the students in front of the library.

"I don't understand," whispered Lisanne. "You seem so…"

Her words trailed off.

"Normal?" he finished for her, his tone bitter.

Her skin reddened, and she had to admit he'd guessed right.

"How do you … how do you do it?"

He licked his lips, looking around him again. He couldn't talk to her here, not with everyone watching, maybe listening.

"Can we go somewhere—get away from here?" he asked, his tone pleading.

"Yes, of course."

He was relieved that she agreed immediately. He nodded, and started back across the quad, his jaw tight, tension rolling off him in waves.

Lisanne had to practically run to keep up as Daniel strode rapidly across the campus.

"Where are we going?" she asked, breathlessly.

He didn't answer, but she soon realized he was leading her toward the student parking lot.

She nearly lost her nerve when he walked toward a shiny, black motorcycle. Reaching into one of the saddlebags, he pulled out a helmet and passed it to her without comment.

"Um, I've never done this before," she said, waving her hand helplessly toward the machine, and biting her lip.

41

He didn't smile.

"Have you ever ridden a bicycle?"

"Of course!"

"It's like that. Just hold on."

He swung his leg over the bike gracefully and held out his hand. Accepting, putting her hand in his, putting her trust in him, Lisanne clambered on behind. She reached around, searching for the grab bar. There wasn't one, and to make the point clear, Daniel fastened his hands over her wrists, and pulled her arms around his waist.

His body felt warm and very solid as Lisanne gripped him tightly, squeezing her eyes shut when the engine started with a throaty roar. She squealed when he kicked the stand and pulled away onto the road, her eyes snapping open.

He accelerated hard, and Lisanne clung on, giddy with the speed, exhilaration, and a little fear.

They rode for about 15 minutes, Daniel weaving recklessly in and out of the light traffic. Despite the assault on her senses, Lisanne gradually began to get used to the sensation and started to enjoy being close to Daniel. Then the memory of the circumstances that had taken them there came crashing back, and her throat closed up.

Maybe she'd got it horribly wrong. But then why had he looked at her like that? Why had he begged her not to tell anyone? As if she would! Why was he so upset?

The bike began to slow, and Daniel pulled up beside a cheap looking diner that had been designed to resemble an old train car.

The sudden silence as he cut the engine was startling. Lisanne took a deep breath and reluctantly unlocked her hands from his waist.

Without a word, he dismounted and pulled off his helmet.

Lisanne tried to swallow, but the anger and pain in his face had been replaced by a mask of coldness. She passed him her helmet in silence, then followed him into the diner. She was surprised when he held the door open for her. That small act of politeness helped to ease the constriction that was building in her chest.

He dropped into a booth at the back, and Lisanne followed, reluctant for the forthcoming confrontation, but anxious for the truth about this beautiful, complicated boy.

A middle-aged waitress immediately walked over with a jug of coffee that looked strong enough to curl the hairs on a buffalo's chest, and poured two cups without being asked.

"Thanks, Maggie," said Daniel, tiredly.

"Anything for you, handsome," she said, with a fond smile and a wink at Lisanne.

She strolled away before Lisanne had got up the nerve to ask for cream. She watched with fascination as Daniel added three packets of sugar to his coffee, stirring the steaming brew moodily.

She picked up her own mug and took a sip. The coffee was strong, but not as unpleasant as she'd been expecting.

Daniel leaned back in the booth and closed his eyes.

He looked so lost and vulnerable, but then his eyes opened and he stared down at her, his expression once again icy.

"What do you want from me?"

He repeated the words he'd spat at her in the quad, but now his voice was a cool monotone.

Lisanne shivered.

"I just want to know … if I was right."

"Why do you care?"

"I just … it could be dangerous … if people don't know about … you."

He raised his eyebrows at her in disbelief.

"Dangerous?"

"Yes," said Lisanne, trying to hold her nerve. "In the library, you didn't hear the fire alarm, did you?"

"Are you asking me or telling me?"

"Um, asking you?"

He sighed, and studied the table with undue interest. Needing something to do with his hands, he poured a small pile of salt onto the table and began drawing patterns with his finger. He tried to pull his thoughts together, wondering how much he could tell her, how much he could trust her.

Lisanne bit back the trivial words that would have told him to stop making a mess on the table. Daniel was going to talk to her—she knew it—and she didn't want to interrupt him.

"I usually sit with my back to the wall so I can see what everyone else is doing," he said, at last. "That usually clues me in."

He looked up at her.

"You wouldn't move, and I had to sit opposite you so I could lip read what you were saying." He shrugged. "I'm more careful when I'm by myself."

Lisanne felt horrible. Her refusal to swap seats, her bitchiness, all the unfair thoughts she'd had about him. He *wasn't* a liar. He *wasn't* a jerk. But she, Lisanne, she was a first class bitch with a smug, selfish streak a mile wide.

"I'm sorry," she whispered.

He nodded and sighed again.

"Yeah, I get that a lot."

He looked down, and pushed the pile of salt in another direction.

Lisanne put her hand over his, forcing him to look at her.

"I'm sorry because I've been a bitch to you."

He gave her a small smile, and gently slid his hand free, dropping it to his lap.

Embarrassed, she pulled her hand back, too, and they both sipped at their coffee to have something to do—something that would alleviate the ghastly silence.

"So ... you can lip read?" she said, at last.

He nodded, watching her face.

"Is that ... is that why you don't take notes during lectures?"

He nodded again. "If I tried to take notes, I'd miss half the lecture."

"But isn't that really hard?"

He shrugged. "I'm pretty good at remembering stuff: I write

the notes up later. They offered me computer-assisted real-time captioning, but … I'd rather do it my way."

"So your tutors know?"

"Yeah."

"Anyone else?"

"At school? Only you."

"I don't understand—why are you trying to keep it secret? It's not something to be ashamed of? I mean, you've done amazing to get this far…"

"Don't!" he snarled. "Don't fucking patronize me!"

"I wasn't! I…"

"Yes, you fucking were. You're just like all the rest. I've 'done amazing'—is that what you said? Why should it be any more 'amazing' for me to go to college? I'm deaf, not stupid."

It was the first time either of them had said the word, and Lisanne blanched.

"I didn't mean it like that! I'm sorry, I…"

She stared into her coffee cup and felt tears sting the back of her eyes. She couldn't seem to say anything without making it worse. She couldn't imagine how hard it must have been for him. She knew how tough she was finding college, but at least she was normal. Then she hated herself for thinking like that. Even so, his challenges must be so much harder than her own. And then she realized how terribly lonely it must be—not to be able to join in a group conversation, not to be able to talk about the latest songs or bands, not overhearing the funny or weird remarks other people made, not to be able to play her violin, not to be able to hear her own voice, her own singing. She couldn't imagine life without her music, without sounds.

But that was the reality of Daniel's life. No wonder he wrapped himself in a façade of hostility, trying to keep everyone away from him.

"I saw you dancing at the club," she said, suddenly remembering his dirty dancing, and feeling confused, "with your girlf … with that girl. How did you…?"

He smiled tightly. "I can feel it," he said. "I can feel the beat

45

of the music through the floor, the vibrations. No one ever notices ... that I'm deaf ... when I'm in a club—no one can hear for shit in those places either. I fit right in. It's the one place you could say I have an advantage. Other people have to shout to be heard—I can read their lips."

His tone was biting.

"Can you ... um ... can you hear anything at all? I was just wondering because you sound so..."

"You were going to say 'normal' again, weren't you?" he said, accusingly.

Lisanne bit her lip and nodded slowly. "Sorry," she mumbled.

"And you still wonder why I don't want anyone to know?"

She looked up, seeing only pain and frustration in his eyes.

"Because I don't want to be defined by this," he said, his voice soft. "When people know that you have ... a disability—Christ, I fucking hate that word—they treat you differently. Half the time they don't even know they're doing it. I hate all the fucking stereotypes." He dropped his head into his hands. "I hate it. I really fucking hate it."

Lisanne didn't know what to say or how to behave. It was hard to take in that he had this life changing ... problem, issue, disability ... what was she supposed to call it?

"I'm so fucking pathetic," he mumbled. "Two weeks: I managed to ... just two weeks before someone—before you—guessed."

Lisanne looked him in the eye.

"If it hadn't been for the fire alarm, I'm not sure I would have noticed." She gave him a small smile. "I'd have just carried on thinking you were a jerk for ignoring me, sometimes."

His face softened slightly and he tried to smile, although it seemed to get stuck around the corners of his mouth.

"But Daniel: I don't get why you'd rather people think you were a jerk than ... think that you're deaf."

He shrugged.

"Jerks are normal. Being deaf ... that makes me different. I don't want to be different."

Lisanne ran her eyes up and down his tattoos and fixed her gaze on his pierced eyebrow.

"I think you do."

"What?"

"I think you do want to be different. The way you look."

He stared at her and shook his head slowly. "You don't understand."

"I'm trying to."

"Yeah, I guess you are."

"Will you ... will you tell me about it? When it started? I mean, you weren't born deaf, were you?"

"What do you want—my fucking life story?"

"Yes, if you can manage not to cuss with every other word."

He looked at her in amazement, then laughed out loud.

"You're funny!"

"Glad I make you laugh!" she snorted, although she wasn't really mad. It was good to see him smiling again.

But his smile faded quickly.

"I don't want anyone else to know. I mean it: no one."

"I promise, Daniel. Besides, it's your secret to tell—not mine."

He nodded slowly.

"Guess I'll have to trust you."

"Guess you will."

"Fine, but I'm going to need another damn coffee."

"Hey—no cussing! You promised!"

"I can't even say 'damn'?"

"I'd rather you didn't."

"Your old man a preacher, by any chance?"

Lisanne rolled her eyes. "So cliché! You think just because I don't like cussing that I must be a Holy Roller? Now who's stereotyping?"

He was saved a reply when Maggie came by to top up their coffee mugs.

"You want anything to eat with that, Danny? Or maybe for

your friend?"

Daniel looked at Lisanne. "You hungry?"

"Not really, but thanks."

"We're good here, thanks, Maggie."

"I'll get you your usual," she said, "and don't you roll your eyes at me Danny Colton. I know that you never have any food in the house."

"Thanks, Maggie," he mumbled, sounding chastened as the waitress stalked away.

Lisanne raised her eyebrows.

"Danny, huh?"

He grimaced. "Yeah, well, she's known me since I was a kid. She's the only one who calls me that."

"I don't know—I think it suits you, Danny."

"Keep it up, preacher's kid."

Lisanne scowled and Daniel couldn't help laughing at her again.

"So, how come your chose this school?" she said, trying to make conversation.

He shrugged.

"It's got a great business program, good for economics. And I got a partial scholarship. You?"

"It was more Mom and Dad's choice. I knew I wanted to do music and there's a music education program, so I'm training to be a music teacher."

"Is that what you want?"

"Not really, but it's close enough."

When Maggie arrived with a plate of eggs, bacon and grits, Daniel tore into it like a starving man.

"Wow, I guess you really are hungry," said Lisanne, her eyes about bugging out of her head, amazed by the speed with which he was inhaling everything in sight.

"Mmm," he said, over a mouthful of eggs and bacon. "Didn't get around to eating yesterday."

"What? Not at all."

"Uh-uh," he mumbled, shaking his head.

"Why not?"

He swallowed the last morsel and reached for his coffee.

"Haven't done any grocery shopping. Besides, it never lasts long, so there's not much point."

Lisanne shook her head, confused.

"Doesn't your mom buy the groceries?"

As soon as she asked the question she realized she'd yet again put her giant-sized foot in it.

"Both my parents died—over two years ago now," he said, staring at a spot on the wall behind her. "It's just me and Zef now—my brother."

The breath stuttered out of Lisanne's lungs.

"How?"

"Car accident."

All she could do was nod in appalled sympathy. Daniel had been born with intelligence and good looks, but within a few years he'd lost his parents, his hearing, a huge chunk of pride and dignity, along with hope, it seemed.

Lisanne couldn't begin to understand how he functioned at all, let alone got up in the morning and came to school to study. He must be strong, she decided. Very strong.

Her heart swelled with admiration for him, then burned with pain for the hand life had dealt him.

"I'm sorry," she repeated, helplessly.

He shrugged.

"Life sucks."

He stretched his arms above his head, and his t-shirt rose up and tightened over his chest. Lisanne's cheeks began to heat, and then she felt horrible for having faintly lustful thoughts when he'd been baring his soul to her. She was a terrible person.

"What about you?" he said. "What's your story?"

"Nothing interesting," she said, quickly.

"Tell me anyway."

"There's really nothing to tell."

He frowned. "So you get to grill me about my life, but you won't say anything back."

"No, I meant … it's just boring. What do you want to know?"

"Tell me about your family."

She sighed.

"My parents are Monica and Ernie. They're both high school teachers—math. I have a younger brother, Harry: he's 13. He's a complete pain in the … well, a pain, but I miss him anyway. He's into the usual stuff: football, computer games, and just getting into girls." She shuddered. "He has a poster of Megan Fox on his wall. Mom told him he was objectifying women, but I think Dad kind of likes it—the poster, I mean."

"Yeah, well, she's hot!"

"Ugh! You're such a *guy*," she jeered.

He winked at her, and she couldn't help grinning at him.

"Who do *you* have posters of on your wall at home?" she teased him.

"Why? You wanna see my bedroom?" he asked, raising one eyebrow, the one with the ring through it. "Because I gotta say, I didn't think you were that sort of girl."

Lisanne stared at him, utterly without words.

He smirked, concluding that he'd won that round of verbal jousting.

"You ever been kissed, LA?" he said, leaning forward and staring into her eyes, a smile hidden behind them.

"Don't be a jerk!" she snapped.

"Thought not," he said, smugly.

"I've been kissed," she stammered. "A lot."

It was a damned lie, but there was no way she was going to admit that to *him*.

"Good to know," he said, sitting back, smiling.

"Well, what about you?"

"Yeah, I've been kissed. A lot."

She rolled her eyes.

"I meant do you have a girlfriend?"

"Why, you offering?"

"I don't know why I bother," she huffed.

He smiled back at her.

"No, I don't have a girlfriend. Anything else you want to know?"

Lisanne chewed her lip.

"Ask me," he prompted. "I won't answer if I don't want to."

"Fair enough." She paused. "Well, I was wondering … when, um, when did you … when did … I'm sorry, it doesn't matter."

His playful expression vanished, and Lisanne could have kicked herself.

"We keep coming back to this shit, don't we," he said, his voice angry. "This is why I'm sick of it, why I hate talking about it. It's so fucking fascinating to everyone else, but this is my life and I know what I've lost. Every fucking day I know what I've lost. I see you going to rehearsals with Roy and the guys and it fucking slays me. I'll *never* have that again; I'll *never* hear that music. And you know what? I'm beginning to forget. Sometimes I think I hear music in my head, but I'm not sure anymore."

He closed his eyes, then spoke again. "Do you think it's like that for blind people? I mean, if they used to be able to see … can they remember colors? Do they think in color, dream in color? Sometimes I think I can hear music in my dreams…"

Lisanne's throat closed tightly, and she felt responsible for making him feel like this. And she had a responsibility to answer him.

"Yes, I think they do. I mean, I think I would. You know, Beethoven carried on composing even after he went deaf."

"Yeah, like no one's ever said that to me before," he said, scathingly.

"It doesn't make it any less true," she said, quietly.

He sighed.

"My … condition … is called idiopathic sensorineural hearing loss—which means they don't have a fucking clue. They think maybe it was a virus, but they don't really know. It began after I started high school. The first thing was that I got into trouble: teachers said I wasn't concentrating, or I was being a smart-ass and not answering them. One teacher really had it in for me, Miss Francis. She had one of those fucking irritating high-pitched voices, and I couldn't hear a fucking thing she was saying. You lose the high sounds first—low tone reception takes a bit longer. I was too dumb to tell anyone I was having problems."

He paused and looked down.

"Then my grades started dropping. I got into fights and my parents got called in a ton of times. One of my teachers was the first to guess what was going on. I was sent for tests … by the time I was 15, I had moderate to severe hearing loss."

He scrubbed his hands over his face.

"The school said they couldn't 'deal' with me anymore. So … my parents sent me to a *special* school. When they… when they died, I had just under two years left, so … I graduated, and I swore that I'd never live like that. I didn't want that 'disabled' tag—'differently able' for fuck's sake. I fucking hate it." He paused. "I lost just about all my hearing then. I have some hearing in my left ear, but I'm not sure about that anymore. I didn't hear that fucking fire alarm. Maybe I could hear a damn bomb going off—I don't know."

Lisanne didn't realize she'd been holding her breath until her lungs began to hurt.

"And … hearing aids don't help?"

Daniel pulled a face.

"Not really. They work for some people. I tried digital hearing aids but they didn't provide enough amplification, and voices sounded muddy and distorted. The analog ones were better—but not by much."

"But it would help a bit?"

"Sure, if you want people to treat you like a fucking moron."

"Not all people!"

"Don't fucking tell me what it's like. People say shit like, 'Oh, you talk really well', like they're fucking patting me on the back or something."

"So … there's no … no hope? The doctors…?"

He shook his head. "Nah. I'm one of their 'worst case

scenarios'. Memorable, you might say."

Lisanne felt slightly sick, but plowed on.

"You mustn't give up hope, Daniel. Scientists make breakthroughs all the time. You could … I don't know … take part in a trial or something. What about those implants I've heard about?"

He shook his head again.

"I used to think like that, but I've had enough of being a fucking lab rat. I've spent so much time in hospitals and clinics, having different tests, being fitted for different hearing aids—each one more fucking useless than the last one. I couldn't stand going through all that again … the hope. It fucking kills you."

He looked so broken, that Lisanne wanted nothing more than to try and comfort him, but before she could think of anything, he shook his head, as if to clear it.

"Fuck me," he said, "that sounded like a freakin' soap opera. Do you wanna go do something fun?"

Lisanne's head was spinning from his change of mood.

"Okay," she said, uncertainly. "Like what?"

"Trust me?"

"No."

He grinned.

"What have you got to lose?"

"Um, my life, my reputation, my sanity?"

Daniel laughed.

"Is that all? Come on. I'll get you back to your dorm room in one piece. Can't speak for your reputation if you're seen with me, though."

Lisanne pretended to sigh.

"Guess I'll have to live with that."

Half an hour later, Lisanne was staring in open-mouthed amazement, her jaw firmly on the floor.

Seriously? He'd taken her to an arcade?

"What are you? Thirteen?" she said, in utter disbelief.

"No, baby, I'm all man," he said with a smirk, winking at her. "Want me to prove it?"

She crossed her arms across her chest and tried to look stern. Daniel just grinned at her.

"Aw, come on! It'll be fun. We can eat chips, drink soda, and shoot up stuff. What's not to like?"

He grabbed her hand and pulled her inside. His excitement was infectious—he was like a little boy, his eyes shining. Lisanne had to admit she liked this playful side of him. He was so serious most of the time.

He changed ten dollars into tokens and handed her a pile.

"Uh-uh, I think I'll watch you."

He grinned at her and headed for a machine called MotorStorm Apocalypse.

"This one's awesome."

For nearly an hour, Daniel played on various games. She was amused watching him act like an overactive kid; he reminded Lisanne of her brother. Every time he won or scored highly, he turned around and gave her a huge grin. He even persuaded Lisanne to take him on at Project Gotham Racing, and then kicked her ass in all four city racetracks.

Refusing a rematch, she wandered off to get the promised chips and sodas with a ten dollar bill that he insisted she take from his wallet, then they sat on a couple of plastic chairs and watched a group of junior high kids fight over Ridge Racer.

Lisanne had to admit that despite herself, she'd had fun. The one thing that disturbed her was that it was so easy to forget Daniel was deaf. Several times she'd spoken to him when he'd had his back to her, before remembering to tap him on the shoulder.

She could see how easy it would be for people to find him unresponsive or rude. She sort of understood what he'd said about not wanting people to know, but she didn't really get why he'd rather have people think he was a jerk. She remembered the proverb her mom had drummed into her: you have to walk a mile in another man's shoes before you judge him.

She sighed, realizing she had a lot to learn.

Eventually she decided that it was getting late and that she'd promised Kirsty they'd go out together tonight. A large part of her would have been happy to stay with Daniel, but a promise was a promise.

He offered to take her back to her dorm room, and Lisanne accepted gratefully.

But when he dropped her off, his face was anxious.

"Um, Lisanne—you won't say anything to anyone, will you?"

"No, I promise. Like I said, it's not my secret to tell," she repeated.

He looked relieved.

"So, we should reschedule our study session," she reminded him.

"Yeah, I guess we should. Give me your phone—I'll program in my number."

Wordlessly, Lisanne handed her phone to the hottest guy in college, trying not to smile as he punched his number into her contacts list.

"Just give me a cool ringtone, okay?" he said, an amused look on his face.

"I'll give you Celine Dion," she said. "You'll never know."

An incredulous look passed over Daniel's face, then he threw back his head and laughed.

"You are one tough woman—I like it."

Then he slung his leg over the saddle of his bike, and took off into the darkening sky.

With his words ringing in her ears, Lisanne hugged herself, then skipped back to her dorm room.

He likes me!

Before she could put her key in the lock, the door was yanked open and Kirsty dragged her inside.

"Do not tell me you just had a five-hour study date with Mr. Tall Dark and Deliciously Dangerous!" she yelled.

Lisanne laughed nervously.

"Kind of. We studied for a while..." *a very short while, she thought.* "Then we hung out for a bit. That's all."

"Shut up! So, was it like a date? Did he kiss you? Did you get some tongue action? Spill!"

"No! I told you—we studied and then took a break. He's ... nice."

"*Nice*?! Oh, you do not get away with saying that the *hottest* guy on campus is *nice*! Please!"

"Um, well, he gave me his phone number, but that's so we can set up another study date."

Kirsty's eyes nearly rolled out of her head, they were so wide open.

"He gave you his *phone number*? Oh my God! I'm so jealous! Promise me next time you'll screw him senseless until he's cross-eyed and can't walk without crutches—then give me all the details, with written notes. Is he well hung?"

"I can't believe you said that!" shrieked Lisanne.

"I'm compiling a dossier," said Kirsty, pulling out a sparkly purple file. "It lists the names of the twenty hottest guys on campus with all their details. Daniel and Mr. Red T-shirt are equal first, and I need some vital statistics. How tall is he?"

Lisanne capitulated, deciding it was easier to go along with Kirsty's crazy plan than attempt to fight it.

"Um, well, he's taller than my dad, I guess, but not by much, so he must be about six-two."

"Excellent," said Kirsty, licking the end of her pencil and writing in her notebook. "Eye color?"

"Hazel with gold and green flecks—and really long eyelashes."

"Hmm, so you got quite close," said Kirsty, raising an eyebrow.

A light pink heated Lisanne's cheeks. "I was sitting opposite him in the library like forever—I couldn't help *but* notice."

"Oh, okay. Tats?"

"Well, yes. I didn't get a good look at all of them, obviously..."

"Obviously..."

"But he's got them on both arms and maybe across his back. I'm not sure."

"Hmm, interesting. Nipple rings?"

"What?!"

"That's the rumor—that he's got two nipple rings."

"I … I…" stammered Lisanne.

"Oh, well, see if you can find out for next time. And find out if he has any other piercings—other than his eyebrow, of course."

Lisanne's face was scarlet. "I can't ask him *that*!"

"I can let you have a copy of the checklist to give to him if you like," said Kirsty, looking almost serious.

Lisanne shook her head so hard she was afraid she'd dislodged her brain, along with all rational speech.

"How often did other girls check him out?"

That question was easier to answer.

"Huh, *all* the time."

"So ten out of ten for being eye-fuckable," confirmed Kirsty.

Lisanne had to give her that one.

"Oh! Does he have a tongue piercing?"

Lisanne screwed her face up trying to remember if she'd seen any sign of a stud in his tongue.

"I don't think so."

"Pity. I might have to deduct points for that."

"Yeah, but he has a motorcycle."

"Oh, God, yes! I can't believe you rode on it. You're so lucky, Lisanne."

The comment sobered her immediately. Yes, she was lucky. She was damn lucky. She had a family who loved her; she had her hearing. And she had her music.

Daniel had lost all of those.

Kirsty's dossier was meant to be fun, but Lisanne couldn't help wondering how differently Daniel would be judged if people knew the truth.

Daniel had no choice but to trust Lisanne. The thought pissed him the hell off. He knew from experience that most people let you down sooner or later. Sure, she seemed like she

57

was on the level—she seemed nice. But he didn't *know* her, and that made him nervous.

All he could do was wait and see.

CHAPTER 4

Sunday dragged painfully.

Lisanne sat in her room, catching up with the Everest of homework that her professors had seen fit to pile on during the first two weeks of the semester.

Even Kirsty was taking things seriously, sitting at her desk with her laptop in front of her, eyes squinting at the screen.

At least Lisanne had a rehearsal with Roy and the rest of the *32° North* guys to look forward to. Roy had even offered to give her a ride. Lisanne had thought that one over for a while, but she decided that having two scary looking tattooed men visiting her dorm room in the same week might get her something worse than a reputation.

"If it gets late, call me and I'll come pick you up," Kirsty offered kindly. "Any time up until midnight is fine. Jeez, if you're not done by then, you won't have any voice left to speak of!"

Lisanne agreed gratefully and set off to catch the bus.

Roy opened the club's door after she'd pounded on it for a good three minutes.

"Sorry, baby girl. Didn't hear you. Mike had the amps turned up to 11."

He grinned at his own joke, and Lisanne smiled as he swept her into a rib-cracking hug.

"We're gonna warm up with some Etta James before we go onto the new stuff. It's always good to mix in some oldies to get the audience going. You know *Something's Got A Hold On Me?*"

"Sure, didn't Christina Aguilera cover it a couple of years back?"

Roy frowned. "Yeah, but Etta did it better. Hey, that rhymes!"

"We could try *Dirrty*?"

He looked at her sideways. "You think you can pull off a song like that, baby girl?"

Lisanne blushed and looked down. "I know the melody," she said quietly, feeling like a fool. *Of course*, she couldn't pull off being sexy. That was a lost cause.

The rehearsal went well and they were beginning to get a pretty good set together—it was a little bit conservative for Lisanne's tastes—although she kept that thought to herself. About three quarters of the songs were a mix of old and modern classics with some indie rock thrown in, but the rest were original. Carlos, the bass player, could sing a good harmony and his voice blended well with Lisanne's.

But she was still curious about one thing.

"I really like the new material," Lisanne said, casually. "But you've never said which of you wrote it. I really like *Last Song* and *On My Mind*—those are beautiful."

"A friend," said Roy. "He doesn't play anymore."

Lisanne looked him in the eye. "Do you mean Daniel?"

There was a sudden silence, but Lisanne held her ground.

"You know him?" said Roy, cautiously.

"He's in one of my classes. We're working on an assignment together. He told me ... some stuff."

"Yeah, Dan wrote those songs," said Roy, at last. "He carried on writing songs until about a year and a half ago. Kid was a genius." He shook his head. "But don't ask him about it because he won't talk to you. Understand?"

Lisanne nodded. Yes, she understood.

The confirmation stunned her. It was only what she'd suspected for a while now, but hearing that it was Daniel who had composed those beautiful songs hurt her heart in ways she didn't understand. She could only imagine how she'd feel if she lost her music—it was such a huge part of her life. What would it be like for your world to end like that—a slow descent into silence? She couldn't bear it—she'd go mad.

It was amazing that Daniel was as together as he seemed—so controlled. And then Lisanne thought about the effort it must take to appear like that. She remembered his flashes of rage when she'd made assumptions about him. Not that she blamed him. In fact, she blamed herself for her casual stereotyping. Hell, no wonder he didn't want anyone to know about him. And she realized how many value judgments she made every single day based solely on appearance: she'd assumed Kirsty was vacuous because she was pretty; she'd assumed Roy was a scary, violent criminal because of his size and his tattoos; and she'd assumed Daniel was a jerk because he kept people at arms' length. She didn't want to think about how shallow that made her.

Lisanne was glad to accept Roy's offer of a ride back to the dorms, grateful that she didn't have to call Kirsty out so late, and too tired to care what anyone thought should they see her with him.

They were quiet for most of the ride, and Lisanne was content to simply stare at the washed-out colors of the night, buildings bathed in an amber neon glow.

Eventually, Roy cleared his throat, announcing to Lisanne that he had a question for her.

"You must know Dan pretty well if he told you about himself," he commented carefully.

"Not really. Not well."

"Hmm, because he almost never tells anyone who hasn't known him for years."

Lisanne shrugged, not wanting to explain that she'd uncovered his secret by accident.

"Like I said—we're working on an assignment together."

"Hmm," said Roy again, but didn't push her.

He let her out at the dorm rooms, simply saying that he'd see her at the next rehearsal. His face was thoughtful as he drove away.

Kirsty was propped up in bed reading a book when Lisanne dragged herself through the door.

"Good rehearsal?"

"Yeah, it's going really well," replied Lisanne with a tired smile.

"Great! Because I'm getting together a load of people to come see you when you have your debut."

"What? Not … not people from school?"

Kirsty rolled her eyes. "Duh! Do I know anyone else? *Of course* it's people from school. Everyone's really excited to see you. I've been telling them how amazing you are."

"Kirsty! You've never even heard me sing! Why would you say that?"

"I'm being supportive. We're roommates and that's what roommates do. Besides, I know you'll be awesome—Roy told me you were the new Adele when I met him at the club."

Lisanne was taken aback.

"Roy said that?"

"Sure! And a load more stuff that I promised not to tell you in case you got up yourself."

Lisanne shook her head. "No! Please don't tell me! It's going to be bad enough falling flat on my face without having people from school see it. Please, Kirsty, not the first gig. Maybe one later in the semester."

"Uh-uh, I'll be there, cheering you on. Besides, Vin wants to see you in action, too."

"Who's Vin?"

"Red T-shirt guy!" said Kirsty, with a giggle. "I saw him in the cafeteria today and he asked me out. We're going for dinner and a movie tomorrow."

"That's great! He's really cute."

"Yes, he is. Although I seem to remember you said he was 'okay' but not your type. Of course, we all know who's *your* type, don't we? How is Daniel?"

Lisanne pretended to be very busy unpacking her purse, which as it only held her cell phone and wallet, took some serious acting skills. She couldn't pull off indifference very well. Insouciance was harder. And casual could just fuck off.

"We're just doing this assignment. He probably won't even speak to me when we're finished."

Kirsty didn't reply, which made Lisanne look up. Her roommate was leaning back with a small smile on her face.

"Want to take a bet on that, roomie?"

On Wednesday morning, Lisanne got a text from Daniel.

* D: Want to study and smuggle chips in library later? *

She smiled to herself. Playful Daniel was her favorite. No, wait, Sexy Daniel was number one, but playful was good, too.

She texted back immediately.

* L: Yes to study but what do I get
for not reporting serious biblio violation? *
* D: You drive hard bargain!
Ok—you choose flavor, I'll buy. Good enough? *
* L: thinking about it *
* D: playing hard to get? *
* L: who's playing? *
* D: Are you sexting me? *

"Oh my God!"

He was *definitely* flirting with her.

* L: shock! *
* D: bbq flavor? *
* L: and cheesy chili. 4 PM. Don't be late. *
* D: wouldn't dare ;) *

Flirting, possible sexting, *and* a winking smiley.

The next two hours were tortuously slow. Never had Lisanne's classical music composition seminar seemed so deadly dull. Root chords, dominants and subdominants didn't even have the usual frisson of BDSM to enliven the proceedings. Professor Hastings behaved as if he was curing cancer, and neither a giggle nor a raised eyebrow was allowed under his watchful, querulous gaze.

Eventually, Lisanne was released—ten minutes late. Damn it! Daniel would have a field day with her being late.

Her shoulder bag thumped painfully against her hip as Lisanne jogged across the campus to the library. The quad outside was filled with people hanging out and enjoying the Fall sunshine.

She hurried inside, searching the occupied tables, looking for his trademark spiky black hair.

But when she saw Daniel, he was talking to the redhead who'd been draped all over him at the club. A cold feeling crept up from the pit of Lisanne's stomach as she gazed at the beautiful, curvaceous girl in front of her. She couldn't help wilting under the weight of comparison with her own meager figure.

"I'm sure I can think of something more fun than studying," the girl said slyly, leaning forward to give Daniel a view over her impressive assets.

"I'm meeting someone for a study session, Terri."

"I'll write you a permission slip. You can study later."

Then she bent down and whispered in his ear: a flirtation that had the opposite effect from the one she'd hoped for. Daniel leaned away from her, regarding her coolly.

"I'm busy, Terri," he said curtly, then looked past her when he saw Lisanne.

"Hi," she said, quietly. "Sorry I'm late. My class ran over."

Terri turned and glared, a sneer on her lovely face.

"You're kidding! A study date with a bookworm? When you get bored of her, call me."

She stalked off, tossing her magnificent mane of hair over her shoulder as she went.

Lisanne wished someone would dig a big hole so she could quietly fall into it. Then they could shovel the dirt on top and plant some grass. Maybe a few flowers.

"Don't let her bother you, Lis. She's just a bitch," said

Daniel, softly.

He crumpled up a piece of paper as he spoke, and Lisanne hoped that Terri's phone number was scrawled across it.

"It's okay," she said shrugging it off, even as she felt her throat tighten uncomfortably.

In truth she was used to girls like Terri talking to her with such condescension. Didn't make it sting any less, though.

"No it isn't okay!" he said, crossing his arms over his chest, a movement that caused his biceps to bunch up under his t-shirt.

Lisanne licked her lips as they continued to stare at each other in silence, then she remembered where she was, and turned to pull out her books, notepad and laptop.

"So," she began, without daring to look at him, "a model for corporate governance within a framework of societal responsibility. Fun times."

She glanced up as Daniel cracked a smile. "Yeah, and don't forget the chips."

Then he winked at her and she felt some of the tension fade away.

"You're so bad!" she said, rolling her eyes.

"Better believe it, baby."

Ninety minutes later, Lisanne's head was ready to explode. Even though Daniel had patiently explained again (and again) the theory of subsistence marketplaces and poverty-based market opportunities, the words and phrases all blurred into one, making less and less sense.

"I'm going to flunk out of this course, I know it!" she groaned, stabbing her pen into her notebook hard enough to break the tip.

"No you won't," said Daniel, calmly. "I won't let you. You'll be fine—it's just a lot of new stuff to take in."

Lisanne shook her head.

"It's like doing one of those dumb math problems: three people are driving at 20mph in a car carrying two gallons of gas and a horse doing yoga, when a car traveling at 30mph with two clowns drinking cola collides, what time is it in Tokyo? It doesn't make any sense and the only answer I ever come up with is *who cares!*"

Daniel laughed. "A horse doing yoga? Did I read you right? I think you need coffee."

"Yes," she moaned. "I need caffeine, intravenously."

He smiled. "I know just the place."

While he gathered up the empty chip bags, Lisanne continued to moan and hold her head, just in case it really did split in half and her brain dribbled across the table.

She was surprised into motion when she felt his strong fingers around her wrist.

"Come on," he said, with a smile. "IV coffee coming up."

Lisanne followed him out of the library, grateful for his caffeinated intervention, but more astonished by the way his hand had felt on her skin—almost as if his touch burned. She was also horribly aware of the surprised stares that followed them across the campus.

Again.

If Daniel noticed, he didn't say.

As before, his bike was waiting for them in the student parking lot.

"Miss me, baby?" he said, his tone soft and loving.

Lisanne couldn't help laughing at the blissful expression on his face.

"Are you really talking to your motorcycle?"

"Sure! She's the only woman in my life, aren't you, baby?"

Was it unreasonable of Lisanne to feel jealous of an inanimate object? Because at that point, she wanted to push the bike to the ground, stamp all over its shiny bodywork, and laugh like a hyena while she did it.

Daniel ran a loving hand over the polished chrome and grinned up at Lisanne when he saw her shaking her head.

"What can I say? She's beautiful—and she doesn't talk back. Or eat all my chips."

"I did not!" huffed Lisanne, guiltily.

Daniel smirked at her, then turned back to the bike.

"Don't be jealous, baby. She's only a human."

"What sort of motorcycle is this?"

He shook his head in disbelief at her ignorance.

"She's a 1969 Harley Davidson XLCH Sportster," he answered. "Rebuilt her myself—one thousand cc engine. V2, four-stroke ... too much information?"

Lisanne nodded, looking amused. He swung his leg over the saddle and held out his hand.

"Come on. Sirona doesn't like to be kept waiting."

"You *named* her?"

"Of course. She's too beautiful not to have a name."

Boys and their toys.

"Does it mean anything?"

"Sirona is a Celtic goddess. She rules over healing."

He shrugged, and Lisanne felt a pang. Did that mean Daniel hoped he'd be healed? Was he awaiting some miracle that would restore his hearing? She watched him carefully. Whatever pain he suffered, he held it inside. How strong must he be to do that? She didn't know. She couldn't imagine.

In silence, he passed her the spare helmet and fastened his own. He nodded, and she latched her arms around his waist. This was, by far, her favorite part of riding with him. She snuggled into his solid warmth, tightening her grip.

A short trip later, and they were back at the diner.

Lisanne was a little disappointed; she'd imagined they were going somewhere different—somewhere fresh and exciting. But then she realized that she was being stupid and selfish. It was no surprise that Daniel preferred to go somewhere he knew. He had enough challenges in his life without wondering if he'd be able to lip read a new waitress in a new coffee shop.

He led her to the same booth as last time, and like last time Maggie sauntered over to serve them.

"Back again, Danny. You just can't get enough of my coffee, huh, kid?"

He winced slightly at the diminutive of his name, but didn't bother to correct her.

"Hey, Maggie."

"And if your girl is going to be a regular, you ought to darn well introduce her."

His girl?

"Yeah, sorry. This is Lisanne. Lisanne, Maggie."

"Hi, Maggie," she said, feeling shy.

"You treat him good, honey," said the waitress. "He's a royal pain in the ass, like most men, but he's one of the better ones. I'll get you two of the specials."

Lisanne had no idea what the 'specials' were but she found Maggie too daunting to ask. Instead she watched as the woman poured them each a coffee—black—ruffled Daniel's hair, and wandered away.

She couldn't help giggling at the chagrined expression on Daniel's face.

"I can see why you keep coming here, *Danny*."

He groaned. "God! Don't you start! I was just beginning to like you."

A warm glow heated Lisanne from the inside and damn it if she didn't feel her traitorous cheeks turn pink.

Daniel sipped his coffee, then looked up and smiled again.

"Roy says rehearsals are going well."

"Um, yeah, I think so. I mean, they seem pretty pleased. I don't know. I'm sure I'll be a bag of nerves on the night."

"Nah, you'll be fine. He says you're a natural. He'd know."

"I'll probably make a complete fool of myself, trip over the cables, electrocute everyone, and break a leg—all before the opening chords."

Daniel laughed. "At least no one would ever forget it."

"Oh no," she moaned. "It's going to be a nightmare. And Kirsty—my roommate—she's getting up a group of people from school to come. I wish she wouldn't but it's too late to stop her."

For some reason Daniel didn't look pleased, but he twitched a shoulder and said, "She's just being a friend."

"Yeah, she's pretty awesome."

"Is she the girl you sit next to in Business class?"

"Yes."

"Huh. She's hot."

Lisanne's heart shuddered. Was this the reason why he was being so nice to her? He was really interested in Kirsty? Yeah, and why was that even a surprise to her?

Lisanne stared down into her coffee. "She's got a boyfriend," she blurted out, even though it wasn't strictly true since Kirsty had only had one date with Vin so far.

"Yeah?" said Daniel, without much interest.

Lisanne closed her eyes. He was probably the kind of guy who didn't care whether a girl had a boyfriend or not. He could still have whoever he wanted.

By the time Maggie returned with the specials—chicken-fried steak with gravy, mashed potatoes, and biscuits—Lisanne had lost her appetite.

"Guess you filled up on chips, huh?" said Daniel, watching her push the untouched biscuits across her plate.

Lisanne didn't reply, and continued staring at the ruins of her meal.

"You could have had anything from the menu," he said, gently. "Maggie just knows what I like. I'm sorry—I should have told her to wait and see what you wanted."

"No, it's fine," she said, quietly. "Actually I'm kind of tired. I think I'll grab a taxi. You don't have to take me back."

Daniel frowned.

"It's no problem. Besides, I was the one who brought you out here."

"It's fine," she said again, not meeting his eyes.

"For fuck's sake, Lis!" he said, crossly. "What's crawled up your ass?"

"Nothing!" she said, hotly. "I'm fine." Which was a big fat lie. "I told you. I'm tired."

"Whatever," he muttered, coldly.

He ducked out of the booth to pay the check before Lisanne could say anything.

Lisanne was miserable. She felt 33% angry; 33% hurt; 33% dumb; and 0% surprised. She didn't know what happened to that last 1%—she really hated math.

She tugged on her jacket and dug out her cell phone to call a cab. But long fingers reached over her shoulder and pulled it from her hand.

"What are you doing?"

"I said I'd take you back and I will," said Daniel, stiffly.

"No thanks."

He growled with frustration.

"Why are you being such a bitch?"

"I can't imagine," she said, coldly.

She knew she was being unfair—it wasn't like she was his girlfriend or anything. But, come on! He was talking about checking out her roommate in front of her. Did he think her feelings didn't count even a tiny bit?

He tried one last time.

"I'm guessing I've done something to make you mad, but I have no fucking clue what it is."

"Give me my damn phone, Daniel!"

Looking furious, he tossed it back to her. She fumbled and came close to dropping it on the floor.

Now she was pissed as well as upset.

"You could have broken it!"

"I didn't know you couldn't fucking catch for shit," he snarled back at her.

"You're such a jerk!" she hissed, tears leaking from her eyes.

He stopped suddenly.

"Are you crying?"

"No!"

"Yes, you are."

"Leave me alone, Daniel," she said, her voice shaky.

Lisanne stormed out of the diner, ignoring the curious or concerned stares of other customers, and turned her back on Daniel, not wanting to see him or talk to him.

He grabbed her by the shoulders and spun her around.

"Will you just tell me what the fuck is wrong?"

Lisanne stuck out her lip mulishly and Daniel dropped his shoulders in defeat.

"Just get on the damn bike, Lis."

Wondering whether it was worth arguing the point, Lisanne stood with her arms wrapped protectively around her body.

Daniel's face morphed from anger to resignation.

"Do what you want. I'll wait till your cab gets here."

Mentally, Lisanne was giving herself an ass-kicking for being so damn stubborn. Victory in the battle of wills had come at a very high cost. She scrolled down to the number of a local taxi firm and dialed.

"They'll be here in five minutes," she said, in a small voice. "You don't have to wait."

Daniel didn't speak, just leaned against his bike, gazing off into the distance, his face an unreadable mask.

Lisanne stood in awkward silence, fiddling with her phone just to have something to do with her hands.

She was both relieved and resentful when the cab arrived. Then puzzled and confused when Daniel opened the door for her and handed the driver two ten dollar bills to pay the fare.

Lisanne didn't even have a chance to thank him before the driver pulled away.

She replayed the afternoon in her head. It had been fine until he'd admitted that he thought Kirsty was hot. Lisanne knew that her little temper tantrum had been nothing more than plain old jealousy. Daniel hadn't done anything wrong: she, on the other hand, could probably have won the bitch of the year award.

She chewed on a lip, wondering what to do—wondering if there was any way of salvaging the situation.

After writing and deleting at least four different messages, she finally picked one that said enough but not too much.

* L: thank you for paying for the taxi *

There was no reply.

CHAPTER 5

Lisanne didn't see Daniel at all the following day—and he didn't text her back.

Kirsty had accepted her explanation of being 'tired' without question, although she'd thrown Lisanne several penetrating glances. She'd shown her support by plying Lisanne with candy and cookies—no questions asked.

It wasn't until Friday that she saw Daniel again. It was just before their shared Business class. Lisanne was keyed up, her apology prepared and practiced so she was sure she wouldn't mumble, or have an embarrassing episode of word vomit.

But all her thoughts were sucked out along with the air in her body, when she saw him outside the lecture hall in a steamy liplock with a blonde girl.

Someone yelled out, "Get a room!" and Kirsty gave Lisanne a sympathetic look, squeezing her arm gently. But she didn't say anything and Lisanne was grateful for that.

Kirsty led them to the back of the hall in the two empty seats next to Red T-shirt guy—Vin—then made the introductions.

"Hey, baby," he said, gazing with warm eyes at Kirsty.

She kissed him quickly on the lips.

"Vin, this is my extremely talented and wonderful roommate, Lisanne."

"Good to meet you, 'extremely talented and wonderful' roommate," he said, with a smile. "Me and the guys are looking forward to hearing you sing on the weekend."

Lisanne pinked up rapidly, throwing a desperate look at her friend.

Kirsty grinned back and Lisanne managed to mutter a strangled, "Thanks!"

Vin winked and hooked his arm around Kirsty's shoulder.

Lisanne had to admit that he was kind of nice and, for a football player, not at all cocky. There were those dratted stereotypes again.

And he was obviously nuts about Kirsty. It would have been sweet—if it weren't for the fact that it made Lisanne want to commit an act of violence on the nearest piece of furniture. But the innocent chairs blinked back at her with the benign air of planks of wood. Instead, she confined her violent impulses to stabbing the keyboard on her laptop as she set up a new doc file.

Daniel strolled in a few minutes later, a smear of lipstick on his left cheek. He did his usual trick of throwing his jacket onto one seat and his shoulder bag onto another. Lisanne ducked her head down. She didn't want him to catch her staring. But when she looked up again, she saw his head turning toward the front and had the distinct impression that he'd been looking for her. But had he?

Professor Walden walked in and the lecture began. Lisanne managed to make some sensible notes but her attention was only half there, at best.

Fifty minutes later, Lisanne still hadn't decided what to say to Daniel, but she didn't get the chance either. As soon as the lecture finished, Kirsty claimed her attention by telling Vin all about Lisanne's upcoming gig, and by the time she could get away without being too rude, Daniel had gone.

Her apology would have to remain unsaid: unless she wanted to be a coward and send it by text. So she took the simple way out.

She did nothing.

The weekend passed in a haze of rehearsals, homework, and spending time with Kirsty and her friends. Unfortunately, that meant spending time with the ghastly Shawna, too, but Lisanne had the pleasure of seeing that nobody else seemed to enjoy her company either. In fact, she distinctly saw Vin roll his eyes at some bitchy remark Shawna had made, and he'd winked when Lisanne caught his eye.

Vin and Kirsty were fast becoming inseparable, but Lisanne noticed that Kirsty made every effort to make time for her roommate, as well—she was more than grateful for that. Lisanne had come to the conclusion that being on her own sucked. Right now, she hated her own company as much as she hated her guilty thoughts.

She still hadn't fixed the Daniel situation—a situation that she'd dug for herself—so she decided to man up and text him.

* L: library tomorrow? 4 PM? *

Okay, maybe 'man up' was putting it too strongly.
Daniel's reply was even briefer.

* D: Fine *

Four letters and no winking smiley. Definitely no flirting or sexting. And, was he deliberately mimicking her words of a week ago: *fine*? If he was, Lisanne knew she deserved it. Her penance was to feel like shit and spend five bucks on chips and cookies. She owed him.

The next day, she took her place at their usual table, feeling anxious and uncomfortable. When someone touched her shoulder, she squealed and jumped.

Daniel slouched into the seat opposite her and muttered "Hi" without waiting for her to reply.

He looked tired, which was accentuated by the fact that he hadn't shaved. She realized the stubble was hiding a dark bruise on one side of his jaw. Maybe he'd gotten into another fight.

She touched his hand lightly and he looked up at her.

"I'm sorry about last week. You're right. I was being a bitch. Can we start over?"

He gave a lopsided smile.

"Yeah, sure. It's not been the same without you yelling at me."

Lisanne breathed out in a long, relieved sigh.

"I brought cookies and chips."

"Do I get to eat any this week?"

"If you're quick," she said.

"I'm always quick."

Lisanne raised an eyebrow, and Daniel's eyes widened as he realized what he'd said.

"God! Don't ever repeat that! I'll completely deny saying it."

"Your secret is safe with me," she teased.

He nodded, his face serious.

"I know it is. Thanks."

His tone surprised her and she had to look away from his intense gaze.

They worked peacefully, the only interruption being the rustle of illicit chip bags.

But when they finished up, there was no offer of coffee, no offer of a ride on Sirona, just a smile and a casual, "See ya next week."

"Daniel, wait!"

But he'd already turned his back and was walking away. Lisanne leapt up from her chair, hearing it clatter backward as she tried to grab his arm.

Daniel turned around, surprised.

"What's up?"

"Daniel, I … I…"

"What is it, LA?"

She was surprised to hear him use Roy's silly nickname for her, but it gave her enough confidence to speak.

"Will you come—on Saturday? To the gig? I know you can't … but … I'd like … will you?"

His mouth twisted in distaste and he shook his head.

"Lis, don't…"

She immediately stepped back.

"I'm sorry," she said, at once. "That was selfish of me."

He scrubbed his hand over his face in frustration.

"I just ... I *can't*..." he said, his voice tense, as if he was in pain.

"I know. I'm sorry. Really. Forget I said anything. I ... I'll see you in class on Friday."

He nodded, but didn't reply. As he walked from the library, Lisanne could see that his shoulders were slumped and his head hung down, as if pulled by a great weight.

Stupid! Stupid! Stupid! Stupid and cruel, her conscience chided.

Sighing and internally berating herself, she stuffed the rest of the cookies and chips into her bag, piled up her books and laptop, and dragged herself back to her room—where she proceeded to finish the cookies, and went to bed feeling nauseous.

But on Thursday morning, Lisanne woke up feeling worse. She was bathed in sweat, her throat was dry, and her tongue felt as if it had been lying at the bottom of a parrot's cage.

She made a rush for the bathroom, then crawled back to bed, groaning loudly. She could just about manage to drink water without throwing up. She turned off her phone and slept for several more hours. At the end of the school day, Kirsty arrived and was horrified to see the sweaty, shivering mess.

"Why the hell didn't you call me?" she said, angrily. "Jeez! You look horrible."

Lisanne moaned and clutched her stomach.

Kirsty sat on the edge of her bed and felt Lisanne's forehead.

"Ugh, you're all clammy, but you're not too hot. I think it's just stomach flu. Stay in bed and I'll make you some herbal tea. My mom always makes it with ginger—it's good for settling bad stomachs."

Kirsty wanted to cancel her own plans for the evening, but Lisanne insisted that all she needed to do was sleep, and that it would be as boring as hell for Kirsty to stay in and watch her.

They agreed on a compromise: Kirsty would go for dinner with Vin as planned, but come back by 10 PM to check on the patient. She was as good as her word, dosing Lisanne with more herbal tea, and fortifying her with crackers.

By Friday, Lisanne was feeling a little better, but Kirsty decided for her that another day resting in bed would seal the deal.

"Besides," she insisted, "you want to be well for the gig. We can't have you throwing up on stage—that would be too much like punk rock."

As she walked out of the dorm room to their Business class, Kirsty called over her shoulder, "I'll say 'hi' to Daniel for you," then laughed as she saw Lisanne's jaw drop.

Twenty minutes later, Lisanne was just falling asleep again when her cell phone beeped, waking her thoroughly.

Irritated, she opened the message. Her heart gave a happy jolt when she saw it was from Daniel.

> * D: heard you sick? You need anything?
> Can come by after this? *

A smile lit her up from the inside out. *He wanted to make her feel better. He cared about her.* And then the realization hit. If he came over, he'd see her looking like a reject from a drug ed video—or something that had been dug up and ought to be reburied. Her longing to see him warred with her vanity. Vanity won.

Gritting her teeth, she sent a text back.

> * L: Thanx. Feel gross but better than yesterday.
> Won't subject u to fugly parade. LA xx *
> * D: Am open-minded ;)
> Seriously—you need anything? *

He was *so* sweet.

> * L: I'm good. Kirsty looking after me
> like momma bear. See you next week? LA xx *
> * D: ok. Be good *

Daniel had told her to 'be good'. She sighed—as if she'd ever been anything else. She wanted to be just a little bit bad. Or rather, she wanted to have a little bit of bad—a Daniel-shaped slice of wickedness. Just a small taste. Or a large one.

She sighed again.

By Saturday, she was feeling semi-human, which was a huge step up.

"Well, you don't look too gross," was Kirsty's verdict.

Lisanne suspected she was being kind.

But she managed to eat some breakfast, and had soup and a roll for lunch.

Operation 'Make Lisanne Look Smoking Hot' began four hours before the gig. Kirsty had wanted to start earlier, citing stomach flu ickyness required drastic action, but Lisanne had taken herself off to a practice room in the music block to warm up her voice by singing scales—something she absolutely refused to do in front of Kirsty.

Lisanne's nerves, never particularly resilient, were tap dancing up and down her spine, sending quivering shudders throughout her entire body.

When her cell phone started beeping every 30 seconds with texts from Kirsty, Lisanne dragged herself back to the dorm room.

It was a nightmarish version of Dress Up Barbie, where every lotion, potion, spray and powder in Kirsty's scarily comprehensive makeup arsenal, was lavished on Lisanne. Three hours of pampering was followed by Kirsty unveiling the outfit she'd decided should adorn her creation.

"I can't wear that!" gasped Lisanne, shocked beyond words.

She stared at the dress that Kirsty was holding out like a proud game show hostess. Well, calling it a 'dress' would have been a vast exaggeration: it was more like a scrap of material with bondage style leather laces up the side. It was strapless, backless and damn near skirtless.

"Nonsense," said Kirsty, firmly. "You'll look amazing. You'll look *hot*. Daniel won't be able to take his eyes off of you."

"He won't be there," Lisanne answered, sadly.

"What? Why the hell not?!"

Lisanne shrugged, feeling guilty and knowing that Kirsty couldn't possibly understand his reasons. She wondered again at the price Daniel paid, when everyone assumed he behaved like a jerk.

"Um, I think he was busy," she replied, lamely.

Kirsty muttered something under her breath, and thrust a pair of knee-high boots at Lisanne. This time, she didn't even try to argue, but wondered if you could get vertigo from five inch heels.

Lisanne sat on the bed, taking deep breaths to try and quell her nerves—if only a little—while Kirsty poured herself into a deep red halter top and skinny jeans.

Her cell beeped and she glanced at the message, hoping it would be from Daniel. But it wasn't.

* Wish I could be there.
Break a leg! Rodney xx *

Lisanne smiled to herself, happy that her high school friend had remembered it was her big night, and was about to reply when a knock at the door had her heart thumping painfully.

"Hey! Two gorgeous girls," said Vin, with a surprised look.

He swept Kirsty into a hug but she yelled out, "Don't smudge my lipstick."

He laughed.

"Okay, okay! I don't won't to get my ass kicked. Lookin' good, ladies. Your chariot awaits."

Kirsty took his arm, and he offered his other to Lisanne.

Gratefully, she hooked her hand through his, and hung on for dear life as she tottered toward his car.

Luke, CJ and Manek, three of his football buddies, were already squeezed into the back seat. Lisanne had no option but to hop onto Kirsty's knee in the passenger seat.

Luke sighed.

"Oh man, that is so close to one of my fantasies coming true."

Kirsty snorted.

"From what I've heard, fantasies are the only things you've got coming—true or otherwise."

The others laughed and Lisanne managed a weak smile. She felt as sick as a dog.

They parked half a block away from the club and Lisanne had an entourage to escort her to the back door.

Unfortunately, that meant that they had to walk past the waiting line. They all turned when someone called Kirsty's name.

Shawna.

Ugh.

"I called your cell like a thousand times," she said to Kirsty, accusingly.

"Oh, I must have put it on silent by mistake," came the even reply.

But Shawna wasn't put off that easily, and threaded her arm through CJ's. He looked rather surprised and raised his eyebrows at Vin, but didn't say anything.

"This is so cool!" said Kirsty, as the bouncer escorted them in through the back. "It's like being VIPs! Well, Lis, you are a VIP tonight. See you out front, honey. Knock 'em dead!"

Kissing Lisanne on the cheek, Kirsty whispered in her ear, "Deep breathing, sweetie. You know you're great—you just have to show everyone else now."

She gave her another hug, and vanished toward the front of the club where the noise was increasing decibel by decibel.

Lisanne felt a tiny bit relieved when she saw Roy.

"Whoa, baby girl! You scrub up good. Phew! You look too hot to handle. How you doin'?"

"I feel like I'm going to throw up," she said, honestly.

"Nah, you'll be fine. As soon as you set foot on that stage, you'll be awesome."

Daniel stood outside the club, sucking hard on his smoke.

He'd been watching from across the street when Lisanne had arrived. His eyes had almost dropped out of his head and rolled into the gutter along with his thoughts, when he saw her barely there dress and sky-high heels. He had to admit she looked pretty damn hot. Not at all like the shy girl that he met every week in the library. Although he kind of liked her, too.

He wasn't pleased to see her linking arms with a couple of jocks. Nor had he been able to tell which of them she was with, and that bugged the shit out of him.

He dropped his cigarette to the pavement and ground it out with his heel. His chest felt tight with frustration, and he wanted to spew bitter words and rant at the powers that be.

Some days he could almost accept the hand he'd been dealt. Shit happens. Sometimes you were at the back of the line, but sometimes you were right at the front. Some days he could just say to hell with it, to hell with everyone, and get on with his life. But some days he wanted to snarl and yell and scream his fury at the unfairness of it all.

Today was one of those days.

When Lisanne had asked Daniel to come to the club to see her, he'd felt physically sick. He'd wanted to run and hide, and it had taken everything he'd had to remain standing talking to her in the library. She had no idea what she was asking of him: how could she?

Torture could be so innocent.

Slowly, reluctantly, Daniel made his way to the front of the line, passing irritated clubbers as they waited impatiently. The doorman waved him along without a second glance, and Daniel made his way toward the bar.

He would need a drink if he was going to get through the evening without hitting something. Or someone.

A couple of girls eye-fucked him from the opposite end of the bar, but he didn't return their interest.

Ordering a bourbon and beer chaser, he waited for the change in ambience that would announce the arrival of the live music.

He made his way to the back of the crowded room and stood aloof—watching but not joining in, seeing but not caring. He really fucking hadn't wanted to come tonight, but he hadn't been able to stay away either.

He could feel the adrenaline building in the club, the atmosphere thickening like smoke. He knew how she'd be feeling now: that heavy tension that could only be released by letting the music flow through you, letting it pull all the threads of your body to weave a tapestry of sound.

He watched as trembling legs carried her onto the stage, her terrified eyes shooting left and right, as if she was searching for somewhere to hide. She stood hunched over the microphone, her chest rising and falling rapidly. He could see that the crowd was undecided whether or not they'd accept the terrified-looking girl, who hung onto the microphone as if it would save her from an angry mob.

But then the bass throbbed into life, and Daniel could feel the vibrations of the drum kit pulse through his body.

And she started to sing.

Her face lit up and she began to breathe. It was like watching a flower open and turn its face to the sun. She poured her heart and soul into the song as she commanded the stage.

He stood alone, watching the crowd, watching her, feeling the music through his body—hearing nothing.

Daniel pulled out his phone and snapped a picture of her lifting her voice, the crowd beneath her howling their delight.

And then he turned and left. It was too much. And it was far, far too little.

Everyone agreed that Lisanne's debut had been a triumph.

They'd started with Etta, then rocked into Adele's *Rolling in the Deep*, which had people leaping up and down, chilled out with *Hey Love* by Quadron, tried out some of their own material which had been amazing, and finished with some indie classics and, of course, Alicia Keys *Fallin'*.

They hadn't attempted *Dirrty* and, bearing in mind what

she'd been wearing, Lisanne was relieved.

She was covered in sweat, half her makeup rubbed off onto her hands, exhausted and exhilarated—her body was buzzing.

"You were awesome, Lisanne!" shouted Kirsty, barging into the shabby dressing room and hugging her senseless.

"Way to go, Lis!" said Vin, joining in the group hug and kissing her on the cheek.

Lisanne smiled and grinned and said all the right things.

She'd loved being up on the stage. She'd loved hearing the cheers of the crowd as her voice hit every high note. She was happy Kirsty had been there to see it all and see her through it. She was glad that Vin and his friends had approved and toasted her with bottles of beer. She was delirious that it had gone well, and she was relieved that Roy and the guys had given her a universal thumbs up. But through it all, she'd hoped that Daniel would come.

She'd scanned the crowd but couldn't find his face.

That was okay. That was fine. She hadn't really expected him to come. She should never have asked.

When Daniel cut the engine outside his house, he felt wrung out. He hadn't been back to the club for a live music night since … well, not for a long while.

He climbed the steps to his house, not surprised that the front door was hanging wide open, people he didn't recognize spilling out onto the street. They could have been friends of Zef's, or they could have been customers. Sometimes it was the same thing.

He swiped a six-pack from a table, not caring who it belonged to, and trudged up the stairs to his room.

He stared with distaste at the girl asleep—or passed out—in the hallway.

Thank fuck he had his own bathroom that he could keep locked; otherwise living there would have been intolerable.

He opened the bedroom door using his key, and locked it behind him again. He was vaguely aware of music thumping through the house because of the vibrations that traveled up through the floor. It was the only advantage to being deaf: noise couldn't keep him awake at night. It was a small mercy—but something was better than nothing.

He snapped the tab on the first beer and drank it down in one go. Then he turned on his laptop and downloaded the photograph of Lisanne from his camera phone. Damn, if she didn't look hot in that outfit, but seeing her sing—he'd never seen anyone look more beautiful. She looked like she fit inside her own skin. He hadn't seen her so at ease before—she glowed.

He printed out the picture and stuck it on his notice board among the photographs of his family. Then he turned off his laptop, toed off his boots and sat in the dark, drinking beer until sleep or oblivion took him.

CHAPTER 6

Kirsty and Vin had insisted that the party wasn't over. Lisanne's triumph needed some serious celebration, no matter that all she wanted to do was go back to her room and crash for 12 hours.

"You are so not raining on this parade, missy!" shouted Kirsty, grabbing her arm.

"You don't want to argue with her, Lis," laughed Vin. "I thought you'd have known that by now."

"Yes, but…" began Lisanne.

It was no use. They piled into Vin's car, followed by two taxi loads of other students they'd met at the club, and went back to his fraternity house.

Lisanne had never considered that she'd be the kind of girl who could get invited to a frat party, but Vin's friends were fun and surprisingly friendly, and they drank and danced until dawn.

They did. But Lisanne found a sofa in a dark corner and lay down with a pile of coats on top of her and slept, hearing music in her dreams, seeing a pair of laughing hazel eyes.

When she'd finally gotten home, it was Sunday and the clouds were tinged pink with the coming dawn.

Kirsty and Lisanne were standing arm in arm outside the dorm rooms, breathing in the pure morning air.

"How does it feel?" said Kirsty, quietly.

Lisanne tried to find words to sum up the chaos of emotions that had coursed through over the last few hours.

"I don't know," she said, at last. "I feel different, but the same. Happy, but sort of calm. It's hard to describe."

85

"You were amazing out there, I'm so envious," said Kirsty.

Lisanne laughed but Kirsty tugged her arm.

"I mean it. You really moved people with your singing. People look at me and think they see straight through me."

Lisanne stared at her. "But you're so beautiful!"

Kirsty gave a small smile. "It's not false modesty, Lis, I know I'm pretty." She shrugged. "But most of the time that's all they see."

Lisanne shook her head. "That's not true. You've been an amazing friend to me—I see how thoughtful you are and how kind. Vin sees it, too. He's crazy about you."

Kirsty's eyes brightened. "You think?"

"I *know*," said Lisanne, with certainty. "I've seen the way he looks at you—he adores you. But he *sees* you, too. And *I* see you."

Kirsty smiled. "By the way, did you know Daniel was there tonight—last night?"

Lisanne was stunned: her eyes flickered up to Kirsty.

"Daniel? But he said he wasn't going?"

"Guess he changed his mind," said Kirsty, with a knowing look. "Shawna tried to speak to him and he totally blew her off."

"Oh," said Lisanne, unsure how to answer that.

"He was by himself," said Kirsty, encouragingly.

Lisanne couldn't help smiling to herself.

"Come on," said Kirsty. "We need to get some beauty sleep."

When Lisanne woke up, it was nearly lunchtime and her stomach growled, reminding her that she'd missed breakfast as well as dinner the night before.

Despite everything, she felt refreshed and relaxed.

She peered at her cell phone. It was 12:00, and Kirsty was still buried under her duvet. Then Lisanne noticed that she had a text message from Daniel.

* D: Roy said you were amazing.
U looked great! *

He thought she looked great?

Lisanne's cheeks heated immediately, and the warm feeling spread throughout her body. She stretched out in her bed, a huge, ridiculous smile on her face. *He thought she looked great!* Okay, so Kirsty had spent several hours getting her into a presentable condition, but still. *Great!*

Kirsty finally rolled out of bed an hour later and they spent a quiet afternoon catching up on homework and doing chores. It hadn't taken long for reality to hit, but Lisanne didn't mind—it was soothing to do ordinary things.

By Monday, most of the euphoria had worn off. Several people had come up to her to say they'd enjoyed the gig, and one or two had asked about the next one. Roy had vaguely mentioned playing elsewhere in town, but there was nothing definite planned.

Lisanne was just about to visit the campus coffee shop for a quick hit of caffeine before heading back to her dorm room, when she heard raised voices. Across the quad, she saw Daniel in some sort of argument with two students who looked old enough to be seniors. From their body language, she could see that it was a tense stand-off, possibly a precursor to a fight. She didn't know what to do, but simply acted on pure instinct, hurrying over.

Daniel's voice was angry.

"I said no, man! Stay the fuck away from me."

"Oh, come on. Everyone knows your brother is the guy around here. Stop pretending you're fucking Snow White."

Daniel turned to walk away, but the bigger guy grabbed his shoulder.

Daniel pulled back his fist but then saw Lisanne running toward him. Instead of swinging, he stepped back and took a deep breath.

"Don't start what you can't finish," sneered the other student. "Nice that your little girlfriend is protecting you."

Daniel's face creased with anger and Lisanne had to grab hold of his arm to drag him away.

"Don't! He's not worth it!" she said, urgently.

She wasn't sure if he'd understood her, but Lisanne pulled him back. She kept tugging his arm while he kept his eyes firmly fixed on the two students, who continued to jeer at him.

"What was that about?" Lisanne said breathlessly, once they were a good distance away.

Daniel was still looking over his shoulder, so she tapped him on his hand.

"What?" he snarled.

Lisanne dropped his arm, her face shocked by this angry tone.

"Sorry," he muttered. "Sorry."

"It's okay," she said, faintly. "What was it all about?"

He shook his head. "They're assholes."

Lisanne was pretty certain there was more to it than that, but as she hadn't heard how the argument had started, she thought it was wiser to let it go.

"Do you want to get a coffee?" she said, quietly.

He shook his head again, ran one hand through his hair and tugged at his eyebrow ring with the other.

"No. I need to get off campus."

There was an awkward pause.

"Well, okay. I'll see you Friday then?"

He looked down at her quickly. "Do you want to come with me? Just take off for a couple of hours? I don't know—go somewhere?"

"Um, okay," Lisanne said hesitantly, thinking of the pile of homework she still had to tackle. "Where do you want to go?"

Daniel closed his eyes. "Anywhere."

When they reached his motorcycle, he passed her the spare helmet and soon they were leaving the city behind them, heading east.

Houses and shops flew past, and Lisanne couldn't help wondering how much over the limit they were going. She was dreading that at any moment, she'd hear the shrill sirens of a police cruiser behind them. What were the penalties for speeding? Could a passenger get into trouble? She had visions of phoning her mom and dad to bail her out of jail. It was too horrible to contemplate. She knew *exactly* what they'd think of that … and what they'd think of Daniel.

God, how fast was he going? They were going to get into an accident, never mind getting pulled over.

She squeezed his waist more tightly and, ironically, that only seemed to spur him on to go faster.

When Lisanne felt brave enough to open her eyes again, she could see the ocean rising up in the distance, gray and massive.

By now, Daniel had slowed down considerably and Lisanne realized they were traveling parallel to the boardwalk. She and Kirsty had talked about coming down to the shoreline and checking out the coffee shops, but Lisanne was very happy to be doing it with Daniel instead.

Eventually, he drove into a parking lot and pulled off his helmet

He breathed in deeply and seemed to relax several degrees.

Giving Lisanne a small smile, he climbed off and held out his hand to her.

She scrambled awkwardly, then stood still, taking in her surroundings.

"It's beautiful here," she said, a feeling of peace spreading through her.

"Yeah. I like coming out to the ocean when I'm…" He stopped suddenly, unable or unwilling to continue what he'd been going to say. "You want a coffee?"

"Sure, my treat," she said, smiling away the uncomfortable moment.

"No way!" he said, pretending to be appalled. "We have to celebrate for last Saturday. I'm buying."

"But it was your gas that got us here!"

"Do you always argue this much?" he grinned, raising his eyebrow so that the small silver ring he wore glinted in the sunshine.

Lisanne put her head to one side, and smiled back. "Yep.

Pretty much."

He rolled his eyes. "Like I couldn't have guessed. I'm still buying."

They wandered down the boardwalk until they found a small café that was selling coffee and donuts. It also had an outdoor patio area, stretching onto the boardwalk, and it was plenty warm enough to sit outside.

Daniel sighed happily as he sank his teeth into the jam filled pastry. It was gone in about three bites and Lisanne caught him eyeing hers.

"Don't you touch my donut!" she threatened. "I'm dangerous when you try to keep me from my sugar rush."

"Yeah, and you've got a thing for chips, too. Don't think I didn't notice," he shot back at her.

"If you're that hungry, get yourself another donut, but just take your eyes off of mine, mister."

He laughed, but took her advice and waved to the waitress, ordering two more donuts for himself.

Lisanne's eyes grew wide.

"You're going to be hyper from all that sugar," she warned him. "Either that or your teeth will fall out."

"Jeez, chill!" he said. "You're sounding like my kindergarten teacher."

She scowled and he leaned back in his chair, laughing at her.

"I can't help it," she said, petulantly. "I'm sensible. Mom says I was born middle-aged."

"Yeah?" he said, leaning forward and planting his elbows on the table. "Well, you didn't look middle-aged on Saturday night—you looked hot. Every guy in that place had a boner for you."

Lisanne stared and blushed, her eyes dropping to the table, too embarrassed to speak.

"Just sayin'," he smirked, stuffing another piece of donut into his mouth.

"Thanks, I think," she mumbled. "Kirsty did it—hair, makeup, that dress." Then she looked up. "I'm glad you came: I didn't think you would."

He grimaced then flicked his eyes away.

"I wasn't going to."

"I know. But thank you anyway."

He nodded slowly.

As they finished their coffee, Daniel wiped the last grain of sugar from his lips. Lisanne couldn't help sighing, watching his long, strong fingers brushing across his face.

He caught her staring.

"What?"

"You missed a bit."

She started to reach out, but hesitated at the last moment. Daniel blinked, then scrubbed both hands over his face.

"Okay?"

She nodded. "Yes, you're good."

He smirked again. "Oh, no, baby. You've got that wrong."

Lisanne rolled her eyes.

"You're such a *boy*."

He leaned down with a smile on his face, and whispered into her ear.

"Man, not boy."

She felt his warm breath tickle her skin, but it was several seconds before his words sank in. She shivered, whether with cold or pleasure or something else, she didn't know.

They strolled along the boardwalk, close but not touching, in companionable silence. Every now and then, they'd stop to look in a shop window or admire the way the colors of the sea swirled and changed with every passing moment.

But too soon, gray clouds started to roll in and heavy drops of rain began to patter down around them.

"Ah, hell," said Daniel, frowning at the threatening sky. "We're gonna get seriously wet."

He was right.

They ran for his bike, but there was no way they could outrun the storm.

The rain was lashing down and they were both soaked to the

skin, as Daniel raced back along the highway.

He was slightly better off, his leather jacket giving him a little more protection, but his jeans were plastered to his legs and he could feel water seeping into his boots.

Hunched behind, sheltering her body with his, Lisanne huddled into him, her violent shivers sending tremors through his own body.

It was crazy to continue getting soaked, trying to make it to the dorms, when his own place was closer. They were both half drowned and frozen, and the rain on his visor was making it dangerous. They'd be better off going to his place than carrying on driving to the dorms. Plus, he knew for a certain fact that it would be easier to dry clothes at his place. No one would be using the washing machine or dryer there—no one ever did.

He pulled off the highway one exit early. Lisanne was so numb that she didn't even notice, until they were rumbling down a residential street in a part of town she didn't know.

Daniel cut the engine and clambered stiffly from the bike, pulling Lisanne with him.

"Where are we?" she stuttered between shivers, as he tugged her up the steps to the porch.

"My place. I thought it was just dumb to carry on getting soaked. You can dry your clothes here and get warmed up."

She nodded shakily, but when she followed him inside, her eyes bulged—and she stared at the couple in the lounge who were smoking from a bong.

"Is that…?"

"Friends of Zef's," he muttered, not wanting to get into it.

They passed another couple who were gazing vacantly into space with glazed eyes, and Daniel wondered if bringing her there was a mistake.

He had no idea where Zef was.

He motioned for Lisanne to follow him up the stairs, and she clung to him as if he were the last life raft on the Titanic.

He pulled out his room key and pushed the door open for her, then locked it behind them.

"Why have you locked the door?" she whispered, her expression suddenly wary.

His eyes narrowed in confusion, then he realized how it looked from her point of view.

"What? No! God, no, Lis! How could you think … it's this place … people wander in if the door isn't locked. That's all. I'm sorry. I didn't mean to scare you."

She shook her head and tried to smile, while her face was still frozen and her teeth chattering.

"No, sorry. It's just…" she paused, swallowing whatever she'd been going to say, and looked around her. "You have a nice room."

"Thanks," he said, sounding too casual as he watched her nervously wrap her arms around herself.

Then Lisanne's eyes fell on an acoustic guitar. She looked back to him, blinking rapidly.

"You play?"

He pulled a face, picking up the guitar by the neck and tossing it unceremoniously into his closet.

"Not anymore."

"Sorry," she whispered again, internally berating herself for being such an idiot. *Of course* he didn't play anymore.

To cover the awkward silence, Daniel rummaged through his chest of drawers and tossed her one of his t-shirts.

"Put this on and I'll go put your clothes in the dryer. It won't take long." He shot her his sexy smile. "I'll turn my back."

Flushing slightly, Lisanne peeled off her soaking clothes until she was standing in just her underwear. Hastily, she pulled on his t-shirt, which hung to the middle of her thighs. She couldn't help lifting it to her face and breathing in deeply. It smelled like him, his cologne clinging to the material, along with a faint trace of cigarette smoke. She looked over her shoulder, but he was as good as his word and had kept his back turned. She'd expected nothing less. Lisanne tapped him lightly on the shoulder.

"I'm done."

He smiled, and his eyes flashed appreciatively up and down

her legs.

"Sorry," he said, catching her look. "I'm a guy." He shrugged and winked at her, then scooped up her wet clothes, which had left a damp patch on the bare floorboards.

"I'll just be a minute. Lock the door behind me. I'll knock when I get back."

While he was gone, Lisanne took a moment to examine his room. It was much tidier than she'd imagined, and the sheets on his bed were clean and fresh. He had a small bookshelf that was crammed with textbooks from school, and paperbacks by writers she'd never heard of. A lot of them had foreign names, Russian maybe. Stacked up next to them was a pile of toilet paper. Odd.

In the corner, there was now a space where his guitar had been, and Lisanne felt horribly guilty for having mentioned it. Sometimes she only opened her mouth to change feet, she thought acidly.

Then she saw there were half a dozen photographs tacked to a notice board. There was a picture of a younger looking Daniel and a slightly older guy she assumed was Zef. They looked alike, with the same black hair and hazel eyes. There was a photo of his parents, and a family picture of the four of them together—they were laughing.

Then her heart skipped a beat when she peered closer. Daniel had included a picture of her among the family photographs. It was from the gig. In it, you could see clearly that she was singing her heart out. She didn't even know he'd taken it. She wouldn't even have known he'd been there if Kirsty hadn't mentioned it, although he *had* texted her later.

A mix of emotions rushed through her. He'd never heard her sing—and never would—but he'd wanted to keep that particular image of her. She didn't understand. Surely that would be the most painful thing for him to see every day?

A light tap on the door brought her back to herself.

"Yes?" she said, hesitantly, and then felt like an idiot. He couldn't hear her, of course.

She opened the door cautiously, and Daniel walked in

carrying two mugs of coffee.

"Thought you might need this."

"Oh, lifesaver!" she gasped, wrapping her hand around the hot cup.

"Sorry," he said. "There's no milk in the house. Someone must have drunk it."

He shrugged.

"How can you stand to live like this?" Lisanne blurted out.

He frowned at her. "It's my home."

"God, I'm so stupid!" she croaked. "Sorry, Daniel."

He twitched a shoulder but he still looked hurt.

"I mean it," she said, touching his arm lightly. "I am sorry." Then recoiled slightly. "Ugh! You're all wet and clammy!"

He smirked at her.

"Yeah, rain will do that to you."

"I thought you were going to put your clothes in the dryer?"

"Well, I've put yours in. I thought you'd want to get out of here as quickly as possible." He gave her an apologetic smile. "I'll do mine later."

"Well, you should take them off, or you could get sick."

"Are you trying to get me out of my clothes, Lis. Should I take the hint?"

She slapped his arm and huffed as he continued to grin at her.

"Just messing with you, kiddo. Turn your back while I change. No peeking!"

Muttering to herself, Lisanne turned her back, listening to the rustle of material as Daniel pulled off his wet t-shirt and jeans. She couldn't deny it was a turn-on, hearing him remove his clothes while she was standing in the same room. Her body heated at the idea. And then a thought struck her: this might be her best chance to show him that he meant more to her—more than just a friend. She was desperate to know if he felt the same. Sometimes she thought so, despite the other women she'd seen him with. There was the photograph, too, but still…

She took a deep breath and turned around.

He was standing with his back to her, wearing a pair of dark gray boxer briefs. She studied the muscles of his broad back as they rippled and flexed under his skin. She followed the outline of the tattoos across his shoulders and let her eyes drift down his narrow hips, firm ass, and his long, strong legs. He was beautiful, but to Lisanne it was the beauty on the inside that she loved the most. It made her bold.

Maybe he felt her eyes on him because suddenly he turned around, looking at her in surprise.

"Sorry! Sorry! I ... I just ... I just wanted to see," she mumbled, her flaming cheeks highlighting her extreme embarrassment.

He cocked his head to one side, staring at her, but didn't speak.

She couldn't meet his questioning gaze, so she allowed her eyes to wander over his chest. She gasped softly when she noticed the tiny, silver rings he wore in each nipple. It was so unexpected and erotic. It was so Daniel. Wishing she was brave enough to step forward and touch him, Lisanne cursed herself for being such a coward. Kirsty would have. Kirsty would have taken that step, not shuffled from foot to foot like a stupid little girl.

Her eyes dropped further down and she was hypnotized by the bulge in his briefs.

When he spoke, she nearly jumped.

"Have you ever seen a man's cock?"

Her mouth dropped open, then she gave a small nod. "On TV."

He smiled. "Baby doll watches porn?"

"No! God, no! Well, maybe once—at a friend's house."

"Did you like it?"

"Not really. It was a stupid film—the plot was awful. There was no storyline at all."

He laughed gently. "Yeah, well, I don't think that's the point of it."

She flushed. "I guess not."

She was suddenly reminded that she was still staring at him—at one particular part of him. She was shocked when she realized the bulge had grown considerably larger. Her eyes flickered up to his, and he gave a small shrug.

"Have you ever touched a man's cock?"

She shook her head wordlessly as he continued to gaze at her. She couldn't tear her eyes away from him—and she didn't want to.

"Do you want to touch mine?"

Lisanne's heart began to sprint. What was he asking her?

"I … I don't know."

He stood for a moment, looking at her, then dipped down to pick up the sweatpants that he'd dropped.

"Daniel, I…" she waited until he was looking at her again. "Daniel, I…" but she wasn't sure what she wanted to say.

He gave a small smile.

"It's okay, Lis. It's cool."

"No! I mean, I want to…"

"Want to what?"

She didn't answer. Instead she took a step toward him and tentatively laid her hand on his chest, above his heart.

His eyes fluttered closed and he breathed deeply, the movement gently lifting Lisanne's hand as his lungs expanded.

When he opened his eyes again, they were nearly black, and burning with desire. No man had ever looked at Lisanne like that and it took her breath away. A slow heat began to pulse between her legs and she knew that she wanted him. She wanted Daniel to be her first.

Slowly, he raised his right hand, resting it gently against her cheek.

"What do you want, Lisanne?"

"You," she whispered.

He swallowed, and she was fascinated watching his Adam's apple bob up and down in his throat.

"Are you sure? You don't get to have your first time again, baby doll. This isn't how I'd imagined it."

A small smile pulled at the corner of her lips.

"You've imagined it … with me?"

He grinned at her.

"Are you fucking kidding me? You are *hot*. I've wanted you since I met you, but I figured you just wanted to be friends. That's cool. I like having a friend who's a girl."

Lisanne's smile faded. She wasn't sure how she felt about that. But he said she was hot. That meant he liked her, didn't it?

"Can I just … can I touch you?"

He nodded slowly, his eyes following her hand as it moved shakily to his waistband.

Softly, she laid her hand over his crotch and felt his heat and hardness. He inhaled deeply.

"You are so fucking sexy," he said in a low, deep voice.

She stared at him, amazed, but he didn't repeat his extraordinary words.

Feeling bolder, she rubbed her hand over him again and he groaned.

"Oh, sorry!" she cried out, stepping backward.

He grinned at her.

"Nothing to be sorry about, baby doll—only that you're fucking killing me here."

"Sorry!" she muttered again.

He shrugged. "I'll live."

He reached for his sweatpants again, but she laid her hand on his arm. He looked up at her, puzzled.

"Can we just lie down together?"

He raised his eyebrows.

"Okay, but this isn't why I brought you here, Lis. You know that, right?"

She nodded.

"I know."

She lay down on the bed and, after a moment's hesitation he climbed up next to her. He slid his arm around her shoulders and pulled her in for a hug. Her right arm automatically rested on his stomach and he hummed happily.

He nearly leapt off of the bed when she stroked his semi once more.

"Fuck!" he yelled. "Lis! You've got to give me some warning, baby. You'll give me a fucking heart attack!"

She giggled nervously but kept stroking him.

He leaned up to look at her.

"Do you mind?" she whispered.

"Fuck, no!" he said, gazing at her with amazement.

"I want to see it," she said.

This time he didn't hesitate. He lifted his hips and pushed his briefs past his knees, then thrashed with his legs as he kicked them off.

His hard cock leapt up to his stomach, where it bobbed contentedly.

Nervously, Lisanne ran one finger up the large vein and jumped when it twitched at her. She felt rather than heard Daniel's chuckle.

She ran her hand over him again, and heard his deep breaths as he sucked in air through his nose. His skin felt soft and smooth, but also hot and hard beneath her fingers. She squeezed and Daniel shifted his hips upwards into her palm.

"Is that okay?" she asked nervously.

He didn't answer and she realized his eyes were closed, his breaths becoming shallow.

Tentatively, she moved her hand up and down, pulling a moan from deep within his chest.

"Fuck, Lis!" he whispered. "Can you go a bit faster?"

She moved her hand up and down more quickly, enjoying the way his erection thickened and heated beneath her fingers.

"Nnhhmm," he groaned, encouraging her to move still faster.

A bead of pre-cum glistened on his tip and, entranced, she ran her thumb over it.

Daniel swore loudly and started pumping his hips into her hand, his head pressed backward into the pillow, his mouth open.

She moved her hand more quickly, watching his face with fascination as his orgasm began to build.

"I'm gonna cum. I'm gonna cum," he chanted.

Lisanne kept going and suddenly, three jets of pearly liquid shot from his tip, startling her. Daniel called out loudly, then lay still.

His chest heaved, and his eyelids were screwed shut. Lisanne let her eyes drink in his masculine beauty. She felt proud of herself. *She'd* done that. *She'd* made him feel like that. Not some other girl. Not one of the skanks who hung around him all the time.

She lay back on the bed and Daniel pulled her into a careful hug, nuzzling his nose into her hair.

"That was awesome, baby doll," he whispered.

After another minute he sat up and grinned down at her.

"You made a real mess of me—want to clean me up?"

Lisanne wrinkled her nose and shook her head. Daniel chuckled and reached over his bedside table for some of the toilet paper he'd had piled up.

He saw the expression on her face and shrugged.

"I keep it locked in here or it disappears."

He wiped himself clean and tossed the tissues into a waste basket.

"Come here."

Lisanne willingly snuggled into the warmth of his firm chest as he pulled the sheets over them.

"This is nice," he said, quietly.

Lisanne smiled as his free hand stroked her hair. She thought she'd die of happiness when he placed a gentle kiss on the top of her head.

She felt bereft when he sat up.

"Lis, can I ask you something?"

"Um, yeah?"

"Have you ever made yourself come?"

Her cheeks flushed pink. "No!"

Daniel shrugged. "Just sayin'. Lots of girls do."

Lisanne blinked. "Yeah, I guess. But … I…"

He brushed his nose against hers. "Do you want me to?"

"Do I want you to what?"

"Make you come."

"Um, won't it hurt?"

He raised his eyebrows. "No. Why would you say that?"

Lisanne wasn't sure if she could blush any redder. It made it so much harder to have this conversation, knowing that Daniel had to see her face as she spoke.

"Because … because I haven't had sex before."

A look of understanding passed over his face and his lips twitched in a smile.

"No, baby. You don't have to have my dick inside you to have an orgasm. Although I'd really fucking like to try that one day. I can make you come with my fingers if you like. Or my tongue."

"Your t-t-tongue!" she stuttered, unable to stop herself. Then she hid her head in her hands. "Oh God, I'm such a loser!"

He pulled her hands away from her face. "Can't lip read you like that, baby," he said, with a frown.

"Sorry. Sorry. I'm just … I don't know what to say."

"Say yes. I'll make it good for you, I promise. Just my fingers, no tongue."

He waved his jazz hands at her and she had to smile.

"Okay, I guess."

He smiled back. "Could you wound my ego any more, baby doll?" Then his expression became serious. "Can I take your t-shirt off?"

"N-no. I'd rather you didn't."

"Okay," he smiled. "No problem. But you'll let me touch your tits, won't you?"

"Um, all right."

He placed a gentle kiss on her lips. "I won't hurt you, baby doll. I just want to make you feel good."

Lisanne lay back on the bed, her body filled with tension.

Daniel stroked her hair and kissed her lips again, gently tugging her lower lip with his teeth, until she opened her mouth a fraction.

His warm, wet tongue stroked her lips and traced the outline of her mouth. She opened a little more, and his tongue caressed hers, pulling sparks of pleasure from her. She moaned softly and he hummed quietly into her mouth.

She wrapped her arms around his neck and pulled his head down, letting him deepen the kiss.

His hands rested lightly on her waist, then he pulled his lips from hers and planted a path of soft kisses down her throat and over the t-shirt, nuzzling her breasts softly.

She gasped slightly and he looked up when he felt her move.

"Okay?" he whispered.

She nodded quickly and he continued kissing down her chest, pushing the t-shirt up from her waist so he could kiss and lick her exposed stomach.

Her fingers gripped his shoulders as his head moved lower.

"I ... um..."

He lifted his head to look at her. "What did you say, baby? Did you say something?"

"I ... I don't want you to kiss me *there*," she said, nervously.

"I won't if you don't want me to, but I'd like to kiss your sweet little pussy one day."

Lisanne was so embarrassed she didn't know where to look. All she could do was close her eyes.

"Lis, look at me," Daniel ordered.

Reluctantly, her eyes fluttered open.

"Don't be embarrassed with me, Lis. I just want to make you feel good. Just my fingers, I promise. Will you let me?"

"Okaaay," she said, softly.

He kissed her again and she moaned into his mouth, as his tongue tangled with hers. This time she kissed him back, and the growl he released made her triumphant. His hands drifted back to her chest, and his long fingers gently teased her nipples through the soft fabric of the t-shirt.

By her thigh, she felt his cock twitch into life again.

Gradually, her nerves fell away as his tongue worked its magic on her mouth and neck, sucking and nipping, turning her on in ways that amazed her. His hand continued to play with her nipples, occasionally cupping her breasts and massaging them gently.

She reached down and gripped his thickening length, but he pushed her hand away.

"No, baby doll, this is about you."

Lisanne felt her panties grow damp as Daniel continued his sensual assault on her body. It was behaving and moving in ways that were unfamiliar to her, her hips lifting automatically to his touch, as if his own body was summoning hers.

His fingers began to toy with the edge of her panties and Lisanne moaned, barely recognizing the feral sound that fell from her.

Daniel felt the vibration of her moan and took this as encouragement. He slipped his hand inside her panties, causing Lisanne's shallow breaths to catch in her throat.

"You're so wet, baby doll," he said softly into her shoulder. "You're wet for me and one day I want to push my hard cock inside you and feel that sweet tightness all around me, but right now you're going to ride my fingers."

His thumb circled her clit, making Lisanne's body arch off the bed. Quickly, he slipped his index finger inside, sliding it in and out. To Lisanne, it felt like a jolt of electricity passing through her body as the level of arousal took her by surprise.

She groaned and he caught the sound with his lips, pushing his tongue inside her mouth as his finger moved inside her body. Then he added a second finger, and started pumping them slowly as his thumb continued to massage her.

The sensation began deep in her belly, fizzing out to her thighs and toes, causing her muscles to twitch and convulse.

Her body arched again and she cried out.

"That's it, baby doll," whispered Daniel, spurring her on. "Let it go. Let it all go, baby. I'm here. I'm here."

She tried to bat his hands away, sure that she couldn't take anymore, but he pressed his body over hers, forcing his chest against her breasts.

"Ride it, baby," he said, his voice strained. "Fuck my fingers, baby doll."

Lisanne's orgasm ripped across her, spirals of pleasure shooting through her body like quicksilver.

"Oh, God!" she cried out. "Oh, God!"

As her body floated back to earth, Daniel slowly removed his fingers, straightened her panties and tugged her borrowed t-shirt into place.

When Lisanne finally opened her eyes, Daniel was watching her, a calm, focused look on his face.

She blushed even redder when she realized he was sucking his fingers.

He saw her expression.

"You taste real good." He held his hand out to her and wiggled his fingers. "Want to try?"

"No!" she said, shocked.

He grinned at her. "Your loss. So, how was that for you?"

"I ... I..." she stammered. "Um, good?"

Daniel laughed. "Don't go over fucking board or anything!"

Lisanne gave a nervous chuckle. "Sorry, I'm still ... I mean ... that was ... I don't know *what* that was, but it was ... *amazing*. I can see what all the fuss is about now. I mean, I didn't know that ... I mean, wow!"

He smiled. "It gets better: trust me."

Lisanne couldn't imagine how *anything* could be better than that. But then she thought back to his dirty mouth, and all the things he'd said he wanted to do to her. Yeah, she'd definitely like to try that.

Daniel leaned back, pleased with his afternoon's work. In truth, he'd been more than a little surprised when Lisanne had come on to him. Obviously he knew she was a virgin, and he'd thought that she was the type who planned on staying that way until she met Mr. Right. He hadn't wanted to abuse her trust.

But her body was lush, even if she hadn't let him see her naked. And that damn dress she'd worn on Saturday—seriously hot. The fact that she'd wanted to whack him off had surprised the shit out of him. But damn, if it hadn't been good to have her hands on him, playing him like her instrument. And the way she'd responded to his touch had been a real fucking turn-on.

He wasn't sure what she wanted to happen next, but he really hoped she'd let him sleep with her. Not today, perhaps, but soon. Wrapping his arms around her and feeling her head on his chest, knowing he had nothing to hide from her—that made his body feel light in a way he'd never known before.

And seeing her come—that had been pretty fucking amazing. She had no idea how sexy she looked, splayed out beneath him. Yeah, he really wanted some more of that. Did that mean she would be his girlfriend? Did he *want* a girlfriend? He definitely had no idea what she wanted either. Then he frowned: maybe she just wanted him for a fuck buddy—someone to get the pesky business of her virginity out of the way. She wouldn't be the first woman who wanted his cum but not his conversation.

Distracting him from the dark direction of his thoughts, Lisanne stretched like a cat and leaned up on one arm so he could see her face.

"I feel all sort of disjointed … I don't know … disconnected … sort of like I'm floating. It's weird."

"Good weird?"

She smiled. "Definitely good weird." She kissed him quickly on the cheek. "I can see why you've got your reputation—it's very well deserved."

Daniel felt like she'd punched him.

Lisanne saw the softness disappear from his face, and he scowled at her. "What?"

She swallowed nervously as she saw the sudden anger on his face.

"Well, you've always got girls falling all over themselves to sleep with you. You don't even have to *try* to get a girl. I'm just saying … I understand."

Daniel rolled off of the bed and started pulling on his jeans. He couldn't explain his anger even to himself. It wasn't like she said anything that was untrue. But she had to understand that this had been more than a casual fuck to him. They were *friends*, for Chrissake.

"Where are you going?" said Lisanne nervously, then cursed herself for talking to his back again. It was unforgiveable that she kept forgetting.

She tapped him on the shoulder, but he wouldn't turn around and look at her.

"I'll get your clothes from the dryer," he mumbled, and before she could think of what to say, he was gone.

She leaned against the headboard, wondering why he was so upset. What had she said to make him behave like that? She hadn't made any demands of him. Even though she was desperate for him to say that they were exclusive, she didn't want to sound needy or be unrealistic. He hadn't asked her to throw herself at him.

She chewed on a fingernail nervously, feeling relieved when the door opened.

But it wasn't Daniel. It was a man in his mid-twenties with sleeve tattoos covering both arms, multiple piercings, and a furious look on his face.

Lisanne pulled the sheet tightly around her, acutely aware that calling out for Daniel wouldn't do any good.

"What did you do to him?" snarled the man.

Lisanne stared at him, her heart beating frantically.

"Answer me!" he shouted. "Why is my little brother looking like you just shot his fucking puppy?"

"I ... I..."

"I am so sick of you bitches treating him like a fucking toy. He's got feelings, for fuck's sake! But maybe you don't care about that."

Lisanne was shocked into silence. She had no idea what had caused this outburst, and why Daniel's older brother was looking at her murderously.

His eyes narrowed. "You're *her*, aren't you? The singer. I *told* him to stay away from you. I *told* him you'd rip his fucking heart out. You're dangerous. Why can't you just leave him alone?"

Lisanne felt tears prick her eyes, and she fisted the sheet in her hands, looking anxiously at the door, waiting for Daniel to come and tell his brother that he'd got it all wrong.

"I'm fucking warning you," snarled Zef, "I'll..."

But whatever he was going to threaten her with, his words ground to a halt when Daniel reappeared.

"What's going on?" he said, seeing his brother's anger and Lisanne's fear.

Nobody answered.

"I said, what the fuck's going on?" he repeated angrily, the volume rising.

Zef turned to face him.

"Just having a quiet chat to your little woman, bro. No biggie."

Daniel looked at the scared girl on the bed. "Lisanne?"

"We were just talking," she murmured, dropping her eyes to the sheets.

Daniel pulled a hand through his hair in frustration.

"Don't do that!" he spat out. "Don't treat me like a fucking moron!"

Zef laid a soothing hand on his shoulder but Daniel shrugged it off. Then he threw Lisanne's dry clothes at her.

"Get dressed," he commanded. "I'll take you home."

He walked out, leaving Zef and Lisanne staring at each other.

When Zef closed the door, Lisanne dressed quickly, wiping the tears from her eyes. The afternoon had been the best of her life until Daniel had suddenly gone all weird on her. And now his brother hated her, too. It was so confusing.

She tiptoed down the stairs, stepping over a man who appeared to be curled up asleep on the last step.

Daniel was zipping up his damp leather jacket. He didn't even look at Lisanne, simply opening the front door and pulling his bike keys out of his pocket.

Ignoring the light drizzle that continued to darken the sky, Daniel swung his leg over the motorcycle. He still hadn't looked at Lisanne, and simply waited until she climbed on behind him. She tentatively wrapped her arms around his waist, but he didn't respond. This time, the roar of the engine wasn't comforting; instead it was a punctuation mark to her distress.

Daniel drove with reckless speed toward the college, then stopped abruptly outside her dorm room and waited for her to dismount. She handed him her helmet and he dropped it into his saddlebag. She leaned in to kiss him goodbye, needing some sort of closeness, but he pulled away and drove off before she could speak.

"I wondered how long it would be before he realized you were an uptight bitch," said a voice.

Lisanne turned around to see Shawna leaning against the wall, a smug expression on her face.

"Colton finally came to his senses, huh? Saw he could do better, right? Or maybe you're just a lousy lay."

Lisanne couldn't reply, her brain and body overloaded with emotion. She ran back to her room with Shawna's words echoing in her ears.

The room was dark, and when Lisanne turned on the light switch, the brightness dazzled her. Feeling dazed, she sat on her bed, her shoulders slumped. Then she saw that Kirsty had left a note saying that she'd be back at 8 PM if Lisanne wanted to share pizza.

Pizza? As if she could even think about eating. She *had* to know what the matter was with Daniel. She *had* to know.

Feeling desperate, Lisanne pulled out her phone and sent him a text.

> * What's wrong? I don't understand.
> Text me, please. LA xx *

She waited and waited, but he didn't reply.

CHAPTER 7

Daniel was going over 90mph when he caught the flicker of blue and red lights in his mirrors. He cursed loudly and colorfully as he pulled over to the curb. After fighting with Lisanne, his day didn't show any signs of improving.

The cop got out of the cruiser, wearily shaking his head, and motioned for Daniel to take off his helmet.

"Do you know how fast you were going, son?"

"No, sir," Daniel replied, truthfully.

"Well, my speed gun is telling me 91mph. That's pretty reckless, don't you think."

Daniel nodded. "Yes, sir."

"You want to tell me why you were going that fast?"

Forgetting all the advice that Zef had given him should he ever be arrested, Daniel said the first thing that came into his head.

"I had a fight with my girlfriend. I wasn't thinking."

The cop looked at him, sympathetically.

"Well, I can understand, but the speed limit here is 55mph. Now, I'm a nice guy, so I'm not going to arrest you, but you will be getting a speeding ticket, son. License and registration."

Daniel pulled them out of his wallet and handed the documents to the officer, without speaking.

"Wait there," instructed the police officer, as he ambled back to his cruiser and ran Daniel's details through his computer. Whatever he saw made him frown.

He walked back to Daniel, scratching his head.

"According to my records there's a Detective Dickinson who

wants to speak with you at the station. I'm going to have to take you in."

Daniel swallowed hard, a cool shiver rippling down his spine.

"What? What for? I've never heard of that guy?"

"Can't tell you that, son, but you're going to have to come with me. Look, I'm not arresting you, so just take it easy, okay?"

Daniel didn't even try to argue. He knew there was no point.

The cop sighed—sometimes he hated his job. The kid really did look as if he had the weight of the world on his shoulders.

"That's a nice bike you've got there. Sportster, huh? Rebuild?"

Daniel nodded.

"You do that work yourself, son?"

"Yes, sir. Took me two years."

The cop held in another sigh.

"Well, we'll just have to leave your motorcycle here for now. You won't be at the station long, and you can call a friend to bring you back to pick it up. Or I could get it towed, but that would end up costing you more…"

Daniel shook his head, and the cop sighed again before helping him into the back of the cruiser. At least he hadn't been handcuffed.

Daniel felt sick to his stomach. He could expect a hefty fucking fine, which there was no way he could pay right now— unless he sold his bike. The bike he'd worked on for two years. Or dip into his college fund. Either way, Zef would have his balls.

Fuck! Fuck! Fuck!

And he only had his own stupid dumb ass to blame.

If things weren't bad enough already, they got a whole lot worse when he arrived at the police station.

The nice cop wrote up his notes while a bastard fuckwit of a sergeant nearly turned cartwheels, when he learned that Daniel was Zef Colton's brother.

"Well, isn't this interesting. You're the little brother, huh? About time we saw you in here. Your brother is on our

Christmas List. Let's try and make you welcome. We can find a nice, cozy cell with your name on it, and I think my colleague Detective Dickinson would like to talk to you."

"I want to make a phone call."

"I'm sure you do. You can wait."

The sergeant looked back to the computer screen and typed something.

"Now empty out your pockets," he said, still looking at the computer.

Unable to see the man's face, Daniel just stood there.

"I said, empty your damn pockets!" shouted the cop, looking up, his face creased with anger.

"What for? I haven't been arrested."

"You're pissing me off, Colton, which is pretty dumb. Watch your smart mouth or you'll be arrested on suspicion of a DUI."

God damn it—he was fucked.

"I want to make a phone call."

"Later."

The nice cop looked irritated, but Mr. Really Not Fucking Charming was the senior officer. Throwing Daniel a sympathetic look, the nice cop walked away, shaking his head.

Daniel put his smokes, lighter, wallet, keys, and change into the box in front of him. The contents were logged and tipped into a clear plastic bag.

"I need to text someone to go get my bike. I've left her…"

But his words trailed off as the officer pulled Daniel's cell phone from his hand and shoved it into the bag with the rest of his belongings, then he was escorted into an interview room, by the man he assumed was Detective Dickinson.

The detective looked tired and crumpled, but his eyes were sharp, and his mouth curled with disgust as he stared at Daniel.

Roughly, Dickinson pushed him into a chair.

"Well, well, Zef Colton's little brother. Another apple that didn't fall too far from the tree, huh? Bet your mom and dad would be really proud."

"Fuck you!" snarled Daniel.

"You've got a dirty mouth, kid. And you really don't want to piss me off."

"I want my phone call," said Daniel, in a sullen tone.

"We can just have a little chat first," said the detective, in a bored voice. "It'll be in your best interest to answer my questions. Of course, you're free to walk out any time … but I really wouldn't recommend it."

Daniel really didn't think it would be in his best interest to answer anything either, but he was worried about the repercussions of just walking the hell out of there.

"Look, kid," said the detective, in a more conciliatory tone, "Answer a few questions and the speeding fine just disappears. I can make it go away. I'm not after your brother—I'm after the asshat who's been flooding the streets with cheap crystal meth. Who's your brother's supplier?"

Daniel was silent. Zef had always told him that he just dealt in some weed and coke. He didn't know whether or not to believe Dickinson, but he really didn't want to.

"Come on, kid. You want that shit on the streets? I know you're in school, trying to stay clean. It's your brother who's fucking things up for you."

"You don't know anything," said Daniel, hotly.

Dickinson smiled. He could tell he had the boy rattled.

"Do you know how crank works?" asked the detective. "It destroys dopamine receptors in your brain, so you can't feel pleasure. Then there's psychotic behavior, paranoia, hallucinations, death. But before that happens, the blood vessels constrict, it cuts off the steady flow of blood to all parts of the body. Do you know what that means? Your body doesn't heal right. It starts with bad acne, sores, that kind of thing. Maybe you've heard of 'meth mouth'? The mouth's acids eat away at the tooth enamel, so your teeth rot and fall out. Nice. You want to be responsible for that?"

Daniel closed his eyes, shutting out the words that made him want to vomit. He didn't believe the shit that Dickinson was pissing in his ear, but he didn't want to know any more either.

He jumped when Dickinson slapped his hands down hard on the back of Daniel's chair.

"I want my fucking phone call!" snapped Daniel, whose patience was running pretty damn low.

Detective Dickinson threw his hands in the air.

"Fine, make your call."

"I want to send a text from my phone."

"No, you can use the phone out there."

Daniel began to panic. He'd have no way of knowing whether or not Zef had answered the phone. He didn't even know if he'd still be at the house.

Lisanne. He'd call Lis. She always answered his texts quickly. He prayed she'd take the call.

Thank fuck he knew her number off by heart.

He dialed and counted to ten into the receiver, hoping that she'd understand … understand that he had no clue if she was there listening to him, or if a machine was picking up the message or … God, he just hoped she wouldn't hang up. He hoped she'd wait for him to leave a message.

"Lis, it's me. Daniel. I'm in a whole shitload of trouble. I got pulled over for speeding. I'm at the police station. Can you get a message to Zef for me, please, baby? His number is 912-555 0195. I'm sorry I got mad at you, baby. I'm so fucking sorry."

Then he hung up, not knowing if she'd heard him. He knew the smart thing to do would be to tell Dickinson that he couldn't hear what the fuck he was saying. But he couldn't bring himself to give the bastard the satisfaction.

Dickinson continued to fire questions at him, even though they weren't answered. Concentrating on controlling his breathing, Daniel closed his eyes, willing the tension and anxiety away.

Eventually Dickinson gave up and left him in the interrogation room 'to think about it'.

It was nearly 1 AM and Daniel had resigned himself to spending the night. He wondered if he'd gotten the wrong number for Lisanne, or maybe the message hadn't recorded, or she hadn't heard it. Maybe she was too angry with the way he'd treated her to care. He had no way of knowing.

He spent a restless night by himself. At one point he was allowed a bathroom break and through the barred windows he could see that pale light was leaking into the gray sky, the blackness fading with the dawn.

Sometime after 7 AM, Dickinson came back. He paced back and forth spewing out his questions. Daniel kept his eyes fixed on the table most of the time, but every now and then he'd glance up.

After another hour, even the detective's furious energy had waned, and he rubbed his eyes tiredly.

"Fine. You're free to go," snarled Dickinson, at last. "I'm sure I'll be seeing you again, *little brother*. It's only a matter of time before you're part of the family business—if you're not already."

Daniel stood up shakily as he was led out of the room by Dickinson who watched with narrowed eyes.

He collected his belongings, relieved that the assholes hadn't arrested him.

Lisanne woke up with light leaking through the curtains above her bed. She rolled onto her side and grabbed her phone.

"Holy shit!"

She leapt up, vaguely aware of Kirsty's sleepy grumbles from the other side of the room.

"Kirsty! Get your ass out of bed! I put my phone on silent— we've slept right through. It's nearly 8:30!"

Hurriedly, Lisanne pulled on her robe, picked up her towel and caddy, and trotted to the bathroom.

The water was cooler than usual, and she shivered under the puny flow. At least it had woken her up.

Kirsty, however, had fallen back asleep.

"Come on, lazybones. Rise and shine," said Lisanne, as she twitched Kirsty's duvet.

"Gerroff," was the mumbled reply.

Lisanne shrugged. They went through the same routine every

day. If it wasn't for Lisanne, Kirsty wouldn't have made any of her morning classes.

Lisanne pulled on jeans and a long-sleeved t-shirt, then turned her phone on. There was a missed call from a number she didn't recognize, and one voice message.

As she listened, all the color drained from her face. Her knees gave way and she collapsed onto the bed. Daniel had left the message *last night*.

She played the message again and scrawled down Zef's number. She had to call back four times before he picked up.

When he heard who it was and why she'd called, he wasn't happy. Which was putting it mildly. Especially when Lisanne insisted on coming with him, threatening to go directly to the police station if he didn't pick her up.

Zef was furious when they finally reached the police station.

"Stay here!" he barked at Lisanne, who was sitting stiffly beside him.

'Furious' was probably the understatement of the year. Rage poured from him in heated pulses, his face was flushed and his teeth were clenched as he saw Daniel being led out by one of the police officers.

He looked at Zef with a guilty expression as he put his wallet away.

"Are you a fucking idiot?" Zef hissed at Daniel. "Because you're fucking acting like one! I do all this shit so you can stay clean, then you go and fuck it up like this."

"I'm sorry, man. I wasn't thinking."

"That is stating the really fucking obvious."

He grabbed Daniel's arm and dragged him outside, where the too interested cops couldn't see. Then he pushed him up against the wall, his hands bunched around the collar of Daniel's t-shirt.

"Get off!"

"Not until I've knocked some fucking sense into you!" snarled his brother.

Daniel shoved him hard and Zef took a pace backward, swinging a fist at the same time. It caught Daniel on the cheek and he fell sideways, landing awkwardly on one knee.

Pain shot through him and he was glad he hadn't had his tongue between his teeth, or he'd have bitten the damn thing clean off.

Lisanne leapt out of the car the moment Zef had pushed Daniel against the wall. She was too late to stop their fight, but she was damn sure she wouldn't let it go any further. She tried to help Daniel up as Zef stood behind her, panting hard.

Daniel felt hands on his shoulder again and he automatically pushed them off.

Lisanne tried to soothe him.

"It's me, Daniel. It's me."

He looked up and saw her face creased with concern.

"Baby doll!" he gasped, leaning his head against her body as her arms wrapped around him.

"Fuck, I'm sorry, bro!" said Zef.

Lisanne turned on him, violently.

"Don't you touch him! Leave him alone!"

She helped Daniel stand, holding his arm as he staggered slightly.

"Just get in the damn car," said Zef, stiffly. "I'll take you to get Sirona—if she's still there."

"Take Lis home first," Daniel muttered.

Zef looked as if he wanted to argue, but held back whatever he was going to say.

The drive was silent, violence simmering between the two brothers. Lisanne could see Zef glancing in the rearview mirror, his face dark and hard. Beside her, Daniel was leaning back with his eyes closed, a red mark blossoming on his cheek.

When they reached the dorm rooms, Lisanne gently stroked Daniel's face to make him open his eyes.

"We're here," she said, softly. "Do you want to come in? Kirsty could drive you home later."

Zef started to argue, but Daniel shot his brother a look.

"Yeah, I'd like that, Lis. Sirona can wait."

He climbed out of the car awkwardly, rubbing his sore knee.

With a final, furious look, Zef drove off, tires screeching, leaving the pungent smell of burning rubber hanging in the air with his disapproval.

Lisanne was worried about Daniel. He was quiet, and the fire that she so loved seemed to have dimmed.

He dragged himself up the stairs to her dorm room, his shoulders slumped and his head hanging down. Maybe it was just tiredness, Lisanne told herself. He couldn't have slept much, being in a police station all night. She felt guilty again—while she'd been snuggled up in her own bed, he was dealing with God knows what.

She pushed open the door, relieved that Kirsty was out at morning classes. Tugging his hand, she led Daniel to her bed and pushed him gently, telling him to sit.

"I'll make you a coffee," she said, quietly.

He nodded but didn't speak, instead unbuckling his boots and lying back against the pillows. By the time Lisanne had made the coffee, he was fast asleep, curled up on his side.

Carefully, she eased down onto the bed next to him, and picked up her book to read, occasionally sipping her coffee. Daniel sighed heavily and wrapped his left arm across her waist, pushing his head into her hip.

In silence, studying his face, Lisanne could see the tiredness, with dark rings visible under his eyes. His cheeks were covered in stubble and she blushed, wondering how his light scruff would feel if they kissed again.

She crossed her legs at the ankle and drank some more coffee, willing her body to relax. Today she seemed to be permanently turned on—her body tuned to Daniel, ready for sex.

She could hardly believe it. She didn't know it was possible to feel like that. She didn't know that girls could be as horny as guys. But that was the truth.

And then she felt selfish for having those thoughts, when he'd been having such a horrible time. Right now, he needed her friendship. She frowned, wondering if that was all he'd ever want from her. But yesterday ... that had gone far beyond friendship.

She looked down at him again. His soft lips were parted, his bruised cheek slightly swollen. Lisanne kicked herself for not having gotten him some ice. Not that she'd have had time: he'd fallen asleep right away. His eyes trembled slightly under the closed lids and she wondered what he was dreaming about. The long, dark lashes were fanned out across his cheeks and, if it hadn't been for his stubble, he'd have looked much younger.

Lisanne sighed and tried to turn her attention back to her book. Daniel didn't move except to hook his left leg over hers, so for nearly two hours, she read, with Daniel curled around her. She loved the fact that in his sleep he seemed to crave her. She wished it was the same when he was awake.

Suddenly the door flew open, making Lisanne jump. Kirsty burst in with Shawna tagging along behind her.

"Oh, God! Sorry!" said Kirsty, coming to an abrupt halt, her eyes wide, fixed on Daniel.

Shawna's face resembled someone who'd sucked up a quart of lemon juice.

Daniel shifted sleepily and then sat up, yawning.

"Oh shit, sorry, baby doll. Did I fall asleep? What time is it?"

"Three o'clock," said Lisanne.

"Crap. Sirona! I should get going," he grumbled to himself. "Hey, Kirsty."

Kirsty waved, while Shawna crooned, "Hi Daniel," in a sickly singsong voice.

Of course, her tone was completely lost on him, even if her flirty look wasn't.

"Shawna," he said, with a curt nod.

Lisanne was too distracted to care that Shawna was being her usual bitchy self. Her main concern was *him*.

"Should I make you another coffee? Yours is cold now."

He shook his head, mumbling about *business* to take care of. Lisanne grimaced, wondering what that might entail. And he definitely needed a ride.

"Kirsty, could you drive Daniel?"

"What happened to your motorcycle?" asked Shawna, rudely interrupting Kirsty's answer.

Nosy bitch, thought Lisanne.

"Sure, no problem," said Kirsty, reaching for her keys.

That was one of the things that Lisanne had come to love about Kirsty. She acted like a cheerleader on helium half the time, but when she could see something was important, she didn't hesitate to help.

But Daniel rubbed his eyes and yawned again.

"Nah. S'okay, thanks. I've got some things to take care of," he repeated, stretching his arms above his head, and innocently flexing his muscles in a way that made Shawna drool openly. "I'll text Roy. He'll give me a ride."

He swung his legs over the bed and started to pull on his boots. Lisanne felt the loss of him next to her immediately.

Before he left, he smiled at her and kissed her hair.

"I'll see you in class tomorrow, okay. Text me later?"

"Sure," she said, trying to smile.

He winked, nodded at Kirsty, and completely ignored Shawna, who didn't even say goodbye but turned and trotted after him, firing questions to his back.

As soon as they'd gone, Kirsty swept into interrogation mode.

"Oh my God! Are you guys fucking? That was so sweet the way he was curled up around you. Wow! Daniel Colton! Is he really good in bed? On a scale of one to ten, how would you rate him?"

Lisanne flushed red and tried to laugh it off.

"We're just friends, Kirsty."

"Bullshit! I *saw* you, Lis. He's *totally* into you. And it's obvious how you feel about *him*. Wow! Well, now you can give me the details."

Lisanne shook her head.

"I have a violin lesson to get to. I'll see you later."

Kirsty pouted. "Fine! But you're not getting off the hook that easily, missy. I want to know *everything*. By the way, why did he need a ride?"

"Oh," said Lisanne, feeling uneasy. "He, um, he had bike trouble."

Which wasn't a complete lie.

She grabbed her violin case and her shoulder bag with her music scores, and hurried out of the room.

Her concentration had gone to hell and Professor Crawford raised his eyebrows in surprise. All Lisanne could do was apologize again, and promise to try harder next week.

It didn't help that she'd heard a text message pop up on her cell phone, and she was burning with curiosity to see if it was from Daniel.

As soon as her lesson was finished, before Professor Crawford had even closed the door behind him, Lisanne dove into her bag to find her phone.

The text had been from Daniel.

* Thanx *

She looked at the short message and felt tears in her eyes. How dumb was that? He'd sent her a text. He'd thanked her— what was the damn drama?

Irritated for being so pathetic, she dragged her weary ass back to the dorm room. Unfortunately, Kirsty was still there, and attacked her the minute she walked in the door.

"Spill! What's with you and Daniel? Are you guys dating?" Then she looked at Lisanne more closely. "Because if you are, you look kind of miserable."

Lisanne sighed. "It's complicated."

"Of course it is," said Kirsty, sympathetically. "He's a guy— their brains are wired differently. Well, most guys' brains are wired to their dicks, so that's pretty straightforward."

Lisanne tried to laugh, but her heart wasn't in it.

"I don't really know what we are," she said, honestly. "We're friends, I know that. And sometimes I think we're more than that, but ... I just don't know."

Kirsty nodded. "I get it. Mixed messages, huh? You know I'm not going to tell anyone anything, right, Lis? I mean, not even Shawna. I know she acts like we're BFFs, but I'm not dumb. She's kind of a bitch to you. But that's because she's jealous. She'd love to be getting some Daniel Colton shaped action. She doesn't get what he sees in you—oh, I don't mean it like *that*," she said, hastily. "It's just you don't act all flirty and … you know what I mean."

"Thanks, Kirsty … I think. I just…" Lisanne sighed again, having no clue how to finish the sentence, let alone explain her feelings to Kirsty.

"Okay, well let's do the checklist."

Lisanne couldn't help laughing at that: Kirsty and her damn checklists.

"Has he kissed you?"

"Yes."

"Tongues?"

"Um, yes. Once."

"Just once? When was that?"

Lisanne blushed. "Yesterday."

Kirsty nodded encouragingly. "Well, that's good."

Good. Amazing. Sensational. Out of this world.

"It is?"

"Sure! You guys have been friends since the start of the semester—sort of. So if you've only just done tongues, that's progress."

"Oh, okay."

"Has he taken you on a date?"

That was a tough one. They had been out together, but neither of them had ever called it a date.

"Um, no, yes, maybe. I'm not sure."

"Oh," said Kirsty, in a way that indicated this wasn't good.

"Oh?"

"Honey, if you're not sure it was a date, then it wasn't. A guy has to *ask* you on a date for it to be a date. It's different from just hanging out together."

Lisanne sighed. That sounded logical.

Kirsty continued.

"So, when you kissed, did ya do anything else?"

Lisanne shifted uncomfortably. "Like what?"

Kirsty rolled her eyes. "Like, did he feel you up at all?"

Lisanne's face flushed, thinking of the awesome orgasm that Daniel had given her.

Kirsty smiled smugly. "I'll take that as a 'yes' then." Her smile faded. "There's really only one answer, Lis—you have to *ask* him where you stand. Guys can be pretty dumb. You have to say, 'Hey? Is this a date?' Or, 'Hooked up with any other girls lately?' You know, make it clear."

"I don't know if I can do that."

"Why not?"

"Well," said Lisanne, twisting a stray thread from her t-shirt around her finger, "What if he says 'no'? What if he isn't interested in me?"

"Then he says 'no', but at least you won't be pining for something that isn't going to happen. It's like ripping off the band-aid—you gotta do it fast because it'll hurt less in the long run."

It sounded like good advice: Lisanne just didn't know if she'd be brave enough to do it.

"Have you slept with him yet?"

Lisanne shook her head.

"Do you want to?"

Lisanne looked up into Kirsty's kind eyes.

"Yes, but not if it's because he feels sorry for me."

"Oh, sweetie," said Kirsty, patting her hand. "All guys want sex—that's a given. But you have to decide if that's all *you* want. And I *know* you, Lis. You're the kind of girl who wants the whole package. And Daniel … look, he seems nice—he's different with you—but he doesn't have a great track record. He's definitely the love 'em and leave 'em type."

"But if I sleep with him, maybe he'll…"

"Don't even *think* that! I mean it, Lis. Some girls are fine having one-night stands. Whatever. Good for them. But you're not like that. And you'll feel shit about yourself if you do it. It's just not worth it. Look, I can see that Daniel cares about you—I mean, you guys are friends. And that's good. Sex can really fuck things up." She giggled when she'd realized how that sounded, and Lisanne couldn't help smiling. "Yeah, well, you know what I mean."

"So what do I do?" asked Lisanne, her smile worn away.

"Wish I could tell you, hon. Talk to him. You'll figure it out. Look—Vin and I are going to that new Mexican place with a bunch of his frat house friends. You'd be doing me a favor if you come with us."

"Thanks, Kirsty, but I think I'll just have a quiet night in."

"Okay, if you change your mind, text me. But don't wait up."

"Pajama party with Vin?"

Kirsty winked. "Something like that."

It had taken him a while to shake off Shawna. Girl was persistent, but he'd seen the way she treated Lisanne and he wasn't the least bit interested in someone who was such a bitch—and hot she was not.

Daniel stubbed out his smoke when he saw Roy's battered Dodge Ram pull up.

"What's up? Where're your wheels, man?"

Daniel sighed. "I got pulled over for speeding. I thought I was gonna get arrested for reckless driving, but the fuckers were more interested in Zef."

Roy shot him a look.

"I didn't give them anything."

"But they didn't hold you," said Roy, suspiciously.

"Fuck, man! You think I'd say something—about my own brother?"

"About your brother, no."

Daniel looked at Roy incredulously. "You think I'd sell *you* out?" He knew that Roy sold a little weed on the side.

Roy chewed on his words for a while before he answered.

"No, I guess not."

Daniel was slightly mollified but still annoyed that Roy could even think he'd do a deal with the cops. He didn't want to ask him if Dickinson was right about the meth-dealing. The larger part of him didn't want to know. Ignorance wasn't bliss, but it could be a damn sight more comfortable than an ugly truth.

"Anyway, they did hold me. Had my ass in a police station all last night."

"Cops rough you up?" said Roy, his eyes flicking over Daniel's face.

Daniel angled the truck's rearview mirror toward him and saw the dark bruise on his cheek.

"Fuck. No, that was Zef."

Roy sighed. "He worries about you—you're his little brother."

Daniel stared out of the window and didn't reply. Roy tapped his arm.

"Where we going, man?"

"Sirona. Cops made me leave her at the side of the road. Fuck knows what's happened to her."

"Aw, hell! Why didn't you tell me? I'd have got her for you."

"Cops took my phone."

Roy sighed. "How much was the fine?"

"A thousand dollars."

"Oh, yeah? And where are you gonna find that kind of spare money?"

"College fund."

"Oh, man! No wonder Zef was whaling on you. He takes that shit pretty damn serious."

"It's no big deal. I've got three years of school yet. I can work summers in the garage. I'll earn that back easy."

"Just make sure you do."

"Fuck, Roy! When did you turn into Martha Stewart?" Roy laughed out loud and Daniel couldn't help grinning. "Okay, bad example—how about Dave Ramsey?"

Roy pointed up ahead and Daniel's smile widened. Sirona

was parked where he'd left her and still had two wheels. Things were looking up.

"Thanks, man," he said to Roy.

"No worries. Stay out of trouble."

Daniel climbed out of the truck and thumped on the side. Roy peeled away, giving Daniel the bird as he drove off.

"Fucker," Daniel grumbled to himself.

But running his hands over Sirona's chrome, he began to feel better.

"Hey, baby. Miss me?"

She was hard work, this motorcycle. Not like a modern Japanese import. Nope, no easy push button start for his baby.

He bent down to turn on the gas, pulled out the choke, opened the throttle fully, primed it with a couple of kicks, then he felt the vibrations as the kick-start made her spring alive, pulsing through his body. He could feel her.

He rode home, keeping within the speed limit the whole way. He couldn't risk losing her again.

But his good mood didn't last long. As soon as Zef heard him pull up, he was outside and in Daniel's face. Roy stood there, grimacing.

"Tell me you're fucking joking?" shouted Zef. "You're using your college fund to pay that fucking fine?"

Daniel stood his ground as Zef's eyes blazed with fury, and Roy looked more than a little uncomfortable.

Daniel glanced over to his brother's friend. He didn't blame Roy—Zef would have found out sooner or later.

"Mom and dad saved that money for you to go to school and get your degree. They didn't work their butts off so you could piss it up against the wall to pay for a fucking speeding ticket."

"I know that!" Daniel yelled back. "But I didn't have a choice. I worked on Sirona for two fucking years so I wouldn't have to take the bus—I'm not going to sell her to pay some shitty fine."

"Then you shouldn't have got caught speeding, you dumb fuck!"

"Do you think I don't fucking know that?!"

"No, I don't. And why the hell are you dating that singer? That is just fucking mental! Do you want to be reminded every day? Because I remember you bleeding all over me when you couldn't play your music any more, and now you're dating a *singer*?"

"We're not dating, we're friends. We…"

"Bullshit!"

Roy stepped between them, placing his massive hands on their chests and pushing them apart.

"Take it down a notch, guys. It's done now. No use having a shit fit."

Zef glared at him. "Butt the fuck out, Roy. This is family business."

"No, it's *my* business," snapped Daniel, "and I'm outta here."

He turned on his heel, needing some space. He had to get his head together and there was only one person he wanted to see.

* D: can I see you? Are you alone? *

Lisanne's reply was instant.

* L: K out with Vin. Am home alone. LA xx *

Feeling relieved, he pulled his bike around, heading for the dorms, and to the one person who seemed to understand him.

Just a quick stop at the liquor store first.

It wasn't open house hours at the dorm rooms, so Daniel snuck in via the fire exit that the girls kept open, allowing their boyfriends to visit. It was the worst kept secret on campus.

He knocked on Lisanne's door and she opened it immediately.

"Hi."

"Hi. Are you okay? Did you get your bike back?"

He nodded wearily as she pushed the door open wide. He walked in, kissing her quickly on the cheek, and slumped down on her bed.

"Yeah."

"So, it was all okay?"

"Pretty much."

He couldn't face telling her that he'd had to spend a chunk of money from his college fund, or that Zef had told him not to date her. That shit was just too raw to talk about.

"I brought beer," he said, shrugging out of his leather jacket and pulling a six-pack from a paper bag.

"Oh! Um, I don't really drink."

"S'okay. I do." He snapped the tab on the first can and chugged almost half of it.

Lisanne watched him nervously, wondering if he simply wanted somewhere to get drunk. He looked up and saw the expression on her face.

"Sorry. I should have asked. Do you mind?"

"Um, no. It's fine."

He sighed. "Shit, I'm doing everything wrong. Sit with me?"

Lisanne climbed onto the end of the bed and sat cross-legged, facing him.

"Look, I'm really sorry about how I was before. You know, yesterday. I just … fuck, this is hard." He stared down at his fingers.

Lisanne waited for him to continue

"It was really good yesterday. Before … I wasn't expecting … I mean, we're friends, right? And I don't want to do anything to fuck that up. But I don't want you to think that what we did … ah, shit."

His stumbling words ground to a halt again. But he was trying. He was really trying.

"Why were you so mad at me?" she said, quietly.

He met her gaze. "Because you made it sound like it was nothing. Like I just go around getting off random girls."

"Don't you?"

Daniel scowled at her. "No!"

"How many girls have you slept with this semester?"

127

"Other than you?" he said, raising his eyebrows.

They were both thinking of him falling asleep on her bed that morning.

"You know what I mean, but if you want me to rephrase: How many girls have you had sex with?"

He chewed his lip for a few seconds, thinking hard, and took a large gulp of beer.

"Three."

"Altogether?"

"Three this semester."

Jeez!

"How many in total?"

"Um…"

There was a long, uncomfortable pause.

Lisanne stared. "You don't know?"

"Christ! Give me a break! I don't exactly mark notches on my bedpost!"

She folded her arms across her chest. "Make a guess. A wild stab," she added, sarcastically.

"Maybe thirty."

Lisanne swallowed.

"Maybe thirty-five," he said, quietly.

She'd guessed it would be a high number, but it was still quite a shock.

"Oh," she said, trying to keep her face blank, but knowing he could probably read her expression perfectly.

"Why are we even talking about this?" he muttered, as much to himself as to her. Then he looked up. "But you're only the second girl I've ever *slept* with," he added.

"What do you mean?"

He rubbed his hands over his hair in frustration.

"In case you haven't noticed, I don't date. Girls don't want to date me—they just want to fuck me. And I like fucking. But none of them *know* about me: you're the only one. The others never stick around long enough to find out."

"You mean you never give them the chance."

"Whatever. It's the same thing."

"Not really."

"Fuck, Lisanne! I'm trying to say … I want…"

"What?"

"You're not making this easy…"

"Sorry, it's just intimidating."

"What is?"

"All the girls you've slept with. It makes me feel…" she hesitated, fishing to find the right words to express how desperately inexperienced and inadequate she felt.

"What does it make you feel?"

Lisanne ran through a list of words in her mind: pathetic, uptight, *a virgin*.

"What does it make you feel, Lis? Because it's all bullshit. You … me … it's just *different*, and …yesterday, when you said about my *reputation*…"

Suddenly, Lisanne had a light bulb moment—she understood. "Oh! I hurt your feelings yesterday?"

He shrugged one shoulder.

"Daniel, I'm so sorry."

He looked down at her bedspread. "I like you."

"You do?"

He groaned with frustration and irritation.

"Of course I fucking do! I'm here, aren't I?"

That was all Lisanne wanted to know.

Taking a deep breath, she uncrossed her legs and crawled up the bed. Halting in front of him, she brushed her lips against his.

His eyelids fluttered closed and he sighed softly.

Encouraged, she knelt across him and bent down, placing another gentle kiss on his lips.

Daniel slipped his arms around her waist and nuzzled her neck, humming quietly. Then he pulled her down so she was lying across his chest. He ran his hands downwards, stopping just below the small of her back, placing soft kisses on her throat.

He let his head fall back to the pillow, and tucked her into his side for a cozy hug, one hand softly stroking her hair, occasionally turning so he could brush his lips over her temple.

Lisanne was bitterly disappointed. Where were the burning touches she'd experienced from him yesterday? Where was the dark fire in his eyes? Was this it? Were they just friends after all? What did 'like' mean anyway?

He was being gentle with her but Lisanne didn't want gentle. She wanted *him*. All of him. And she wanted to know once and for all if he wanted her.

She hooked her thigh over his hip, pushing herself into him so her leg was almost wrapped around his waist.

Daniel paused in his tender kisses and looked up at her.

"Lis?"

She didn't answer, but nervously slid her fingers under his t-shirt. He blinked in surprise, then his eyes fluttered closed as she ran her hands over his stomach and chest, tugging gently on his nipple rings. She could feel he was hardening beneath her. It was thrilling.

But then he grabbed her wrists and pushed her back slightly, sitting up so he could see her face.

"What are you doing, Lis?"

"Just … you know."

"Baby doll…"

"I *want* to, Daniel. *I* want to. Please."

He groaned and closed his eyes.

She didn't wait for him to speak, but pressed her lips hard against his, waiting for his mouth to open. When it did, she could taste beer and nicotine, but it was still the best feeling. She pushed her tongue into his mouth, hoping that enthusiasm would make up for what she lacked in technique.

His grip on her wrists lessened, and then his hands brushed up her arms and into her hair.

Gently, but with building passion, he stroked his tongue against hers, controlling the moment, showing her how sensual it could be, taking it slowly. His lips were soft and warm, and she could feel the prickle of his stubble against her skin.

Lisanne's body throbbed with pleasure. She had no idea kissing a guy could make her feel so much. She was overflowing with sensations and emotions, as if her skin would split open, unable to contain everything she felt, her lungs too big for her body.

Daniel rolled onto his back, taking her with him so she was lying across his body. His hands sculpted her waist, massaging her hips with his fingers.

Then he cupped her ass and pulled her tightly against him. His erection was hard against the fabric of his jeans.

"You sure, baby doll?" he whispered.

Lisanne's brain was deliciously disconnected from the parts that moved, and she hesitated. Daniel pushed her back a few inches so he could read her face.

"Hey," he said, softly. "It's okay. You're not ready."

"I am!" she snapped, slapping the pillow next to his head in frustration. "I am *so* ready it's giving me a headache! Just *do it* already!"

He blinked at her.

"I'm just ... I'm just *nervous*, okay!"

By now she was yelling.

Daniel was trying to hold back a smile and not doing a very good job of it.

"Um, Lis, you don't have to yell at me or beat me up."

She frowned. "Are you laughing at me?"

"Kinda, I mean, it's pretty damn funny, you yelling at me that you want sex and you want it now."

"I'm not yelling!" she yelled.

"Yes, you are."

"How do you know?" she said, allowing the volume to drop by a couple of decibels.

"Because your face is all scrunched up," he said, with a grin. "It's cute."

"Oh!" she said, her voice dropping to a whisper as her skin heated to the point where the room ought to have caught fire.

She flopped onto her back, cursing the genes that made her

whole body blush with embarrassment.

"Hey, I'm sorry, okay," he said, sitting up and looking down at her.

Lisanne pulled the pillow over her face and groaned with defeat and dissatisfaction. She felt Daniel tugging at the pillow, and she allowed him pull it from her. She knew how much he hated it when he couldn't see her face.

"I'm sorry, baby. Lis … I'm flattered, you know, that you want me to be your first. I just … I don't want it to be something you'll regret. I don't want you to regret *me*."

She heard the anxiety in his voice and opened her eyes.

"I wouldn't. I won't."

He rubbed his face.

"Shit, you're making this hard."

"Am I making *you* hard?"

Her voice came out in a sultry, slutty purr that bore no resemblance to her usual voice whatsoever. It was like having an out-of-body experience, watching some vixen trying to seduce him. She had *no idea* where those words had come from.

Daniel raised his eyebrows, and a slow grin stretched across his face.

"I can't believe you said that, Lis. Should I be scared?"

"Yes," she said, in a low voice.

The grin dropped from his face, and he looked so surprised that Lisanne almost laughed.

For a moment she thought she was going to get her way after all, but after taking a deep breath, he swung his legs off of the bed and stood up.

"What?" Lisanne was startled. "Where are you going?"

"Come on," he said, holding out his hand. "Let's get out of here, because if we stay, I'm gonna end up fucking you every which way."

Why did his dirty words sound so erotic?

"Would that be a bad thing?" she said, in a small voice.

"No," he said, sighing and rubbing his face again. "But right now I want to take my girl out. Besides, I could do with a shower and a shave, and a night sleeping in a comfortable bed."

Something fluttered in Lisanne's chest, and she only heard the first of the two sentences.

"Your girl?"

He frowned.

"What? Yeah, if you want."

Lisanne remembered Kirsty's words, as she stared at him doubtfully.

"So, is this like a date?"

"Um, yeah?"

He didn't sound sure, and Lisanne's fluttering heart stuttered softly to a halt.

"Are you sleeping with anyone else?" she said, needing to know despite herself.

When she saw the look on his face, she could have willingly yanked out her own tongue and used it for fish food.

"What the fuck, Lis? You really think I'm that big of a jerk!"

His eyes were dark with anger and hurt.

She'd done it again.

"Daniel, I'm sorry! I just … shit, can we just erase the last two minutes? Please?"

He shoved his hands in his pockets and glowered at her.

"No," he snarled. "I'm not sleeping with anyone. I'm not fucking anyone. At all."

She cringed at his tone and his words. From somewhere inside, she called on the strength to be honest—to say it straight.

"I just … I just don't think I could share you," she sniffed, her eyes filling with tears.

His face softened at once, and he pulled her toward him.

"Sorry, baby," he breathed into her hair. "I'm shit at this whole boyfriend thing. Fuck, can we get out of here? I need a smoke."

Lisanne gave a wobbly smile, and forced back the tears that were still threatening.

"Where do you want to go?"

He shrugged.

"Anywhere you like? You wanna get something to eat? I'm starving. The food in jail sucked ass."

"Um, well," said Lisanne, hesitantly, "Kirsty was meeting Vin and some of his friends: we could meet up with them if you like?"

Daniel looked down and frowned.

"I don't think so, Lis. Groups are really hard for me. I ... I can't join in conversations that easily."

"Just try it," she said, encouragingly.

"No, really. It's too hard. I mean, it's bad enough with just one person. I have to guess half the time. I mean, understanding what someone is saying is only 40% about the lip reading—the rest is body language and context. Sometimes it can be a goddamn nightmare."

"But I thought ... I mean, you do it so well."

"Because I don't want ... I don't want anyone to know. But seriously, Lis, have you any idea how easy it is to mix up 'where there's life, there's hope', with 'where's the lavender soap'?"

Lisanne wasn't sure whether or not it would be appropriate to giggle. She stood there with her face frozen.

"And 'elephant shoes' looks like 'I love you', which could be really fucking embarrassing. And people get freaked out when I stare at their faces all the time. I mean, I can read you because I've gotten to know you pretty well, but new people ... and anyone with a strong accent—I'm totally screwed."

Lisanne realized that Daniel was starting to sound slightly panicky. It was upsetting to see him anxious when he was usually so in control.

She laid her hand on his cheek to calm him

"They've gone to that new Mexican restaurant. There won't be that many of them. If you don't like it, we'll just stay for one drink and go."

Daniel took a deep breath, purposefully trying to slow his racing heart.

"No way anyone will believe you're 21 even with fake ID," he said, shifting uncomfortably, playing for time.

"Probably not," she said, with a smirk, "but they serve *virgin* cocktails."

He grinned at her, and she saw his body relax a little.

"Yeah?"

"Besides," she said, continuing to stroke his face, "we can always ignore everyone and just make out."

Suddenly, he grabbed Lisanne by her hips and pushed her up against the door so her head thudded softly against the wood.

And then he kissed her until she thought she was going to pass out.

"W-what was that for?" she gasped.

"Just 'cause," Daniel replied, equally breathlessly.

CHAPTER 8

Daniel pulled up outside the Mexican restaurant, staring through the window at the bright room and people beyond the plate glass. But he didn't cut the engine. From the soles of his boots to the roots of his hair, his whole body was urging him to get the hell out of there. His heart was thundering so hard, it was nearly pounding out of his chest.

He'd spent the last three years avoiding *exactly* this sort of situation. It was different with Roy and the guys. They'd all been around as he'd started to lose his hearing. They knew his limitations and how to adjust their behavior around him. But here, none of them knew. Which was just how he'd set it up—except he'd never intended to spend much time mixing with other students from school. It was tiring enough just going to lectures and lip reading that shit for nearly an hour at a time. He hadn't even told Lisanne that he was so fucked by the end of a school day that he mostly just went home and slept.

Now she was asking him to break all his carefully constructed rules. He was out of his depth—and he was fucking terrified.

He felt her small hand rub his arm, soothing him, as if she understood how he felt. Slowly, he pulled off his helmet so he could speak to her.

"I don't think this is such a good idea, Lis."

She scrambled off the bike and pulled his face around, so he had to look at her.

"Five minutes," she said. "And if you want to go, just say, 'elephant shoes'."

He snorted in amusement. "'Elephant shoes', huh?"

She nodded and gave him a small smile.

He pulled out a smoke and lit it hurriedly, inhaling deeply, trying to calm himself the fuck down. Then he tossed it to the sidewalk and took a deep breath.

"Fuck it," he said. "Let's do it."

The restaurant wasn't crowded, and perhaps only half the tables were being used.

The hostess walked over briskly, a hungry expression on her face that Lisanne had come to recognize all too well when women looked at Daniel. At her *boyfriend*.

"Table for two?" asked the woman, checking him out as she spoke.

"No, that's okay, thanks," answered Lisanne. "We'll be joining our friends."

Her head turned as she heard Kirsty's laugh right across the room. She was with a group of five people sitting around a circular table.

Lisanne took Daniel's hand, looking up at him and smiling. His face looked rather tense, his jaw clenched tightly, but he tried to smile at her.

"Okay?" she said, softly. "Five minutes—that's all."

He nodded stiffly, then followed her across the restaurant.

"Hi!" said Lisanne brightly, inwardly cringing at the way her nerves made her sound like a game show contestant.

Kirsty's jaw dropped in surprise, but she recovered quickly.

"Yay! You came! Everyone—this is my roommate Lisanne. And this is her … this is Daniel."

Lisanne was relieved to see that Shawna wasn't there. As Kirsty had said, it was all Vin's friends.

"Hey, good to see you again, Lisanne," smiled Vin. "Daniel," he said, standing up and holding out his hand.

Lisanne discreetly nudged Daniel in the ribs, and the two men shook hands, quickly doing the guy head nod thing and sizing each other up.

Vin introduced the others, who were all from his fraternity.

It was slightly awkward for a moment, then the conversation

resumed more naturally.

Kirsty scooted over so Lisanne and Daniel could sit down in the booth.

Unfortunately, or fortunately, depending on her fluctuating point of view at any given moment, Lisanne was sitting next to Daniel. It meant she could hold his hand and feel the warmth of his body next to hers, but it made it difficult for him to lip read her.

His body was stiff and he looked like he might bolt at any second. Lisanne laid her hand on his forearm, then slid her fingers down to hold his hand. He smiled down at their intertwined fingers.

When the waitress arrived to take their order, Daniel asked for a beer, as did several of the other guys. Lisanne ordered a Shirley Temple, with a smirk at Daniel.

He leaned down and whispered, "We both know you're not really such a good girl."

Lisanne took a sharp intake of breath, then turned her head so he could see her face. "Maybe it's because you're such a bad influence."

He laughed huskily and leaned down to kiss her hair. Lisanne felt her body overheat, then became aware that Kirsty's eyes were trained on her.

She moved away slightly but grabbed his hand under the table again. He held her fingers tightly.

"So, man," said Vin, "I've seen you in Introduction to Business: what's your major?"

Luckily, Daniel looked over in time to see the second part of Vin's question.

With an uncomfortable jolt, Lisanne realized how truly hard this was going to be for him. She felt guilty for putting him under pressure.

"Economics. You?"

"Really? You look more like…" Vin choked back whatever he was going to say. "I'm doing a degree in Business Administration with Buddy and Rich. Eric is the black sheep of the fraternity—he's a Psych major."

"Yeah," said Eric. "It comes in handy with you guys."

Lisanne knew that Daniel had missed Eric's retort when she saw the fleeting expression of confusion, as everyone laughed at the joke.

She squeezed his hand and, without making a sound, mouthed the words 'elephant shoes' to him. She cocked her head on one side, waiting for him to answer her silent question. He smiled back gratefully but gave a small shake of his head.

When the waitress came back with the drinks, Daniel drank his beer quickly. But he wasn't alone in that—all the guys were in a drinking mood.

The waitress paused with her notebook, ready to take their food order.

Lisanne nudged Daniel's knee and he turned to look at her.

"Do you want to eat here?"

He paused for a moment, then gave another small nod.

Lisanne was pleased, and then immediately questioned his response. Did that mean he was enjoying himself, or was he just doing it for her? She wasn't sure, so she watched him closely. He'd gotten into a discussion with Eric about attribution theory from Psych 101—something that he seemed to know a lot about. Lisanne was surprised—she realized she had a lot to learn about Daniel Colton. And beyond her own feelings, it was clear that Eric was impressed and respected Daniel's point of view.

"Yeah, but we explain behaviors by assigning attributes to them," Daniel argued. "You can't underestimate the external factors."

"Only if we pay more attention to the situation rather than to the individual," said Eric.

"Well, fuck yes!" said Daniel. "If someone cuts me off on the road, I'm not going to say, 'Gee, they must be having a rough day.' I'll say, 'What a fucking jerk!'."

Eric laughed. "I'm with you on that, man."

Rich interrupted their discussion, and Lisanne had to nudge Daniel under the table again to redirect his attention. It made her a little tense, trying to keep track of what Daniel was saying and who he was talking to, as well as concentrating on Kirsty's description of one of her toughest professors. She began to appreciate how stressful and tiring social settings must be for him.

"I've gotta ask, man," said Rich, impatiently. "Is it true what they say about you?"

Daniel tensed immediately. "What the fuck are you talking about?"

All conversation ceased and everyone stared at Daniel's angry face.

Rich raised his hands immediately. "Whoa! Take it easy, dude. I just meant about your, um, your piercings. Did ya really get *other* stuff pierced?"

Daniel's angry expression disappeared and he raised an eyebrow. "Other stuff?"

"Is it, you know, good when you're … you know? Ah hell, don't make me say it, man!" whined Rich, making everyone laugh.

Daniel smiled down at Lisanne. "Should I tell him, baby?"

Lisanne instantly blushed beet red and the guys sniggered. Daniel leaned back, making it clear that he had no further answer to give.

Eric grinned. "We don't cover body art in psych till next year, Rich. Looks like you're going to have to live in ignorance."

Daniel winked at Lisanne. She was still embarrassed and was *definitely* going to have words with Daniel about that. But she loved how relaxed and playful he was, even though 30 seconds earlier he'd looked as if he was going to pummel Rich.

They finished their meals, chatting easily. Lisanne was starting to recognize when Daniel had missed the gist of the conversation, and she automatically began to compensate.

When it came to split the check, Lisanne realized the evening was nearly over. She was desperate to ask Daniel if he was coming back to her room—assuming Kirsty was going back to the frat house with Vin.

But then all her hopes, expectations, dreams and daydreams were dashed. Kirsty yawned.

"Oh my God, I'm never going to make it to my 8:30 in the morning. Lis, you'll have to promise to wake me up in the morning. Just keep prodding me until I move, okay?"

"Oh, I thought…?"

Kirsty shook her head quickly and whispered, "I got my period."

Lisanne gave a weak smile, sighing with disappointment. Daniel caught her eye and pulled her into a hug, placing a gentle kiss on her hair.

It was cooler outside, and there was a breath of Fall in the air.

Lisanne shivered, and Daniel put his arm around her protectively.

"You'll need a thicker jacket than that to ride on Sirona, baby," he whispered. "It can get cold at night, especially in the winter."

She smiled up at him, delighted that he seemed to be suggesting that riding on his motorcycle was going to become a regular occurrence.

Buddy was staring with envious eyes at Daniel's bike.

"That yours, man?" he said, the envy obvious by his tone— and by the way he was almost drooling.

"Yeah."

"Nice ride! What year?"

"Sixty nine."

"No shit! Where'd you get her from?"

Were all motorcycles female as far as men were concerned? Lisanne was amused.

"It was pretty much scrap when I found the frame," Daniel explained. "I did the rest of the work over two summers. I had a job in an auto repair shop."

Lisanne could see that Daniel had climbed several notches in the guys' estimation, and now there was a newfound respect in their eyes.

141

She felt relieved. The evening had gone so much better than even her wildest expectations.

Kirsty grabbed her hand and dragged her away from Daniel, while they guys talked bikes.

"I'm so glad you came, Lis! That was fun. Daniel's really nice and he's totally into you."

Lisanne smiled.

"Vin and the guys were great."

"Except," said Kirsty, with a serious look on her face, "when Rich looked like he was going to get punched by Daniel."

"It was a misunderstanding."

"Just ... just be careful." She held up her hands as Lisanne started to argue. "I like Daniel, I really do. Just ... look I'll see you back home, okay?"

Lisanne turned without hearing another word from her friend, irritated that Kirsty had spoiled the end of a great evening.

Daniel frowned when he saw her. "Okay?"

Lisanne nodded. "Can we go now?"

"Sure, baby."

He said goodbye to the guys, kick-started the mean machine, and helped Lisanne climb on behind him.

Daniel was getting used to the feeling of Lisanne's warm body behind him, as they sped along the road on his bike. Every movement of the motorcycle brought her closer to him, or made her grip his waist more firmly.

He'd never taken a girl on the back of his bike before, only his brother or a couple of guys from the band. But the first time Lisanne had come with him, he'd been desperate to get off campus before he talked to her. Now ... now it just felt good.

He'd been nervous as all fuck when she'd suggested going out for a group meal, but having her by his side, understanding, helping, interpreting, watching his back—she'd made it easier.

He hadn't thought he'd be able to do something like that, let alone enjoy. Yeah, the guy Rich had been a bit of a dick, but nothing Daniel couldn't handle. He felt a looseness in his chest, a lessening of the tightness that he'd felt the first day he started college.

It had been amazing having her sitting next to him, feeling her next to him, holding her hand. Walking out of her room when she'd practically begged him to fuck her had been one of the hardest things he'd ever done. He wasn't even sure he could explain it to himself, but somehow he wanted it to be *right* with her. She wasn't someone he'd use just to get his dick wet and walk away—he didn't want to fuck up with her. But his experience of *dating* was pretty limited: once, briefly, in his first year of high school, and then again for a few months when he was at school in Cave Spring.

Sex he could do—dating he wasn't so sure about. But he'd try. For Lisanne, he would try.

He pulled up at the dorm rooms and cut the engine. It didn't make any difference to him, but he knew Lisanne wouldn't be able to hear, and he wanted to say goodnight to her properly.

He took off his helmet and waited for her to give him the spare.

She was frowning and he didn't know why. He wanted to see her smile.

"What's the matter, Lis?"

She shook her head. "Nothing."

His temper flared instantly.

"Don't do that! Fuck! I miss enough of what's going on around me, without you saying 'nothing' when I can see by your face that you're upset."

Lisanne looked down. He wasn't having that shit. He lifted her chin with his fingers, gently raising her head so she was looking at him again.

"Talk to me, Lis!"

She sighed. "It was something Kirsty said. She told me to 'be careful'. With you. It made me mad, that's all."

Fucking interfering bitch. *Be careful?* What the fuck did that even mean? Maybe it was because he'd been about to punch that

143

guy Rich.

Daniel's latent temper snarled, wanting to lash out at someone. But he knew that Kirsty was right—Lisanne *should* be careful around him. The thought left a sour taste in his mouth that he was desperate to get rid of.

Without warning, Daniel pulled Lisanne toward him, letting his lips crash down on hers. He kissed her with an edge of desperation that he'd never experienced before. After a second of stunned surprise, she was kissing him back. Her tongue, hot and wet, was pressing into his mouth and it felt fucking amazing. His dick leapt to life, hopeful of getting in on the action. He wrapped his arms behind her and pulled her in tightly. He felt dizzy when her hands slid up his back and around his neck, locking them together.

They only stopped when a car horn made Lisanne jump.

"Get a room!" yelled Rich, as Vin parked at the curb to let Kirsty out.

Daniel saw the car and sighed. It was probably just as well they'd been interrupted because things had been about to get damn hot and heavy for outside a public building—at ten o'clock on a weekday night. Not that he cared, but he knew Lisanne would.

"Will I see you tomorrow?" said Lisanne, her face anxious.

"I'll find you in the cafeteria at lunchtime, baby," said Daniel, smiling at the thought. "Okay?"

She nodded contentedly. "Okay."

He kissed her quickly, kick-started Sirona, then rode away, glancing behind him once, seeing her standing alone in a pool of light, watching him.

It wasn't a long ride, but Daniel went slowly, not particularly eager to go home just to get into another scene with his brother.

As usual, there were bikes and cars parked up and down the road. Daniel could feel the front porch vibrating from a bass beat. It was a good thing there was an empty lot on one side, and an old deaf guy on the other. It wasn't an irony that amused Daniel, but he knew it was a lucky break, nevertheless.

He recognized a few of the people that were hanging around—a couple were from the Blue Note. Empty cans and bottles littered the whole ground floor. He barely noticed it anymore. As long as no one bothered him, he didn't much care. Except that now he had Lisanne to consider—he knew he couldn't bring her back there with so many fucking potheads and speed-freaks around. The thought irritated him more than he thought it should.

Mostly, Daniel didn't have much to do with Zef's friends or clients or whoever the hell they were, but tonight he needed a drink.

He slumped down on the dirty couch and picked up the bottle nearest to him: his good friend and namesake—Jack Daniels.

He wiped the top of the bottle with his hand and took a long drink. It had some bite but the burn helped him to think. His head was completely spun with everything that had happened over the last 48 hours. He'd done some sexy dirty stuff with Lisanne; fought with her; gotten arrested; beaten up by Zef. Now, it seemed, he had a girlfriend and was socializing with frat boys who thought he had a cool bike.

It was hard to keep up with the emotional cartwheels.

Zef had been right about one thing—dating Lisanne was not going to be without cost. It had been so fucking painful seeing her sing that night—seeing her sing but not to be able to hear a goddamn note of it. He'd stayed until the end of the first song, but it slayed him to be there. How much harder would it be as time went by? If they were dating—and somehow they seemed to have fallen into it—then it was only fair that he support her with her music. That's what boyfriends did, wasn't it? Supportive shit?

He took another drink and noticed that a cute brunette in her mid twenties was staring at him. When she realized that he'd seen her, she smiled and slowly licked her lips. Part of him would have liked nothing more than to lose himself in a stranger, but another part rebelled, not wanting to have anything to do with her.

He smiled back but gave her a small headshake. She cocked her head to one side. *Are you sure?*

Daniel shook his head again, and stood up, taking the whiskey with him.

Alone in his room, he lay on his bed with the curtains open, staring at the stars. Shortly before 2 AM, and after he'd finished the bottle of whiskey, he passed out.

The next day Lisanne felt so light, so weightless, she could have floated away entirely. Only her classes, and Kirsty's careful avoidance of mentioning anything Daniel related, kept her anchored to planet Earth.

He'd told her he liked her, he'd kissed her, he'd implied that there'd be more rides on Sirona, and he'd promised that they'd meet at lunchtime. A tiny part of her whispered that *of course* he hadn't really meant any of it, and *of course* he wasn't really interested in her: but that was just her usual lack of self-confidence spilling out. It was second nature for Lisanne to doubt anything positive that someone said about her. She was so used to being invisible at school and a vague disappointment to her parents, that being noticed was new. Being wanted, being kissed, being touched like that—it was all so unexpected. She felt giddy with happiness.

But midway through the morning, her fragile bubble of joy was punctured by a text message from Daniel.

> * D: have to meet my tutor.
> Be late for lunch. Later *

So that was it.

Of course.

He just wanted to find a way to let her down gently. Lisanne appreciated the text, she really did. At least he hadn't planned to let her sit there looking like a complete idiot. Just a partial idiot for having thought his words, his kisses—that any of those things meant something.

Lisanne entered the cafeteria feeling as if she had ton weights tied to her shoes. Her heart sank still further when she saw Kirsty sitting on Vin's lap, giggling into his hair, and Shawna flirting with one of Vin's football buddies.

She slid into a chair and pulled an apple out of her bag. It was about all she could face eating even though fifty minutes ago she'd been starving.

"Hey, roomie!" said Kirsty, her eyes sparkling with happiness. "Didja have a good morning?"

"It was okay," she mumbled.

Shawna sniggered. "Anyone would look that miserable if they had to listen to Beethoven and crap all day."

Kirsty frowned and started to say something, but Vin recaptured her attention by kissing her neck and tickling her.

Lisanne took a bite of her apple and chewed sullenly. How could an apple that had looked all juicy and appealing this morning, now taste like sawdust?

She nearly jumped out of her chair when a warm hand stroked her cheek.

"Hey, baby."

Lisanne yelped. "Daniel!"

There was an echo as Shawna purred his name, but he wasn't looking at her so he had no clue she'd spoken. To everyone else it looked like he'd completely blown her off.

Daniel chuckled softly at Lisanne's response and raised a challenging eyebrow at her.

"You expecting some other guy?"

"N-no! But you said you weren't coming?"

"I said I'd be *late*—I didn't say I wasn't coming."

"Oh!" she replied, her brain refusing to construct any answer that required additional syllables.

He smirked at her then glanced at her apple. "Is that all you're eating?"

"Um, yes?"

"Huh," he said, pushing his lunch tray onto the table. "Good

147

thing I got two slices of pizza. I know what you're like with my chips. And I got some salad, as well—girls like that rabbit food shit, right?"

Vin glanced over and laughed.

"You got that right, man!"

Lisanne was stunned by his thoughtfulness, then ashamed of her assumptions about him yet again. This boy! He surprised her constantly.

"Thank you," she said, quietly.

His expression softened. "You're welcome."

He pulled out a chair and leaned in to kiss her hair.

Lisanne felt her face glow. He smelled so good, and his skin looked soft and smooth now that he'd shaved.

The world fell away, and for a moment it was just the two of them.

Then Shawna muttered, "Oh, please!" and the moment was broken.

They chatted about their Business assignment and Vin asked a couple of questions about Daniel's motorcycle as he described it to his friends. But too soon lunch was over.

"Do you want to do something later, baby?" said Daniel, as he slung his messenger bag over his shoulder.

"Um, well," said Lisanne, hesitating. "I, um, I have band practice tonight."

A look of something like pain washed across Daniel's face, then it was gone.

"You want me to give you a ride home after?" he offered.

Lisanne was desperate to say 'yes', but it was just too selfish, forcing him to come to the club when she knew how hard it was for him.

"No, it's okay, thanks. Roy said he'd take me back."

Daniel nodded but he didn't smile. "Text me when you get back so I know you're home safe."

The rehearsal went well. They were all still on a high from the previous Saturday, and full of ideas for songs to extend their set from 45 minutes to an hour.

Roy's cell phone interrupted them.

"Uh-huh. Yeah. Yeah. Got it. How much? Okay. Yup. You got a deal." He ended the call and grinned at them. "We got that booking for the Down Under in three weeks. Graeme heard we were rockin' this place and he wants some of the action. Pay's ninety bucks each."

He launched himself at Lisanne and scooped her into a bone crushing hug. "And it's all thanks to baby girl!"

Lisanne gasped and tried to wriggle free. Roy whirled her around and deposited her on her feet, breathless and dizzy.

"This deserves a celebration!" he said. "Let's crack open the beer!"

Lisanne felt her smile slip. She liked the guys, but they were all older and she knew they drank a lot.

Roy seemed to have forgotten his promise of taking her home. When he offered her a beer she took a small sip and surreptitiously looked at her watch. It was nearly 11 PM already, and she had an early tutorial to get to in the morning.

She wondered whether it was too late to call Kirsty, then remembered that her roommate had planned on seeing Vin.

Lisanne decided to call a cab.

"Um, I'm going to take off now," she said, still hoping that Roy might remember his promise.

But they waved and carried on drinking, seemingly quite content to let her make her own way home. Irritated, Lisanne stood outside and called the cab firm that she used before, but all she got was the busy tone. She tried again a minute later, biting her lip and looking around nervously, but it was the same result.

Then she noticed a man watching her from across the street, and decided it was smarter to wait inside the club. She banged on the door and yelled, but nobody came.

She'd just scrolled down to find Roy's number when the man called out, "Hey, sugar. You want some company? I've got twenty bucks."

149

He crossed the street toward her.

"Pick up, Roy! Pick up!" she muttered desperately.

There was no answer.

She started walking down the street and was terrified when the man followed her. She ran, her heart pounding, fear making her fast.

Someone, there must be someone! But there was no one around, no one she could ask for help.

Stay in well lit areas!

She knew that was important, but every other building was in darkness and the area was rundown and seedy, and all she could hear was the sound of her own echoing footsteps.

With her lungs aching, she came to a halt outside a TV repair shop, where a dim light illuminated the bars on the windows. Her hands shook as she sent a text to Daniel, hoping he'd have his cell phone with him this late.

> * L: can you come get me? Am outside TV shop
> West River St. LA xx *

She breathed a sigh of relief when his reply was immediate.

> * D: wtf?! On way.
> Keep your phone out. 911 if you need *

She slumped down in the filthy doorway, her knees no longer able to support her. Fear pumped through her body, making her shake uncontrollably. She saw the man walking up the street toward her, clearly still searching for her. Squeezing herself into the darkest corner, Lisanne held her breath. The seconds ticked by as the man walked slowly on the other side of the street, peering through the gloom.

Lisanne thanked God for the broken streetlights and clutched her phone more tightly to her body.

Her nerves were stretched unbearably by the time she heard the guttural roar of Daniel's Harley a few minutes later.

He pulled off his helmet quickly.

"Are you okay?" he said urgently, checking her up and down as if he was looking for obvious injuries.

Lisanne nodded but felt hot tears spill down her face from fear, from relief. Daniel pulled her toward him tightly and she sobbed into his chest, feeling the cool leather of his jacket against her face.

Strong arms wrapped around her and he rocked her gently, murmuring wordlessly into her hair. After a minute he gently pushed her away and ran his thumbs over her cheeks, brushing away the tears.

"What happened? Why are you here?"

Lisanne explained briefly, and when she got to the part where Roy started drinking, Daniel swore loudly.

"Motherfucker! I'll kill the bastard!"

He was all for going back to the club and showing Roy just how pissed he really was.

"Please, Daniel. I just want to go home."

Immediately, he looked contrite. "Yeah, sure. Okay."

He handed her the spare helmet and kick-started the bike. Lisanne felt much happier when they left the club area behind and were heading back toward the campus. She snuggled into Daniel's broad back and felt his hand brush over hers as she pushed her fingers into his jacket pockets.

Once they were at the dorms, Daniel insisted on walking her to her room, which meant sneaking in through the fire exit. Lisanne desperately hoped no one would see them—she'd had enough drama for one night.

She'd just pushed the key in her lock, when the door sprang open, with an anxious looking Kirsty bearing down on her.

"There you are! I've been so worried!"

Then she saw Lisanne's red eyes and tear marked face with Daniel standing behind her, and immediately pole-vaulted to the wrong conclusion.

"What have you done to her?" she hissed, pulling Lisanne behind her and pointing at Daniel accusingly.

"Nothing!" he snarled, fury etched into every plane of his beautiful face.

"Kirsty," whispered Lisanne, "he saved me."

"What?" snapped Kirsty, whirling around. "Right—I want to know everything. You sit over there," she ordered Daniel, "and you," she said to Lisanne, "tell me everything."

"Fuck that!" growled Daniel. "I don't take orders from you."

"Daniel, please," gasped Lisanne. "I can't take any more tonight."

"Can't you see you're upsetting her!" shouted Kirsty.

"You're not helping!" said Lisanne, fresh tears stinging her eyes.

Daniel and Kirsty eyed each other angrily. Eventually, he walked further into the room and sat stiffly on Lisanne's desk chair.

She told the story again quickly, almost smiling when Kirsty's reaction to Roy's irresponsible behavior was the same as Daniel's, although with slightly less profane cursing.

Kirsty shook out her long hair and stood up.

"I apologize, Daniel," she said, formally. "I jumped to conclusions."

"Yeah," he said bitterly, staring her down. He turned to Lisanne, his expression still angry. "I'm going to take off now, baby doll. Will you be okay?"

"Yes, I'm fine," she said, with a weak smile. "I mean nothing happened. I just panicked. I'm sorry."

He looked at her seriously. "I don't want you wandering around those streets at night," he said. "Next time wait inside the club. Fuck Roy, I'll come get you. Okay?"

"Okay," she said. "Thank you."

He kissed her on the cheek, shot another angry look at Kirsty, and slipped out of the door.

"That boy can't accept an apology," said Kirsty, as soon as Daniel had gone.

"*That boy* shouldn't have needed one," Lisanne shot back.

Kirsty looked at her in surprise.

"Lis! You turn up here, over an hour late, bawling your eyes out with Daniel looking like he wanted to kill someone—what was I supposed to think?"

Lisanne closed her eyes tiredly.

"You just assumed that he was in the wrong. He *saved* me, Kirsty. If you just knew how amazing he is…"

She stopped abruptly.

"Whatever," said Kirsty. "I'm just glad you're safe. *Don't do it again!*"

Then she gave her a huge hug.

"Now go get ready for bed. You look as exhausted as I feel."

"Yes, Mom!"

Ten minutes later, Lisanne was pulling the duvet around her when her cell phone buzzed with a text.

* D: sleep well, beautiful.
See you at lunch tomorrow. *

CHAPTER 9

Lisanne did sleep well and was one degree short of blissful when someone knocked on the door the next morning, minutes before she and Kirsty were due to leave for class.

Kirsty was applying her usual industrial layers of glossy lipstick.

"It's for you," she said, without looking away from the mirror.

Lisanne rolled her eyes. Kirsty was Ms. Popularity on campus—it was sure to be for her.

She pulled open the door and a sophomore that she dimly recognized was leaning against the door.

"Which of you's dating Zef Colton?" she said with a yawn, drumming her chipped fingernails against the doorjamb.

"Um ... do you mean Daniel Colton?"

The girl looked bored. "How the hell should I know? Yeah, are you her?"

"I guess."

"Okay, finally. So I'm after a wrap—something for the weekend."

"Excuse me?"

"Hello! Am I talking Egyptian? What can I get for thirty bucks?"

Kirsty strode to the door and pushed her finger into the girl's face.

"You've got the wrong fucking room, lady. Nobody here deals, now get the hell out!"

Kirsty slammed the door on the annoyed woman and stared

154

at Lisanne.

"What was that all about? Tell me you're not dealing drugs for Daniel."

"What? God, no! Kirsty, no! I never … Daniel hasn't … no!"

Lisanne was incoherent with shock.

That girl had thought she could buy drugs from their dorm room?

She saw that her hands were shaking and hastily sat down on her bed, before her knees buckled.

Kirsty stared at her, but her expression softened when she realized how upset Lisanne was. "Okay," she said, in a more measured toned. "And you're not hiding anything in our room for him?"

"No!"

Lisanne's voice was shrill.

"You have to talk to Daniel about this."

Lisanne nodded numbly, and Kirsty chewed on her lip before plowing on.

"Has Daniel ever offered you drugs? Weed, anything?"

"No." Lisanne's voice had dropped to a whisper.

"Good. Keep it that way, sweetie."

Kirsty headed out for class, leaving Lisanne shaken and very worried.

She sat for a few more minutes, letting her breathing slow, then picked up her backpack and headed out. Her expression was grim. She had no idea how she was going to bring this up with Daniel.

Lisanne was distracted all day. She was afraid Daniel would blow her off if she said something to him. She decided to wait until they had more time to spend together, which was easier said than done.

Lisanne was constantly busy: running between classes, band practices, and trying to keep up with her homework load. She managed to snatch brief moments with Daniel, over lunch, or a coffee before class, but it was all hurried. She didn't mention the unexpected visitor, but it was on her mind. Without meaning to, she kept an eye open for anything that showed Daniel *was* dealing. It was tiring and upsetting and she didn't know what to do about it. So, in the end, she did nothing, and said nothing.

She had received a short text message from Roy, apologizing for leaving her in the lurch and promising not to do it again. She strongly suspected that Daniel had had something to do with that, but neither of them mentioned anything, so she let it go.

They were sitting drinking sodas after their Friday morning Business lecture, when Vin and Kirsty joined them.

Lisanne was disappointed that Daniel and Kirsty didn't seem to have gotten over their spat, instead maintaining a cautious civility around each other; but Vin and Daniel had talked bikes for hours and were well on their way to becoming friends—a fact that seemed to irk Kirsty.

"Hey, guys," Vin said, as they walked into the cafeteria. "We're going to get a few people together and head out to the beach tomorrow. You want in?"

Lisanne looked hopefully toward Daniel before she answered. She didn't want to put him under too much pressure. But she was disappointed when he shook his head straightaway.

"Can't, man. Gotta be somewhere."

"No problem," said Vin.

"That doesn't mean *you* can't come, Lisanne," said Kirsty, sharply.

Vin gave her a warning look which Kirsty pretended to ignore, then carried on making plans for the outing.

Vin assumed that whatever Daniel had planned also involved Lisanne. But as far as she was concerned, it was the first time Daniel had mentioned being busy at the weekend. Disappointment made her brusque.

"What are you doing? You didn't mention anything before?"

He looked annoyed as he replied quietly, "I'm busy."

"Doing what?" Lisanne persisted

"Not here," he muttered.

"Fine," she said, huffily. "Let's go. You can tell me outside."

Vin waved as they left, but Kirsty just watched them go without comment.

Lisanne led Daniel toward an empty patch of grass in the middle of the quad. It was pleasantly warm and many of the students were sitting outside enjoying the weather. Despite the peaceful surroundings, Daniel looked tense and unhappy, but Lisanne wasn't in the mood for backing down. They were supposed to be dating: shouldn't he tell her if he'd made weekend plans without her?

She sat opposite him and waited.

"What's the matter?" she said, in a slightly milder tone.

Even though Daniel couldn't hear her, he could read her face easily.

He frowned at her, then dropped his gaze and started to pick at one of the laces on his boots.

"I've got an appointment at the clinic," he mumbled without looking up.

Lisanne was taken aback. *What? A clinic?* She immediately thought of STDs—she couldn't help the wayward direction of her thoughts.

"What sort of clinic?" she said at last, when Daniel didn't seem inclined to add any further detail. Of course he didn't answer, and she had to nudge his foot so he'd look up. "What sort of clinic?" she repeated.

He seemed surprised by her question.

"The hearing loss clinic," he said, quietly. "What did you think I meant?"

"Oh," she said, stupidly. "Why?"

He shrugged. "I go every six months for a checkup. It's a waste of time: they just tell me the same shit. I'm deaf—that's not gonna change."

"Oh," she said again, wishing she could think of something supportive to say—or at least something that didn't make her sound like an idiot.

Then she had a brainwave: this could really help her to understand. Lisanne took a deep breath.

"Can I come with you?"

Daniel looked stunned. "What?"

Lisanne sat up straighter. "Can I come with you?"

"Fuck! Why would you want to do that?"

Lisanne looked away for a moment, gathering her thoughts.

"So I can understand more," she replied, looking back at him. "Please, Daniel. If I'm supposed to be…" she paused. "If I'm supposed to be your *girlfriend*, I want you to be able to share things like this with me."

He seemed conflicted. Lisanne forced herself to stay silent, letting Daniel decide.

"It's the other side of town," he said, grudgingly.

"I don't mind that," she said, gently. "But only if you want me to come."

He fiddled with his lace a bit more, then pulled out a cigarette and lit it.

"I don't want it to change things," he said, blowing the smoke away from her.

"Why would it do that?" Lisanne asked patiently.

He shrugged. "It always does."

"I don't understand."

"I know." Daniel let out a long sigh. "The appointment's at 11:15. I'd have to pick you up at 10:45."

She put her hand over his and he glanced up.

"I'll be ready," she said.

When Kirsty saw Lisanne that evening, she seemed determined to give her a hard time for not coming to the beach with them.

"Well, why is it such a secret where you're going?" she said, irritation coloring her voice.

"It's not a secret," Lisanne replied sharply, if not entirely truthfully. "It's just something private Daniel has to do. It's not for me to say."

"It's not anything *illegal*, is it?" snapped Kirsty. "Because if is, don't let yourself get dragged into it."

"What?" said Lisanne, shocked. "Daniel isn't into anything illegal!"

"Are you sure about that? Because that's not what I've heard, not forgetting our little visitor the other day."

"Since when do you listen to gossip?"

Kirsty stared back stonily.

"I don't usually, but I've heard it from several different places now. Too many for it to be a coincidence."

"What *exactly* have you heard?"

"That he deals drugs," said Kirsty flatly, raising her eyebrows.

"That is such bullshit!" shouted Lisanne. "How could you even *think* that? I've never seen him do anything more than smoke a cigarette!"

"Don't be naïve, Lis," said Kirsty, her voice chilly. "Have you forgotten that skank who tried to buy drugs from you?"

"She asked for Zef, not Daniel. You *heard* her! He can't help what his brother does."

Kirsty folded her arms, her face full of disbelief.

Lisanne suddenly remembered everything she'd seen at Daniel's home, but she wasn't going to admit that to Kirsty. Daniel had never done *anything* like that in front of her.

"You don't know everything about him, Lis," said Kirsty, her voice becoming heated.

"I know the important things!" shouted Lisanne. "He's sweet and kind and takes care of me!"

Kirsty snorted. "Just because he puts on a good show, that doesn't make him squeaky clean. He acts like he's stoned half the time—not listening and always staring, all intense and..."

Lisanne cut her off. "You don't know what you're talking about, Kirsty. Drop it now."

Her voice was dangerously quiet and Kirsty looked surprised.

"I'm looking out for you, Lis," she said, in a more reasonable tone. "You're my friend. I don't want him to hurt you."

Lisanne took a deep breath. "Daniel won't hurt me. You have to trust me on this. His brother ... well ... I don't know. But Daniel doesn't have anything to do with that. I promise you."

Kirsty shook her head and sighed. "If you say so. Just ... just be careful, okay?"

Lisanne nodded stiffly.

She hated fighting with Kirsty, but she was *so* wrong on this.

The next morning, Kirsty was trying hard to act naturally around Lisanne, but it was obvious she was still on edge.

Lisanne did her best to ignore her hyper roommate, more focused on what the morning would bring.

"You can always meet us out there later?" pleaded Kirsty. "You know, when you've finished your *private* thing. Just text me—I'll tell you where we are."

Lisanne gritted her teeth.

"Maybe. I don't know."

Kirsty sighed and threw up her hands as if to say, *Have it your own way.*

Lisanne slipped out of the door, too keyed up to take any more sharp looks or knowing gazes.

She sat on the curb outside waiting for the now familiar sound of Daniel's Harley. She was humming along with *This Fire*, a track by one of her favorite bands, Birds of Tokyo, when Vin drove up in his brand new Expedition SUV.

She pulled out her ear buds as he walked over to her.

"Hi, Lis! How you doing? Changed your mind about coming with us?"

Lisanne smiled and shook her head.

"No, but thanks."

"Pity, it's going to be fun. Are you waiting for Dan?"

Lisanne nodded and Vin looked at her carefully.

"And you didn't want to wait inside?"

Lisanne looked up, seeing nothing judgmental in Vin's face.

"Kirsty doesn't approve," she said, pulling a wry face. "It's ... quieter if I wait out here."

Vin squatted down on the curb next to her.

"She's just trying to look out for you, Lis. Dan seems like an okay guy, but I guess you must have heard what they're saying about his brother? That's why he's gotten into all those fights this last week."

Lisanne looked up, pinning Vin with a fierce stare.

"What fights?"

Vin's ears turned red and he looked uncomfortable.

"Um … just a couple of guys throwing a few punches—nothing to worry about."

"What?!"

"Look, Lis, it's like this. Some people—assholes mainly—assume that if one brother is dealing, then the other must be, too. But I haven't come across a single person who's actually seen Dan with drugs or bought anything from him, which makes me think it's all bullshit. But he's being tarred with the same brush, and his first thought is to beat the shit out of whoever's doing the asking. That's why Kirsty worries about you."

Lisanne didn't know what to think.

"Daniel isn't … he doesn't…"

Vin sighed.

"Even if he isn't, he must know what his brother's doing. He could get into a whole load of serious trouble—and so could you."

He gave her a sympathetic look, then stood up and made his way to the dorm rooms, leaving Lisanne fumbling with her overflowing thoughts and emotions.

In the distance, the sound of a motorcycle engine grew louder. Lisanne took a few deep breaths and tried to quell her stomach's natural inclination to turn a few somersaults.

Daniel pulled up next to her and lifted his visor, but he didn't cut the engine and he didn't dismount. He simply handed her the spare helmet without speaking, and jerked his head to indicate that Lisanne should climb on.

She'd known the morning would be stressful but she hadn't thought it would be this bad: first what Vin had told her; now Daniel stressing out.

Daniel hit the throttle and they took off so quickly, Lisanne had to grab him to stop herself being jolted off the back.

He drove for about 20 minutes before pulling up in the

parking lot of the city hospital. When he cut the engine, finally there was silence. For Lisanne it was a relief—it made no difference to Daniel.

He locked their helmets in the leather saddlebags and carefully met her gaze.

"If you don't want to stay, there's a cafeteria in the main part of the hospital."

Lisanne was confused.

"Why wouldn't I want to stay?"

He shrugged but didn't answer.

Lisanne took his hand and he looked down at her, surprised.

"Let's go," she said.

Daniel felt dread seep into his bones. *This* would be the day when she'd decide she couldn't date a deaf guy. *This* would be the moment that she'd run.

He led her around to a side door with a large, blue and white sign that announced 'Hearing Loss Clinic'.

"I'll need my hand, Lis," he said, pulling his fingers from her grasp.

His rejection hurt, but she didn't say anything. Daniel was radiating enough tension to make Lisanne bite her tongue.

But she was wrong—about Daniel rejecting her.

The clinic's reception was already occupied by two families with a bunch of kids who were probably still in elementary school. In complete silence, they appeared to be chatting away animatedly, communicating through sign language.

One of the youngest kids turned to stare, then gave Lisanne a big smile and raised his hand to his head in what looked like a salute.

Lisanne smiled and waved back, but the child looked confused.

Suddenly she realized that Daniel was moving his hands quickly in a series of confusing shapes.

"You ... you can do sign language?"

He raised his eyebrows.

"Well, yeah. I went to a deaf school for nearly three years.

What do you think we did? Draw pictures?"

She tried to ignore his blunt sarcasm.

"What about lip reading?"

"Not everyone can lip read, especially if they were deaf pre-lingual."

"Um, pre-lingual?"

He gave her his full attention.

"If a kid is born deaf or becomes deaf before they've learned to speak, it's a lot harder to learn to lip read. Not impossible, just a lot harder. Most deaf kids are brought up signing."

"Oh," said Lisanne, anxiously. "I see. What did you just say to him?"

"I told him that you were hearing and couldn't sign."

"Is everyone here deaf?" she whispered.

"Not everyone, honey," said one of the mothers, kindly. "Is this your first time?"

Lisanne blushed and gave an awkward laugh. "Is it that obvious?"

"Pretty much, but don't worry about it. You'll get used to it," she said, glancing at Daniel, then giving Lisanne a warm smile.

Daniel was still in conversation with the young boy. Something the boy had signed made him smile and throw a wicked look at Lisanne.

"Trevor!" snapped his mother, signing as she spoke. "That is rude! Apologize to the young lady."

The boy made a fist with his right hand and drew a circular motion in front of his chest.

"He's saying 'sorry'," Daniel translated for her.

"Oh! How do I say, 'that's okay'?"

"Make an 'O' shape with your hand—yeah—that's it. And you make a sign like a pair of scissors for the 'K' by pushing up your middle finger and dropping your index finger."

Feeling self-conscious, she copied the gesture, and the boy smiled.

"By the way," she asked, somewhat belatedly, "what did he say?"

"You sure you want to know?"

"Yes!"

"He asked me why you were so dumb—because you couldn't sign."

"Oh!" gasped Lisanne.

Daniel smirked at her. "I did warn you."

She thumped his arm. "You set me up!"

He leaned down and whispered in her ear. "You're fucking sexy when you're mad."

Lisanne felt her skin flush as her mouth opened and shut with confusion. She was glad he was in a better mood, although she had no idea how it had happened. Except that here, he was the same as everyone else—she was the odd one out.

"Will you teach me?"

"Teach you what?"

"Sign language."

Daniel frowned. "What for? I only ever use it when I go to these fucking places."

"Please ... how do I say, 'I hear you'?"

"Are you fucking kidding me? How many deaf people do you know, Lis, because I'm telling you, that's the most useless thing ever."

Lisanne swallowed and looked down. She felt his gentle fingers on her cheek.

"I'm sorry, baby doll. These places just ... okay, I'll show you."

She gave him a weak smile.

"You say 'I' by pointing at yourself. For 'hear' you just tap your ear twice, and 'you'—just point at the person you're talking to."

"That's it?"

"That's it."

Suddenly the video screen flashed and everyone looked up. A name was displayed and one of the moms stood and corralled her brood, before heading off down the corridor.

"Teach me something else," said Lisanne, drawing Daniel's

attention back to herself by nudging his knee.

"Like what?"

"How do I say, 'My boyfriend's Harley is cooler than yours'?"

Daniel laughed.

"Like this," and he flipped the bird.

"Stop that!" she hissed, grabbing his hand before one of the remaining children saw it. "Behave!"

He leaned into her and ran his nose along her cheek. "Can't do that, baby doll. Not around you."

The video screen flashed again and this time Daniel's name came up.

His smile disappeared and he sighed heavily.

"You can stay here if you want," he offered again, almost hopefully.

"No. I'm coming with you," Lisanne said, insistently.

He shrugged as if he didn't care, and Lisanne tried not to feel hurt. She knew it was just his way—an act.

They walked down a corridor with regimented doors, until they found number five.

Daniel didn't knock but walked straight in, which Lisanne found surprising.

She followed him into a room that was small and white, with medical posters tacked to the walls: several had cross sections that showed the inner workings of the ear. One picture was of a beautiful sunset. Perhaps it was to make the place seem friendlier.

The man they'd come to see stood up and smiled at Daniel, then cast a surprised look at Lisanne.

He made a quick movement with his hands, clearly asking a question, and Daniel signed back.

Lisanne was shocked. She'd expected a normal consultation. *Normal?* She cringed, just for thinking the word. She'd expected a spoken consultation. *How dumb was that?* She kicked herself for embracing yet another stereotype—automatically assuming that the doctor would be hearing.

Instead, the entire conversation was held in sign language.

She started paying attention when she saw that Daniel was introducing her.

"Lis, this is Dr. Pappas—my audiologist."

She tried to remember the sign for 'hello' and gave a rather cack-handed half salute that made the doctor smile.

"Hi," she said shyly, holding out her hand, as he saluted her back.

"Hel-lo, Lis," said the doctor, in a slow, robotic monotone. "It is good to meet you."

Lisanne struggled to understand what Dr. Pappas was saying and looked anxiously at Daniel.

"It's okay," he said, quietly. "I've told him this is all new to you."

The doctor tapped Daniel's arm and signed something else.

Daniel shook his head quickly, but the doctor seemed to be insisting.

"For fuck's sake," Daniel muttered, earning him a rather shocked look from Lisanne. "He says that if you have any questions, just ask. But not too many, please, baby?"

"Oh, okay," she said, softly, having absolutely no idea what she'd ask or where to start.

The doctor tapped Daniel's arm again and they started signing rapidly. Lisanne sat silently, utterly bewildered, at a loss to understand a single thing. Perhaps this was how Daniel felt when he was among a group of people he didn't know—isolated, unaware, excluded. Or perhaps this was how Daniel felt most of the time. Her heart thumped painfully and she had to stop herself from rubbing her chest to ease the stabbing sensation.

Dr. Pappas passed Daniel some headphones and they ran through a number of tests. Lisanne watched Dr. Pappas' computer screen as various charts appeared.

When they'd finished with the headphones, they carried on their conversation.

She watched Daniel and Dr. Pappas carefully. At first their

body language was relaxed, but as the conversation progressed, she saw that it was becoming increasingly heated. Dr. Pappas kept looking at Lisanne, as if he was asking Daniel something about her.

She jumped when Daniel suddenly shouted, "No!"

"What is it?" she said, nervously.

He ignored her, signing furiously at the doctor, who seemed equally determined.

Suddenly Daniel crossed his arms and scowled.

"What's wrong? What's happened?"

"Lis," intoned Dr. Pappas. "Ask Dan-i-el to tell you about coch-le-ar im-plants."

"I said no!" Daniel roared. "Come on! We're getting the fuck out of here."

He grabbed Lisanne's wrist and pulled her out of the chair.

She threw a hasty look at the doctor, who smiled sadly and gave her a small wave.

Daniel towed her down the corridor, refusing to speak or explain. When they reached the parking lot she yanked her hand free.

"Daniel! Talk to me! What just happened in there? What was he telling me to ask you about?"

"Nothing."

"No! It wasn't nothing."

"Just drop it, please, Lis."

He grabbed his hair as if he wanted to yank it out, and screwed his eyes shut.

She reached up and stroked his face, trying to calm him.

"Daniel, you get so mad at me if I don't tell you everything—now you're doing the same to me. Please—I want to understand."

His eyes blazed, but then he dropped his head in resignation. When he looked at her a few seconds later, she could see the pain in his eyes.

"Okay, okay. But not here. I fucking hate hospitals. Let's just go, okay?"

She nodded and placed a gentle kiss on his lips.

"We could get some takeout and go back to your place?"

He shook his head. "No, not there. Place was jammed when I left. Can we go to your room? Kirsty's at the beach, right?"

"Of course. I'll make you a coffee. We just need to buy some food."

They stopped at a convenience store and picked up sandwiches and chips before heading back.

It was open house hours so at least Daniel didn't have to sneak in, although several girls stared curiously at him and Lisanne.

By the time Lisanne turned her key in the lock, she felt exhausted. It had been another morning spent on Daniel's emotional rollercoaster. The only thing that stopped her from feeling sorry for herself was the look of bitterness on his face as he'd run from the hospital. Whatever he and Dr. Pappas had argued about, it had really upset him.

Daniel dropped his jacket on the floor and, without a word, flung himself down on Lisanne's bed. He threw one arm over his eyes and lay still.

Lisanne wasn't sure what to do. She decided to give him a minute, hoping he'd talk to her when he was ready. She puttered around the room, taking off her sneakers and hanging up her jacket as well as Daniel's. She pulled the food out of the paper bag and placed it next to him on the bedside table. Then she stroked his arm and placed a gentle kiss on his bicep.

When he lifted his arm to look at her, she kissed his mouth, letting her tongue flick along his top lip.

His surprised expression turned into a sexy smile.

"I thought I was being invited for coffee?"

She pulled a face. "You really want coffee?"

He laughed. "Yeah, I'm actually kind of thirsty. And hungry."

"I've got some cookies, too."

"Chocolate chip?" he asked, his eyes lighting up like Christmas.

Lisanne laughed. "As it happens, yes!"

She reached into her cabinet and threw an unopened packet to him. Then she realized she was out of coffee. Completely.

"Uh, Daniel, I don't have any coffee!"

His expression was amused. "So you brought me here under false pretenses?"

She crossed her arms, a little embarrassed, then inspiration hit. "But I've got that beer you left behind the other day. It's not cold, but…"

"Better not, baby doll. If I get stopped by the cops again on the way home and they smell alcohol on me, I'll be in a shitload of trouble."

Lisanne took a deep breath. "You can stay here—for the night. Kirsty won't be coming back. I mean, if you want to."

Daniel stared at her.

"Are you sure?"

"Y-yes."

"C'mere."

Nervously she walked toward him. He sat up and swung his legs off the bed, then pulled her down so she was sitting on his lap.

"Lis, I promise I'll make it good for you, baby doll, but only when you're ready. Yeah, I'd really like to stay but we don't have to do anything, okay?"

"Okay," she said, her voice a little shaky.

"Good. Now where's that damn beer?" he said, planting a noisy kiss just below her throat.

She pushed him away playfully and dug the beer out from under her bed, where she'd hidden it.

She looked up and watched in fascination as Daniel kicked off his boots. Then he peeled off his socks and launched himself backward onto her bed again, patting the space beside him.

She crawled up next to him and he pulled her into his chest, kissing her hair. She felt his muscles contract and ripple as he reached over to grab a beer. He popped the tab and offered it to Lisanne first.

"Okay, just a sip," she said.

She realized this was going to be awkward. Snuggling into him was wonderful, but they couldn't carry on a conversation like that. Wondering what she wanted more—to talk, or to cuddle—she had a couple of sips of beer, then passed it back to him.

He took a long drink, tipping his head back. She watched his Adam's apple move as he drank, and wondered what it would feel like under her tongue.

Before Daniel had even placed his beer back on the bedside table, Lisanne slid her fingers under his t-shirt.

He looked down at her.

"Will you take it off?" she said, shocked by her own forwardness.

Giving her a small smile, he pulled the t-shirt over his head from the back of the neck.

Lisanne could have sworn she heard a few seams rip, but she didn't say anything. He tossed it onto her chair and sat back on the bed.

"Am I allowed to eat something now or do you want to keep undressing me?"

Lisanne laughed, hoping it sounded—or at least looked— vaguely natural.

Trying to act casual, she threw a packet of sandwiches at him, watching with amusement as he devoured them in a couple of bites.

"What?" he mumbled with crumbs on his lips. "I'm hungry."

Shaking her head, Lisanne ate her own sandwich more slowly and let Daniel have the lion's share of the chips. But when it came to chocolate chip cookies, she insisted on an equal division of the spoils.

"Don't come between me and my cookies," she said with a challenging look, daring him to have more than his fair share.

He laughed and pretended to look scared.

Lisanne didn't want to spoil the banter, but there was a big elephant in the room that they weren't discussing. She wasn't sure how to bring up Dr. Pappas' words to her. But she *needed* to know … to understand.

"Daniel…" she began. "About what Dr. Pappas said…"

He frowned and looked down, his mood changing rapidly.

"Lis…"

"Please, I just want to understand. What did he mean?"

For a moment she thought he was going to refuse to explain, but instead he took a deep breath.

"He was talking about a cochlear implant."

"Cochlear?" Lisanne tested the unfamiliar word.

He nodded. "It's part of the inner ear. I can give you all the technical shit but basically it processes sound. There's an implant that's been developed that can give back some hearing. It doesn't work for all deaf people—it depends on what caused the hearing loss."

"Would it work for you?"

"Maybe. Dr. Pappas thinks so."

Lisanne was confused. If the doctor thought it could help Daniel to hear again, she couldn't imagine what he was waiting for.

"You don't want to?"

"No, I fucking don't!"

Lisanne was shocked by the vehemence of his reply. She pushed her finger into a worn patch on the knee of her jeans.

"I don't understand. Why wouldn't you?"

"Because!" he shouted, then lowered his voice. "Because it means having a fucking chunk of metal drilled into your skull, and a magnet shoved under your skin so you can clip on a receiver that's attached to *another* fucking hearing aid. And after all that, there's no guarantee it would work. I told you—I'm sick of hospitals." His voice dropped to a whisper. "I'm sick of being different."

"But you could hear again?"

"*Could. Could* hear. Nothing's definite."

Lisanne wasn't sure how far she should push him, but she still didn't understand why he was so against trying.

171

"Wouldn't some hearing be worth it? Isn't it worth trying?"

He looked at her angrily.

"You think I'm broken, don't you? You think I should be *fixed*. You want me to be normal. I'll never be your version of normal, Lis. I'll never be like you—like them."

He waved his arm around, to emphasize his point.

She felt tears start in her eyes.

"I'm not trying to fix you, Daniel. I just want you to be happy. I love you just the way you are."

He blinked at her, looking shocked. Lisanne held her breath when she realized what she'd said. She hadn't meant to say it. She didn't even realize it was true until that moment.

"You ... you *love* me?"

His voice was faint, disbelieving.

Lisanne nodded slowly, afraid to take her eyes away from his beautiful face.

"But ... why?"

He looked lost, confused, so unsure of himself: Lisanne felt her heart tremble.

"Because you're kind, and good, and sweet, and funny. Because I feel happy when I'm with you. You make me feel protected, safe." She shrugged. "You're everything."

His voice was bewildered. "But why?"

Lisanne shook her head, unable to speak any further.

She crawled up the bed and he automatically wrapped his arms around her shoulders and pulled her toward him. She lay with her head on his chest, listening to the frantic pounding of his heart.

His skin was warm and silky, inviting Lisanne to place gentle kisses over his torso.

He shivered under her touch and pulled her in tighter, making it hard for her to move. Needing to keep touching him, she traced the tattoo on his left shoulder with one finger. It was a bird, bursting from flames—a phoenix in red and gold: the symbol of rebirth. The tail feathers curled around to the top half of his chest, resting just above the small silver ring that pierced his nipple. Further down his arm, there were dark blue swirls that looked like waves and in between them, tiny musical notes in black.

She knew that on his other shoulder, he carried a dragon in a Celtic design of sea-greens and blues. She pushed away from him so she could see it again.

A sinuous lizard coiled itself from his elbow to the top of his arm, silvery gray smoke curling from its nostrils.

"It's beautiful," she breathed. "You're beautiful." She let her finger drift over his bicep. "Why a dragon? Does it mean anything?"

He nodded slowly, one had stroking her back in long, languid, featherlight touches.

"The dragon means wisdom, and the ability to go through different worlds."

Different worlds.

Lisanne thought she was beginning to understand, but Daniel didn't make it easy.

She followed the dragon's tail thoughtfully, Daniel's eyes watching her.

"You've got another tattoo … on your hip. I saw it … last time."

He nodded, his eyes so dark and sensuous, the hazel eclipsed.

"Do you want to see it again?"

Lisanne wasn't sure if they were still talking tattoos, but managed to murmur, "Yes."

Daniel unbuttoned his jeans and pulled the zipper down. Then he pushed a corner of the denim away to reveal his hipbone and two Kanji in black ink.

"What do they mean?"

"It's Japanese. It says 'nozomu'. It means hope or wish."

Lisanne traced the outline with her index finger and his body quivered under her touch.

Suddenly, he pulled her hand away.

"What?"

"Lis, you're making it hard for me to stop from fucking you here and now," he said, breathing heavily.

She froze, then looked up at him.

"What if I don't want you to stop?"

He hesitated, trying to read certainty in her steady gaze.

"Don't say it if you don't mean it."

"I do. I do mean it."

He growled low in his throat, suddenly pulling her face to his lips and kissing her cheeks, her chin, her throat, her mouth.

Lisanne gasped and wound her hands behind his neck, kissing him back passionately. She felt his tongue slide into her mouth, tasting faintly of beer, her brain fogged with lust.

His hands tugged on the bottom of her t-shirt and Lisanne pulled it over her head. Daniel moaned at the sight of her bare flesh and sank his face between her breasts and nuzzled them softly, letting his teeth pull at the cup of her bra.

The breath caught in her throat as for the first time in her life, she had the sensation of a man's hot mouth on her bare nipple. His tongue rolled over and around the tight bud and his teeth grazed the flesh, making Lisanne arch her back. With a quick, practiced movement, Daniel snapped the fastening on her bra and pulled the straps over Lisanne's arms, tossing it to the floor.

Then he rolled her onto her back, bracing himself on his forearms, his left knee between her thighs, and began to feast on her breasts.

Lisanne's senses were overwhemed as his hard, heavy body pressed into hers. She couldn't help wanting to stroke his broad back as he hovered over her. She felt his muscles shiver as she touched him, running her fingers all the way down to the curve of his ass cheeks.

A long sigh left his throat as he sucked her skin gently.

Barely coherent, she forced her hand inside his jeans and started to push the waistband over his hips. He leaned away from her and sat up long enough for him to kick the pants and his briefs free.

They didn't speak as her hands reached for him, and he sighed again as she wrapped her hand around him.

He kissed her down her body, forcing her to let go of him. Then his fingers unhooked the button on her jeans, and he pulled the zipper down. Without moving them off of her, he slipped a finger inside her panties and groaned when he found her wet.

Lisanne gasped and arched her hips into his, feeling his erection pushing against her stomach. She couldn't imagine how that would feel *inside* her—everything she'd read, everything she'd heard made her afraid it would hurt. But she didn't want to stop. She couldn't.

His fingers pumped gently inside her, his thumb pressing against the warm, tight flesh. His mouth mimicked the movements on her neck and shoulders, gradually increasing the speed. She tried desperately to assimilate everything she was feeling, but her mind was overpowered by sensation.

Her hips bucked onto his hand and the same slow burn, the fizzing of her blood, that she'd felt before, began again.

"Daniel!" she gasped. "Daniel, I … I…" but her thoughts and words were swept away as her body took control.

This orgasm was even more intense than the last. The intimacy they'd found by sharing their doubts and fears, maybe that was the reason.

She hadn't run. And he was still there, with her.

Daniel stroked her face.

"Lis? Lis? Do you still want me?"

His voice was filled with tension.

"Yes," she said, the breath shuddering in her lungs. "I want you."

Daniel tugged off her jeans, followed by her panties, surprising her when he leaned down to kiss her pubic bone, nuzzling her wiry hair.

"You smell so good," he said, his voice hoarse. "Can I taste you?"

"Uh … uh … I don't know…" she gasped.

"Please? It'll feel good, I promise."

She nodded, bewildered, and he smiled at her.

To Lisanne's extreme embarrassment, his head disappeared between her thighs and she felt his hot tongue between her lips. When he flicked her clit, he drew a long moan from her.

Embarrassment fled, and Lisanne was pulled under again by the extremes of her responses.

Her fingers clawed at his shoulders, making him look up.

"Are you ready?" he asked, his voice tight with need.

"Y-yes, I think so," she whispered.

He closed his eyes for a moment.

"Be sure, Lisanne."

"Yes, I'm sure. Please, Daniel."

The need in her own voice surprised her.

He pulled away from her and reached down to the floor to find his jeans, plucking out his wallet and grabbing a condom. He sat on the edge of the bed, ripping open the foil packet. Lisanne watched, fascinated, as he rolled the thin film of rubber over his erection, tugging it into place securely.

"Okay?" he said again, his eyes locked on hers.

She stroked his arm. "Yes."

He climbed back onto the bed, his body shadowing hers.

Lisanne screwed her eyes shut and grabbed the duvet and sheet with her fingers, waiting for the invasion.

Her eyes flickered open in surprise when she felt soft kisses drifting across her chest and neck.

"Relax," he breathed. "It's going to be fine, baby." He rubbed his nose across her cheekbone. "Kiss me, Lisanne."

The way he said her name freed something in her mind. She wrapped her arms around his neck and pulled his mouth toward hers.

He kissed her with such intensity, with such certainty and ardor, that her whole body flamed under his touch.

Gently, he pushed her knees into place and settled himself between her legs. Using his left hand, he coaxed her knees upwards, stroking her thighs.

She felt his tip probing at her entrance and he pushed inside a short way.

Lisanne tensed immediately.

"Relax," he breathed onto her lips.

She took a deep breath, and as she did so, he moved into her with a quick thrust.

Lisanne cried out as a brief spark of pain shot through her.

Daniel held himself without moving.

"Are you okay?" he asked tightly, staring down into her eyes.

"I … I think so."

He moved his hips slowly, and sank a little deeper into her. She gasped as the strange and alien feeling filled her. Her flesh burned, but tiny shivers of desire skittered around the edges of her consciousness.

"Tap my arm if you want me to stop," hissed Daniel, his eyes scrunched shut.

He started to pull out slowly, then push back in. Out and in, long, supple strokes.

Lisanne's body stretched and pulsed around him, and he groaned.

He continued to move carefully, establishing a slow, steady rhythm.

"Fuck, you feel so damn good, baby doll. Nngh, shit…"

Lisanne opened her eyes and gazed down at herself, hypnotised by the way their flesh was initmately connected, his length glistening with the proof of her own arousal.

She looked up, and saw his eyes fixed on hers, full of dark heat. He circled his hips and she cried out again, this time with pleasure.

"Oh!" she breathed out, the sound faint on her lips, as she watched his eyelids flutter.

She gripped his biceps and Daniel opened his eyes.

"Okay, baby?"

"Oh, God, yes!" Lisanne gasped out.

He kissed her roughly and his hips began to move faster, the rhythm faltering slightly as he neared his own orgasm.

His breathing became erratic and he couldn't help himself from thrusting hard, despite the promises to himself that he wouldn't lose control.

"Shit, I'm coming," he gasped.

He felt the tightening in his balls as Lisanne's flesh quivered around him. She cried out again, and he felt it vibrate through her chest. It was too much.

He reared up, his back arching as he thrust into her one last time, trembled and was still.

Panting hard, he rested his forehead on her neck, and felt her soft hands in his hair. He took a deep breath to try and steady his racing heart, then reached down between them and made sure the condom was still in place as he carefully pulled out of her.

He noticed there was blood on the sheets and on his hand as he tugged off the condom and tied it in a knot, before dropping it onto the floor.

Concerned he'd hurt her, Daniel leaned up on his elbow and stared at her flushed face. Gently he stroked her cheek.

"Are you okay?"

She nodded, smiling up at him.

"Sure?"

She raised her fingers to his lips and pushed them into a smile.

"I'm sure."

"Did it hurt? Did I hurt you?"

"A little, but it's okay. It felt…" but Lisanne had no words.

Instead she smiled her answer and kissed him lightly on the lips.

Relieved, Daniel lay back, one hand behind his head.

Lisanne was struggling to define how she felt. Amazing, for one thing, but confused how pain—and it had hurt as he'd pushed inside her—how pain could bring such pleasure. Feeling him inside her, around her, surrounding her … *seeing* him move inside her—it had been extraordinary. And yet part of her felt the same: she was still Lisanne—music major and major nerd.

She now knew that no matter how many times you read about the mechanics of making love with someone, it could never really explain the feeling. Girls at her high school had either raved about it or said it was horrible and painful.

Lisanne was definitely in the former category—it hadn't felt like sex, it had felt like love. And, coming after her declaration to him, she knew he'd made love to her.

She snuggled into him, trailing her fingers over his chest and tugging gently on his nipple rings.

Then she leaned up to see his face.

"Why did you have your nipples pierced? Didn't it hurt?"

He smiled.

"Yeah, a bit. It was intense."

"But you like it?"

"Especially when you do that, baby doll. It's a fucking orgasm waiting to happen."

She grinned.

"What if I do this?"

She leaned down and sucked them into her mouth one at a time, teasing the tiny rings with her tongue.

When she looked up, Daniel's eyelids had fluttered closed.

He opened one eye and smiled.

"Fucking hot!" he said. "You've given me a semi doing that."

Lisanne gazed down and saw that the sheet was tenting slightly below his hips.

"Wow! That was quick! Um, I don't think … I'm a bit sore."

"It's okay, baby," he said, a smile tugging at his lips. "I can't help getting hard around you. It'll go away if I can think about math or something."

Lisanne snorted and giggled. "Math?"

"Yeah, or something. C'mere."

She lay across his chest and he stroked her back in soothing, loving touches.

They fell asleep in each other's arms.

CHAPTER 10

The sky had turned a deep, dark blue, streaked with purple by the time Daniel woke up.

For the briefest moment he couldn't remember where he was. Then he felt Lisanne's warm body curled up on his chest, and the memories came flooding back.

He lay still, his chest filling with warmth.

She hadn't run.

She hadn't told him she couldn't date a deaf guy.

He'd shown her the reality at the clinic—he'd even talked to her about cochlear implants, for fuck's sake.

And then she'd let him have sex with her, let him be her first. She'd *wanted* him.

It had been amazing. The screwing had been good, sure, but it was more than that. Because she *knew* him—she knew *him*. She knew everything, and she still wanted him.

It was hard for Daniel to take in.

Since he'd first started to lose his hearing, he'd convinced himself that no girl would want him if they knew. That had begun his long line of hookups and one-night stands—leaving them before they could leave him when they found out the truth.

But not Lisanne.

Somehow she'd battered her way through all the walls and defenses he'd erected, not even knowing she was doing it.

She was extraordinary.

He stroked the soft skin of her shoulder, amazed that she'd fallen asleep curled up around him, her hair fanned out across his chest. So trusting.

He realized his cock was rock hard against her thigh. That was nothing new: he woke up most mornings like that and, depending on whether he was running late or not, usually did something about it in the shower. He'd really liked to have found a use for it with Lisanne, but she'd said earlier that she was sore, and he didn't want to hurt her.

He shifted uncomfortably and she stretched sleepily, unconsciously rubbing herself against him. Daniel tried hard to concentrate on some algebra, but it wasn't easy when a beautiful, naked woman was lying next to him.

She blinked a couple of times, and her skin turned pink as she realized that Daniel was lying beside her, equally naked.

He saw the moment her memories spilled into her mind and he tensed: maybe *this* would be the moment when she ran.

"How long did we sleep?" she said, squinting to see the time on her cell phone.

"About five hours," he said, quietly. "It's nearly seven. Are you okay? How do you feel?"

She laughed huskily.

"Like someone rearranged my bones," she said, holding her hand over her mouth as she yawned.

He tapped her shoulder.

"Say that again, baby. I couldn't see your lips."

"Oh, sorry," she frowned then stretched again. "I feel like I've spent the morning at the gym. Everything hurts."

She saw the look on his face and regretted the way she'd phrased it.

"I don't mean it like that, Daniel. I'm a bit sore, that's all."

His mouth formed into a flat line.

"You're not sorry, are you? I mean, about what we did?"

Lisanne smiled shyly, then kissed him softly on his lips.

"No, I'm not sorry about *that*. It was … wonderful."

Daniel felt his whole body loosen. *Wonderful.* He could live with that.

"Um, could you close your eyes just for a moment? I need to get my robe," she mumbled.

He stared at her in disbelief.

"Lis, we just fucked halfway into next week and you don't want me to see your ass?"

She blushed even redder.

"I know, just … please?"

Shaking his head, Daniel closed his eyes. He didn't like doing it, not just because he had enjoyed seeing her body at last, but because it deprived him of another of his senses. With no sound and no sight, it was just blackness and it scared him. He gripped the sheet and duvet tightly, wanting to be able to feel *something*.

He jumped slightly when she touched his arm.

"Sorry," she whispered. "I know it's dumb…"

He smiled reluctantly.

"It's okay. I get it. Kind of."

Lisanne looked at him, gratefully. "I'll be back in a minute."

She slipped out of the door and Daniel sighed. His erection was still showing signs of hoping for another play date with Lisanne. Staring at it with irritation, he swung his legs off of the bed and searched for his clothes. He pulled on his briefs and tucked his semi inside, cursing it softly. Damn thing never listened to him.

He was just zipping up his jeans when Lisanne returned.

She ran her eyes over his body hungrily, and frowned when she realized he was dressing.

"I thought I'd take you out for dinner."

"Can't we just stay here?" she said, yawning again.

He laughed lightly. "We could, but I'll want to fuck you again and I don't think that's a good idea right now. He glanced back at the bed, wishing he'd thought to cover up the blood that showed on the white sheet.

Lisanne followed his gaze and looked horrified.

"Ugh! That's gross!"

Daniel caught her arm and made her look at him.

"It's not gross. It was amazing. I'm just sorry I hurt you."

Embarrassment made her stiffen in his arms.

"It can't be the first time you've slept with a *virgin*."

His lack of response was all the answer she needed. She sat down on the bed, heavily. She wondered how it had been for *him*—after all, he was used to girls with so much more experience. And it wasn't possible to have *less* experience than she'd had.

Shawna's words from a few days ago came back to her: *maybe you're just a lousy lay*. Her shoulders sagged. Maybe now he'd *had* her, he'd lose interest.

Daniel was worried by the conflict of emotions he saw on Lisanne's face.

"Baby, talk to me," he said, quietly.

"You've slept with so many people," she said, sadly.

Was that all that was bothering her? He tried to find the words that would reassure her.

"Do you know why?"

"Because you could."

He shook his head and twined his fingers with hers.

"No. Because I knew they wouldn't want me once I was deaf. After … it … I don't know. It was … easier."

Lisanne stared at him.

"But … but you're beautiful—and hot—and all the girls want you," she said, confused.

"They want what they *think* I am," he answered. "They don't know I'm *disabled*." He spat the word out bitterly.

Lisanne was silenced. Was that how he saw himself?

"Daniel, I…"

He closed his eyes, refusing to look at her.

She stroked his cheek and let her finger trace around his beautiful, sad mouth. But he turned his face away from her.

She kept touching him, coaxing him gently. Finally, he turned to look at her.

I hear you, she signed with her hands.

He smiled and placed a soft kiss on the end of her nose.

Then her stomach gave a loud rumble, and she rubbed her eyes tiredly.

Tapping his shoulder, she stood up.

"Come on then. Let's go get something to eat. I'm starving." She laid a gentle kiss on his pouting lips. "All that exercise has given me an appetite."

Daniel gave her a wry smile. "Better than going to the gym?"

"Way, way better," she laughed.

He let her tug him to his feet, then he wrapped his arms around her waist.

"You are so amazing," he said, into her hair.

Lisanne didn't know if she was supposed to hear him or not.

She pushed him away gently.

"Elephants shoes," she breathed.

His eyes widened, and he smiled at her.

They settled on dinner at Taco Bell, on the basis that it was both nearby and cheap.

Daniel was halfway through his steak burrito when Lisanne casually mentioned that her parents would be in the city the following week.

"They've been on at me to visit the campus and see my dorm room. So, I was wondering, maybe we could all go out for lunch or something on Saturday? Or coffee? Maybe."

He stopped mid chew, sure that his face must look as horrified as he felt.

"You want me to meet your parents?"

Daniel felt the need to clarify, because he was damned if his brain was processing her words accurately. Lisanne nodded warily.

Shit! She really did want him to meet her folks. How the hell was he going to get out of that one? Then he thought about how much it must mean to her to ask him. They were dating now: she wasn't some random girl he'd screwed. His stomach churned, thinking about all the things that could go wrong. Then an image of his own parents came to him, and Daniel couldn't help thinking how much his mom and dad would have liked to meet her—how happy they'd have been that he'd found someone.

He swallowed his food and took a large gulp of soda before he answered.

"Okay," he said, quietly. "I'd like to meet your parents."

"Really?" Lisanne beamed at him.

God, he loved it when her whole face lit up like that.

"Yeah. They've got a pretty amazing daughter—it would be good to meet them."

Although he very much doubted that they'd feel the same about him. Daniel was no fool, and he could imagine just how *not* pleased her folks would be when they met him. Was *unpleased* a word? He had a feeling it was about to be invented—probably next Saturday. But if Lisanne wanted him with her, he'd do anything to make her happy.

Lisanne looked so surprised and delighted, he couldn't help smiling back.

"So ... have you told them? About me? About us?"

"Well," she said, looking at him sideways with a sexy smile. "Mom knows that I've been working with you on the Business assignment. I *may* have mentioned to her that you're really cute."

"Cute, huh? Not awesomely hot? Or fucking amazing in bed?"

Lisanne immediately flushed beet red and Daniel smirked to himself, enjoying her embarrassment every time he mentioned anything to do with sex.

"Um, no! And my mom definitely won't be hearing that any time soon!" she said, adamantly.

"Huh. So no tongues in front of them? I don't know, baby doll, do you think you'll be able to keep your hands off of me?"

"You are so bad!" hissed Lisanne, trying not to laugh, but rather shocked all the same.

Daniel grinned at her and winked.

She sat back and sighed. He looked so deliciously bad boy sitting there, with his pierced eyebrow and his tats peeping out from under his t-shirt. That boy was sex on legs. And now she knew what she was talking about.

Truthfully, she was still feeling sore, but gosh, it had been worth it. She felt changed beyond recognition, and that everyone ought to be able to tell just by looking at her. She cringed when she thought about how she'd cope with Kirsty asking how they'd spent their day. It was going to be *so* obvious. And she'd definitely have to do some laundry.

But at least she wouldn't have to face Kirsty until tomorrow—she had another whole night to spend sleeping with Daniel.

Sleeping with Daniel!

Her toes curled up ecstatically at the thought.

When they arrived back at her room, Daniel had to sneak back via the fire exit. He tapped on her door and she let him in.

He grinned at her.

"There was a fucking line of guys waiting to get in," he laughed. "Jeez, I thought we were going to have to take numbers or something!"

He pulled her into a hug and nuzzled her neck. Then he leaned back to look at her.

"What's the matter?"

Lisanne smiled nervously. "I don't want to, um, you know. Not tonight. I still feel a bit…"

"Hey, it's okay," he said, stroking her face with his thumbs. "I told you—we don't have to do anything you don't want."

"Really?" she said, relieved. "Because I've read that guys think about sex every 15 seconds or something."

He laughed loudly, his eyes dancing with amusement.

"Yeah, or more often than that around you, baby doll. Jeez, where do you read this stuff?"

Lisanne didn't answer, suddenly becoming very busy hunting for clean sheets in her closet.

Daniel watched her for a moment, then helped her make up the bed with fresh linen.

"By the way," she said, deliberately and obviously changing the subject, "where does Zef think you are?"

Daniel raised his eyebrows.

"Zef? I've no clue. Why would he care?"

His question pulled her up sharply. Zef didn't care? Then she realized that Daniel didn't have anyone who cared whether or not he went to school or got good grades—or even whether or not he got up in the mornings. The thought made her unbearably sad. She flung herself at him, wrapping her arms tightly around his neck.

"Hey," he said, surprised. "What's all this? I mean I like it, a gorgeous woman throwing herself at me. I was just wondering if there was a particular reason."

"No," she mumbled into his chest. Then looking up, she repeated, "no reason."

His face said he clearly didn't believe her, but he let it go.

"Okay, baby, I'm going to sneak off to the men's room now. If I'm not back in ten minutes, it probably means I'm in the dean's office having my ass handed to me."

Lisanne gave a shaky smile.

Daniel pulled the door open a crack, winked at her and slunk out, closing it quietly behind him.

For a moment she stood dazed, then gave herself a mental kick. She pulled off her clothes, changing into a baggy t-shirt and robe, collecting her towel and caddy.

Daniel returned in far less than the allotted ten minutes, grinning at her attire.

"Bunny slippers?" he snickered, staring at her feet.

"My mom gave them to me!" said Lisanne defiantly, her face flaming.

"Nice!"

Trying to maintain some dignity, Lisanne said, "I meant to ask if you wanted to borrow my toothbrush."

Daniel grinned at her, knowing that changing the subject was her favorite way of dealing with his teasing.

"Got my own," he said, pointing to the back pocket of his jeans, as he tugged his t-shirt over his head.

"But … but…" stuttered Lisanne. "You didn't know you'd be staying here!"

Daniel tried to hide a smile—and failed utterly.

"I keep a spare with Sirona," he said, raising his eyebrows.

Lisanne spluttered futilely while he continued to smirk at her.

Then he leaned down and planted a soft kiss full on her lips.

"It doesn't mean anything, baby doll. Been doing it for years."

"Oh!" huffed Lisanne, not entirely sure if that made it better or worse.

She hid her glowing face and shuffled off to the bathroom, the ears on her bunny slippers waving as she walked.

When she came back, looking calmer even if she didn't feel it, Daniel was already in bed. He grinned up at her, looking the picture of ease, his hands behind his head, his glorious, muscled chest bare.

Lisanne's throat dried and she started to feel warm in all the right places—or wrong places, considering she still felt a pulse of faint pain between her legs.

Her eyes followed the contours of his chest, down to his defined abs and muscled stomach. The boy was built! She realized her eyes were lingering on the sheet below his waist. When she finally dragged her eyes up to his face, he was watching her with an amused expression.

"Your eyes are bugging out, baby doll," he said, with a smile.

"Why do you call me that?" she said, crossly.

His smile faltered.

"Don't you like it?"

"Not much," she lied. "It makes me sound like a toy. Besides, Roy calls me 'baby girl'."

Daniel's eyes darkened dangerously. "You never told me that."

"You didn't ask."

"Fine," he said, with a scowl. "I won't call you that anymore."

"Fine," she said, her irritation rising to match his.

She stomped around the room, annoyed with herself and Daniel's over-reaction. Every time she snuck a glance at him, he was frowning at the far wall. She sighed—sometimes it was hard work having a boyfriend.

She tried to remember what her mom had said about never

letting the sun set on an argument—particularly as she'd set it in motion.

"Hey," she said, walking to the bed and leaning down to kiss him, "I don't mind that much."

His mind was clearly elsewhere because he spat out, "If that asshat lays a finger on you, you'll tell me, right?"

Lisanne blinked. He was *jealous*?

"Roy's never touched me, not like that. I mean, he gives me a hug, but he's just being friendly."

Daniel's eyes narrowed even more.

"I mean it, Lis. If he does one more thing that makes you uncomfortable…"

He left the threat hanging in the air, but the look on his face made Lisanne shiver. For the first time, she could believe some of the things people said about him. He looked dangerous.

"Roy hasn't done anything," she said, firmly. "But there was something I wanted to ask you about."

"What?" he said, his face still angry.

"I heard you got into some fights this week."

He didn't try to deny it or pretend he didn't know what she was talking about.

"Yeah, what about them?"

"You didn't tell me."

He shrugged.

"Why didn't you tell me, Daniel?"

"Why would I?" he snapped. "It wasn't anything to do with you."

Lisanne felt her temper beginning to rise as quickly as his. Two minutes ago she was feeling fully fed and sleepy, and looking forward to spending her first night with her boyfriend: now she was just pissed.

"It's nothing to do with me that my boyfriend's brother is a drug dealer?" she hissed, her tone incredulous.

Daniel's eyes were fiery.

"Don't go there, Lis."

"Why not? Everyone else seems to know! I don't think there

isn't anyone who *hasn't* warned me not to date you because of it! I even had some skank come to my room and try to buy drugs from me."

Shock, hurt, and anger flared in his eyes, and Lisanne immediately regretted what she'd said.

"What?!"

"Yes, some sophomore heard that we were dating and came to *my* dorm room to buy 'something for the weekend'."

Daniel rubbed his hands over his face, and when he looked up his eyes were stormy.

"Kirsty threw her out," Lisanne went on. "You have to do something about Zef. You have to stop him…"

"Fuck this!" he snarled, leaping out of bed.

He started pulling on his jeans.

"Daniel…" Lisanne said, hesitantly.

"No!" he shouted, making her jump. "No! You don't get to judge him! You don't know what he … I don't have to listen to this fucking shit."

He turned his back and continued dressing hastily, thrusting his bare feet into his boots. Lisanne knew she had about five seconds to fix it—she had no clue how.

She tapped his arm but he wouldn't look at her. So she forced herself in front of him and grabbed his face.

"I'm sorry!" she said, quickly. "I'm sorry. I worry about you."

He tried to pull himself free, but Lisanne hung on, as a cold, creeping fear took over her body.

"Please, Daniel!"

Finally, he looked at her. "He's the only family I've got."

His voice was low and raw, and Lisanne felt physical pain when she saw how much she'd hurt him.

"I'm sorry," she whispered again, even though the words seemed deeply inadequate. "Please don't go."

He stared at her, indecision clear on his face.

I hear you, she signed.

He closed his eyes.

Defeated, Daniel sat back down on the bed, resting his

elbows on his knees. His head hung down and he wouldn't look at her.

"It was three days after my seventeenth birthday when Mom and Dad died," he said, his voice soft with grief. "Zef could have just stuck me in a foster home or something, but he didn't. He became my legal guardian when he was 22. He really had to fight for me—the fucking social workers said because I had *special needs*, that he wasn't competent, for fuck's sake. As if he hadn't lived with all that shit for years. Luckily the judge asked me what I wanted, and they let me stay with him."

He looked up at Lisanne, his eyes pleading. "He's my *brother*."

Daniel's voice cracked on the last word, and he dropped his eyes to the carpet. Lisanne knelt down in front of him and took his face in her hands.

"Thank you for helping me understand," she said, at last. "I'm sorry I … I'm just sorry. Okay?"

He nodded and rubbed his eyes. Lisanne was shocked to see tears.

"Come to bed," she said, gently.

He nodded again, kicked off his boots and threw his jeans back on the floor. Then he lay on the bed, staring up at her.

Quickly, Lisanne pulled off her robe and slipped into bed beside him. He wrapped his arm around her and she lay on his chest, listening to the deep, even sounds of his beating heart, gradually slowing, as his breathing calmed.

She reached out with one hand and turned off the light.

They lay quietly in the peaceful darkness, and Lisanne was just falling asleep when she realized something: Daniel hadn't denied that his brother was a drug dealer.

She lay awake for a long time listening to the soft sounds of his breaths.

Waking early, the first thing Lisanne saw were Daniel's hazel eyes smiling down at her.

"Hey, beautiful. This is a great way to wake up."

He relaxed back onto the bed and kissed her softly, letting his lips drift across her throat—sweet, loving, undemanding. But despite the gentleness of his touches, they seemed to arouse her entire body.

She wondered if it was too soon, whether or not she'd still be sore. She *felt* okay, but she had no idea how she was supposed to feel emotionally: sort of shy, sort of sexy, sort of weirded out that she'd lost her virginity—and to Daniel.

On the other hand, it was pretty obvious how he was feeling—or one part of him, at least.

Lisanne reached down and wrapped her hand around his hard length. Daniel's eyes flew open with surprise, and Lisanne heard his sharp intake of breath.

"S-sorry!" she stuttered.

"Hey, don't apologize! It feels freakin' amazing to have your hands on me like that."

She continued stroking him firmly, and Daniel breathed deeply and his eyelids fluttered. He gazed out through his long lashes, his mouth slightly open. Then he leaned over and kissed her deeply, sweeping his fingers over her breasts. Lisanne shivered as he moved his head down and took her in his mouth, his warm lips sensual on her body.

She moaned, hoping that he'd feel from her chest, the vibrations of desire.

Starting where he'd left off the day before, Daniel made love with a new sweetness and intensity that surprised them both.

Lisanne felt her body respond to his touch, his taste, the heavy weight of him on her. She called out his name as he buried himself inside her.

He stared down into her face, his eyes dark and passionate as his body moved, pushing deep inside her. Lisanne felt a delicious tremble begin in her body. She called out again, and she had to shut away the painful thought that he'd never hear her call his name. Never. He'd never know the sound of her voice.

Tears sprang to her eyes and he kissed them away as his body told her how much he cared.

Afterward, warm and sated, their bodies twined together like wild flowers, Lisanne stroked Daniel's smooth skin and smiled to herself.

He was right—it was a great way to wake up.

The peaceful moment of complete connection couldn't last.

For one thing, Lisanne really needed to pee. And for another, she felt very sweaty and sticky and desperately wanted to shower. And she *still* felt embarrassed walking around naked in front of him. She knew it was dumb, after everything they'd done—things that made her blush to just think about.

Daniel didn't have any of the same hang-ups, but then again, everything about his body was beautiful. The word 'chiseled' might have been invented for him. He was quite content to wander around her room buck naked, completely relaxed and at ease. He'd even pushed the window wide open, shivering slightly, as he hung out as far as possible to smoke a cigarette.

Lisanne couldn't stop herself from ogling him. Was it really uncool to ogle your own boyfriend? She didn't know. But every now and then Daniel would catch her staring, and give her his sexy trademark smile. Except that at times it was definitely more of a smirk, apparently knowing that her thoughts had just gone straight to the gutter. Again.

Eventually he pulled on his jeans and hunted around for his t-shirt, which, for some unknown reason, had found its way under Kirsty's bed.

"Back in a minute, baby," he said with a wink, slipping out of the door.

While he was gone, Lisanne pulled on her robe and set about straightening up the bed. It seemed to need a lot more work than usual, and Daniel was already tapping on the door before she'd finished.

"Fuck! Let me in!" he said, looking irritated.

"Why? What happened? Did you get caught?"

"You could say that," he said, wryly. "That girl Shawna practically dragged me into her lair."

"What?!"

"She said she had something heavy that needed moving in her room. Probably her butt."

Lisanne giggled at the expression of distaste on Daniel's face.

"I would think you were used to that—girls trying to drag you away to do wicked things to you. I kind of like it myself."

Daniel rolled his eyes.

"*That* girl can't take no for an answer."

Lisanne frowned as Daniel continued to shudder.

"Has she ... you know ... tried something before?"

Daniel pulled a face.

"Yeah, every time she sees me, especially if you're not around. Sometimes when you are. It's getting kind of old." He paused, alerted by the angry look on her face, that it was time to stop talking about Shawna. "So, baby d ... Lis, can I take you to breakfast?"

"Okay, but I need to shower. I won't be long."

Daniel groaned.

"What?"

"Girls always say they won't take long to get ready, but they always fucking do."

"I don't," she said, defensively.

"I'll time you!" he said, with a challenging look on his face.

"Fine. If I'm ten minutes or less, *you* pay for breakfast."

"Deal."

Lisanne rushed, she really did, but she ended up being the one to pay for breakfast after all. By one damn minute.

"This isn't a fair bet," she complained, staring at Daniel's loaded plate as he tucked into bacon, beans, eggs, and hash browns. A huge stack of toast followed.

Her dollar pancakes and fresh fruit looked meager by comparison.

Daniel winked at her.

"You made the bet, baby d ... Lis."

"Oh for goodness sake! Call me what you like. I'll just call you ... Danny."

He scowled at her. "That's a pussy name."

"And 'baby doll' sounds like a sex toy."

Daniel choked on his hash browns, and Lisanne blushed as realization dawned of *exactly* how that sounded.

Maggie wandered over to refill their coffee cups and stayed to shoot the breeze for a minute. Lisanne was starting to be less nervous of her. She particularly enjoyed hearing Maggie tease Daniel about things he said and did when he was a kid.

"You should have seen him when he was 14, Lisanne. He was the cutest lil thing. Musta gotten his first tube of hair gel 'cause he had it all spiked up. He spent damn near an hour checking himself out in the window and fussing with it. And I swear he used to practice talking to girls by hitting on me."

They both ignored Daniel's muttered comment, "Hell, no!"

Lisanne laughed.

"What sort of lines did he use?"

"Let me see, oh pretty cheesy stuff, ya know: 'You sure lookin' nice today, Maggie. You lookin' tired, Maggie, come and take your break with me. Did you get your hair fixed, Maggie, 'cause you're lookin' mighty fine today'."

Daniel shook his head, his eyes wide with embarrassment and the tip of his ears red.

"Jeez! Give me a break, Maggie! I was fourteen!"

"And a heartbreaker even then, Danny. But you should have seen him the day he came in after getting his first tattoo…"

Daniel groaned and stood up.

"Come on, Lis. We've got to get going."

"But I want to hear the end of that story!" said Lisanne, trying not to laugh.

Maggie winked at her, pinched his cheek and patted his arm.

"You bring your sweet girl back here soon, and I'll tell her how *that* one ended with you passing out at the table."

Daniel practically ran to the door.

As soon as they left the diner, he fixed Lisanne with a desperate stare.

"If you value my sanity, don't ever mention this again, please, baby."

"Oh, I don't know, *Danny*, because you're the *cutest lil thing!*"

It was wonderfully relaxing doing ordinary couple things like have breakfast together, and Lisanne was happy to enjoy it to the fullest. But too soon the world claimed them back. Daniel dropped her at the dorms, and left to catch up on his homework, while she wondered which pile of her own work to attack first.

Kirsty returned just before lunch, describing the fun day they'd had at the beach and the amazing, impromptu party at the frat house later on.

"So, what did you do?" she said, with an appraising eye. "Did you have a good time?"

Lisanne simply nodded, afraid that her voice would give her away.

"Oh my God!" breathed Kirsty. "You did it, didn't you?"

"I don't know what you mean," Lisanne mumbled, unconvincingly.

"You slept with him, didn't you! You totally slept with Daniel!"

There was no point Lisanne trying to deny it—her face told the entire story.

"Oh. My. God!" repeated Kirsty, shaking her head. "So that was the *private* thing you were doing with Daniel! I can't believe you didn't tell me!"

"It wasn't planned," said Lisanne weakly, but Kirsty didn't believe her.

"Well," she said, "how was it? Did you come?"

"I'm not telling you *that!*" gasped Lisanne.

"You totally did!" shrieked Kirsty. "How many times? Once? Twice? *Three* times? No way!"

Lisanne shook her head. "I'm not discussing it, Kirsty. It's private."

Kirsty giggled. "Not for much longer. Shawna will bust a gut! She's been crushing on Daniel for like, forever!"

"No!" snapped Lisanne. "It's nobody's business but mine and Daniel's!"

Kirsty just grinned at her. "Oh, take it down a notch, missy. And a word to the wise—morning sex is awesome. Just sayin'. Anyway, I won't have to tell anyone: it's just so *obvious* that you've been making the beast with two backs. I can't say I blame you—I always said Daniel had a great body."

For some reason Kirsty's words annoyed Lisanne. Yes, Daniel had an amazing body, no doubt about that. But there was so much more to him.

"He's a nice person, too," she said, quietly.

Kirsty threw her a look.

"Sorry, Lis," she said. "I know you're crazy about him."

Which was the closest Kirsty came to an apology.

The week that followed was full on for both Lisanne and Daniel.

She had three evenings of rehearsals with the *32° North* guys, and although Daniel insisted on giving her a ride home each time, they barely had a chance for more than a brief make out session as he dropped her off. Sometimes a whole day would go by when she only caught glimpses of him across the quad, or snatched a hurried sandwich with him in the cafeteria.

Daniel had a huge paper for one of his Economics professors, and as that was his major, he was taking it seriously.

Most of Lisanne's lunch breaks were taken up with orchestra practice, something all music majors were expected to be involved in.

Kirsty was working hard, too, littering their dorm room with scraps of materials, and sketches of clothes designs.

Daniel texted Lisanne constantly, but she was amazed how much her body craved him physically. All the moments her brain wasn't occupied with work or music practice, she found her mind drifting to all the things they'd done—which almost always made her blush—sometimes at immensely inappropriate times.

She hoped to have a chance to do more sexy stuff with Daniel during the week, but he simply said he couldn't take her back to his place, and with Kirsty working hard at her desk, they had no choice but to wait.

Lisanne was stunned to wake up from an incredibly erotic dream on Friday morning with her body tingling.

"What's the matter?" mumbled Kirsty grumpily, opening one eye. "Why are you making such a racket?"

Lisanne had no words to answer that question.

By Friday evening, she was exhausted and ready for some downtime.

Kirsty was staying with Vin, so she and Daniel had the dorm room to themselves. They spent the evening making out—as well as discussing, yet again, suitable topics of conversation for when Daniel met Lisanne's parents the following day—and eating takeout.

"Is Harry coming, too?" Daniel asked, hoping that having Lisanne's little brother there would make things a bit easier. It always helped having another guy around—he didn't count Lisanne's father as he definitely wouldn't be on the home team.

But Lisanne shook her head.

"No, he's got some basketball game to go to."

There went Daniel's first line of defense.

He sighed.

"And don't tell them about Sirona," said Lisanne, looking anxious.

"Should I tell them I like to ride her hard?" he said, raising an eyebrow.

Lisanne ignored him.

"They'll go crazy if they think I'm riding around on motorcycles," she continued. "They think they're dangerous."

"I'm not going to lie to them if they ask me," said Daniel, frowning at her.

"You don't have to lie—just don't tell them everything," she pleaded with him. "You're studying economics: be economical with the facts!"

He began to feel like he'd be better off facing Joe McCarthy than Ernie and Monica Maclaine.

"And try not to swear—or blaspheme. They don't like that."

"Why don't you just give me a list of what I *can* say," he said, with a sullen look on his face.

"Oh," said Lisanne. "That's a good idea."

Daniel rolled his eyes, but luckily she didn't see him do it.

"Economics—they'll like that. And business studies. That's fine. And the math, of course." She chewed her lip, desperately trying to think of any other suitable subjects. "Sport!" she said, suddenly. "Do you play any sport? My dad's always watching it on TV. He's a sport nut."

"I'm a champion at fucking."

She smacked his arm. "I'm serious!"

"So am I!" He grinned at her. "I played football in high school."

"Really?"

"Sure!"

"What position?"

"Quarterback."

"You … You were a jock?"

Daniel laughed. "Your words, baby."

"So how come you didn't try out for the college team?"

"You're kidding, right?" He rolled his eyes again. "Didja forget I'm deaf?"

Lisanne blushed. The truth was she was so used to being around him, making sure she faced him when she spoke, that it *was* easy to forget he was deaf. He hardly ever made mistakes lip reading her, and although she noticed he spoke far less when other people were around in case he'd misread them, nobody else had guessed his secret. She immediately felt guilty.

"No," she said defensively, if untruthfully.

Daniel smirked at her. She *hated* that he knew when she was lying, but he didn't call her on it.

"But you played in high school?"

"Lis, it was a *special* school. We got in the huddle and signed." Tired of the topic, Daniel yawned and stretched. Lisanne couldn't help being fascinated by the way his t-shirt tightened over his body. "Did you know the huddle was invented by a deaf guy?"

199

"I don't know much about football," she admitted.

"Doesn't matter: not many people who do like football know that either."

"Oh," she said, feeling more ignorant and challenged by the second. "Aren't there any deaf NFL players?"

"There've been two: Bonnie Sloan in the seventies, and Kenny Walker was a defensive linesman for the Denver Broncos. That was over 20 years ago. Not since then."

"Oh," said Lisanne, again.

"So, can I show you my other favorite sport now?" Daniel said, bored of the subject, his face alive with new mischief.

"What's that?" she said, cautiously.

"I told you—fucking!"

He grinned as he tugged off his t-shirt.

As usual, Lisanne couldn't help her eyes being immediately riveted to his chest—a fact that Daniel was more than happy to use to his advantage.

"Wanna play, baby?" he said, undoing the top button of his jeans, so they hung a little lower on his hips.

Lisanne nodded, then squealed as he dove at her, throwing her onto the bed.

After that, neither of them was capable of speaking in full sentences for several hours.

CHAPTER 11

Lisanne woke up to the delicious sensation of light kisses peppering her back. She giggled as Daniel's hand slid across her hip and over her stomach, pulling her back tightly into his chest.

She felt his substantial morning wood poking her in the ass and couldn't help wiggling her hips, making him groan.

She rolled over until she was facing him, and reverently traced the outline of his lips with her finger.

"Good morning," she whispered.

"Yes, it is," he said, happily.

She kissed him softly and a rumble of desire escaped from his chest. Kirsty was right to insist that morning sex was so awesome. Lisanne loved seeing his face softened by sleep, the hard exterior worn away with the night.

It was still such a novelty to have a man in her bed—and what a man!

She pulled back from him so she could fully appreciate his beauty, following the swirls of his tattoos across his arms, letting her fingers drift down the hard planes of his chest, over the muscles of his abs. Then she licked his nipple rings and sucked them gently, causing a soft moan to rise from his throat.

Smiling to herself, she pulled the sheet lower, letting her finger tremble over his belly button, then drift below.

He took a deep breath.

"When did you get to be such a bad girl?"

She turned to look at him, and smiled.

"About the time I met you."

He laughed gently. "Good. I like it."

Feeling brave, she reached down to stroke his erection, and heard the breath hitch in his throat.

She gasped a little when it twitched in her hand.

She pulled the sheet down to take a closer look.

"It looks so cute, when it jumps like that."

Daniel's voice was filled with horror.

"You did not just call my cock 'cute'!" he huffed. "Come on! Awesome, amazing, enormous—those adjectives are fine—but not cute. Give my dick some dignity for fuck's sake!"

"He's sweet!" giggled Lisanne.

Daniel groaned and hid his head under the pillow.

"What are you doing to me, woman?"

Suddenly there was a loud knock at the door.

Daniel felt Lisanne's body tense, and he pulled his head out from under the pillow.

"What's the matter, baby?"

"Kirsty's outside. She must have come back early. She *promised* she wouldn't," Lisanne complained.

"Damn cockblocker!" growled Daniel. "She has lousy fucking timing." He sighed. "I'd better put my pants on."

He half fell out of the narrow bed and scrabbled through their assorted clothes to find his jeans.

Lisanne couldn't help watching the amazing floor show. Dear God! That boy could be a model. A nude model. An erotic model.

Her flesh heated at the thought, but another loud knock thudded at the door and, reluctantly, she turned to answer it.

"I'm coming!" she grumbled, pulling on her robe and padding to the door. "Kirsty, you…"

Her words cut off suddenly as the smiling face of her parents appeared in view.

"Surprise!" called her mother. "Oh, it's so good to see you, honey. We were so excited we left early. Goodness! What are you doing in bed at this time of day? Are you sick?"

"Mom…" she stammered, as her mother pushed past her and entered the room.

Daniel had his back to the door, with no clue as to what was happening. He was still pulling his t-shirt over his finely muscled back, then bent down to buckle up his boots.

"Hey, Lis. What time are we meeting your folks? I want to go home and grab a shower—try and make a good impression—although you know they're not going to like me, right?"

He turned around with a grin on his face: a grin that vanished when he came to face to face with Lisanne's shocked parents.

Her father strode into the room.

"What's going on? Who is this boy?"

"Dad, I…"

Daniel swallowed, then straightened his shoulders. He walked forward and held out his hand toward Lisanne's father.

"Daniel Colton, sir. I'm pleased to meet you and Mrs. Maclaine."

Lisanne's father looked Daniel up and down and then deliberately turned his back, ignoring Daniel's outstretched hand.

Lisanne was mortified as she watched Daniel's face flush with anger and humiliation.

"Dad!"

"We'll talk later, young lady," announced her father. "I suggest you tell your *friend* to leave."

Lisanne looked helplessly from her father to Daniel.

"It's okay, Lis," Daniel said, softly. "I'll see you later, baby. Text me?"

She nodded wordlessly. Daniel looked at her sympathetically and placed a swift kiss on her temple, earning him a very dark look from Lisanne's father.

"Mrs. Maclaine," Daniel muttered as he walked past Lisanne's mother, who was suffering an unaccustomed case of muteness.

The door closed quietly behind him, and Lisanne was left at the mercy of her furious father.

"So that was Daniel," said her mother, the first of them to break the ominous silence.

Lisanne nodded miserably.

"And … he spent the night here."

Lisanne nodded again.

"I see. Well, I think we have some serious talking to do."

"Good God, Monica!" shouted Lisanne's father. "Is that all you have to say to your daughter, when it's clear she's been *entertaining* that young man in her room. *Sleeping* with him. Acting like a…"

"Dad!"

"Ernie—this isn't helping," said her mother, quietly.

"Then you talk to your daughter, because I have nothing to say to her."

He stormed out of the room, leaving an ugly atmosphere behind him.

"Just let him calm down, dear," said her mother, sadly. "He's a bit shocked. We both are. But you know, fathers and daughters don't mix with daughters and their boyfriends. I … I take it you are … sleeping … with Daniel."

Lisanne nodded tiredly.

"I see. Are you being safe?"

"Mom!"

"It's a fair question, Lisanne. If you're old enough to be indulging in intercourse, you're old enough to answer questions about it. I don't want to worry about being a grandmother at my age."

"God, Mom!"

"Please don't take the Lord's name in vain, Lisanne."

Lisanne took a deep breath.

"Yes, we're being safe. Daniel wouldn't…" she stopped abruptly.

"Do you love him?"

Her mother's question surprised her. Had she seen something that made her ask?

"He … he's everything. If … if you just gave him a chance, Mom. He's so amazing. You don't even know. He's really smart and sweet and kind, and he treats me like gold."

"I'm sure, dear, but the way he looks … your father will take some persuading." Lisanne's mother sighed. "I'll talk to him. You get dressed. We'll see you outside in 10 minutes."

She patted her daughter's arm and kissed her cheek.

When she was alone, Lisanne's head dropped into her hands. The most important meeting of her whole life couldn't possibly have gone more wrong. She always knew that Daniel was going to be a difficult sell as far as her father was concerned, but now … he'd never give him a chance. Her mom, well, maybe, but everything had been made so much harder.

God, it really couldn't have been worse. They'd been about to *do* it when her parents had walked in. Well, at least that disaster was averted. But only just. What a goddamn nightmare.

Daniel cursed his luck—or lack of it—as he strode purposefully toward his bike. He really hoped he would bump into Roy or Vin's asshat friend, Rich. Anyone would do, because right now, he'd have enjoyed beating the shit out of someone. He wasn't picky.

Lisanne's father had looked at him like he was dirt. And her mom: she'd looked so shocked—disappointed, too.

Daniel knew he wasn't good enough for Lisanne, but he'd really hoped her parents wouldn't agree with him.

"Fuck my life," he muttered.

He rode home cursing himself, cursing them, and wishing he could erase those last few minutes. Lisanne had looked so crushed. He wouldn't be surprised if they didn't persuade her to dump his sorry ass.

Just to make matters worse, the house looked like it had been trashed. Again.

There were empty bottles and cans strewn across the front yard, and the porch door was hanging off its hinges. He stepped over what looked like splatters of blood, and guessed there must have been a fight the previous night.

He retreated to his own room and checked his cell phone. There was no word from Lisanne. Guess it looked like lunch was off the menu.

He pulled out his sweatpants and sneakers and took off for a long, calming run. He tried not to assume the worst about Lisanne, but he had to admit it wasn't looking good. Fuck. For the first time in a long time, he'd been accepted by someone who wanted him just as he was, without trying to change him. He didn't count the whole 'don't swear in front of my parents' as anything serious.

He ran along the sidewalk, pushing himself harder, needing the endorphins to drive away the pain he was feeling in his chest, when he thought about Lisanne telling him they were through.

Unfortunately, by the time he returned an hour later, the place hadn't miraculously cleaned itself. In daylight, it looked like the dump it was. He knew his parents would be disappointed—it had been an ordinary, blue-collar family home when they'd been alive.

Cursing quietly, he rehung the porch door, then hunted around in the garage until he found some garbage bags, and started clearing up the front, tossing all the cans, bottles, and empty cigarette packets. He worked his way around to the back, but when he saw it was in a worse state, he gave up.

At least the house was empty for a change.

He dragged himself upstairs, feeling pissed and bad-tempered. Checking his phone again did nothing to improve his mood—still no message from Lisanne.

Sighing, and feeling all types of sorry for himself, he stripped off his clothes and dumped them in the laundry basket, then wrapped a towel around his waist and unlocked the bathroom door. It was like being a damn prison warder, wandering around with keys for all the rooms—the ones he wanted to keep from being torn apart.

He waited for the shower to get hot, but his wait was futile. It looked like the boiler was either out of oil or the power had gotten cut off again. He tried the light. Nope, that was working—must be out of oil. He made a note to check later in case Zef had stuffed some unpaid bills in his bookcase. Daniel shivered under the cold jet of water and decided he'd have to make more use of the campus fitness center and their superior facilities.

If he could have afforded to, he'd have moved out. It didn't feel much like home.

Lisanne dressed quickly. Her brain was whirling, trying to think of what she could say to her parents, some argument that she could offer, *something* that would make them listen to her when she talked about Daniel. But she had nothing. Her brain was a thought free zone.

She'd wanted this first meeting to go well. And now … she was *so* screwed.

Her parents were waiting in the reception area when Lisanne felt brave enough to leave her room. Her mom was sitting in a vinyl covered easy chair, while her dad stood tight jawed, staring at the flyers tacked to a notice board.

Lisanne groaned inwardly—it was going to be a long day.

"Well," said her mom, brightly, "let's go see this campus of yours. Show us the music faculty, darling."

Lisanne was grateful to her mom—at least she was trying.

She showed them the practice rooms, where the college orchestra rehearsed, and the hall where they'd perform their end of semester presentation pieces. They looked at the other faculty buildings, the fitness center, and the library. Finally, they entered the cafeteria.

Lisanne waited for her father's interrogation to begin. He started off with the easy questions: how did she get on with her professors; was she studying hard; what was her roommate like; was she keeping up her grades.

Good, yes, nice, and yes.

There was a long pause.

"So, tell us about this boy…" said her dad.

"He has a name," Lisanne snarked back.

"Tell us about Daniel," said her mother, crisply. "Where's he from?"

"He's local."

"Hmm," said her father, as if being a local was a cause for deep disapproval. "What's his major?"

"Economics and business studies, with a minor in math." Lisanne socked that one out into the park.

Her father didn't blink.

Lisanne's heart sank. She'd hoped that with both her parents being math, teachers that Daniel's minor would win him some points. Not so far.

"And he's in your Introduction to Business class?"

"Yes, we were assigned to work on a project together. He's really smart," muttered Lisanne. "He's a straight A student."

"What's his grade point average?" said her father, with an air of keen disbelief.

"Really high: 4.0, I think," she said, with the kind of exaggeration that could be called an outright lie. The truth was, Lisanne had no clue. She just knew that without Daniel she'd be flunking out of Introduction to Business.

"That's nice, dear," said her mother, who seemed to be acting as a referee between her husband and daughter. "How long have you two been seeing each other?"

"Seeing as it's only the fifth week of the semester, I'd say the answer speaks for itself," snapped her father.

"Lis?" prompted her mother, encouragingly.

"Nearly three weeks."

"*Nearly* three weeks! And she's sleeping with him already!"

"Now, Ernie…"

"No, Monica. I'm ashamed of her—and so should you be. We brought you up better than this, Lisanne."

He stood up abruptly and stalked off.

Lisanne felt tears pool in her eyes. She blinked them away, hurriedly. Her mother patted her hand.

"Give him time, sweetie. He'll calm down."

"I really like Daniel."

"I know, honey. And he likes you?"

Lisanne nodded, but her mother caught the look of

uncertainty on Lisanne's face.

"Oh, sweetie! You're sleeping with him and you're not sure how he feels about you?"

Lisanne shook her head and looked down.

Her mother swept her up into a hug, ignoring the curious eyes of other students who were lining up for their lunches.

"Lisanne, sweetheart!" said her mom, tucking Lisanne's hair behind her ears and looking her in the eye. "Are you … are you sleeping with him because you think that'll make him like you more? Did he tell you that?"

"No! No, Mom, it's not like that. I just … I really like him," she repeated lamely. "He's really amazing, if you'd only give him a chance."

"Well, I'd certainly like to get to know him more," said her mother, rather coolly. "But I don't think it had better be today, not with the mood your father's in. Come on, let's go find him and then we can have some lunch."

Food was the last thing on Lisanne's mind, as her stomach twisted unhappily.

She left the cafeteria with her mom. The plan was to head downtown so they could see a bit more of the area, and the sights surrounding the campus.

Her father was waiting outside with a look of suppressed rage on his face. Lisanne felt more like a prisoner who was being escorted by her guards than a daughter with her parents.

She would have happily sunk through the ground into the nether regions of hell, because anything was worse than this purgatory. At that moment she spotted Kirsty and Vin walking toward her, hand in hand.

Kirsty waved.

"Who's that, darling?" asked her mother.

"My roommate, Kirsty. And Vin, her boyfriend."

"She looks nice," said her mother, in a neutral tone.

"She is," agreed Lisanne, miserably.

"Hi, Lis!" chirruped Kirsty. She held her hand out to Lisanne's mom and dad. "You must be Mr. and Mrs. Maclaine.

Lisanne's been so excited about your visit. I'm Kirsty, her roomie, and this is Vincent Vescovi."

They all shook hands. Kirsty couldn't help but notice the awkward silence and the glowering looks. She babbled, helplessly, trying to find some way to fill the gulf of unvoiced antagonism that seemed to be deepening by the second.

"So," she said, her voice tinged with concern for Lisanne, "did you see our awesome concert hall yet?"

"Yes, it was very impressive," replied Lisanne's mother.

"Great!" chirped Kirsty, half an octave higher than usual. "And are you guys going to meet Daniel now because Lis said that you were all going for lunch?"

There was a stony silence, and Lisanne's heart sank to her boots.

"We've already met," grated her father through gritted teeth.

"Oh, super," said Kirsty, throwing nervous looks toward Lisanne.

"Well, we'll let you folks go enjoy your visit," said Vin, tugging gently on Kirsty's hand. "Say hi to Dan for us."

"Okay," mumbled Lisanne. "Bye."

"See you later, Lis," said Kirsty, with one last desperate look at Lisanne, and an overly bright smile at her parents.

"She seems nice," said her mother, faintly.

Her father said nothing, simply striding ahead, as if determined to leave the contaminated campus as quickly as possible.

Lisanne and her parents spent a miserable lunch in a small Italian restaurant, chewing their way through food that none of them wanted, and probably couldn't taste. Conversation, such as it was, was carried on by Lisanne's mother.

At the first opportunity, Lisanne went to the bathroom and sent a text to Daniel.

* L: so sorry about my dad.
Having lunch from hell at Benito's.
See you later? LA xx *

She waited for a moment, but he didn't reply.

"Well," said her mother, when she returned. "This has been … nice."

Neither Lisanne nor her father commented.

"We must do this again some time. Maybe when Harry's free. He'd like to see where you're going to school, Lis."

"Sure, Mom," mumbled Lisanne, without much enthusiasm.

"And we'll see you at Thanksgiving. That's only five weeks away. You'll be ready for some home cooking by then, I'm sure, won't she, Ernie?"

"Hmmph," he said, then stood up to pay the check.

They both watched him stalk off to accost the cashier.

"Perhaps you should come home in a couple of weeks," said her mom, dropping her voice. "He'll have calmed down by then. It'll do you both good."

"I can't, Mom," said Lisanne. "I've got a … concert coming up. I can't miss rehearsals."

Lisanne felt a tiny speck of relief—she hadn't told them about *32° North*. She couldn't imagine how her father would react if he knew she was singing in dives and hanging out with the criminal looking Roy.

"No, no, of course not. Well, it was just an idea. You're welcome anytime, darling, you know that. Well, we'll drop you back at the dorms and head off now. It's a good three hour drive and you know Dad doesn't like driving in the dark."

"Sure, Mom. No problem. Thanks for coming."

"And Lisanne: do talk to your young man—to Daniel. Honesty is so important in a relationship. You must tell him how you feel."

Lisanne hung her head.

"I know. Thanks, Mom."

They followed her father toward the exit, but a loud and very familiar sound made them look out the window at the same time.

Lisanne didn't know whether to laugh, cry or run when she saw Daniel pull up at the curb.

211

He looked straight at her, before pulling off his helmet.

"My goodness! Isn't that...?" said her mother.

"Oh, shit!" muttered Lisanne.

She watched as Daniel hesitated at the door of the restaurant for the briefest moment. Then he pulled it open and strode in.

"Hey, baby," he said, throwing her a smile. "I thought I'd say goodbye to your folks before they left, and see if you wanted a ride home."

He turned to stare at Lisanne's father, whose face was turning from white to red to purple with astonishing speed.

"Stay away from my daughter!"

"I can't do that, sir," replied Daniel, evenly but firmly.

Lisanne's father gaped at him.

"I'm sorry that we met the way we did, and I didn't mean to disrespect you—either of you—but your daughter is very special and I care about her. I'll leave when *she* tells me to, not you."

Throughout his speech, Daniel kept his voice low and calm, but there was no doubting the challenge in his eyes as he gazed at Lisanne's father.

Her dad started to huff and bellow, but it was her mother who laid a soothing hand on his arm and replied.

"Well, it certainly wasn't the best of circumstances, Daniel, but we appreciate you apologizing. You seem like a very..." she eyed his piercing and tattoos apprehensively, "like a smart young man, so I hope you'll understand when I say that we want nothing but the best for our daughter..."

"She deserves it," said Daniel, hotly.

"Yes, she does," agreed Lisanne's mom, a small smile twitching at her lips. She held out her hand. "It was nice meeting you—more formally."

A faint blush colored Daniel's cheeks, and he scrubbed his palm over the back of his jeans before he shook hands.

Lisanne's father stood in outraged silence as his wife kissed Lisanne and gave her a tight hug.

"I think you got the answer to your question, darling," whispered her mom. "Now for goodness sake, be safe on that motorcycle."

Then she dragged her husband to the car. Lisanne could hear his raised voice for nearly half a block.

Daniel let out a lungful of air, and turned to her with an amazed grin.

"Wow!" Lisanne said, softly.

Daniel's smile softened as he gazed down at her.

"And you came without body armor! My hero!"

"Yeah, us heroes do stuff like that," he said nonchalantly, but the twinkle in his eye gave him away.

"You're definitely my white knight," she said, standing on tiptoe and kissing him on his beautiful lips.

He dropped his nose into her hair and nuzzled her neck, causing Lisanne to shiver.

"Does that mean you were a damsel in distress?" he asked, letting her go.

"You better believe it!"

She spoke so quickly, Daniel couldn't help laughing.

"That was the longest morning of my whole life." Lisanne sighed as she looked up at him. "Thank you for coming to rescue me. I didn't mean for you to do that when I texted you—but I'm really glad you did." She looked at him thoughtfully. "You really charmed my mom."

He grinned at her, clearly delighted.

"What can I say, baby d ... Lis? Women find me irresistible."

Lisanne laughed and playfully slapped his arm.

"Oh for goodness sake—just call me 'baby doll'. I can live with that."

"Yeah?"

"But being irresistible to women isn't going to work with my dad, so you'd better come up with a plan B."

Daniel didn't look fazed.

"Don't need to, baby. Your mom is my backup. And if she's anything like my mom was, she'll talk him around."

Lisanne was surprised—she'd never heard him speak about his parents before.

"What was she like?" she said, shyly.

Daniel smiled, although his eyes were distant. "Her name was Rebecca and dad was Adam. Mom was the best. Shit at sign language—always confusing 'yellow' with 'I love you', which got pretty weird sometimes, but she tried really hard. She always said I could do anything I wanted to do."

His smile faded.

"Come on, I'll take you back to the dorms."

"Sorry," said Lisanne, running her hand down his jaw to cup his neck.

"'S'okay," he said, quietly.

They rode back to the dorm room on Sirona, with Lisanne's arms wrapped tightly around Daniel's waist. She was still stunned at her mother's behavior—even to the point of not getting too bent out of shape knowing that her only daughter was riding around on a motorcycle.

Daniel kept one hand cupped loosely over hers for sections of the short journey, but when they arrived, his mood seemed to have shifted again.

As soon as Lisanne had dismounted and removed her helmet, he grabbed her waist and pulled her toward him, kissing her hungrily then biting at the base of her neck, just above her shoulder.

"Can I come in with you?" he growled against her skin. "I really want you, Lis."

She could feel his need as he rocked his hips into her.

The pile of homework she had waiting was no competition for the raw desire in his voice.

Peeling herself off of him, they rushed through reception, and took the stairs two at a time.

It was the hardest thing in the world for Lisanne to find her key in her purse, while Daniel was pressing hot kisses to the back of her neck.

They almost fell through the door when she finally got it opened.

"Eager much!" Kirsty's caustic voice vaguely penetrated

Lisanne's lustful haze. "I'd say get a room, but I guess you already have."

Daniel swore softly under his breath and discreetly adjusted himself, while Lisanne tried to calm her hammering heart.

"Oh, sorry, Kirsty," she said, breathlessly. "I thought you'd be with Vin."

"No, he has a frat thing tonight. Guess you're stuck with me."

Daniel pulled a face and tugged Lisanne toward him.

"I'll take off now, Lis."

"Where are you going?"

"Home. Text me later?"

"Can't I come with you?"

He shook his head, and an expression that Lisanne didn't recognize darkened his eyes.

"No, baby doll. Not tonight. We can do something tomorrow maybe?"

"I'd like that."

Feeling flustered with Kirsty's judgmental eyes on her, Lisanne kissed him lightly on the lips. It wasn't enough for Daniel. Ignoring Kirsty, he kissed Lisanne deeply, then rested his forehead on hers.

"Later," he said quietly, and slipped out of the door.

Kirsty primly ignored Lisanne's glowing face. "He seems … enthusiastic."

"Um…"

"How was lunch? Did your parents have fun?"

Lisanne knew Kirsty was fishing, but she didn't care.

"You mean apart from them arriving early and finding Daniel half dressed in my room?"

Kirsty's eyes opened wide.

"No way! Well, that explains the weirdness."

Lisanne nodded.

"It was awful. Dad pretty much threw Daniel out and wouldn't talk to him or anything. I spent the whole morning feeling like a slut or a criminal or something. Mom was trying to get Dad to calm down, but it was pretty intense."

Kirsty looked appalled and sympathetic all at the same time.

"I thought things seemed kind of strained when I saw you."

Lisanne laughed mirthlessly.

"Yeah, you could definitely say they were strained."

"Oh crap! And then I had to go and put my great hoof in it and ask if they'd met him! I'm so sorry, Lis! I had no idea."

Lisanne shrugged.

"Don't worry about it—by that point I didn't think things could get any worse. But then Daniel turned up at the restaurant where we were having lunch."

"Oh. My. God! What happened?"

"He rescued me."

"What?"

"Yep. Rode up on his bike and told my dad that the only person who could make him leave was me." Lisanne's voice dropped to a whisper. "He said that I was special and that he cared for me."

Kirsty's face could have been used on a poster for an Edvard Munch exhibition. She was shocked. Or stunned. Amazed. Aghast. Astounded. Bewildered. Stupefied. Maybe even stumped.

"Oh wow! Truly?"

"Yes, he was amazing."

"Oh my God!" she repeated faintly. "That is the most romantic thing I've ever heard! That boy is *totally* into you."

Lisanne smiled.

"I know."

CHAPTER 12

Daniel was wound up badly after leaving Lisanne in her dorm room.

Having met her parents—twice—and having told them how much he cared about her, and really putting it all on the line, he'd wanted nothing more than to reassure himself that she was really his, in the only way he understood. But the bitchy cockblocker had been in the way. Again.

He badly wanted to get laid right there and then, just to be free and stop all the fucking *feelings* that were choking him, but he couldn't do that to Lisanne. It was *her* body that he craved, *her* hands on his cock, *her* mouth against his, and no one else would do. He'd had wilder sex, he'd done it in ways and places that Lisanne couldn't begin to imagine, innocent as she was, but *none* of those times, *none* of those women had come close to making him feel what he felt when he was inside her.

He'd almost wavered in his decision not to take Lisanne back to his place, but he knew it wouldn't be right.

He didn't know why—and Zef never told him anything, muttering about 'need to know'—but things had really amped up at home. It seemed that every night was party night lately. He didn't want to risk Lisanne having anything to do with it. The least he could do was shelter her from that shit.

Since Daniel had had his run-in with Detective Dickwad, he'd kept a casual eye open for any sign of Zef dealing meth. He didn't think his brother would get involved like that, but he also knew that some his brother's suppliers weren't the kind of people anyone said no to. Not twice. But so far, all he'd seen was

217

normal stuff—the unholy trinity of booze, weed, and speed.

With sex off the menu, Daniel wanted to get shitfaced or stoned. Either way, he intended to spend the evening numb and trashed.

Despite the fact it was still only mid afternoon, it was party o'clock when Daniel pulled up outside his house. He didn't recognize the three guys sitting on the porch drinking from bottles containing a colorless liquid—gin, vodka, or moonshine, for all he knew. But the way they eyed up Sirona made him wheel her around to the side of the house, and lock her away in the garage.

He had a few possessions that were important to him including some books and photographs that had belonged to his parents, but the only items that were of any value were his $2,700 Martin guitar, and Sirona. When Lisanne had asked him about the Martin, he'd slung it in his closet, unable to speak. He'd retrieved it only after she'd left, and had since packed it away carefully in a hard carry case. The beautiful rosewood instrument now resided in the attic space above his bedroom. He didn't want to look at it, but he didn't want to have it too far away either. How dumb was that? He knew he should sell it and take the money. But it had been a gift from his parents. He just couldn't cut that tie. Not yet.

The living room was a scene straight out of a disaster movie. Bodies lay comatose across the sofa and floor, and the place stank of tobacco and spilt liquor.

One guy was smoking a joint, letting the ash fall onto the destroyed carpet. Daniel lifted it straight out of the man's limp fingers.

"Hey!" the guy protested weakly.

Daniel ignored him and headed to his room, swiping a bottle of bourbon along the way. It wasn't Jack but it would work just as well.

He took one toke of the joint and found that the guy had made it wet. Too fucking gross. He wiped his mouth, stubbed it out, then reached into the drawer of his bedside table for his blunt wrappers.

After it was remade, he sucked in the smoke appreciatively. One thing he could say for his brother: he always got the good shit.

Daniel was just taking a slug of bourbon when he felt his phone buzz in his hip pocket. He expected it to be a text from Lisanne, but it wasn't.

> * C: Hey D! Am in Sav for weekend.
> Meet tomorrow? Your diner, lunch?
> Don't say you busy or will come to find you. lol. Cori x *

Fuck. Just what he didn't need.

He hadn't seen Cori in a while, but he knew how single-minded she was. She knew where he lived, too, and he was damn certain she'd come to find him like she threatened if he didn't show. At least the diner wasn't somewhere other students went. It should be fairly safe to meet her there. Besides, he hadn't seen her for a while—it would be good to catch up.

Then he swore softly. It would mean cancelling Lisanne. His body craved her, and the cockblocking roommate definitely hadn't helped. He sighed. He needed Lisanne, but he owed Cori. And no way he wanted the two women to meet. He texted Corinna first.

> * D: Ok. 12. *

And then Lisanne.

> * D: Sorry. Have to do stuff tomorrow.
> Lunch on Monday? *
> * L: Ok. Miss you. Thanks for today.
> You were amazing! LA xx *

Now he felt like a jerk as well. He picked up the bottle again and poured raw bourbon straight into his throat, welcoming the bite.

It was late morning when Daniel woke up. Daylight poured through the window as he squinted upwards. When he moved, his stomach pitched and rolled as if he were onboard a storm blown ship.

The bottle of bourbon glinted at him innocently, sunlight catching what was left of the amber liquid and throwing golden rainbows across the walls.

Daniel groaned as he sat up and held onto his head, feeling as if his brains would leak out at any moment. Moving hurt and his head throbbed. But the bourbon had been effective: he couldn't remember a single thing since Lisanne's text the previous afternoon.

He glanced at his cell phone. Goddamnit! It was already 11:30. He'd been asleep or passed out for 16 hours.

He dragged his sorry ass into the shower. The water was still cold, which made his teeth ache. He *really* needed to get hold of Zef and find out what the fuck was up with the hot water.

As he wheeled Sirona out of the garage, he hoped like hell he wouldn't get stopped by the cops again—there was every chance his blood—alcohol limit wasn't strictly legal.

He was only a few minutes late when he got to the diner—but Cori was already looking irritated, restlessly tapping a spoon against the table. She completely ignored the irked looks thrown at her by other customers.

When she saw him, she glanced impatiently at her watch. Daniel groaned internally.

She looked the same: beautiful—well, stunning—and frowning at him with exasperation. *That* look was familiar, as well. Her ash blonde hair was long and straight, framing a delicate face, with enormous blue eyes. Eyes that were snapping with annoyance.

C: Where the fuck have you been?

"Yeah, good to see you, too, Cori."

C: Sign me, asshole! You know I hate lip reading.
D: Fine. How are you? You look good.
C: Better than you. You look like shit.
D: Give me a break. Heavy night.
C: No kidding. I ordered food.
D: No thanks.
C: That bad? Sucker.

Maggie strolled over with a jug of coffee. Daniel could have kissed her.

"Thanks, Maggie. Damn that smells good."

He wrapped his hands around the steaming cup and breathed in the rich aroma.

"You going to introduce me, Danny, or did y'all forget your manners along with your razor this morning?" she said, swiping a finger across his stubbly cheek.

"Gimme a break, Maggie. This is Cori—you've met before." He glanced over at Cori, who was smiling at Maggie. "She says 'hi'."

"Don't give me that, Danny. She said a lot more than 'hi'. Spill."

Daniel groaned. *Goddamn women.*

"She said, 'Hi, I met you two years ago when he was nursing a different hangover.' Happy now?"

Maggie looked at Cori and winked. Both women laughed, and Daniel felt like laying his head on the cool surface of the table.

"I'll get you guys your breakfasts now," said Maggie, ignoring his mutterings of not being hungry. "By the way—what happened to the other one? I liked her."

Daniel glanced over at Cori, who was watching him intently.

"She's good," said Daniel, shortly.

Amazingly, Maggie took the hint and strolled away.

C: Who was she talking about? What girl?
D: No one you know.

C: Duh! Obviously. She must be special if you brought her to your diner. Tell me.
D: A girl I met at school.
C: And?
D: That's it.
C: What's her name?
D: L-I-S-A-N-N-E.
C: Tell me about her.
D: No.
C: Why not?
D: Why do you want to know?
C: Why are you being so defensive?
D: I'm not.
C: Yes, you are. What's the big mystery?
D: Fuck off.
C: Don't be a dick, although I know that's hard for you.
D: Give me a break.
C: Touchy much! How's Zef?
D: Haven't seen him for a couple of days.
C: Tell him I said hi.
D: If I see him.

"Here you go, guys. Extra grease for you, Danny," said Maggie, lowering two breakfasts to the table.

Daniel's stomach growled and Maggie hid a smile.

"Enjoy!"

Unsure whether the overwhelming sensation was nausea or hunger, Daniel tackled a small piece of bacon and, finding it delicious, proceeded to scarf his food.

Cori ate more slowly, throwing him puzzled looks every now and again. She tapped him on the arm.

C: What's up with you? And don't say 'nothing'.
D: Just tired. Bit hung-over.
C: It's more than that.

Daniel dropped his fork to answer more fully.

D: Just … school and … things are pretty intense at home. Always people hanging around.

C: More than usual?

He nodded, and picked up his fork to carry on eating.

C: Are you worried about Zef?

D: I don't know what he's getting into.

C: What do you mean?

D: I got arrested and…

C: WHAT?!

D: Speeding.

C: Idiot.

D: I know.

C: The cops?

D: Made it sound like Zef was dealing M-E-T-H.

C: Is he?

D: Don't know. He says it's better for me not to know.

C: Crap.

Cori sighed, then gave her own breakfast some attention. After a moment she thought of another question.

C: You know why Zef deals…?

D: Don't remind me.

C: Looks like I have to.

D: Fuck. He knows he doesn't have to anymore. I think he likes it. Easy money.

C: Not if the cops are onto him.

D: I told him what the dickhead cop said.

C: And?

D: He told me it was none of my business and what I didn't hear wouldn't hurt me.

C: Funny guy.

D: Laughed my ass off.

C: Your ass looks fine to me.

D: Keep your hands to yourself.

223

Cori winked at him and Daniel managed to smile back.

C: Apart from Zef, how's life? How's school?
D: Good. Tiring. Lip reading all day.
C: Ass.
D: Yeah? At least I don't have to wave my hands around 24/7.

Cori slapped his arm and Daniel laughed.

C: I still think you look miserable for someone who says school is 'good'. Is it this girl—the one you won't tell me about?

Daniel ignored her and stared pointedly at Cori's full plate.

D: You talk too much.

It wasn't surprising that Daniel had finished eating long before her.

C: Only because you won't say anything.
D: Fine. How are things at Cave Spring?
C: Same old, same old. The football team sucks without you. Did you get on the college team?
D: Haven't tried.
C: Are you kidding? Why the hell not?
D: Didn't try out.
C: But you love football! I don't get it.

He shrugged.

C: Seriously. What gives?
D: Too busy.
C: Bullshit!
D: Drop it.
C: No! Not until you tell me what's really going on!

Daniel slumped back in his seat. He didn't want to get into this with Cori, but she was as stubborn as all hell. He should know: they'd dated on and off—mostly off—for five months. Somehow they'd managed to remain friends afterward, but she acted like she still owned his ass.

C: I know you. Talk to me.
D: I'm flying under the radar here.
C: What the hell does that mean?
D: I haven't told anyone I'm deaf.

There was a stunned pause while Cori stared at him.

C: What? Why?

He shrugged again.

C: Are you ashamed or something?
D: No! I'm just tired of the way hearing people behave when they find out—start acting like I'm dumb or something. You know what that can be like.
C: So you're hiding it? Hiding yourself? Do your professors know?
D: Yes, but that's all.
C: Is that why you didn't try out for the football team?
D: I just wanted to start fresh—no preconceptions, no stereotypes.
C: You're still denying it, aren't you?
D: No!
C: Yes, you are. You pretend like you've accepted it, but you haven't. You're such a hypocrite!
D: No, I'm not!
C: What about this girl? Does she know?
D: Yes. Not that it's any of your business.

He stared at Cori angrily.

C: That's something. Tell me about her.

225

D: She's ... nice.
C: Oh, please! You can do better than that. What's she studying?

Daniel didn't reply.

C: Come on—what's the big mystery?
D: Music.
C: What?
D: She's a music major. A singer.
C: Jesus. You are one sick bastard.
D: Why?
C: Because you're a masochist. You're such a fool—always wanting what you can't have. Look at you, hiding away, pretending you're like them. You're not and you never will be. We've been over and over this shit. Quit hiding away what you are!

"What am I, Cori? What the fuck am I then?" he asked angrily.

She sat and glared at him.

C: A coward.

He stood up suddenly and shook her arm off when she tried to stop him.

"No. Fuck you! You don't get to tell me how to live."

He threw some bills down on the table, then strode out of the diner.

Lisanne was deep into her book on the history of sonatas when she heard a knock at the door. Kirsty looked up from her laptop where she'd been Googling Clifford Coffin.

"You expecting someone, Lis?"

"Not really," she replied, swinging herself off of the bed. "But it's probably MJ from my History of Composition class—she mentioned wanting to borrow my notes."

Lisanne pulled open the door and found Daniel standing there, looking upset and agitated.

He didn't speak, just pulled her into a tight hug, and rested his head against her neck.

"Hey, what's wrong?" she said, stroking his hair.

Of course, he didn't reply.

She waited until he seemed calmer, then pushed him away gently and repeated her question when he could see her face.

"I'm sorry, baby. I know you're studying and shit, but…" he ground to a halt when he saw Kirsty frowning at him from above her laptop.

Lisanne looked over her shoulder and Kirsty's eyes dropped to her computer, although the way she sucked her teeth was audible to Lisanne.

"I'll get my jacket," said Lisanne, quietly.

She followed Daniel down the stairs, and was surprised and pleased when he took her hand.

"Where do you want to go?"

He looked down for a second.

"Do you mind if we just go to the cafeteria and grab a coffee?"

"No, that's fine. Are you okay?"

He shrugged, but his expression told her that he wasn't.

When they'd got their coffee and were sitting opposite each other, Lisanne reached out and touched his wrist.

"What's the matter?"

Daniel leaned back in his chair and scrubbed his hands over his face.

"I met a friend for lunch—an old girlfriend."

Lisanne felt a shiver run down her spine. That was the 'stuff' he mentioned in his text? *What was coming next?*

"Okaaay," Lisanne said, carefully.

Daniel gave her a lopsided smile.

"We haven't dated for like two years, Lis. She went to my old school." He looked around to see if there was anyone near enough to overhear them. "The deaf school."

Lisanne nodded, still unsure why meeting an *old* girlfriend had upset him so much.

He took a deep breath.

"She ... she said I was being a coward—by not telling anyone about myself."

Lisanne's intake of breath was sharp.

"She called you a coward?"

He nodded unhappily.

"That's ridiculous!"

Daniel gazed at her warily, and Lisanne took both of his hands in hers.

"You are the bravest person I know."

He looked doubtful.

"You are! You're sweet and funny and kind and so strong. The way you stood up to my dad—that was ... that was ... you're amazing and wonderful and so brave."

Daniel ducked his head down, embarrassed by her effusiveness.

"Fuck!" he managed to say, made incoherent by her words. "You left out 'awesome in bed'."

Lisanne raised an eyebrow.

"That goes without saying!"

Daniel smirked at her.

"Still like hearing it."

"Fine. You're awesome in bed. Happy now?"

He smiled wistfully.

"I guess. It was just such a fucking kick in the guts. She said I haven't come to terms with being ... what I am. I don't know—maybe I haven't. It really sucks."

"Your friend, when did she lose her hearing?"

Daniel shook his head. "She was born deaf."

Lisanne couldn't help thinking, *So she doesn't know what she's missing.* But it was too cruel to say out loud. And she was aware that some of her angry feelings toward this girl were because she'd been Daniel's *girlfriend.* Not just one of his random women, but someone he'd dated in high school. More than that—

someone who'd been there as his deafness became more pronounced, and when his parents had been killed. How could she compete with the closeness that came from all of those important shared experiences?

"Well, she's wrong. About you. And if I ever meet her…"

Lisanne left the threat of potential mayhem hanging in the air.

Daniel tried to smile, but a sigh left his lips instead.

"I don't know. Maybe she's right. I haven't really stayed in touch with anyone from my old school. Just her. I don't have any deaf friends. I mean, who am I kidding, right?"

Lisanne bit her lip.

"Daniel, I don't really know anything about this—it's all new to me. But maybe you should talk to someone about it?"

"You mean a shrink?" he snarled, his temper sparking instantly.

"No," said Lisanne, patiently. "I was thinking of Dr. Pappas, actually. But counselors help lots of people. It doesn't mean you're crazy." She rolled her eyes. "Seriously, it could help just to talk it through."

"I *am* talking it through," he said, testily.

Lisanne frowned. "I meant with someone who understands what you're going through."

Daniel scowled. "Whatever."

Lisanne crossed her arms.

"For goodness sake! I can't say anything right, can I? I just don't feel like I'm *enough* to talk to you about this."

His expression softened at once. "Sorry, baby doll. It's been a bad day and a really shitty weekend."

Lisanne reached out and stroked the back of his hand.

"Oh, I don't know," she said, gently. "Seeing you stand up to my folks was pretty great. Definitely the highlight of my weekend."

Daniel didn't return her smile. "I meant what I said," he replied, his face serious.

"I know. I spoke to my mom this morning. She was pretty

229

impressed with you."

"Yeah?" he said, his face lightening immediately.

"And she agrees with me—she thinks you're cute."

Daniel laughed. "Okay, weird enough." Then he changed the subject. "You want me to drive you to your rehearsal tomorrow night?"

"Um, no, that's okay. But could you pick me up after? We should be finished by ten."

"Sure, baby."

They chatted for a while longer, then reluctantly agreed that they had a ton of homework to get on with.

Daniel walked Lisanne back to her room, then kissed her until she was giddy before waving her goodbye.

Kirsty was still glued to her laptop, but glanced up when Lisanne walked in.

"Everything okay in Wonderland?"

Lisanne was taken aback by Kirsty's sarcasm, and immediately her desire to defend Daniel bubbled up, molten and hot.

"It is now," Lisanne snapped. "Why are you so down on Daniel?"

"I've told you," Kirsty shot back.

"Look, he stays away from whatever his brother does. He doesn't have anything to do with it."

"So you admit that the brother is … involved."

"I don't admit anything! I met him once for about five seconds—that's all. But I *do* know Daniel."

"You're taking an awful lot on trust, Lis," said Kirsty, more quietly.

"Yes, I am."

Kirsty sighed.

"Look, my dad's a lawyer so I know how this works. If his brother is dealing, the fact that Daniel is living with him and there are drugs there, that could make him criminally liable. And if he's seen his brother selling drugs, Daniel could be charged based on probable cause. At the very least, he's an accessory after the fact, and if he doesn't tell the police, they could say he's obstructing a police investigation. I'm assuming he's smart enough to deny any knowledge…"

She stopped when she saw how pale Lisanne looked. She stood up immediately, and walked over to give her a big hug.

"I'm sorry, sweetie, really I am. Just … just promise me that you won't go to Daniel's house."

Lisanne sat down heavily.

"I don't think that will be an issue. I went there once weeks ago, but he hasn't taken me there since. He hasn't said anything except that it's not a good idea."

Kirsty let out a deep sigh.

"Well, that's something. Look, you know I don't totally buy Daniel's good guy act, but I'd have to be blind not to see how much he cares about you. You've really done a number on that boy, Lis. I'm just saying *be careful*. Okay?"

Lisanne nodded slowly.

"I know. Thanks, Kirsty."

Kirsty's words revolved around in Lisanne's head for most of Sunday night, leaving her tired and grumpy when she woke up the next day.

She dragged her way through her classes and didn't even have the relief of catching up with Daniel at lunch. He'd texted her to say he was involved in some tutorial thing and he'd see her at the Blue Note that evening.

Lisanne sighed. At least she had the rehearsal to look forward to, and what with the next gig coming up at the weekend, they needed as much practice as they could get.

She struggled through her American Folk Music class, and nearly fell asleep in her pasta when she ate her dinner alone in the cafeteria. Then she stood at the bus stop, dozing, until her ride rumbled up and carried her downtown to West River Street.

The Blue Note still looked like a dive, but at least it was familiar.

Mike opened the door for her, his laconic face almost cracking a smile. He was a different person when he was playing his drums—wilder, less restrained. Lisanne understood that— she felt the same when she sang; or rather, singing affected her in the same way.

By 10 PM, she was exhausted but feeling happier.

Thank goodness the rehearsal had gone so well—she'd definitely been in need of some good news after the intensity of the weekend.

Roy picked her up and swung her around.

"You're our lucky charm, baby girl! Things sure been goin' our way since we met you."

Lisanne was laughing and trying to wriggle free when they both heard a snarling voice behind them.

"Put her the fuck down!"

Roy let Lisanne slide free and then turned to frown at Daniel, who was standing with his hands fisted, an expression of fury on his face.

"You talkin' to me, Dan?" said Roy, his voice dangerously quiet.

Daniel ignored him and spoke to Lisanne. "You coming or not?"

"Um, okay," she said, quickly. "I'll see you on Wednesday."

The guys nodded, all except Roy, who was still standing in a defensive position.

Lisanne hurried after Daniel, who was stomping through the club, anger rippling from him. She grabbed hold of his arm, forcing him to stop.

"What's wrong? Why did you yell at Roy like that?"

"Isn't it fucking obvious?"

"Not to me."

He took a deep breath.

"I didn't like how he was touching you. And you let him!" he said, accusingly.

Lisanne was stunned. *He was jealous?*

"Daniel, you know Roy's like that with everyone. He practically breaks my ribs every time we get good news."

He met her eyes, his face relaxing slightly.

"Good news?"

"Yes, we've got the gig at the Down Under in three weeks."

He dragged his hands through his hair and looked apologetic.

"It's this place," he said, at last. "Being here makes me a little crazy."

Lisanne felt horrible and selfish for making him come to the club, just for the piercing reminder of what he'd lost.

Tentatively, she walked toward him and wrapped her arms around his neck.

"Sorry," she whispered. "Sorry."

He rested his forehead against hers. "Me, too." After a moment, he looked up. "Come on, I'll take you back."

It was a short ride to the dorms but even so, Lisanne was chilled to the bone. Daniel had been right about needing a warmer jacket.

She shivered and he looked at her anxiously.

"You okay?"

"Just a bit cold. I'll be fine. Do you want to come in? I could make you a coffee…"

"Will Kirsty be there?"

Lisanne smiled and shook her head. She knew exactly what he meant.

"No, she's at Vin's. Working on their business studies assignment."

She raised an eyebrow at him and he smiled.

"Yeah, that thing's a bitch."

"So, you want to come in and … study?"

He grinned. "It's kind of late for … studying."

"But I promised you a coffee first—that should keep you awake for… studying."

"Do you actually have any coffee this time?"

"I have no idea."

Daniel shook his head, smiling. "You make a man an offer he can't refuse, baby doll."

Lisanne was pleased: that had been the general idea.

She walked in the front entrance, then met Daniel at her door as he snuck in through the fire exit. It felt wonderfully naughty and liberating, sneaking a boy into her room at night.

He caught her as soon as the door was closed and proceeded to kiss her thoroughly. Then she turned the tables and pushed him suddenly so he fell back onto her bed.

He laughed delightedly as Lisanne threw herself at him.

After that, there were no words.

CHAPTER 13

The following Saturday, Lisanne's gig with *32° North* went well.

The sound crew had done a really good job getting the balance right and the audience were enthusiastic.

Daniel stayed for the whole set, watching from the back with Kirsty and Vin. If it hurt him to be there, he didn't show it.

When Lisanne came off stage, her makeup running with sweat, and her heart pounding from the adrenaline rush, he wrapped his arms around her.

"Proud of you, baby. You looked amazing up there."

"I have to agree with Daniel," said Kirsty, pulling Lisanne toward her. "You were awesome."

Daniel smirked at her and Vin couldn't help laughing.

"Well, she was!" said Kirsty, defensively.

Daniel lifted his hands, "Hey, not arguing with you!"

Lisanne rolled her eyes. "Honestly! You two!"

Vin gave her a quick kiss on the cheek. "I agree with both of them—you were totally rocking, Lis. So, hey, look—I've talked them into holding a truce—and making a trip to the Island tomorrow with a bunch of guys I know. You in?"

Lisanne blinked at Daniel, who was holding back a small smile."

"You said yes?"

"Sure, baby doll. I thought you'd like it."

"Wow! Of course I like it!" and she flung herself at Daniel, who caught her easily. "Thank you," she whispered as she kissed him on the lips.

"What did you say?" he asked, frowning slightly.

"I said, thank you. Thank you for doing this."

"Sure, no problem."

Vin had given them a ride, so they all piled into his SUV to take Lisanne and Daniel back to the dorm room, and Kirsty to his frat house.

During the twenty minutes it took for them to drive back, Kirsty talked relentlessly about the 'awesome' party that Vin's frat house buddies were organizing just before Thanksgiving.

"And it's going to be so much fun to really dress up. The guys will be in tuxes, so that means something slinky for me. Lis, you totally have to come shopping with me."

"I don't know, Kirsty. You're much better at that than me."

"I know," replied Kirsty, "I am the shopping queen. But you should come—it'll be fun. Shopping plus food—what's not to like?"

Daniel hadn't caught any of the conversation because Kirsty was sitting in the front seat and he couldn't see her mouth. And even if she hadn't been, it was almost impossible to lip read in the low, flickering light of streetlamps, as they drove along the night-time roads. Instead, Daniel had been gazing out of the window, a distant look in his eyes.

"What?" he said, when Lisanne touched his knee. She spoke slowly and clearly.

"Kirsty wants me to go dress shopping with her."

Daniel pulled a face.

"Some people like shopping," Lisanne said, gently.

"Whatever. Clothes are just to stop my ass from hanging out. They only have to fit."

And he didn't see or hear Kirsty's dismissive snort either. Which was just as well. But then she leaned over the back of her seat.

"Hey, Lis, did I tell you I'm going to my grandmother's in Suffolk for Thanksgiving? She always does an awesome lunch with apple-parsnip mash, and squash with cream and sage. Double yum! I'll be like this huge afterward."

She held her hands out to indicate an enormous belly.

Lisanne laughed.

"Yeah, my mom always does a big spread, too. We usually get loads of cousins dropping in—it gets a bit crazy and…"

She stopped abruptly, feeling awful for talking about her family's plans for Thanksgiving when she knew Daniel didn't have any family, or plans. She could have kicked herself for not cutting the subject as soon as Kirsty had brought it up—even though he hadn't heard it.

"A bit of crazy is good," said Kirsty, oblivious to Lisanne's sudden tension. She looked at Daniel and asked politely, "What are you doing for Thanksgiving, Daniel?"

He caught 'Thanksgiving' and guessed the rest.

"No, no plans."

Kirsty clearly thought that his curt answer was rude, because she bulldozed on.

"So, you're just going to lie in bed and forget Thanksgiving exists?"

"Kirsty…" said Lisanne, a warning in her voice.

"No, enough's enough, Lis! I'm trying to be polite and he can't be bothered to give a proper reply? That's just pathetic."

"Daniel's parents died two years ago in a car crash," Lisanne blurted out angrily.

There was a horrified silence.

Daniel was the only one who didn't know what had been said, but he saw Kirsty's expression morph from combative to shocked.

"Oh … oh! I'm so, so sorry, Daniel! I had no idea. Lis never said. I … I'm so sorry."

He looked to Lisanne for a translation of the conversation.

"Your parents. She didn't know."

"Oh."

He shrugged and stared out of the window again, but when Lisanne held his hand in her lap, he didn't pull away.

Kirsty was sitting quietly in the front, stoically ignoring Vin's angry glances. There were no more attempts to talk.

When Vin pulled up outside the dorms, Daniel got out without speaking and Lisanne muttered a simple, "Night."

But as Daniel turned to walk away, Vin rolled down his window and reached out with his right hand.

"Sorry about your parents, man."

Daniel stared at him for a moment, then shook Vin's hand.

"Thanks," he said, quietly.

As Vin's car pulled away, Lisanne grabbed Daniel's arm, forcing him to look at her.

"I'm so sorry. I didn't tell her because ... well, it was private."

He smiled tiredly.

"It's okay, baby. I don't want people feeling sorry for me, whatever the reason." He let out a deep breath and forced out a smile. "See you upstairs in five."

"Good luck with that, buddy," said another student, in a disgruntled tone, as he walked away from the girls' dorms. "They've put a security guard on the fire door—guess the dean got wise to it."

"And the hits just keep on coming," muttered Daniel. "Looks like we'll both be sleeping alone tonight, baby doll." He sighed. "Guess I'll see you in the morning." He gave her a small smile, "We have a beach party to go to."

Lisanne wanted to sulk and stamp her foot. It had been a fantastic night—the gig had gone really well, and now everything had fallen apart. All she'd wanted was to fall asleep on Daniel's chest and wake up for some awesome morning sex. Now her plans had been ruthlessly quashed.

He rubbed her arms and kissed her lips gently.

"See you at 9:30. Night, baby."

Then he shoved his hands in his pockets and walked slowly toward the lot where he'd left Sirona. Lisanne felt bereft and filled with sadness for him. He looked so alone.

She slept badly, tossing and turning and waking several times. In her dreams, she kept seeing Daniel walking away from her. It was upsetting.

As soon as her cell phone started chirruping at 8 AM, she sent a text to Daniel.

> * L: slept horribly without u.
> No fun : (see you later. LA xx *

His reply made her smile.

> * D: See you SOON *

She dashed into the shower before other girls from the dorm started lining up. Then she stood wrapped in a towel, staring at her wardrobe, wondering whether it would be warm enough to wear shorts. When her phone rang, she briefly considered ignoring it. The caller ID showed it was her mom and she didn't have time for a long talk right now. Sighing, she answered, praying for a short conversation.

"Hi, Mom. How are you? How's Dad? What's Harry up to?"

"My! Someone's in a hurry this morning! And I'm sad to think it's not because you're going to church."

"Yeah, kind of busy. A bunch of us are going out to the Island. It's supposed to be hot today—maybe as high as 70. Should I wear shorts?"

"Are you going on that motorcycle of Daniel's? In which case you definitely need long pants, my girl!"

Lisanne shook her head. "No, Mom. Vin's driving us—Kirsty's boyfriend. He's got a brand new SUV—totally safe."

"Well, I'm glad to hear that. Wear shorts and take jeans, then you've got everything you'll need."

"Okay, thanks, Mom."

"Honey, I know you're in a rush, but I just wanted to ask you very quickly about Thanksgiving—you haven't said which day you're coming."

"Oh," said Lisanne. "Um, Mom, I was going to talk to you about this, but now's not a good time."

"What do you mean, Lisanne?" said her mother, in a sharp voice.

"I thought I'd stay here for Thanksgiving. With Daniel."

There was a long silence. Lisanne held her breath.

She hadn't discussed anything with Daniel, but having heard everyone excitedly talking about their plans for Thanksgiving, she couldn't bear to think of Daniel stuck here with just Zef. She didn't even know if he'd want to see her, and blurting this out to her mom now had been impulsive to say the least.

"Lisanne, you know Thanksgiving is an important holiday for our family. All the cousins make an effort to be there—it's the one time we really see each other. And Pops and Grandma Olsen are coming a long way to spend some time with *you*. Your father and I would rather you be here with us."

Lisanne felt horrible. "Mom, I know. But … He'll be here all by himself and I can't just leave him."

"Why isn't he spending time with his family?"

"He only has his older brother, and Zef will be busy with his … friends."

"What about Daniel's parents? Where are they? Won't he be with them? After all…"

Lisanne had to interrupt.

"Mom, no. Daniel's parents … they were killed in a car accident. Two years ago."

"Oh my!" her mother gasped. "That poor boy!" Then there was a long pause. "Just wait a moment, sweetheart—I'm going to put you on hold."

Lisanne huffed ineffectually as she held the silent phone to her ear.

After what seemed like forever, her mother came back on the line.

"Well, I just spoke to your father: we want you to bring Daniel to stay with us for Thanksgiving. No one should be alone at this time of year."

"What? Dad agreed to that?" Lisanne's tone was disbelieving.

"Yes, he did," said her mom, decisively. "So could you please ask Daniel—he'll be more than welcome."

"Um, okay. Thanks, Mom."

"I'll talk to you later, honey. Have a lovely time at the beach."

The call ended and Lisanne stared at her phone, wondering if she'd just imagined the whole conversation. Surely she couldn't invent a universe where her father would willingly invite *the boy she was sleeping with* to come and stay in his house. It was too weird. Good, definitely—but weird.

After the initial shock wore off, Lisanne began to be excited by the idea. She'd like Daniel to meet her family in a more acceptable way. The question was, would he come?

When she heard the rumble of Daniel's motorcycle, she realized she'd spent nearly 20 minutes staring at her wardrobe. Hurrying, she pulled on a pair of cut off shorts and a tank top over her tankini, and tied a plaid shirt in a knot at her waist. Then she pushed a pair of jeans into her backpack along with sunscreen, a paperback, and a large beach towel big enough for two.

Daniel was leaning on the saddle of his bike. With his sunglasses covering his eyes, and casually smoked cigarette hanging from his lips, he looked like a movie star.

And then Shawna made her appearance.

"Hi, Daniel! I didn't know you were in on this. That's so cool! Oh wow, did you get a new tattoo?" and she trailed a finger down his bicep.

Daniel twitched his shoulder in an irritated gesture.

"You know I'm with Lisanne, right?"

Shawna gave a fake giggle and batted her false eyelashes at him. Daniel's gaze grazed her breasts as he wondered if they were fake, too.

He turned away, but not before Shawna had guessed the direction of his look and leapt to the wrong conclusion.

"I'll keep your side of the bed warm," she whispered.

Daniel didn't hear her. He'd seen Lisanne, and a huge smile lit his face as his eyes swept up and down her bare legs. It was the least he'd seen her wear outside either the bedroom or the stage.

"I like!" he said, with a grin.

On cue, Lisanne blushed.

"Um, thanks. Didn't you bring something to swim in?" she said, gazing at his empty hands.

"Sure, baby doll. You want to see?"

He opened the top button of his jeans and pulled down enough of the waistband to reveal a band of dark blue cotton.

"Daniel!" hissed Lisanne, her eyes darting around to see if anyone was watching.

Shawna's eyes were drawn like magnets to the exposed skin that he was carelessly flaunting.

Daniel laughed.

"Nothing you haven't seen before, baby."

And he pulled her into a hug.

Shawna tossed her hair over her shoulder and sucked her teeth.

The small drama was interrupted by the arrival of Vin and Kirsty.

The SUV pulled up to the curb, followed by a convoy of three other cars, all crammed with kids from the college.

"Ready to catch some rays!" shouted Kirsty, happily.

One of the other drivers came hurrying over to Vin's window.

"Hey, man. I'm seriously overloaded. Can you take one more?"

"I don't know, Paul. I've already got three in the back."

"We're good, Vin," said Daniel, surprising them all. "Lis can sit on my knee."

Vin smiled. "You heard the man—everyone in."

One of Vin's football buddies, an enormous cheerful guy called Isaac, sandwiched himself in the middle, squashing Shawna into the door.

Lisanne perched awkwardly on Daniel's knee.

"Are you okay," she asked nervously. "Won't I cut off the

circulation in your legs? I'm pretty heavy…"

He laughed lightly. "No, baby doll. Best seat in the house. Just relax."

He settled her comfortably and proceeded to suck the soft skin at the side of her neck.

Isaac elbowed him. "Hey! I don't want to see you mauling your girl all the way to the beach, man!"

Daniel smiled. "You can have Shawna. She's available."

Lisanne hid a giggle, while Isaac eyed a furious Shawna warily.

"Hey," said Vin, "no mauling for anyone—car rule."

"Since when?" murmured Kirsty, raising one eyebrow.

Vin just smiled. "Lis, we need your iPod for some cool tunes. Pass it over."

Lis handed it to Kirsty, and the car was soon filled with the rocking sounds of Gin Wigmore.

"I don't know this one," said Kirsty, after several more songs.

"This is Lykke Li."

"Licky who?"

Lisanne smile. "Lykke Li—she's Swedish."

"And who was that one before?"

"Asa—she's sort of soul jazz, from Paris, France."

"And the one before that?"

"Birds of Tokyo."

"From Japan?"

"From Perth, Australia."

"What about good ole US rock?" snorted Isaac.

"There's some Linkin Park on there."

"Outstanding!" yelled Isaac, who seemed easily pleased.

Lisanne liked sharing her music but felt uneasy knowing that Daniel couldn't. He gave her a quick smile and spent the rest of the ride gazing out of the window. It was his default position on car journeys.

The trip was short and uneventful, if Lisanne discounted Shawna's sulky presence. Daniel half heartedly obeyed Vin's new car rule, and contented himself with kissing her hair and resting one hand on her bare thigh.

Lisanne was fizzing with happiness. She'd never had a boyfriend before, never been to the beach with a bunch of friends, never made out in a car. She felt as if the whole world was filled with possibilities when Daniel was at her side. She felt safe and adventurous all at the same time.

She wriggled on his lap and leaned down to kiss him.

"What's that for?" he said, grinning up at her.

Lisanne shrugged. "I'm happy."

His grin widened, then he kissed her back.

"Car rules!" chanted Isaac and Vin at the same time.

Lisanne pushed Daniel gently.

"What?" he said, opening his eyes.

"Car rules," she said, with a smile.

"Yeah, well, you're a bad influence," he replied, his eyes flashing with humor.

The temperature began to rise along with the sun, brilliant in a flawless blue sky. Vin turned on the air conditioning but Kirsty begged for open windows instead. He agreed immediately, unable to deny her a single thing.

"It's too windy back here," grumbled Shawna. "It's messing up my hair."

"We're going to the beach, Shaw. You know, sand, seawater?"

"It's drying out my skin," she moaned.

"Okay, fine," said Kirsty, shaking her head as she rolled the window back up.

When they arrived at the beach, they spilled out, happy and yelling excitedly. The other cars parked behind them and they started unloading the trunk.

The sand was a pale gold, the color and texture of unrefined sugar, and the light breeze tugged at Lisanne's heart. She felt ridiculously happy and when she turned to look at Daniel, wanting to share the moment, the grin on his face made it feel like her body couldn't possibly contain such pure joy.

The sound of cursing distracted her. Isaac had dropped a heavy cooler on his foot—and from the sound—and weight—of it, it was filled with beer. More and more beer coolers were unloaded, as well as an array of food.

"Um, Kirsty," she said, quietly. "I feel really bad—I didn't bring anything. Can I give you some money or something?"

Kirsty smiled and shook her head. "No, we're good. Tell you what, there's a store over there—why don't you buy some more chips. You should see these guys eat—there's never enough chips."

Lisanne was grateful to her friend. Kirsty knew that she didn't have much money, but chips she could manage.

She tapped Daniel on the shoulder. "I'm just going to buy some chips and a bottle of water. You want anything."

He shook his head. "No, I got it, baby," and he strode across, selecting three enormous family size bags of chips and a large bottle of water.

He was almost hidden by the chips as he walked back, making Lisanne laugh. She took a bag from him and they followed the others to the shoreline, staking out an empty patch of sand.

Vin and his buddies had already stripped down to their swim shorts, and Isaac was spinning a football on his finger. Shawna stood with her back to the ocean, enjoying the view of near naked male flesh, while Kirsty laid out an enormous beach towel and proceeded to rub sunscreen into her arms.

Vin hurried over to her, muttering something about, "My job," which made Kirsty giggle.

"Come on, man!" yelled Isaac. "Football! You playing or what?"

"Or what," replied Vin, rubbing sunscreen over Kirsty's back.

"Aw hell," muttered Isaac. "What about you, Dan? You wanna play some ball?"

Lisanne nudged Daniel's arm as he dropped the bags of chips next to the food coolers.

"Isaac's asking if you want to play football," she said, quietly.

The gleam in his eye, followed by a wistful expression, hurt Lisanne's heart.

"Go on," she said, encouragingly. "It's only a beach game. Just have a go. You can always come back and rub lotion into my back."

He smiled, "Always up for that, baby." He took a deep breath. "Okay, what the hell." Then he turned toward Isaac. "I'm in!"

Isaac whooped and high-fived the guy standing next to him.

Daniel unbuckled his boots and peeled off his socks. Lisanne watched, dry mouthed, as he yanked off his t-shirt and dropped his pants.

"Oh my God," gasped Shawna. "He really does have nipple rings!"

Everyone turned to stare, but Daniel didn't know why. He froze.

"It's okay," Lisanne said, reassuringly. "They're just admiring your, um, chest jewelry."

A knowing smirk passed across Daniel's face. "Just so long as you like it, baby doll."

"You know I do," she said, her face suddenly becoming hot enough to fry an egg.

He leaned down and kissed her hard, leaving her breathless and flushed throughout her entire body.

She sat down, fanning herself.

"Hot?" asked Kirsty, a wry expression on her face.

"Definitely," agreed Lisanne.

Vin laughed out loud. "Maybe I should get some."

"Don't you dare!" shrieked Kirsty. "It would be weeks before we could, um, I mean, it would hurt for weeks."

Now it was Kirsty's turn to blush.

Lisanne turned to watch the football game that was taking place further up the beach. She didn't really follow football, as a rule, so when Vin whistled between his teeth, she looked at him questioningly.

"Daniel just threw a 30 yard pass."

"Is that good?"

"Yeah," he said quietly, then sat back to watch the game, one hand idly rubbing Kirsty's knee.

Lisanne couldn't really tell what was going on. There seemed to be a lot of shouting, along with some running and catching.

Then Isaac yelled, "touchdown!" and threw himself at Daniel, who looked pleased.

"He's pretty good," said Vin.

Then he stood up and jogged over to join in.

Lisanne watched for a bit longer, but Daniel seemed to be doing okay. She pulled out a battered paperback and settled down on her stomach to read.

Shawna had wandered nearer to the football game, dressed in a bikini that was so small, Lisanne wasn't entirely sure why she'd bothered. She felt too shy to sit around in her bathing suit, especially next to Kirsty, who looked a goddess with her long curls and flawless skin.

After half an hour of burning sun, Lisanne decided to go for a swim. Kirsty was asleep, all the guys were absorbed in the game, and Shawna was still doing her cheerleader impersonation, although it wasn't clear who she was trying to encourage. But at least it meant no one was watching Lisanne. She slipped off her tank top and shorts, hitched the top of her tankini a bit higher, and gingerly made her way over the heated sand to the ocean's edge.

The water rippled over her feet, making it look as if they were bending and flexing like seaweed. She waded further in, letting the water cool her hot skin. She sank down to her knees and shivered slightly as the chill reached her chest. Inching further forward, she leaned into the water and took off in a serene breast stroke.

In the distance, she heard shouting and jeers. She turned her head to see Daniel holding up his hands to the guys, as if he was apologizing for something. Then he turned and jogged along the beach for a short distance, before diving into the water and swimming a fast crawl toward her.

He jumped up next to her, with his dark hair plastered to his head, and the sun glinting on his chest as seawater poured from his shoulders.

"Hey, baby doll. Miss me?"

"Might have."

He pouted. "Only might?"

"Well, you seemed to be having fun with the *boys*, I thought I'd take a swim."

"I know," he grinned at her. "They were pretty mad, but between them and my girl getting all wet, it was no competition."

He pulled her toward him and her legs wrapped around his waist. His hands slipped under her ass to hold her up as he attacked her lips.

She opened her mouth and his tongue swept inside. He moaned and lifted one hand up to the centre of her back, pulling her in more tightly.

When he moved his head back, his eyes were dark with desire. He groaned and shifted her carefully.

"What's the matter?" she said, in a voice so husky she barely recognized it as her own.

"I've got a boner," he muttered. "That's not supposed to happen to guys in cold water. It's you, baby. You're so *hot*—I could fuck you right here. Nobody would know."

Lisanne giggled a little nervously.

"I think people might notice if you suddenly started putting on a condom, unless you can do that underwater."

Daniel groaned again. "Fuck. We're gonna have to get you on the pill, baby. You're driving me crazy."

Lisanne blinked. She wasn't sure how she felt about that. But Daniel didn't notice the change in her expression. He was too busy kissing the top of her chest and sucking her throat gently.

He looked up when Lisanne shifted in his arms.

"What's up, baby?"

"They're waving us to come over and have some food."

"Shit. I'll need a minute," he said, letting her slide down against his body. "I'll just swim for a bit, okay?"

"I'll come with you—I'm not really hungry yet anyway."

Lisanne swam parallel to the beach, while Daniel zoomed a hundred yards out, then came splashing toward her.

As his head broke the water he grinned at her.

"Feeling better? Everything back where it belongs."

"Not sure about that, baby. My dick belongs in you."

Lisanne blushed. He had *such* a dirty mouth. She loved it.

They walked back along the beach, hand in hand, with Daniel leaning down to kiss her every few paces. Lisanne was pretty sure she could have passed for a bright red fire hydrant from his very public display of affection.

"Um, Daniel? We're nearly there now."

"I know," he said, nuzzling her neck. "Your nipples are so hard—I can't wait to wrap my tongue around them."

She smacked his arm and he looked at her in surprise.

"What?"

"Don't!"

"Don't what?" he said, looking confused.

"Don't ... say stuff like *that* in front of people. I'll just die of embarrassment."

Daniel narrowed his eyes at her.

"Are you ashamed of being seen with me?"

"No! God, no! It's just ... when you say all that stuff about sex—I get embarrassed. I'm not used to it," she finished, lamely.

Lisanne was relieved to see that his smile was quickly restored.

"Okay, baby doll, but I can't guarantee I'll be able to keep my hands off of you. Just sayin'."

The others had made quick work of the food, and everyone seemed to have a paper plate loaded up with something.

Daniel's eyes just got really wide when he saw the piles of barbecue ribs, chicken wings and hot dogs. Good food on a regular basis was something of a rarity for him. He was soon digging in happily.

Lisanne preferred the lighter fare of cold pasta and salad.

They settled down onto her towel and enjoyed their food.

"You've got an awesome throwing arm, man," said Vin.

Lisanne tapped Daniel's knee, and discreetly pointed at Vin.

"Sorry, man, what?"

"I'm just surprised you didn't try out for the team. You must have played in high school?"

"Uh, yeah, a bit."

"More than a bit," snorted Kirsty. "Lis said you were your school's quarterback."

There was a short silence while Daniel threw an accusing look at Lisanne.

"Yeah," he said, at last.

Vin frowned. "So how come you didn't try out this year?"

"Yeah, man," added Isaac. "You threw a clean 30 yard pass and damn near out ran Vinny from a cold start."

Daniel shrugged and stood up, tossing his plate into the garbage. Then he pulled a packet of cigarettes out of his jeans' pocket.

"I was busy."

Vin could see that for some reason Daniel was uncomfortable with the subject, so he dropped it quickly. The conversation soon turned to everyone's plans for Thanksgiving.

Lisanne looked at Daniel and mouthed, "Sorry."

He shrugged again, and blew his cigarette smoke away from her.

She cupped his cheek gently until he looked at her. "Sorry, really."

He gave her a lopsided smile. "It's okay. I like that you talk about me when I'm not there—well, if it's good stuff."

"Always," said Lisanne, gently.

His answering smile was shy and sweet.

"Yeah?"

"Yeah. And," she said, taking a deep breath, "there's something else I wanted to tell you, but I'm not sure what you'll think about it."

A small furrow appeared between Daniel's eyebrows. "Go on."

"My mom invited you to join us for Thanksgiving."

Daniel didn't reply—in fact, his face seemed to have frozen halfway through a thought. Lisanne felt herself babbling.

"I told Mom that you were by yourself—and that I wanted to stay here with you."

That got his attention.

"You ... you were going to stay here ... with me."

Lisanne nodded.

"Why?" he seemed genuinely puzzled.

"Because!" she said, rolling her eyes.

Daniel wasn't generally obtuse, but sometimes he really didn't get her.

Lisanne tried again.

"So will you? Come for Thanksgiving?"

Daniel rubbed his hands over his face.

"Seriously? Your old man is going to let me in your house for Thanksgiving ... and he won't shoot me or anything?"

Lisanne giggled at the expression on his face.

"Nope. He'll probably just throw you a hard stare every time you look at me."

"Sounds fun," muttered Daniel, but Lisanne could tell he was trying to hide a smile.

"Can I tell her yes?"

"Will there be turkey?"

"Of course."

"And mashed potatoes?"

"With gravy."

"And pumpkin pie?"

Lisanne smiled. "Trust me—there'll be enough food even for you."

Daniel looked serious.

"That's really great of them, Lis. I mean it. But I don't think so—all those people. I won't be able to ... it's really hard..."

She stroked his arm. "I'll be there and I'll help you. Today's been okay, hasn't it?"

He nodded and gave her a small smile.

"Yeah, today's been great. I know I've missed some stuff, and some of the calls when we were playing football, but knowing you've got my back—that makes it a lot easier. I was going to tell you later, but … thanks. Thank you for today."

Lisanne's mouth dropped open with a soft pop.

"You're welcome," she said, faintly.

The afternoon passed peacefully. Vin organized a complicated game of Frisbee in the water, with three pieces of plastic whizzing over everyone's heads, where no one except Vin was sure of the rules.

More food was eaten, and then most people stretched out for a sleep in the sun before heading back. Daniel had gone for another long swim, racing Isaac and one of the other guys. Then he dripped his way back up the hot sand and planted chilled kisses across Lisanne's stomach. They lay together and dozed comfortably, her head on his chest.

Shawna had arranged to ride back in one of the other cars, which was just fine by Lisanne.

She picked some mellow music from her iPod, and soon the ambient sounds of Cults' *You Know What I Mean* and some Alison Sudol was filling the car. The journey was quiet, with everyone dozing after a long day of sun, sea, and sand.

Suddenly Vin sat up straighter.

"Oh, shit," he muttered. "I'm being pulled over."

Lisanne felt very nervous. She'd never been in a car that had been stopped by police before. Going with Zef to collect Daniel was the closest she'd ever come to a law enforcement officer. She really hadn't wanted a closer encounter.

Daniel twisted to look over his shoulder when Lisanne pointed behind them.

"Fuck," he said, quietly.

Kirsty faced him and shot him an angry look.

"Do you have anything on you, Daniel? Because if you do, this could affect all of us!"

"No, I fucking don't!" he snarled at her.

Vin tightened his jaw but didn't say anything. He pulled over and rolled down the window of his car as the policeman approached.

"Is something wrong, officer?"

"You failed to maintain the lane while you were driving: license and registration," said the man, abruptly.

Vin opened his wallet and handed over his driver's license.

"If you could step out of the vehicle, please, Mr. Vescovi."

Looking worried, Vin climbed out and the cops walked him a distance from the car. They seemed to be questioning him about something and Vin was shaking his head vigorously.

Daniel watched closely and Lisanne knew he was lip reading them. He turned to her quickly.

"Lis, I think they're going to arrest me," he said, his voice strained.

"What?" snapped Kirsty. "How do you know that?"

He ignored her.

"Don't say anything to them—just get a message to Zef as quickly as you can? Please, baby?"

"I don't understand!" cried Lisanne. "You haven't done anything!"

"Do you think that will stop them?" he sneered. "Believe me, when your name is Colton, they don't need a reason."

"Daniel," whispered Lisanne, "is there anything else— anything at all?"

The look of anger and disappointment on his face dried the words in her mouth until they tasted like ash.

The officers returned to the car and ordered them all to get out.

One man took their names, and then he got to Daniel. He didn't even ask to see his ID.

"Turn around and face the car, Colton. I am arresting you on suspicion of possession of drugs with intent to distribute."

Lisanne gasped as the officer cuffed Daniel's hands behind his back. Kirsty caught her arm as she darted forward.

"Lis, no! That won't help." Then Kirsty spoke up. "Excuse me, officer. My father's a lawyer and I know that…"

"Listen, kid," said the smaller of the two policeman, "if I had a dime for every rich kid who told me their dad was a lawyer, I'd be a wealthy man—not arresting punks on the highway. My advice to you is get back in your expensive car, keep quiet, and stay away from street scum like that."

He pointed at Daniel and gave Kirsty a warning glare.

"You have the right to remain silent," said the bigger cop, to the back of Daniel's head. "Anything you say or do may be used against you in a court of law."

Lisanne collapsed against Kirsty, whose arms were wrapped around her, tightly.

"You have the right to consult an attorney before speaking to the police," the cop continued, "and to have an attorney present during questioning now or in the future. If you cannot afford an attorney, one will be appointed for you before any questioning, if you wish. If you decide to answer any questions now, without an attorney present, you will still have the right to stop answering at any time until you talk to an attorney. Knowing and understanding your rights as I have explained them to you, are you willing to answer my questions without an attorney present?"

Daniel didn't speak, and Lisanne knew he hadn't heard a single word.

"I said do you understand these rights?" snapped the officer, and he pushed Daniel's head so it thudded against the SUV's roof.

"Bastard," muttered Isaac under his breath.

Daniel was escorted into the police cruiser. He didn't look back as they drove him away.

Vin walked back to them, white-faced and shaken. The police had completely ignored the reason he'd been pulled over—the bogus accusation of 'failing to maintain a lane'.

Kirsty turned to Lisanne.

"I'm just going to ask you once, Lis—has Daniel got

anything on him? Anything at all?"

Lisanne shook her head.

"He looked so mad when I asked him that!" she said, tears stinging her eyes.

Vin spoke quietly.

"They knew he was in the car."

"What?" snapped Kirsty.

"They knew Dan was in the car. I mean, they didn't ask me his name or anything. That big cop, he just said, 'Has Colton supplied you any drugs today, or in the past?' That was before they checked everyone's ID. They *knew* who he was before they stopped me. Like they were waiting for us."

"I have to call his brother," said Lisanne, softly.

"No," said Kirsty, authority ringing in her voice. "Vin, drive us to the police station."

"What are you going to do?"

"Help Daniel," she said. "Like I said, Dad's a lawyer, and I *know* they can't do what they just did."

"Honey, I know you want to help…"

"I mean it, Vin. I'll get Dad on the phone—he'll tell me what to say."

An hour later, a dazed looking Daniel left the police station escorted by a victorious Kirsty, to the whoops and cheers of Vin and Isaac.

Lisanne burst into tears.

"Hey, baby. Don't cry," he said, wiping her cheeks with his fingers. "It's all good. I'm fine."

Vin picked up Kirsty and whirled her around, as she laughed happily.

"What happened?" choked out Lisanne between her tears.

"Your friend was awesome," said Daniel, with a huge smile directed at Kirsty. "Totally ripped them a new one. By the time we left they were calling her 'ma'am'."

"Thank you very much," said Kirsty, with a delicate curtsey. "I have to agree with Daniel—I was totally awesome. Well, my dad was totally awesome—he talked me through everything I had to say."

"But I don't understand," sniffed Lisanne. "Why did they arrest you? You hadn't done anything."

Kirsty looked serious.

"Honestly, Daniel. I think you've got a case for police harassment. Vin was right—they were looking for you and from what they *weren't* saying, they wanted to use you to get to your brother."

Daniel pulled a face.

"Nah, I'm staying well away from those fuckers."

Kirsty sighed. "Dad says you should get out of town for a while if you can. Have you got somewhere you can stay until this calms down?"

A slow smile lifted Daniel's lips.

"Yeah. Is the offer still open, baby?"

"Excuse me?" gasped Lisanne, completely bewildered by the change of direction.

"Is the invitation for Thanksgiving still open?"

She flung her arms around his neck, fresh tears trickling down her face.

"Yes," she mumbled into his chest, even though he couldn't hear her. "Yes," she said again, looking up at his beautiful face.

CHAPTER 14

Zef stood with his arms crossed as Daniel shoved clothes into his messenger bag.

When he was facing him, he said, "So you're going with *her*—the singer."

Daniel nodded. Although his expression was neutral, his jaw clenched.

Zef scrubbed his fingers over his face, an expression of frustration that his younger brother had seemingly inherited. Then he shoved his hands into his pockets.

"Whatever. It's probably just as well you get out of town for a while."

That was the plan, but Zef's words worried Daniel.

"What's going on? Those cops were really gunning for you. I've been looking over my shoulder ever since—they weren't messing around."

Zef shook his head slowly.

"Things have gotten ... complicated."

Daniel frowned in irritation and confusion.

"I don't get it. We don't need the money. Since ... since Mom and Dad ... the insurance paid off the mortgage and there's the trust for my tuition fees. I've got my summer job in the auto shop—I could work weekends, too. If you got a job…"

"Who's going to give me a job, man? I mean, seriously? With my record? I couldn't even get paid to stock shelves at Wal-Mart."

"Go back to school—finish your degree."

"You don't understand—you're just a kid."

Daniel bristled.

"Is that what you think?"

Zef shrugged then shook his head.

"Nah, man. Not really. I'm just saying that it's more complicated than you think."

"Then *tell* me—I'm sure I can keep up."

Zef pulled a face.

"Look, whatever. Go enjoy Thanksgiving with your girl. Maybe we'll talk when you get back. Come on, get out of here! Enjoy yourself. Don't be a pussy."

Daniel gave a small smile, then his face became serious again.

"But we'll talk when I get back?"

"Yeah, maybe. Now go on—get gone."

Zef pulled his brother into a hug and whispered, "I'm sorry, kid."

He knew Daniel couldn't hear him.

Daniel drove up to the dorms as a crowd of noisy college girls spilled out, shouting and jostling, lugging heavy cases and piling into cars. It was cheerful bedlam. Cheerful for all the ones who were going off to spend time with their families. Daniel felt anything but cheerful—he was as nervous as all hell at the prospect of staying in the Maclaines' house. He'd asked Lisanne if her dad had a gun, ignoring the accompanying eye roll, and even Googled the location of the nearest motel just in case things didn't go entirely to plan.

He kicked the bike's stand and leaned down to pull Lisanne's Thanksgiving gift out of the saddlebags. One of the two gifts he'd gotten her. He wasn't sure she'd like it, but she definitely needed it.

He'd tried to gift wrap it—he'd even bought some expensive paper and ribbon. But then the paper wouldn't fit and the ribbon kept unraveling. In the end he'd used so much Scotch tape that the damn thing looked as attractive as road kill. Which is why he'd stuffed it inside a plastic bag.

He managed to push his way through the crowds of hormonal girls, wondering if getting his ass felt up had been an accident, when he bumped into … what the hell was her name? He racked his brains while her eyes widened as she realized whose chest she was currently eyeballing.

"Oh, Daniel!"

"Hi," he said, amiably.

He started to go around her when she grabbed his arm.

"You made a mistake not calling me back," she said, with a challenging look.

He couldn't help smiling. Girl had balls.

"Happy Thanksgiving," he said, winking at her. "Terri."

She pouted and tossed her long red hair over her shoulder.

He took the stairs two at a time until he was standing outside Lisanne's room. He knocked loudly.

Lisanne yanked the door open, her ears ringing from Kirsty's high-pitched squealing, and grinned up at him, her cheeks pink and her eyes bright. Daniel couldn't help bending down and kissing her sweet lips. The moment skin touched skin, the spark of electricity flared and he couldn't deny it, but deepened the kiss, aching to feel her body pressed against his own.

Several girls milling around in the hallway whistled and called out comments that nice female college students ought not to know, even if they were anatomically correct. Perhaps it was lucky that Daniel didn't hear them, not that he'd have cared. But Lisanne did—her face was scarlet as she tugged him inside and shut the door.

"What?" he asked, bemused.

"Nothing," she lied, then continued as she saw her answer annoyed him. "Just some sophomores eyeing up *my* boyfriend."

Daniel laughed. He liked her being possessive.

Kirsty raised her eyebrows and sighed theatrically.

"Hello! I am in the same room as you guys! I do exist. There is life beyond the Lisanne—Daniel bubble."

"Sorry, Kirsty," mumbled Lisanne.

"Yeah. What she said." Daniel's tone wasn't entirely serious, and he smiled. "Hey, Kirsty. Didn't see you over there."

Kirsty groaned. "Oh God, now I'm invisible. It's finally

happened. The sooner you two get over the honeymoon phase the better for us mere mortals."

"Oh, right!" snorted Lisanne. "And you weren't shrieking because Vin sent you a cute text saying, 'Oh, Kirsty! You're the most beautiful woman I've ever seen. Your eyes are like two sapphires on a really big blue ring, and turtledoves sing every time you enter a room...'"

Kirsty threw a cushion at her.

"Shut up already! He didn't say that—not exactly."

Daniel felt like backing out of the door. The estrogen levels in the room were off the chart and high enough to melt the balls off a brass monkey. Probably. It was no place for a human male.

"Um, yeah, I'll wait for you outside," he said.

"What? No, I'm ready."

Lisanne threw herself at Kirsty and hugged her tightly.

"Text me every day, promise?"

"Of course. And tell me how it goes at your place. Oh and remember what I said—you totally have to have sex in your childhood bedroom," replied Kirsty, muttering into Lisanne's neck.

She gasped. "Kirsty!"

"I'm just saying—it'll be awesome. Trust me."

Kirsty winked at Daniel, who'd been having some inappropriate thoughts of his own when he'd seen his girlfriend kissing another woman, but he hadn't heard the conversation. He shook his head to clear it and suddenly decided it would be wise to hold Lisanne's present in front of him.

Lisanne gave him a strange look, probably because his eyes looked like they were about to dribble down his chest. She picked up a small bag.

"Is this okay?"

"Um..."

"Will it fit in Sirona?"

"Who's Sirona?" asked Kirsty, curiosity coloring her tone.

Lisanne giggled. "His bike."

"He named her?"

"I know!" laughed Lisanne.

"Hey!" said Daniel. "I'm standing right here!"

"Now you know how it feels," muttered Kirsty.

Lisanne grabbed hold of Daniel's hand and tugged him out of the room.

"Bye, Kirsty! Happy Thanksgiving!"

"Yeah," said Daniel. "What she said."

"What's up with you?" Lisanne said to Daniel. "You're acting weird—all sort of wigged out."

Daniel looked around him nervously, pulled her into an empty corner next to the janitor's closet, then thrust the present at her.

"For you," he mumbled. "It's nothing much, and it's not new or anything, so if you don't like it that's fine, but I thought you could use it and … yeah … yeah."

Lisanne's face slowly changed from confusion to comprehension to pleasure.

"You … you got me a present?"

Daniel nodded. "Yeah, but it's pretty crappy. It's not new but I thought … I dunno … you don't have to…"

Shit! Why was giving a girl a present so hard? Because you've never done it before, moron.

"Daniel, I love it."

He stared at her, utterly bewildered. "But … you haven't even opened it."

Lisanne reached up and kissed his cheek. "I love it because it's from you."

The tips of Daniel's ears reddened, and suddenly the ugly carpeting seemed incredibly fascinating.

"It probably won't fit," he muttered, almost to himself.

Lisanne pulled the package out of the bag. She held back a smile as she saw his futile attempts at gift wrapping. Jeez, it looked he'd wrapped it blindfolded—and using his toes.

She tried to tear off the paper, but there was so much Scotch tape, she couldn't make any headway.

"Um, could you help me with this?" she said, biting back an

261

urge to laugh.

"Fuck," muttered Daniel.

When he couldn't tear it with his hands, he used his teeth to rip it open, then handed it back to Lisanne.

Finally, finally Lisanne got her gift opened.

Inside was a black leather biker's jacket, size small. It was worn soft with use, the leather faded and scuffed, the sleeves curved at the elbows by years of wearing.

While Lisanne held out her arms, Daniel slipped it over her shoulders, then pulled up the zipper.

It fit perfectly.

Damn if she didn't look sexy in leather.

"I thought it would keep you warm, when you're on the bike. You don't have to wear it," he said, "but it's safer than your jacket, so I thought…"

Lisanne pressed her lips against his to silence his nervous babbling.

"You can stop talking now," she said, looking into his eyes. "I love it."

Daniel smiled a little unsurely. "Yeah? Because I know it's secondhand and girls don't like that stuff so…" his words tailed off as Lisanne smiled happily at him. "You like it?"

"I love it. I told you."

"Good, because it looks damn sexy on you. Makes me want to do things to you."

"What sort of things?" she said, with a challenging stare.

His arms swept down suddenly and he scooped her up with his hands under her ass, so Lisanne's legs automatically wrapped around his waist. Then he pressed her up against the wall and kissed her hard.

Through the sheen of lust that suddenly enveloped her, she could feel his hips grinding into her thighs.

"I'm going to have you against a wall, baby doll, and all you'll be wearing is that leather jacket."

Lisanne gasped as he muttered the words against her throat.

She fastened her hands around his neck and did some

grinding of her own, drawing out a moan from deep within his chest.

Slowly he let her slide down, his eyes dark and wild.

Suddenly, he grabbed her wrist and pulled her into the janitor's closet and shut the door, leaving them in a darkness illuminated only by cracks of light.

When Lisanne felt Daniel tugging at the button on her jeans, she grabbed his hands and stopped him.

He sighed heavily, and she held him as their breathing slowly returned to normal. After a moment, she cautiously opened the door and stepped outside.

A couple of girls walking past giggled into their hands, and Lisanne knew that the few shreds left of her reputation had just disintegrated, when Daniel followed her out.

"Sorry," he said, not even the slightest bit abashed. "You look so hot."

Lisanne didn't know whether she was more turned on or annoyed that he'd tried to fuck her in a damn closet that smelled of bleach.

"We should get going," she said, raising her eyebrows at him.

"You always get me going, baby," he replied with a grin.

"Daniel!"

"What?"

Wondering how much room for maneuvering the closet really had, Lisanne tugged his sleeve and he followed her down the stairs, laughing quietly. There was absolutely no doubt in her mind, that if she hadn't stopped him, they'd be a hot and sweaty mess by now.

That boy!

Still smiling to himself, Daniel stuffed Lisanne's backpack into the saddlebags.

"Is there anything breakable in here, baby?" he asked, rather belatedly.

"Um, no!" she laughed. "*Now* you ask me?"

He shrugged. "You distracted me."

"You're blaming *me*?"

He grinned. "Yeah, you're totally badass."

Lisanne felt a faint heat in her cheeks. From music major-nerd to badass in half a semester—she liked it.

He handed her a helmet and swung a long leg over the bike, then held out his hand for her.

The roar of the engine was loud, and Lisanne could see heads turning in their direction. A few girls knew that she and the notorious Daniel Colton were dating—but after this, it would be general knowledge. She was pleased, but it made her nervous, too. She wasn't sure why.

She fastened her hands around his waist. It was quickly becoming one of the favorite Daniel places on her list. Although it was quite a long list.

He drove slowly until they reached the interstate, then he really let rip, showing what Sirona could do, and that she was no stately lady, despite her forty-plus years. Lisanne clung on and squeezed his waist extra hard to remind him that he really didn't want to get stopped for speeding again. He must have understood, because he slowed slightly. She could only hope it was below 70mph.

After two hours, riding on Sirona began to lose some of its appeal for Lisanne. Apart from anything else, the vibrations were making her ass numb. She wriggled about uncomfortably and wished for Vin's luxurious, air conditioned SUV. She felt guilty because she knew that Daniel couldn't afford anything like that, and he'd bought her the seriously cool leather jacket to make her more comfortable. She just wished he'd bought her a cushion to sit on, too.

After another 30 minutes she'd had enough. She wanted to stand up. She wanted to walk. She wanted to rub her ass and put her thighs together. She saw a truck stop coming up and tapped Daniel on the shoulder and pointed.

He swung the bike over and headed to the off-ramp. When he finally cut the engine, Lisanne felt like cheering.

She dragged off the helmet, and scrambled from the bike, rubbing her backside gingerly.

Daniel looked like he was trying not to smile.

"You okay, baby doll?"

"No, I can't feel my ass!" she said, grumpily.

"Do you want me to feel it?"

Before she had a chance to answer, he leaned down and massaged her backside, his strong fingers working the soft flesh.

Lisanne groaned with pleasure. He'd definitely missed his calling. He'd be the most amazing massage therapist. *Personal* massage therapist. *Her* personal massage therapist. And she'd be his only client.

"Better?"

"Don't stop," she moaned.

He smiled down at her. "Baby, if I don't stop now, I'm going to want to fuck you in the middle of a truck stop. See what you do to me?"

He glanced down at the front of his jeans and Lisanne was surprised to see a noticeable bulge.

"Oh," she said, softly. "Sorry."

"'S'okay. But I can't wait to get to your place."

Lisanne blinked. "You know we can't fool around at my parents!" she said, an edge of panic in her voice.

A small crease appeared between his eyebrows. "Why not?"

"Because … because…"

Daniel smiled. "I'm not going to do it in front of your parents, Lis. I don't want to give your dad another reason to throw down. We'll wait for them to go out or something."

"Oh," said Lisanne, faintly.

"Unless you don't want to?" he said, his voice suddenly uncertain.

"I do!"

I do? She asked herself. In my parents' house?

"Good," he said, happy and easily appeased.

Lisanne was still wondering what she'd just agreed to as they walked into the small café. Her mom hadn't said they *couldn't*, but she had implied that 'good behavior' was the price of the invitation. She was pretty sure her mom meant no fooling around—which meant no sex.

The waitress strolled over with a jug of coffee, pouring it immediately into the two cups waiting on the table. Lisanne stared at it thoughtfully as Daniel ordered everything that could be fried.

"What?" he said, eyeing her as they leaned back to drink their coffee.

"Hungry?"

"Yeah," he said, smiling. "Starving."

"Didn't you eat last night?"

He looked down at his coffee. "Nah, didn't get around to it."

She tapped the back of his hand. "Well, you'd better get in training because Mom will feed you till you pop."

"Sounds good. I haven't had home cooking since … not for a while."

She stroked his hand. "I know."

"Um, Lis, not to sound like a pussy or anything but…"

He was uncharacteristically anxious.

"Daniel, what is it?"

"Just … just don't leave me alone with your family, okay? It's hard…"

"I think we should tell them—about you. It'll make it easier."

"Fuck no! Your dad already hates me. I don't need to give him another reason."

Lisanne stared at him in confusion.

"Dad won't hate you because you're deaf. I mean, he's not happy that we're … you know … but not because of *that*."

"Lis," Daniel said, patiently. "He won't want his only daughter dating some guy who's not all…"

"Don't say it!" she interrupted, her voice harsh. "Just don't. I want to be with you. That's what matters—that's all Dad needs to know. Anyway," she said, more quietly, "he just wants me to be happy."

Daniel shook his head bitterly.

"Yeah, but not with someone like me."

Lisanne didn't know what to say. Only time would persuade

Daniel. She hoped her dad wasn't too hard on him. Her mom had promised that her father would behave himself, but Lisanne had her doubts. It was only when her mom reminded her that this was the first time he'd had to deal with his daughter being grown up enough to have a boyfriend, that she could see it from his point of view. Sort of.

Daniel was still frowning when his food arrived, but he cheered up immediately at the sight of the enormous plate.

"Grits!" he said, happily. "God, I love this stuff."

He gave the meal his full attention, and Lisanne sat watching him.

His hair had been slightly flattened by the helmet, but spiked up the moment he put his hands through it, which he did often.

He'd changed the ring in his eyebrow to a small, black barbell, although whether that was to make it more comfortable under the helmet, or because it was less obtrusive for her parents, she didn't know.

They finished their meal and then Daniel stood outside for a smoke, while Lisanne paid the check.

They'd had a short but heated argument—she'd persuaded him that as it was her family they were visiting for Thanksgiving, she should pay for any food on the journey up. Daniel agreed only after insisting that he pay for gas.

Lisanne felt like a fool—gas would cost way more than food. Daniel was so much smarter than she was when it came to anything to do with money. Perhaps because he'd had to manage by himself. She couldn't imagine Zef did much to help. The thought made her frown. She didn't want to know exactly what Zef did, and Daniel said it was better that way—she believed him.

When she followed him outside, he was sucking the last hit of nicotine out of his cigarette before grinding the butt with his heel. He saw her and smiled, blowing the last lungful of smoke down his nose like a lazy dragon.

She wondered when would be the right moment to try and persuade him to give up smoking.

"Ready for the next slice of road, baby doll, or do you want me to rub your ass some more?"

Lisanne held in a groan. The truck stop hadn't sold cushions—she'd checked.

Daniel pulled her into a hug and kissed her hair, letting his hands drift down over the curve of her ass. He rubbed slowly and Lisanne felt her body shiver with longing.

He pushed her away gently to see her face.

"Can I come to your room tonight?" he said, holding her hips tightly. "I'll be quiet."

"Um … I don't know."

"Don't you want me, baby?"

"Yes, but…"

He leaned down and kissed her. She could taste coffee and smoke and she *still* wanted him.

"Tonight," he said, daring her to disagree.

Lisanne didn't answer. She was pretty certain her parents wouldn't make it that easy. In fact, now she thought about it, her mom hadn't said *where* Daniel would be sleeping.

Things were sure going to be different this Thanksgiving.

Reluctantly, she climbed back onto Sirona, and Daniel steered them out toward the Interstate.

After another hour of riding and wondering if she'd ever be able to feel her ass again, she would have quite happily dumped his beloved Harley into Peachtree Lake, never to see her … it … again.

She was glad mind-reading wasn't among Daniel's many talents.

They'd pre-agreed signals so she could direct him to her parents' house. Two taps on the left arm meant turn left; two on the right, the opposite; and a squeeze of his waist, slow down; three taps meant stop.

Soon they were traveling down familiar suburban streets, the occasional golf cart crossing their path. It felt strange to be home—even stranger to be arriving on the back of a motorcycle with her boyfriend.

She tapped his shoulder, and Daniel pulled up outside a large, modern house, painted pale blue. The yard at the front was tidy with a large peach tree shading the lawn on one side—it reminded Daniel of how his home had been before his parents died.

They'd just managed to dismount and pull off their helmets when Lisanne's mother came charging down the driveway.

"You're here! I was so worried!" and she pulled Lisanne into the tightest hug, kissing her eldest child repeatedly.

Daniel stood awkwardly, suddenly not knowing what to do with his hands, but wishing he'd had time for a soothing cigarette. He knew *that* wouldn't be a good start to the visit, and he was still holding their helmets.

Damn it. He badly wanted a cigarette.

Then Lisanne's mother released her, and surprised the shit out of Daniel by giving him a quick hug, too.

"Welcome to our home, Daniel."

"Thank you for inviting me, Mrs. Maclaine," he said, shyly.

"Oh, please, call me Monica."

"Okay," he smiled, nervously. "Um, Lis, could you hold these while I get the luggage, baby?"

He handed her the helmets then pulled out Lisanne's small backpack, his own messenger bag, and another plastic bag. Lisanne didn't know what was in that one.

She put the helmets away, then led him toward the front door.

Mrs. Maclaine smiled approvingly when she saw that Daniel was still carrying Lisanne's bag, as well as his own.

Then Ernie came out, and Daniel froze mid-step.

He glanced severely at Daniel before kissing his daughter.

"Good to have you home, honey," he said.

"Thanks, Dad. Um, you remember Daniel?" she replied, somewhat gingerly.

"Daniel," said her father, shortly.

"Mr. Maclaine," Daniel answered, equally shortly.

After a brief pause, her father held out his hand. Daniel put the bags on the floor, and the two men shook hands.

Lisanne's mother let out a sigh of relief.

Stage one complete. No blood was drawn.

"Where's Harry?" said Lisanne, looking around for her little brother.

"Oh, he's over at Jerry's house. You'll meet my youngest later, Daniel. You'll be sharing his room. I hope you don't mind, but Lisanne's grandparents are in our guest rooms. You'll be okay on a cot?"

"Sure," said Daniel, glancing at Lisanne, guessing she'd known about the sleeping arrangements but not told him. "Yeah, a cot's fine, thank you, Monica," he answered, politely.

He decided not to tell her that if he could sleep on a thin mattress in a police cell, he could sleep anywhere.

That kind of shit didn't go down well with parents, he figured.

"Lisanne, if you could show Daniel where he'll be sleeping, I'll make you both a drink. Iced tea okay for you, Daniel?"

"Um…" he hesitated, throwing an appalled glance at his girlfriend.

"I think Daniel might prefer coffee," said Mr. Maclaine.

"Uh, yeah, great," said Daniel, blinking in surprise.

"Coffee for the men folk, honey. You ladies can stick to tea."

Even Lisanne looked surprised, then she enveloped her father in a hug.

"Thank you, Daddy."

"Sure, baby," he said, sounding pleased.

Daniel shut out the fact that Lisanne's dad called her 'baby', as well. That shit was too weird.

Lisanne led Daniel up the stairs and opened a door on the left.

"Um, this is Harry's room," she said.

"You knew about this, didn't you?" he said, accusingly.

Lisanne shook her head.

"Not exactly. Mom didn't say. But I was thinking about it on the way up and I figured it would be either this … or they'd put the cot in the living room."

He sighed.

"Guess I'm lucky it's not in the backyard." He looked at Lisanne. "I want to know where *your* room is."

She laughed nervously, and showed him into a room across the hallway.

It wasn't the frilly, girly room Daniel had half expected. The only word to describe it was peaceful. It wasn't large, but it felt comfortable. There was a closet by the far wall, a chest of drawers, a bookshelf filled with musical scores and ratty paperbacks, and a full-size bed, covered with a pale yellow quilt.

"Nice," he said approvingly, and laid her backpack on the only chair in the room, which was standing next to a simple desk. He stood looking out of the window into the backyard. It was neat and tidy with a freshly mown lawn, and trimmed flower beds. He could see a basketball hoop fixed to the garage wall that formed the edge of the large patio.

Daniel turned to see Lisanne watching him.

"Your folks have got a nice place."

"Thank you," she said, unable to read his expression.

She walked toward him and he looped his arms around her waist, then leaned down to kiss her.

It felt strange kissing him here, in her bedroom, and she pulled away.

"What's the matter, b … Lis?"

She shrugged, and he looked at her warily.

"You … you're not regretting inviting me, are you?"

Lisanne shook her head immediately, and tightened her arms around him.

"No! Of course not. I just … I feel like I don't know how to behave in my own home. It's hard to explain."

Daniel nodded.

"I get it. I felt like that the first time I came back from boarding school. It took a while to feel like home again—I'd changed and I noticed small things that had changed around the house. It was the same but different. It felt weird."

"Yes, exactly!"

She was relieved. He understood.

"Hey," he said, a wicked gleam in his eye, "have you had a guy in your room before?"

"I haven't *had* a guy anywhere before I met you, which you know very well!"

He laughed. "So that's a no?"

"Yes, that's a no."

He smiled his sexy smile, and Lisanne felt her knees tremble. He leaned down and kissed her, his tongue seeking permission.

She opened her mouth and he claimed her.

She knew that's what he was doing, here in her family home, in her bedroom.

But then all thought fell away and she allowed her body to react the way it craved. She grabbed the front of his t-shirt and lifted it up, so she could run her hands over his hard stomach.

He groaned and deepened the kiss further, but then Lisanne heard her mother calling and she pulled away again.

Her face was flushed and Daniel was breathing heavily.

"Mom's calling," she said, huskily.

"Can we ignore her?" he whispered, licking her neck.

Lisanne shivered, and pushed him away for a third time.

"No. She'd send a search party."

"Tonight," he said.

It wasn't a question.

When they reached the kitchen, a tall skinny kid was sitting at the table drinking a soda.

"Hey, loser," said Lisanne, with a smile.

"Hey, nerd," said the kid, without turning around to look.

Daniel hadn't heard the response, but Lisanne's greeting made him smile.

Their mother, on the other hand, was less impressed.

"Honestly, you two! What sort of impression will you give Daniel?"

"The right one," said Lisanne.

"Who?" said the kid.

Lisanne rolled her eyes and poked him in the back.

"This is my brother, Harry."

"Hey, man," said Daniel, holding out his hand to shake. "'Sup?"

Harry stared openly at Daniel's pierced eyebrow and tattoos.

"Jeez, Lis. I thought you only liked nerds."

Daniel smiled and raised his eyebrow at Lisanne. She was about ready to thump her little brother.

Looking all types of gangly and awkward, Harry shook hands with Daniel.

"Is that your Harley out front?"

"Yep."

"No way!"

And Harry insisted on talking motorcycles for the next 15 minutes.

Lisanne sighed. She wished her dad were as easy to please.

Mr. Maclaine re-entered the kitchen and Daniel stood up abruptly, making Lisanne jump. Her father seemed surprised, too.

He nodded at Daniel, who looked about ready to make a run for it—or swing a punch—Lisanne wasn't sure which, but his tension was making her nervous. Her mother looked at them both sympathetically.

"Um, I brought this for you, sir, ma'am, uh, Monica," said Daniel, thrusting the plastic bag at Mrs. Maclaine.

"Why, that was thoughtful of you. But please sit down, Daniel: you're our guest. We want you to relax. Don't we, Ernie?" she said, throwing a meaningful look at her husband.

Lisanne's dad grunted in reply.

With an exasperated sigh, Monica opened the bag and took out a rather squashed box of chocolate covered pralines.

"Crap," said Daniel. "It's melted. Shit. Sorry."

His ears went red when he realized he'd just sworn twice—in front of Lisanne's parents.

Monica's face was a little tight, but Lisanne thought it was because she was trying not to laugh.

"Um, yeah, they were my mom's favorites, so I thought…" his words died away.

"I'm sure they'll be fine," Monica said, with a heartfelt smile. "And I think this is for you, Ernie," she continued, passing her husband a bottle of Jack Daniels.

"You're not old enough to buy liquor," he barked.

Daniel's face closed down. "My brother is," he said quietly, neither admitting nor denying that he'd bought the whiskey.

"Ernie!" Monica hissed.

"Hmm, very thoughtful," Lisanne's dad bit out.

Lisanne wanted to drop her head in her hands. She thought Daniel had had the best idea, when he looked like he wanted to make a run for it.

She held his hand under the table and squeezed his fingers.

"Should we go for a walk?" she said.

What she really meant was: should we get the hell out of here so you can have a cigarette before you blow like Krakatoa?

Daniel nodded, gratefully.

"Yeah, thanks, baby doll."

Lisanne's father didn't look very happy at hearing his daughter's nickname, but after a stern glance from his wife, wisely decided to say nothing about it.

"We're going out for a while, Mom."

"Of course, honey. I'm sure Daniel would like to see the lake. Why don't you take my car? Dinner's at six."

"Thanks, Mom," said Lisanne, kissing her mother on the cheek.

Daniel almost sprinted to the front door as Lisanne collected her mom's car keys. He'd already lit a cigarette by the time she closed the door behind them.

He blew tension out of his body along with a lungful of smoke. Lisanne stroked his back, as if calming a wild animal.

He shook his head.

"Fuck!"

Lisanne gave a small laugh. "It could have gone worse."

"You think?"

"Yes, they could have walked in on us having sex."

Daniel burst out laughing, relieved that Lisanne wasn't pissed at him for swearing, or the way he'd behaved.

"Yeah, that wouldn't have gone down well."

Lisanne wound her arms around his waist and leaned her head against his chest. She looked up as he blew another puff of smoke away from her.

"Thank you for coming," she said.

He smiled as he stubbed out his cigarette.

"'S'okay, baby doll. Come on, let's go see this lake."

Monica's car was a red Honda hatchback and Lisanne couldn't help luxuriating in the wide, comfortable, cushioned seat. So different from Sirona's questionable charms.

She pulled her seatbelt on and waited, while Daniel worked out how to shift the seat back and make room for his long legs.

"Oh God!" she said, as she turned on the engine.

"What, baby?" he said, frowning at her, as she pulled onto the road.

"I can't believe Mom is listening to this radio station! The music is so…"

Lisanne choked on the words when she saw Daniel's face.

"Oh, I'm so sorry! Daniel…"

He nodded at her apology and stared out of the window. Lisanne reached over to turn off the radio, but he placed his hand over hers and pushed it back.

"Lis, I don't expect you to live without music just because I'm around."

"I don't, I…"

"I've seen you do it, baby doll. I've seen you turn off your iPod and stop talking about bands while I'm around. I know music is important to you. Shit, I totally get that. Don't stop listening to music because of me. Fuck, if anything, you have to listen to it for both of us."

Suddenly Lisanne's eyes were too full of tears for her to carry on driving in safety. She pulled over to the curb and covered her face with her hands, sobbing.

Daniel unclipped his seatbelt, moving across to pull her into his arms.

"Don't cry for me, baby doll. Please don't cry."

He spoke the words into her hair as her tears soaked into his t-shirt.

For several minutes, Lisanne cried out all the stress and tension of the day, and the pain she felt from Daniel's words.

He was right, of course. She *had* avoided listening to music or talking about music when he was around, because she hadn't wanted to hurt him, to remind him of what he'd lost. She felt bad enough that he picked her up from all her rehearsals, and had come to all her gigs.

When she was finally hiccuping the last of her tears, Daniel hitched up his t-shirt and wiped her eyes.

"Better, baby?"

She nodded.

"Sorry."

He kissed her hair again. "Don't be. Not for me. Not for caring about me."

Finally, she was composed enough to drive again, but they didn't do much walking when they reached the lake—they simply found a shady tree to lie under. Lisanne rested her head on Daniel's chest, and he drew lazy circles on her shoulder with his fingers.

It was a moment of much needed peace.

Eventually, Lisanne struggled into a sitting position and Daniel opened his eyes, smiling up at her.

"There's a place near here, a sort of outside mini-mall, where we can get a coffee if you like?"

"Yeah, I could definitely go a coffee. This is your home town. Let's see the sights."

Lisanne laughed. "Well, we're sitting by the lake—that's about it. Unless you want to see the golf course?"

"Wow, life in the fast lane," Daniel deadpanned.

Lisanne smiled shyly. "Small town girl, that's me."

He sat up and kissed her on the tip of her nose. "Wouldn't

have you any other way, baby doll."

At the mall, they strolled hand in hand to the nearest coffee shop and sat down outside, enjoying the warm afternoon sun.

Lisanne was hoping that some of the girls she'd known from high school would just happen to walk past. Daniel looked so hot sitting with his Ray Bans covering his eyes, and his t-shirt tight across his muscular shoulders and back. Just once she'd have liked to have been envied by the girls who never gave her the time of day—just for a change. Completely shallow—and she didn't care.

But when the waitress started flirting with Daniel as if Lisanne didn't exist, she changed her mind. It must have been so obvious he was out of her league, that the waitress didn't even try to be subtle.

"What can I get for you folks?" she said, as her eyes roved up and down Daniel's undeniably hot body.

"Lis?"

"Um, I'll have a caramel Frappuccino, please."

"And what can I tempt you with?" said the waitress, sucking her pencil suggestively.

Daniel raised his eyebrows as he replied. "Black coffee, please."

"Oh, I so agree," giggled the waitress. "I can't stand all those fake drinks—I prefer my coffee straight up."

Daniel reached over and took Lisanne's hand in his.

"Yeah? My baby doll likes her drinks sweet—just like her."

Lisanne blushed bright red, grateful and delighted by his public display, but the waitress turned away with an annoyed huff.

"Wow, I can't believe she was hitting on you right in front of me! I mean, come on!"

Daniel gave her his sexy smirk.

"Told you I was irresistible, baby doll," he said, immodestly. "But I only want you."

Lisanne's body began to overheat, so she was relieved when the waitress returned with her iced coffee.

"You folks let me know if I can help you with anything else," she said, sullenly.

Daniel winked at her, which sent the waitress away with a smile on her face.

"You're so bad!" hissed Lisanne.

Daniel shrugged. "Didn't want to ruin her day."

CHAPTER 15

They sat for a while longer, enjoying their drinks and the sunshine. Much to Lisanne's disappointment, none of the girls from her high school seemed to be around.

Eventually, Lisanne sighed and admitted it was time to head back.

"Grandma and Pops will have arrived by now," she said. "That's my mom's mom, and my dad's dad."

"Great," said Daniel, with exaggerated irony.

It was her turn to reassure him.

"They'll love you—besides, I thought you said you were irresistible?"

He shrugged. "Shoulda read the small print."

Daniel tensed visibly as Lisanne drove them back to her house. The relaxed, sexy boy she loved was now spiky and closed off, his fingers drumming restlessly on his thighs.

She reached over with her right hand and touched his knee.

"It'll be fine," she said.

He grimaced and looked out of the window.

But when they arrived back at the house, things got weird.

Pops was standing out front with love in his eyes, as he gazed at Daniel's Harley. Not only that, Lisanne's staid, twinset and pearl wearing Grandma Olsen was waxing lyrical about her first boyfriend who'd had a motorcycle, and talking the ear off of Pops.

"Oh, Marlon Brando had nothing on him. 'What are you rebelling against, Johnny?' 'Whaddya got?' Such nonsense! My boy sure knew how to wear a pair of Levis, I'll say that much for

279

him." She turned and saw Lisanne. "There's my little bunny!" and descended on her, smothering Lisanne with pink-lipstick kisses.

"Hi, Grandma," said Lisanne, embarrassed by her nickname. She could see Daniel smirking at her out of the corner of her eye. "Um, this is my boyfriend Daniel."

Right on cue, she blushed on the word 'boyfriend'.

"My goodness!" said Grandma Olsen, scanning Daniel's tattoos and pierced eyebrow. "Well, you certainly match with your motorcycle. I'm very happy to meet you, Daniel."

"Likewise, ma'am," said Daniel, who assumed they'd be shaking hands.

He didn't know Grandma Olsen.

She pulled him down to her height and planted a loud, pink kiss on his cheek.

Daniel looked taken aback and Lisanne wanted to laugh at the expression on his face.

"Um, this is my grandfather, Pops."

"Pleased to meet you, son. The name's Harold Maclaine, but this little miss called me 'Pops' before she could walk, and it kinda stuck."

They shook hands and then Daniel had to answer dozens of questions about his bike.

"She's called 'Sirona'," added Lisanne, helpfully.

"Who is?" said Grandma Olsen, looking around her as if another person was about to materialize underneath the peach tree in the garden.

"His motorcycle," snickered Lisanne.

Pops looked glassy-eyed. "That sure is a pretty name for a pretty lady."

Daniel smirked at Lisanne, folding his arms across his chest.

"Some people appreciate her charms, baby doll," he said.

Dinner was a noisy affair, and at first Lisanne was worried about how Daniel would cope. But at Pops' request, they were seated at the same end of the table. Lisanne had no idea that a motorcycle fanatic lurked beneath the benign surface of his gray haired exterior.

Poor Daniel was barely permitted to take a bite of the excellent lasagna and salad that Monica had made, before a cascade of questions poured forth.

"I heard that tuning the exhaust is very easy to get wrong on a Harley," said Pops. "The stock 1¾ inch dual header pipes are hard to beat."

Daniel nodded. "Sure, but they're not tunable. SuperTrapp make tunable mufflers. You just need to install baffle cores."

Tunable, untunable, there was nothing musical about *that* conversation: Lisanne tuned out.

She turned to see her grandma watching her.

"Well, bunny, he seems like a very pleasant young man."

Lisanne smiled. "Thanks, grandma."

"Handsome, too, although it's a shame about all those tattoos—and as for that ridiculous piece of metal through his eyebrow, I can't imagine what he was thinking." She patted Lisanne's hand. "You'll be a calming influence on him. You've always been such a sensible girl."

Lisanne winced. For the first time ever, she was glad Daniel hadn't heard what had been said.

Harry, sitting on the other side of Pops, seemed equally taken with Daniel. His eyes kept flicking back to Daniel as he listened to them discussing baffling terms such as cams, combustion chambers and carburetors, with ease and mutual enjoyment.

Lisanne knew her father had little interest in fixing engines— any trouble and he was straight down the auto repair shop.

For Harry, it had been a new experience in male bonding.

After dinner, Lisanne helped her mother clear the table, and Daniel was left to the mercy of Pops and Grandma Olsen. Lisanne regretted having promised him that she wouldn't leave him alone, but really, she had no choice.

She cleared and stacked the plates while her mom loaded them into the dishwasher.

"Lisanne, I swear that young man of yours is in a dream half the time! I called his name three times before he answered."

Lisanne took a deep breath. Daniel's expressed preference was that Lisanne's family didn't know about his deafness. But seeing her mother's amused expression, Lisanne felt she had no choice but to defend him by telling the truth.

"That's because he didn't hear you, Mom."

"Well, I could tell that. I don't know where he was, but it must have been somewhere nice."

"No, Mom. I mean he *couldn't* hear you. Daniel is deaf."

"Excuse me?"

Lisanne almost laughed.

"Daniel is deaf. He started to lose his hearing when he went to high school. He became completely deaf nearly two years ago."

"But ... but...!"

"He lip reads. That's why he doesn't answer you if he can't see your face." Lisanne paused as her mother took in this extraordinary piece of information. "I told you he was amazing," she said, quietly.

Her mother sat down at the kitchen table looking stunned, staring at her daughter as if she was waiting for the punch line.

"He can't hear? At all?"

Lisanne shook her head.

"But how does he manage? At school? In his classes?"

"Like I said: he lip reads then writes up his notes later. He's really smart. He helps me with our Introduction to Business class." Lisanne rolled her eyes.

"But..." her mother was still struggling with the concept. "But he doesn't wear a hearing aid."

"No. They're for people who have some residual hearing. They don't help him. Not anymore."

"Good Heavens," said her mother. "Good Heavens!" Then she looked up. "Is he safe on that motorcycle of his? I mean, if he can't hear the traffic?"

"He's deaf, not blind, Mom," said Lisanne, patiently.

She knew her mom was only asking the questions because

she'd never met a completely deaf person before.

"Is it genetic? I mean, would his children be deaf?" Lisanne's mother flushed red when she realized how that might sound to her daughter.

"No, Mom. The doctors think it was because of a virus—it's not genetic."

"Well … well, that's something."

Lisanne leaned against the kitchen sink, giving her mother time to take it all in.

"What about those implants?" Monica said. "I saw people talking about them on *Ellen*."

"Cochlear implants?"

"Yes, that's it! Could those help Daniel?"

"Maybe," said Lisanne, slowly. "But it's quite a big surgery and there are risks. Sometimes the operation can damage facial nerves. It's rare, but it can happen. And it doesn't always restore hearing of any quality. Besides, it's a bit like saying there's something wrong with Daniel—that he needs to be fixed."

"Oh," said her mother, her mouth opening and closing, lost for words. "But … but wouldn't it help?"

Lisanne gestured helplessly. "Maybe, I don't know. He doesn't like to talk about it."

"Well," said her mother, again. "Does your father know?"

Lisanne shook her head.

"Should I tell him?"

"I guess," said Lisanne. "It's not as if he could dislike Daniel any more than he already does."

Her mother frowned. "That's not fair: your father is trying very hard. It's not easy for him knowing that his daughter … that you're a young woman."

"You mean because I'm sleeping with Daniel."

"Yes, that's exactly what I mean," said her mother, sharply. "I think your father is behaving very well under the circumstances."

Lisanne sighed and looked away.

At that moment Pops came wandering in.

"Everything okay in here, ladies?"

"Sure, Pops," said Lisanne, quietly.

"That's a very interesting young man you've got there," he said. "Knows his motorcycles. Rebuilt Sirona from scrap by the sound of it."

Lisanne rolled her eyes.

"You're not calling her 'Sirona' as well, are you? Because I've got to say, Pops, after riding on her for over three hours, I was about ready to throw it in the lake."

Pops snorted. "No taste some people, unlike young Daniel. Pity he's deaf."

Lisanne stared.

"What … how … when … how did you know, Pops?"

Pops stared back.

"Didn't know it was supposed to be a secret. It's nothing to be ashamed of."

"Well, *I* certainly didn't guess," said Monica, looking slightly miffed.

"But how did you know, Pops?"

Pops smiled. "Friend of mine, Mal Peters. He's damn near deaf. I've gotten used to making sure he's facing me when I'm talking to him. I noticed you did the same thing with Daniel and it got me wondering. Figured the rest out for myself. He hides it well, although I'm not sure why he wants to."

Lisanne stared at her fingers. "It's complicated, Pops."

"Nothing complicated about the truth," he replied, but not unkindly.

"It's how Daniel wants it," explained Lisanne, with a lift of her shoulder. "He says he's tired of people judging him when they know."

Lisanne's mom looked guilty as she listened to her daughter's words.

"Well, well, his choice," said Pops. "I'm going to head for bed now—this old man needs his beauty sleep."

He kissed Lisanne goodnight and waved to Monica.

"Well," said Monica, watching her father-in-law disappear

upstairs, "I suppose I'd better tell your dad. He'll be surprised, that's for sure."

"Thanks, Mom," said Lisanne, giving her mother a big hug.

Then she left Monica in the kitchen, shaking her head tiredly.

Daniel was still sitting at the table with a slightly glazed expression, as Grandma Olsen continued with her blow-by-blow description of her gallbladder operation.

"And the gallstones were the size of walnuts. You certainly don't want to try passing anything that size!"

Daniel winced.

"Well," she said, with a heavy sigh, "I shouldn't eat this late—it's not good for me. I'm going to go and lie down, but nobody get worried if they hear me wandering around in the night. It'll be indigestion—that, or my bowels."

Daniel scraped his hands over his face, obviously wishing he hadn't lip read that last sentence.

"Come on, let's go watch some TV," said Lisanne, pulling him up.

Daniel stood, a grateful expression on his face, and willingly allowed her to lead him into the TV den.

When they'd settled on one of the sofas, she snuggled up to him.

"How was that?" she asked, before planting a soft kiss on his lips.

"Yeah, okay, until your gran started describing—well, you heard her. I thought my lasagna was going to make a repeat performance."

"Sorry about that," she giggled.

Then she sat up straighter.

"Um, Daniel?"

"What, baby doll? You look guilty as all hell. What did you do?" he teased her.

"Pops guessed … I mean, about you."

Daniel's smile faded. "Damn it. I thought I'd nailed that."

"Well, you did, as far as everyone else was concerned, but he's got a friend who's deaf, so he just guessed. Anyway, Mom knows, too. I've asked her to tell Dad."

Daniel sighed. "Don't worry about it, baby. I was dumb to think I could get away with it for the whole vacation."

She kissed his pouting lips, determined to make him forget his disappointment.

They'd had just a few minutes to themselves and Lisanne was cuddled up to Daniel on the sofa, pretending to watch *Arrow*. Really, she was busy kissing Daniel's neck and suggestively rubbing her hand over his thigh.

"You carry on doing that, baby doll, and your dad will have me thrown out," he whispered.

Lisanne giggled.

"Am I turning you on?"

"Lis, you walk into the room and I get a boner," he said, with a smile.

She blushed happily, and was just running her hands under his t-shirt, when Harry walked in.

"Oh, cool," he said glancing at the TV, then plopping himself down on the chair and halting his sister's make out session. "You've got the subtitles on."

"I know," said Lisanne, looking up as her parents came in and sat down on the other sofa.

"Whatever," said Harry, his eyes fixed on the screen.

"It's quite useful having subtitles," said Lisanne's mother, glancing at her daughter.

Daniel caught the look between them and smiled at Lisanne, placing a gentle kiss on her temple. Lisanne's father frowned at the public display of affection, but refrained from speaking. Which was a first.

Shortly after that, Harry yawned and said he was heading for bed. Monica looked pointedly at Lisanne, clearly suggesting that she should do the same.

"Yeah, me, too," said Lisanne, playing along, "it's been some day."

Daniel stood up immediately.

"Sleep well," said Monica. "You'll both feel so much better

after *a good night's sleep.*"

Lisanne caught the message without any trouble. It wasn't like her mom was blessed with subtlety.

As they walked up the stairs, Daniel whispered in her ear.

"I'll see you later, baby doll."

She shivered with longing.

The side of his mouth lifted in a smile and he disappeared into Harry's room. She could hear the low murmur of conversation. Feeling nervous and overwhelmingly *naughty*, she hurried to brush her teeth and wash her face, wondering if there were any other preparations she should make. She ransacked her drawers for something to wear. All her pajamas were so childish—for the first time, she wished she had sexier night wear.

In the end she gave up and pulled on one of Daniel's t-shirts that she'd stolen out of his bag, and changed into some pretty lace panties.

She rearranged the pillows a dozen times before she was satisfied with them. It would be nice to have some room in the bed—at college, she only had a single. This would be a vast improvement.

And she waited.

She stared at her clock as the minutes ticked past, listening to the sounds of her parents going to bed and her grandmother talking loudly to herself. The clock was in the shape of Mickey Mouse's head and for the first time, she realized it was actually kind of scary. The large metal ears were completely spherical so whichever angle you saw them from, they always looked the same. Suddenly it seemed creepy.

She lay down to wait, feeling turned on, nervous and impatient, all at once.

The hands of the clock crept around as the house descended into silence. She felt her eyes weighted with sleep, so she sat up straighter, forcing herself to stay awake.

Her mind began to run through the day: from the tortuous bike ride, her father's ill humor, her mother's refereeing, the flirty waitress, breaking down in the car and what Daniel had said about music. He'd been right, so right. She *had* turned away from music when he was with her. Now she was alone, she had time to think about what he'd said—that she had to hear the music for him, too. She knew he must miss it more than he ever said. Why wasn't he angrier? She'd be angry if she lost her music—hell, she'd be a raving lunatic. How much rage did he hold inside himself? Or had he come to terms with it before he'd met her?

She realized she still had a lot to learn about him—if he'd just let her in.

With too many thoughts still whirling through her mind, her body ceded the battle against emotional exhaustion, and she drifted to sleep.

She woke, shocked and disorientated, when she heard a noise in the room.

"What?!"

She saw Daniel silhouetted against the window. He'd opened the curtains and was staring out at the three-quarter moon.

He turned to look at her, as the moon's light cast shadows across his cheekbones, one corner of his mouth lifted in a smile.

At first she thought he was naked, but as he moved toward her, she realized he was wearing a pair of dark boxer briefs.

He put something on her bedside table, but he didn't speak. She felt the bed move as his warm, hard body slid in next to her.

"Daniel," she breathed.

His silence engulfed her and she realized he couldn't see her lips, even with the moon's faint light. She reached over to turn on the lamp, but he caught her hand and brought it to his lips. She thought he was going to kiss her, but instead he opened his mouth and sucked her fingers one by one, lazily wrapping his tongue around them.

She was panting already, her body tingling for more of his touch.

He released her pinky finger and leaned down toward her. Again she thought he was going to kiss her and she lifted her face eagerly toward him. Instead he licked the base of her throat, laying a trail of wet kisses down to her chest.

She felt his hands pushing up the t-shirt until it was bunched above her breasts, and she gasped as his teeth fastened over her left nipple, and his hand stroked and squeezed the right.

Her body automatically lifted toward him as she inhaled sharply. She felt her hips press into a hard bulge at the front of his boxer briefs.

The silence deepened, and all she could hear was the nighttime concerto as the house settled to sleep, and the twinned breaths, spiraling out of their bodies.

She dragged her nails down his back and heard his soft moan in response. He lifted his head from her breasts and kissed her languorously, his tongue insisting on dominating her mouth.

She pulled him to her more tightly, winding her hands around his neck, feeling his hard weight pressing down on her.

He leaned away from her and spoke quietly.

"I can't read your lips, baby doll. If you want me to stop, just … slap my shoulder or something—I'll get the message."

She pushed him gently and he rolled away from her. She started to tug her t-shirt over her head, and he quickly reached up to help her.

As soon as the material was removed, he pushed her back onto the bed, kissing and sucking her breasts, placing small bites between them, and circling his tongue around her nipples, teasing them until she wanted to cry out.

She jammed her fist into her mouth, overwhelmed by the sensations and the knowledge that this was in her family home, in her bedroom, and that her parents were just yards away—and she was doing all the things her mother and father didn't want to know she did.

He'd reached her belly and was biting her hipbone, swirling his tongue around her belly button. Then his hands drifted lower, tugging at the lace on her panties. She took a deep breath and lifted her ass off of the bed, so he could slide the skimpy material away.

She gasped when his head went still lower and she realized what he was going to do. Before she could say anything, she felt his warm mouth on her inner thigh and the prickle of his stubble, as he carefully parted her legs.

She was mortified. Surely he wasn't going to…? But this was Daniel—and he did. She stifled a cry as she felt his tongue pressing inside her. It was just so wrong—and it felt so good.

His fingers were on her, too, circling, sliding, moving slowly in and out. She gasped again, and her hips bucked as her body bathed in pleasure, while her mind told her it wasn't right.

With the experience of weeks with Daniel, she realized her body was building toward orgasm. Part of her felt like she should stop it before she was dangerously out of control, and the other part had already given up, saturated with the feelings that he was creating.

She jammed her pillow over her head as he opened her legs wider. It was up to her to muffle the sounds coming from her mouth—he would never know how much she wanted to scream his name.

He couldn't hear her but he could feel her, and knew that she was coming hard.

He pulled the pillow away from her face, and swallowed her gasps with his lips and tongue.

"You've fucked my face, baby doll; you've ridden my fingers; now you're going to ride my dick," he whispered.

While her body still trembled, he reached over to her bedside table, picking up the packet he'd left there. As if from far away, she heard the rustle as he pulled out the foil packet and tore it open. Then he stood up, dropped his briefs and sat back on the bed, unfurling the condom over his erection.

She was surprised and alarmed when he rolled her onto her stomach.

"No!" she said, horrified.

He couldn't hear her. Of course not.

But it wasn't what she thought, either. He pulled her up onto her knees and reached between her legs, positioning himself at her entrance.

Relief, surprise, astonishment washed through her.

For a moment she'd thought he was going to do something else entirely, but this was good. This was amazing—it felt so deep and he groaned softly, pushing in and out of her in long, filling strokes.

His fingers gripped her hips tightly, and she could hear the slap of his skin against her body. It was strange not to be able to see him, but this new position felt raw and deep.

She felt her body tremble. He felt it, too, and started to move faster, whispering words she couldn't hear.

His breathing started to become labored, and then she felt his fingers reaching around between her legs once more and she gasped, amazed that her body was responding again.

Her legs and arms gave way as he shuddered into her and, for a moment, she was crushed by his weight.

He pulled out of her carefully and peppered her back with soft kisses.

"Lis, Lis, are you okay? Lis, baby?"

She rolled onto her back, still gasping, and breathed her pleasure into his mouth, kissing him hard.

A small sound escaped him as he kissed her back.

She heard the faint snap as he pulled the condom off, and watched as he tied a knot in the end before dropping it onto the floor.

Then he pulled her back into his chest and they fell into a deep sleep, his arms and legs entwined with hers, expressing with his body what he couldn't say with words.

Daniel woke feeling deeply relaxed. Lisanne's soft, silky skin was pressed against his, and a sense of calm filled him.

He couldn't explain why, but it had been important to him to have sex with her last night. Maybe it was something to do with making sure she still wanted him, even when she was back with her family, away from the heady rush of college independence.

But it had been pretty damn good. There was still a lot more he wanted to try, experiences to explore with her, and he'd have given a case of Jack Daniels to be able to spend a whole day in bed doing just that. But he had high hopes for the future.

He became aware that his usual morning boner was even harder than normal, pointing hopefully in the direction of her smooth, round ass. He groaned as the possibilities ran like a porn show through his mind, but one glance at her ugly Mickey Mouse clock told him that a morning fuck was out of the question, unless he really did want her parents to catch him boning their only daughter.

Reluctantly, he sat up and saw her lips move as if she was saying something, but her eyes remained closed. Frowning, he looked at her mouth again, but he could tell she was deeply asleep, and her words were lost to him.

Sighing, he pulled on his boxer briefs and walked quietly toward the door. With one last look, he stepped out into the hallway and closed the door softly behind him.

He made it back into Harry's room without meeting anyone, and the kid was still asleep.

Daniel scooped up his jeans and headed for the shower. The water was plentiful and hot and he took a few minutes to enjoy life's simple pleasures, and jerk off.

After he'd dried himself, he brushed his teeth and, swiping his hand across the steamed up mirror, decided he'd shave off the two day stubble.

He'd forgotten to ask Lisanne what time her family got up in the morning, so he decided to head out to the backyard for a smoke and wait to see who was awake. But as he left the bathroom, still only wearing his jeans, he bumped into Monica in her robe and slippers.

"Good morning, Daniel. You're an early riser." Then she gasped, her eyes fixed on his chest or, more specifically, his nipple rings. "My goodness!" she said, clearing her throat.

"I hope I didn't wake you," he said, reining in a smirk as he watched her try to pull her eyes up to his.

"Um, sorry, what?" she said, finally managing to snatch her

gaze away from his chest, her face a little flushed. "Um, do come and have some breakfast whenever you like."

"Thanks, Monica. I'll do that."

He returned to Harry's room where the boy was lying on his back, eyes closed and mouth open.

Daniel pulled on a t-shirt and a pair of sneakers, made sure he had his smokes in his pants' pocket, and ran lightly down the stairs.

Monica was standing in the kitchen waiting for a jug of coffee to percolate. She gave a slightly bashful smile as a fully dressed Daniel headed out to the back porch and had his first cigarette of the day.

He was surprised when Monica came out to join him.

She looked nervous and he wondered what she was going to say.

"Um, I don't suppose I could have one of those, could I?"

Daniel blinked in surprise, then handed her the cigarette packet and lit one for her.

"Thanks!" she said, a look of bliss on her face. "Don't tell Lisanne, she'll just start nagging. I'm supposed to have given up, but every now and then…"

Daniel raised his eyebrows. "Hey, not my secret."

Monica smiled. "I'm surprised she hasn't nagged you to give up."

He shook his head. "She's never said anything. I didn't think she minded."

Monica laughed in disbelief. "Really? She hates smoking. Always going on about what a horrible, antisocial habit it is. Oh well, you're lucky not to have her nagging at you—she's tenacious."

Daniel frowned. He wondered why she hadn't said anything to him. Were there other things that she kept hidden? He suddenly felt like he didn't know her as well as he thought, and the feeling bothered him.

"Coffee?" Monica asked.

He'd been looking the other way and hadn't noticed that

she'd spoken.

She tapped him on the arm. "Coffee, Daniel?"

"Yeah, that'd be great, thanks. Black, three sugars."

"Three sugars!" she huffed. "You're so lucky to be able to get away with that."

She wandered inside, muttering to herself.

He followed her in and gratefully accepted a cup of steaming hot coffee, as Lisanne staggered down the stairs looking tired and slightly disheveled. Girl really liked her sleep. He couldn't help grinning at her and as she smiled back, he ran his tongue across his teeth, a knowing look highlighting the sexy smirk on his face.

She blushed instantly and dropped her eyes, clearly reliving some of the things he'd done to her the night before.

Harry wandered in, a useful decoy for Lisanne's embarrassment, and helped himself to a bowl of cereal, mumbling something that may have been a greeting.

Daniel sat down next to him, and Monica told him to help himself. He dug into a pile of toast, smearing it with butter and jelly.

Food seemed to have perked Harry up and he challenged Daniel to a little one-on-one basketball. Daniel laughed and made some disparaging comment about Harry's height, and they were off, playing aggressively on the makeshift court.

Monica watched for a moment, a look of surprised pleasure on her face. Then she turned to her daughter.

"Lisanne, how many, um, piercings does Daniel have?"

Lisanne froze, with her spoon halfway to her mouth.

"Mom!"

Her mother looked embarrassed.

"I just happened to see him coming out of the shower and he hadn't put a shirt on. Well, I couldn't help noticing his … his, um, jewelry."

"So, you've seen his nipple rings," said Lisanne boldly, even as her cheeks reddened.

"Yes, quite."

"And you want to know if he has *more* piercings?!"

Monica's face matched Lisanne's by this point.

"Forget I asked," muttered Monica.

That would take some doing.

Her mother turned to the coffee, just for something to do.

"Oh, I ran into Rachel Brandt at the store yesterday. Apparently she's letting Sonia have a party there tonight. She said you should stop by. Daniel, too, of course."

Lisanne pulled a face.

"I don't know why Sonia would invite me—we were never friends at high school."

"Maybe not," said Monica, firmly, "but Rachel and I *are* friends, so I'm sure you'd be very welcome. Besides," she said, raising her eyebrows, "I'd have thought you and Daniel would like a reason to get away from the oldies for an evening."

It was a fair point. Although Lisanne would have gone some way to avoid Sonia Brandt, she knew Daniel would like a breather. A party could be just the thing. Then something else occurred to her: Sonia was one of the high school crowd who'd never given Lisanne the time of day, turning up with a hot boyfriend … yeah, she really liked the idea of *that*.

"Fine, we'll go, Mom, if Daniel wants to."

"He seems to be getting along with your brother."

"Yeah," said Lisanne, smiling.

It had been a surprise to her how responsive Harry was being. With the rest of the family he mostly just grunted, but Daniel seemed to encourage him to speak whole sentences. Which was almost unnerving.

Ernie entered the kitchen and sniffed the air, his mouth twisting with disgust as he smelt the old cigarette smoke that lingered by the porch.

Monica saw his reaction and made herself very busy putting more bread in the toaster.

"Lisanne," said Ernie, sharply, "I don't want you to be alone in your room with him—with Daniel."

Both Lisanne and her mother looked up. Lisanne was

crimson again.

"Excuse me?"

"Not at all. For no reason. Is that clear?"

"Ernie!"

"Someone needs to say it, Monica," he snapped. "Lisanne: is that clear?"

Feeling mutinous, Lisanne nodded curtly and left the room, furious and embarrassed.

For fuck's sake! She was nearly 19 and her dad was still telling her who she could or could not have in her room? He was such a hypocrite! He knew they were sleeping together, but he just didn't want it to happen under his roof.

Then Lisanne wondered if he'd heard something. She was instantly mortified—perhaps she hadn't been as quiet as she'd thought. Oh God! Imagine if her father *had* heard! It didn't bear thinking about. Did that make *her* the hypocrite?

With her heart hammering, and her befuddled brain existing in a general state of denial, she hurried up the stairs but as she did so, she noticed a burning feeling between her thighs. Slightly panicked, she hurried into the bathroom and stripped off her clothes, examining herself in the mirror.

Holy hell! The skin between her thighs was bright red—stubble burn from Daniel's scruff—between her legs! Would the morning's humiliation never end?

Feeling miserable, she showered quickly and pulled on a pair of jeans, but then found they were far too uncomfortable. She rubbed baby lotion on her the inflamed patches and instantly felt soothed. Digging through her closet, she found a floaty, knee-length skirt that her mom had bought for her, which she'd never worn. She felt a little awkward, being unused to something so damn girly, but it was all she'd got. She matched it with chucks. Great. Sore and style free. Could this day get any worse? Then she thought of the party she'd agreed to go to, and groaned.

Below her window, the sound of laughter drifted upwards, and her face softened as she looked out to see Daniel and Harry relaxed and enjoying themselves. Given the chance, she really believed Daniel could charm anyone. Given the chance, could he even charm her father? Her face fell—it didn't seem likely.

She headed downstairs and sent a long text message to Kirsty, while sitting on the porch watching Daniel and Harry. In truth, she could have watched Daniel play sport for hours, ogling the way his lean muscles moved under his t-shirt.

They finished the game they'd been contesting, and Daniel came over to sit next to her, leaning in and kissing her neck.

Harry rolled his eyes but said nothing. That was his *sister*.

Daniel smiled at the revolted expression on Harry's face and pulled Lisanne's fingers to his lips.

Harry shook his head as he stomped back into the kitchen. He had no idea why a cool guy like Daniel would like his sister, let alone want to *kiss* her.

"So, what's on the menu of today's exciting events," Daniel whispered into Lisanne's hair.

She turned to face him. "You gave me stubble rash!" she hissed.

Daniel took a moment to understand what she'd said. He examined her face and neck, then raised his eyebrows.

"Where'd I do that, baby doll?" he asked, although by the look on his face, he'd already guessed.

Lisanne slapped his arm. "You know where!" she snapped.

He smirked at her and ran his hand over his smooth cheeks. "Yeah? Well, I shaved this morning so we're good to go again."

She shook her head. "Dad knows."

"Knows what?"

"That we were … last night!"

Daniel frowned. "You sure?"

"Yes! He told me I wasn't to be alone in my room with you."

"You going to do what he says, baby doll?"

Which was the crux of Lisanne's problem. *Was she?*

Daniel stood up and stretched, exposing a tanned sliver of skin above the waistband of his jeans.

"Let me know," he said, sounding irritated.

Lisanne grabbed hold of his hand, and he looked down.

"Don't be mad at me. This … it's all *new*. Please…"

Daniel sighed. "I know, I get it. But, fuck! I just want you all the time, baby doll. At school you share a room, and my place is … and now it's the holidays and you're just across the hall. It's driving me crazy. *You* drive me crazy."

Lisanne tingled with pleasure at his words. She didn't think she'd ever be able to hear that enough.

"Do you want to go to a party tonight?" she said, temporarily changing the subject. "It's a girl I went to high school with—my mom is a friend of her mom's. I don't know—would you like to?"

He shrugged and looked back toward the kitchen. "Sure, why not? A party I can do."

At that moment Harry came strolling back out with a can of soda, and plopped down on the porch.

"So, are we going or what?"

Lisanne frowned. "'We'? Who's 'we'? Going where?"

Harry ignored her. "They've got Virtua Racing, Street Fighter II, Mortal Kombat, Call of Duty, Mario Karts, Pacman, Metal Slug—you know: the classics."

"Cool," said Daniel.

"What?" snorted Lisanne.

"Harry's going to take me to the local arcade," said Daniel, winking at her. "You said you wanted me to see the sights."

Lisanne groaned. Spending the morning watching her boyfriend play stupid video games with her little brother was not her idea of fun at all. She'd imagined finding somewhere to go and lie under the trees again, make-out and enjoy some quality time alone. Certainly not with *Harry* tagging along! But it seemed that while she was being lectured by her dad, her boyfriend and her brother had been making other plans.

Just great.

Lisanne had no choice but to agree. At least they'd be away from her parents for a while.

At the arcade, she sat listening to Kate Vigo on her iPod, and texting Rodney who was visiting family in Tuscaloosa, while

Daniel and Harry played something that involved cartoon characters beating the shit out of each other. Fun times.

Lisanne noticed that the arcade was getting a lot busier. That was probably because it was the Thanksgiving holidays, and people were taking time off from school and work. Tomorrow would be the big family day.

Daniel walked over and draped a casual arm around her shoulder.

"We should get out of here," he whispered, while placing a warm kiss on her cheek.

"Really? I thought you wanted to go and do that racing game thingy—not that I'm arguing…"

He gave her a tight smile. "It's going to kick off in here any minute, Lis. We should get your brother out."

"What?" she said, staring around her. "How do you know?"

All she could see were groups of guys playing on the games.

"Trust me," he said. Then to Harry, "Come on, man, we're going to get some burgers and shakes."

Harry bitched a bit, but a lot less than normal. Clearly he didn't want to argue with Daniel. He was hanging on his every word, and was rather resentful of his sister's presence.

They found a café where they could sit outside. Harry ordered his banana milkshake, Lisanne had a chocolate one, and Daniel ordered his usual black coffee—although he then proceeded to 'taste' nearly half of Lisanne's drink. She ended up having to defend it from him before their burgers arrived, and was amused to see Harry wrinkle his nose when Daniel kissed her again.

Suddenly, police sirens pierced the afternoon air. Lisanne and Harry both looked in the direction of the arcade.

"Police," she whispered to Daniel.

He nodded his head.

"How did you know something was going to happen?" she asked, puzzled.

Harry's eyes toggled between the two of them.

Daniel shrugged. "Been in enough fights to know," he said.

Hero worship glowed in Harry's eyes.

Lisanne had a feeling it was going to be hard to get Daniel to herself while Harry was around.

They finished their lunch, and were wandering through the open air mall, when both Harry's and Lisanne's cell phones started ringing.

Lisanne answered hers first.

"Mom? What? No, we're fine. We're fine! Okay, we're on our way."

From the look on Harry's face, his call from their dad was similar.

"What was that about?" he said.

Lisanne shook her head. "I have no idea, but I guess we're going home."

Ten minutes later, Lisanne pulled up on the drive. Both her parents were waiting out front. Ernie looked furious. He wrenched Daniel's door open and pushed him against the car as he tried to climb out.

"What did you do?" he yelled in Daniel's face.

"Get the fuck off me!" snarled Daniel, pushing back, making Ernie stumble.

"Dad!" shrieked Lisanne. "What are you doing?"

"We heard there was a fight at the arcade—police were called and everything. Several teenagers were taken to hospital. We thought … we thought … we were worried," Monica finished lamely.

Daniel's face was full of contempt as he stared at Lisanne's parents, but it was Lisanne who spoke, her voice scathing.

"And you just automatically assumed Daniel had something to do with it. Well, that's just great. Thanks for your support. For your information it was Daniel who got us out of there. He guessed something was going down and we left before anything started." She paused, fury burning through her making her voice shake. "What happened to giving people the benefit of the doubt, Mom? What happened to 'innocent until proven guilty', Dad? If Daniel was one of your high school students you wouldn't be giving him this hard a time."

"Daniel didn't do anything!" shouted Harry, angrily.

Monica looked appalled, standing with her hand over her mouth, and her eyes darting between Daniel and her eldest child.

"I'm so sorry, Daniel," she said.

But with her fingers covering her lips, Daniel didn't know what she'd said.

"I'm getting the fuck out of here, Lis," he growled.

"I'll go with you."

He yanked his bike keys out of his pants' pocket and swung a leg over Sirona. Lisanne mounted behind him without even waiting to pull the helmets out of the saddlebags.

Ernie stood up straight. "Daniel, I apologize. I jumped to a conclusion without knowing the facts. I'm sorry." He looked at his wife. "We're both sorry."

"Sure," said Daniel, bitterly. "Until the next time. I'll never be good enough for you, will I?"

Ernie grabbed his arm. "Really, I am sorry—don't go off like this. Lisanne, please stay."

"No, Dad. You've said enough."

She nodded at Daniel and he leaned down to turn on the gas, then kick-start the bike.

Pops came out of the house, where he'd been standing with Grandma Olsen, both having overheard the whole heated exchange.

"Now then," he said, looking Daniel in the eye. "I hope you're not going to tell me that you're taking my granddaughter on that motorcycle with bare legs and no helmet?"

Daniel glanced over his shoulder at Lisanne.

"Fuck," he muttered.

"Everybody just calm the heck down," said Pops. "Ernie, you sure made a mess of this one, son. Monica, you go on in with the kids. Me and Daniel are going to have some quality time with Sirona, here." He tapped Lisanne on the arm. "You go on in with your mom and dad now."

Reluctantly, still furious with her parents, Lisanne climbed off the bike. Despite the fact her whole family was watching, she wrapped her arms around Daniel's neck and ghosted her lips across his mouth.

He sighed and leaned into her, resting his head on her shoulder.

Lisanne cupped his cheeks with her hands and made him look at her. "Don't leave without me. Promise?"

He hesitated for a moment, then nodded slowly.

She kissed him again and turned to follow her parents inside.

She watched through the window as Pops said something, pointing at the trunk of his car, and Daniel followed him. A moment later, Daniel was carrying a heavy looking toolbox, and Pops was bending over Sirona.

It didn't look like Daniel was going anywhere soon, so Lisanne turned to her parents.

"Thanks, Mom. Thanks, Dad," she said, enunciating every syllable icily. "You've really made Daniel feel welcome. Is there anything else you want to accuse him of while we're here? Maybe that graffiti I saw in the mall, or what about that carjacking that happened last week? You want to blame that on him, too?"

"Honey, we made a mistake. We're sorry," said her mom, a little defensively but still trying to placate her.

Lisanne folded her arms.

"Not good enough, Mom. You know, you and Dad brought me up to treat people with respect. Well, that seems to have just gone straight out the window, doesn't it? Or maybe you just meant people like you, with nice houses, and tidy yards. Maybe it doesn't count if the person has tattoos and piercings … or if he's deaf?"

"That's enough, Lisanne," said her father.

"No, Dad. That's nothing like enough. I'm ashamed of both of you."

And then she burst into tears and ran upstairs.

CHAPTER 16

Several minutes later, Lisanne heard someone tapping on her bedroom door. She guessed it was her mom.

"Honey, can I come in?"

Lisanne didn't answer, but her mom opened the door anyway.

"What do you want, Mom?" she said, her voice cold.

"Just to make sure you're okay."

"Oh, sure, I'm just peachy."

"Sarcasm won't help."

"Won't it, Mom? Well, you tell me what *will* help, because I surely don't know. Daniel has been nothing but polite and respectful, and he's getting along great with Harry and Pops. It's you and Dad who have the problem."

Her mom was quiet for a moment. "You're right, honey. Your dad and I were very wrong to assume that Daniel was involved in that fight at the arcade. All I can say is that we were worried about you and Harry. Now I know that doesn't excuse our behavior, but that was the reason. We've apologized again to Daniel and I believe he's accepted it. Now I'm apologizing to you."

"And Dad?"

"He's ashamed of himself—like you said. Just give him a chance to say he's sorry to you. That's all I ask."

She patted her daughter on the shoulder and quietly walked out of the room.

Lisanne sat up, then pulled herself off the bed, a determined look on her face.

She had a party to get ready for.

"Hey, man," said Daniel, as he strolled into Harry's room.

He was feeling a lot calmer since he'd spent time with Pops. The old man's company had stopped him from doing something spectacularly rash, and although they hadn't talked about anything in particular, just working together on Sirona had taken the heat out of the situation and given him a chance to cool his temper.

Lisanne's parents had both apologized again. Ernie's had been rather stiff, but Monica's had been effusive and heartfelt. She'd begged him to stay for Lisanne's sake, and Daniel had found himself agreeing, albeit reluctantly.

He pulled off his oil smeared t-shirt and dug around in his messenger bag for something clean to wear for the party. There wasn't a lot of choice since Lisanne had stolen his gray t-shirt to sleep in.

When he turned around, Harry was staring at him. Or rather, at his nipple rings.

Daniel was amused. They always provoked extreme reactions in people—he couldn't really see why. After all, it was no different from getting your ears pierced, was it?

"Whoa!" whispered Harry. "Did … did that hurt?"

Yep, always the same question.

"Yeah, some. Not much."

"Isn't it … kind of twisted? Ya know, freaky?"

Daniel laughed. At least the kid had the guts to say what most people just thought.

"It's not everyone's thing. Whatever, man, I like it. Girls like it."

Harry blushed.

"What about your tattoos—did they hurt?"

"Some more than others. Tats near bone tend to hurt the most, like the one on my hip," he said, casually.

Harry gulped. "You have one on your hip, too? Man! That's a lot of tattoos."

304

Daniel shrugged. "My brother has more—on both arms. He said the inside of his wrists hurt the most."

"Is Lisanne going to get a tattoo?"

Daniel raised his eyebrows. "I don't know. She's never said she wanted one."

"Because Mom and Dad would go nuclear."

Daniel smiled. "Yeah, that doesn't surprise me."

He pulled on his last clean t-shirt and saw that Harry was still staring at him.

"Um, can I ask you something?" said Harry, nervously. "Are you ... are you *doing it* with my sister?"

"That's kind of a personal question," said Daniel, seriously.

Harry visibly cringed but plowed on.

"It's just ... because you're kissing and stuff all the time. I've never seen her do that with a guy before."

"Your sister means a lot to me. I care about her."

Harry screwed up his face in disgust. "That's pretty mushy."

Daniel smiled. "Yeah, I guess."

"Um, so ... I was wondering," continued Harry, anxiously twisting his fingers together. "Can I ask you ... about ... stuff?"

Daniel paused, then sat down on the cot bed.

"Shoot."

Harry dropped his head and stared at his hands with a look of abject horror and embarrassment on his face.

"Um ... um..." he mumbled.

Daniel held back a sigh and waited patiently. He was beginning to get an idea about what Harry wanted to ask him.

"What is it, man?" he said, gently.

Harry's face glowed red.

"Um ... when you were my age, did you ... um ... did you ... you know ... um..."

"Whack off?" Daniel supplied helpfully.

"Yeah," croaked Harry, risking a quick glance upwards.

"Sure," replied Daniel easily, glancing at the Megan Fox poster on Harry's wall. "All guys do."

"Oh, okay." Harry paused, then continued his mumble. It

wasn't easy for Daniel to work out what the kid was saying, but the gist of the conversation was all too clear. "How did you know what I was going to ask?" Harry choked out.

Daniel shrugged. "I'm a good guesser." He wondered if that was the end of the conversation.

It wasn't.

"Um, is it true that if you do it … a lot … you can go blind or something?"

"Jeez, man!" said Daniel. "Who's been telling you this shit? The answer's no. Why didn't you just Google it?"

"Dad put a parent block on the computer," Harry said, with a grimace. "And you can't look at school either."

"At a friend's house?" Daniel offered.

"My friend Jerry had some porn," Harry said.

"Cool," said Daniel, hiding a smile.

"Yeah?"

"Sure. Most guys watch porn. Some girls, too."

Harry's eyes were huge. "Girls watch porn?"

"Some, yeah."

"Does … does Lis watch porn?"

Daniel smiled. "Not my secret to tell, man."

"Oh wow!" Harry's face showed surprise and nascent respect for his sister. "Um, so, is it weird to get a boner watching porn when there's another guy around?"

Daniel couldn't help a small smile escaping.

"Embarrassing, isn't it?"

Harry gave a relieved laugh. "Yeah!"

"Look, porn is supposed to make you feel horny. That's kinda the point of it. It's generally not a group activity unless you're like, having a party with beer or whatever. Mostly guys watch it by themselves and jerk off. It's normal. Girls do it, too."

"Girls? H-how?"

Jeez, now he was giving a biology lesson?

"Girls have pussies, right?" Harry seemed to have frozen, as Daniel continued to explain. "Yeah, so their pussies have clits— like a little nub at the front?"

306

Harry looked shocked, although by which sentence, Daniel couldn't tell.

"You rub the clit—or they do it themselves—they come."

"Come?"

"You know—orgasm—man milk."

"Is it … like guys, um…"

"Not exactly, but fuck, it feels good if you're around when it happens. Like I said—it's normal. Girls do it, guys do it."

Harry looked relieved. "I had to do it twice when I came home," he admitted. "After watching the porn movie."

"Nah, that's nothing, man. Lots of guys your age jack off the whole freakin' day. I dunno how any of us ever manage to go to school."

Harry gave a small chuckle and then pulled a face.

"And in my sleep," he groaned.

"Yeah, that happens. Doing the laundry is a nightmare," Daniel agreed sympathetically. "Especially when your mom wants to know why you've changed the sheets when she did it yesterday."

"Yeah!"

"Look, kid. Guys jerk off. A lot. I don't know about by the time a guy gets really old, like 30 or something, but yeah. It's like putting your pants on in the morning—just part of the routine. Know what I'm saying?"

"So, it's *normal?*"

"Yep. Fun and free and nobody gets pregnant—what's not to like?"

Harry laughed nervously.

Daniel remembered when he'd had a similar conversation with Zef. He'd been eleven, although possibly not as clueless as Harry, since he'd discovered Zef's porn stash and examined it thoroughly before being caught. Plus, he then lost his virginity to one of his brother's female friends when he was just slightly older than Harry was now.

It must suck not having an older brother.

He leaned over to reach into his jacket pocket, then tossed

Harry a packet of condoms.

"You might want to practice with these, so when the time comes, you know what you're doing. You don't want to be getting that fucker inside out when you've got your woman all hot and heavy for you."

Harry's mouth popped open but no words came out.

Daniel stood up and headed for the door.

"Thank me in a few years," he called over his shoulder.

Feeling like the day hadn't been a complete disaster after all, he went looking for Lisanne, and banged on her bedroom door.

"Baby doll, it's me."

The door opened and Daniel's jaw met the floor.

His eyes ran down long, bare legs and the *very* short denim skirt; took in the vixen with long, dark lashes, red lipstick and styled hair; and came to rest on tits that were looking very proud of themselves, enticingly covered in a pale blue tank top with spaghetti straps, that clung in all the right places.

Daniel licked his lips. It took a moment before he realized Lisanne was speaking to him.

"Do I look okay?" she repeated, made anxious by his silence.

"Fuck, yeah!" he breathed. "You look incredible, baby doll!"

Lisanne smiled nervously. "I cut up my old denim skirt and it came out a bit shorter than I wanted it."

She tugged at the hem, but it still only just skirted the top of her thighs.

Daniel pulled her toward him and cupped her ass, his fingers lingering under the edge of the cut off skirt.

"You look so fucking hot," he whispered.

"So, you think I look all right?"

Daniel smiled at her, his head cocked to one side. "You just don't get it, do you? I only have to look at you to get hard. Fuck, I want you so bad right now."

Lisanne's face was glowing.

"Um, okay then. I'll see you downstairs in a minute."

Daniel winked at her as she closed the door again. He leaned against the wall and took a deep breath. Being in the Maclaines' house was a giant mind-fuck, but goddamn it, she was worth it.

Harry walked past on his way to the TV den.

"Hey, man," said Daniel. "If you hear me getting up in the night, I'm going to see my girl. You cool with that?"

Harry looked away.

"Yeah, I guess."

Daniel smiled to himself.

"But…"

"Yeah, man?"

"If Dad catches you, I was asleep and didn't know anything about it, okay?"

Daniel held back a smile. "Deal."

To say Lisanne's parents were shocked when they saw her would have been a giant redwood sized understatement.

Ernie's eyes bulged in disbelief, and Monica's mouth opened and closed several times without managing to speak.

"Don't wait up," said Lisanne, hurrying out before viable language skills returned.

Daniel was waiting in the front yard, leaning on Sirona, enjoying a peaceful cigarette. He grinned when he saw her, and stubbed out his smoke.

"Baby doll's ready to party," he murmured into her neck. "You look beautiful, baby."

To Lisanne's hungry eyes, he looked pretty damned appetizing himself.

His jeans were hooked over his hipbones, and his black t-shirt clung to his chest. She could see the tail of his dragon tattoo coiling around his right bicep, just above his elbow. The small silver ring was back in his eyebrow, and his black hair was standing in short spikes.

He opened the car door for her in an old-fashioned gesture that made her giggle, but there was nothing *old-fashioned* about the way he leaned across and ran his tongue along her bare thigh, when he climbed in beside her.

"I want to have you in this car, baby."

Lisanne swallowed.

"Um," she said, unable to frame a reply.

He gave her a wicked grin. "Are you going to start the engine, baby, or are you hoping wishful thinking will get us to the party?"

She shook her head, trying to clear the fog of lust that had descended. *Was it hot in this car?*

With sweating palms, Lisanne managed to turn the ignition key, ignoring Daniel's amused smirk.

They made one stop on the way to Sonia Brandt's house. At Daniel's insistence, Lisanne parked outside a liquor store. She slid down low in the driver's seat, hoping that no one who knew her mom's car would see them. Daniel came out carrying a six-pack and a bottle Jack Daniels.

Lisanne was surprised. She'd never seen him drink anything other than beer, and was annoyed by the little twist of apprehension she felt in her stomach.

When they arrived at the party, Lisanne had to park several hundred yards from the Brandt house, as cars lined the street outside.

The Brandts lived on a wide, tree-lined avenue, with a large mansion style house set back from the road, and a curving driveway leading up to the front door.

People were streaming toward the building, most carrying liquor of some description. Lisanne's apprehension expanded like a balloon in her belly, but Daniel seemed to have cheered up considerably. Whether his relaxed state grew commensurately with the distance from the Maclaines' house, the bottle of Jack that he'd already started drinking, or the prospect of a party, who knew?

Lisanne felt miserable. It was everything she hated: loud, false people; getting drunk; and being ignored by snooty girls from her old high school.

It helped that she was with Daniel, but the old insecurities needed more than a short skirt and a couple of makeup lessons from Kirsty to be fully exorcised.

She took a deep breath to steady her nerves, but jumped slightly when she felt Daniel's fingers gently holding her chin.

"What's the matter, baby doll?"

She shook her head.

"Nothing," she lied. "I'm being dumb."

"Don't bullshit me, Lis," he said, softly. "Talk to me."

Her shoulders slumped. She should have known she wouldn't be able to hide from him.

"This party," she said, waving her hands to indicate their surroundings. "It's not really my thing."

He raised his eyebrows. "Why? I've seen you at the club—you were totally into it."

"That was different," she said. "I could … I could be anyone there, you know? Nobody knew me—I could start over. Here," she pointed her chin at the Brandt's house, "here I'm just a music nerd who plays the violin and is trying to act cool. They know me—they'll know I'm just faking it."

Daniel gave a quiet chuckle.

"Is that what you think? Baby doll, you're hot and sexy and so fucking passionate. There's *nothing* fake about you."

"But…"

"I'm telling you, Lis. I've had *a lot* of women," he said, raising his eyebrows to make the point, "and *none* of them compares to you. You're the real deal."

Lisanne chewed on her lip, and looked doubtfully toward the house.

"We don't have to go," he said, "but if you let them make you feel second class, then they win."

Her head snapped up at his words—she knew he was right.

"Are you channeling Eleanor Roosevelt, 'no one can make you feel inferior without your consent'?"

He grinned at her. "Yeah, baby doll. I'm all for feminism," and he ran his hand up between her legs. "And I'm all for miniskirts—freedom of expression. Fuck, yeah!"

He unbuckled his seatbelt and leaned over, giving him more reach. She gasped as his thumb stroked her *right there*. Then he kissed her, simulating with his tongue what he was doing with his hand.

Lisanne panted into his mouth and when he pulled away, the black of his pupils had burned away the hazel irises.

His eyelids fluttered closed and he took a deep breath.

Lisanne nearly told him to forget the party, that she'd drive them somewhere secluded so he could finish what he'd begun, but another part of her wanted to be the person he thought she was. With him there, maybe she *could* be that person. She wanted to try, at least.

She unbuckled her own seatbelt and opened the car door.

"Let's go," she said.

Daniel grinned at her and winked.

He wrapped his arm around her as they walked toward the house, carrying the beer in his free hand. Much to Lisanne's relief, he'd left the Jack under the seat.

As luck would have it, the first two people they met were the infamous Ingham sisters: cheerleaders, and twin pains in the butt—Kayla and Beth. They did a comic double take when they saw Lisanne, although most of their attention was focused on Daniel.

"What's the magic word, Maclaine?" sniffed Kayla. "This party isn't for nerds, but your friend can come in."

Lisanne smiled pleasantly. "Fuck you. There's two words," and she breezed inside.

"Bad ass," Daniel breathed into her hair.

Lisanne began to enjoy herself.

The entrance hall was heaving with bodies, some drinking, some moving to the pounding music that thundered from hidden speakers. Lisanne recognized a few people from her old high school, but none that she knew well. She planned to lead Daniel through the house out to the pool area at the back. But before she could reach it, Daniel dropped the beer onto a chair and grabbed her hips from behind, moving his body against her. Then he flipped her around, and pulled her hands up to his neck, grinding against her.

He rested his hands on her ass and gently drew her into the dance. Lisanne had never moved like that outside of the bedroom, and that was still very new to her. It was only dancing in the technical sense that they were moving to music. She waited for the familiar flush of embarrassment but instead she felt liberated, wanton and free.

She tugged Daniel's head toward her and thrust her tongue into his mouth. Hearing him groan was the greatest turn on. She ran her hands down his spine, and shoved her hands into the back pockets of his jeans.

They were locked at the lips, and damn near joined at the crotch, and it felt fine.

"Oh. My. God! Lisanne Maclaine?"

Sonia's shriek could have deafened bats in three states.

Lisanne unglued herself from Daniel's willing lips, and looked nonchalantly at the party's hostess.

"Oh, hi Sonia. Thanks for inviting us. Daniel, this is Sonia Brandt; Sonia, this is my boyfriend, Daniel Colton."

"Hello, Sonia Brandt," said Daniel, his eyes flicking in her direction for an insultingly short period of time.

Lisanne ran her hands up under Daniel's t-shirt and he grinned at her, completely understanding the game they were playing. He buried his head in her neck, placing small bites from her earlobe to her throat.

Sonia's face was everything that Lisanne could have hoped for: stunned, disbelieving, and so green with envy that she could have led the St. Patrick's Day Parade.

Up until now, Lisanne had been playing, but the way Daniel was touching her made her think they'd gone straight from the rehearsal to the main event.

Sonia's chagrined face disappeared from view, and Lisanne stopped caring what she thought, or what the Ingham sisters thought, or any of the people who'd belittled, disparaged and discounted her for four, long years.

Daniel must have felt the change, because he began moving more freely with her until they were really dancing, moving sinuously to the rhythm that he could feel through this supple body.

Eventually, Lisanne called a timeout, hot and bothered enough to need a cold drink.

Daniel retrieved his beer and they headed out to the pool.

Lisanne tugged off her pumps that she'd only worn once before to her cousin's wedding, and dangled her feet in the soothing water.

Daniel sat down next to her so she was leaning against the solid comfort of his chest. She felt him sweep her hair away from her shoulder and place beer cooled kisses along her neck. She wanted to thank him for making her come tonight, but to have a conversation, she'd have to move, and right now she was very comfortable.

But it was Daniel who moved, carefully shifting away from her and twisting around until he was facing her.

"Didn't you like high school, Lis?" he said, winding his denim clad legs beneath him until he was sitting cross-legged.

"Does anyone?"

"Yeah, I think some people do."

"Did you?"

He grimaced, and Lisanne could have kicked herself. High school would hardly be on his list of greatest memories—not when it was the time in his life that he'd started to lose his hearing.

"Not so much," he admitted. "It pretty much sucked. I was just … angry all the time. That's why I got into so many fights. Trying to prove that … I don't know … that I was still me." He grinned at her. "Gave my parents a lot of nightmares."

His smile faded and he rubbed at a spot of oil on his jeans.

"They'd be so proud of you," Lisanne said, with certainty. "Going to college, getting your degree."

"They'd have liked you," he said.

"Oh." Lisanne was surprised and her heart gave a happy flip flop.

Daniel chewed on his lip, then reached into his pants'

pocket. She thought he was reaching for a cigarette but instead he pulled out a tiny package, wrapped in the same silver paper that he'd used with such comic results when gift wrapping the leather jacket he'd given her.

"Mom always used to make a big deal about Thanksgiving— said we should think of all the things we were thankful for. The last time…" he took a deep breath, "the last time, when they were alive, I said it was bullshit and I had nothing to be thankful for… but now I've met you, I don't know, I feel like I *am* thankful. So I want you to have this. Thank you for being you. Thank you for putting up with my punk ass—for being in my life."

Lisanne didn't know what to say. With shaking hands, she unwrapped the paper carefully. Nestled beneath was a small gold locket on a short chain.

She stared at him, completely overwhelmed.

"Open it."

Gently, she pried the two halves apart. Inside was a miniature photograph of them, taken during their day at the beach.

"It was my mom's," he said, shrugging. "I wanted you to have it."

He stood up in one smooth move, and took the locket from her hands. Then, crouching behind her, he placed it carefully around her neck and kissed her hair.

She twisted around and caught his face between her trembling fingers.

"Thank you. I don't know what to say."

"Don't say anything," he whispered. "Just wear it, so I know."

She kissed him tenderly, deeply, and the heat flared between them.

"Whoa! Mouse Maclaine! Who knew you could be such a hot piece of ass?!"

Lisanne recognized the voice immediately. Grayson Woods, defensive lineman and star of the high school football team. She'd heard he'd gone to Alabama LSU on a football scholarship. But he was still the foul-mouthed Neanderthal she remembered.

Daniel hadn't heard the comment but he could see from the expression on her face that something was wrong, and it didn't take a genius to work out what was going on.

He stood up slowly, and pulled a cigarette out of his pocket while Grayson eyed him coolly.

"You want to say that again, motherfucker?" Daniel asked in a conversational tone.

Grayson's mouth dropped open, but then a wolfish smile spread across his face.

He'd been surprised when Sonia had told him that the music nerd was here, and even more astonished when he'd seen that she'd transformed into a seriously fuckable piece of tail, but now it looked as if the fun would be in taking out her punk boyfriend, before humiliating her a little more.

"Well," sneered Grayson, "looks like that uptight bitch finally opened her legs for someone and…"

Which was as far as he got before Daniel hit him.

Grayson didn't even see it coming. Maybe he'd had some idea that he'd be able to finish his catalog of insults before Daniel's patience ran out. Live and learn.

Grayson's nose seemed to be spread across his face and leaking two trails of bright blood, before his arms flailed—but failed to stop him falling backward into the pool.

There was a stunned silence and Daniel sucked on his cigarette.

"Motherfucker had a foul mouth," he said calmly, then tossed the butt, watching it bounce off of Grayson's drenched chest.

An ironic cheer went up from some of the guys around the pool, but others looked angrily at the interloper.

Lisanne struggled to her feet and scooped up her pumps.

"Come on," she whispered, tugging on his arm.

She led the way past the side of the house and stopped to pull on her shoes to cross the gravel drive, but Daniel scooped her up into his arms and carried her instead.

As they approached her mom's car, she dug the keys out of her purse and beeped it open so Daniel could deposit her in the driver's seat. When he slid in next to her, his expression was curiously blank.

"You're not mad, are you, baby doll?"

She blinked. "Why would I be mad at you?"

"For hitting that guy."

She smiled. "No, he deserved it. He's done a lot worse to a lot of people over the years. I'm glad you hit him. I'm glad his ugly butt ended up in the pool."

Daniel smiled with relief.

"Thank fuck for that. I thought you were going to chew my ass."

Lisanne raised her eyebrows. "Now that's an idea."

"Baby doll, I'm shocked. Are you flirting with me?"

She laughed. "I'm going to do a lot more than that. I just need to drive this car some place quiet and show you how much I appreciate you being my knight in shining armor. Again."

A slow smile spread over Daniel's face.

"Fuck, yeah!" he muttered.

Lisanne swallowed nervously. It was one thing to sound like she was fearless...

They drove in silence, the car's lights throwing a yellow beam into the trees that fled past in the forest. Daniel's hand dropped to her knee, where his fingers drew mindless patterns on her pale skin.

Finally, she pulled over, and stopped at the side of a lonely, secluded dirt road—one of many that fringed the lake.

They stared at each other for a long moment. Daniel spoke first.

"It's dark, baby. I can't read you right now. But just ... we only ever do what *you* want to do, okay? You want me to stop, you know how."

The sound as she unclipped first her own then his seatbelt was loud in her ears.

She didn't think she was the kind of girl who had sex in cars, but since meeting Daniel her views had broadened to the point of shifting seismically.

And yet, there was no pressure. His touch was gentle and reassuring, not frenzied or demanding. He was letting her lead.

She brought his hand up to her lips and kissed it.

"Thank you," she said, even though she knew he couldn't hear her. "Thank you for everything."

She sucked his fingers into her mouth and bit them gently, making him laugh lightly.

"Baby doll, are you trying to lead me astray?"

She crawled across the seat divide and settled herself on his lap. He hummed happily into her neck, then licked her skin slowly.

"You taste good, baby."

She mirrored his actions, breathing in the scent of his hair, his skin, kissing his cheeks, his eyelids, his lips.

He shifted beneath her and she could feel that he was hard, but he seemed to be content, sprinkling soft kisses across her chest and neck.

When she made her decision, it took her by surprise. *He* might be content to just make out, but *she* wanted to make love to him.

And she did love him. She loved his quiet strength and his patient softness, his humor and his sincerity, his sudden flares of anger, the passion and intelligence he hid behind his hazel eyes and lazy smirk: she loved him skin to core, and the weight of that feeling grounded her and freed her in ways she didn't yet understand.

"I'm going to make love to you, Daniel Colton. I'm going to make love to you here and now because I love everything about you, and I don't care that you can't hear me and I don't care that you'll never hear me sing or play my violin. I'll hear for both of us. I want to share it with you—all of it. I want to share myself with you."

He didn't hear her. He couldn't ever hear her. And she just

didn't care.

He was still nuzzling her neck and rubbing the tops of her arms against the coolness of the night air, when she reached down and brushed her fingers between his legs, teasing the hardness.

His hands fell still and she heard him take a deep breath. He waited, wondering what she was going to do next.

She shifted back on his knees, giving herself more room, and reached down to stroke him again. She felt his stomach tense, but he didn't try to encourage her or stop her—he simply waited.

She unbuttoned his pants and pulled the zipper down. His breaths became more uneven and he couldn't help lifting his hips into her hands.

She pulled his cock free and ran her fingers over its smooth hardness. Daniel groaned and leaned back against the headrest.

"Lis…"

She laid one finger over his lips and continued to stroke him with her other hand. He lifted her off so she was hovering above him, and carefully pushed two fingers inside her, groaning again when he found her wet. With his free hand, he pulled a packet of condoms out of his pocket.

"I don't know what you've got in mind, baby. Do I need these?"

She nodded as he looked up at her.

"Yes," she breathed.

He saw her nod, and quickly unwrapped a condom, sliding it on with expert hands.

She was going to climb off him to remove her panties, but he gripped her hips and shook his head. He pushed the delicate material to one side and lowered her onto him, hissing with pleasure as she sank down.

Lisanne felt powerful and adventurous and so damn turned on she barely knew what to do with herself. Even in the dark she could see the adoration on his face as he pushed up inside of her.

319

They moved together, finding their rhythm in the cramped confines of the car. Even without using his fingers Daniel seemed to know exactly how to move to pull streams of sensation from her. She felt the now familiar trembling inside herself.

Daniel felt it, too, and he started to move faster, harder, his breaths louder in the still air.

Lisanne came first, collapsing onto his neck, and Daniel followed soon after, a strangled moan rolling up his throat.

They sat, joined together, for some minutes before he shifted her away and snapped off the used condom, tying a secure knot around it and shoving it in his pocket. Then he tucked his now limp dick back inside his jeans and pulled the zipper up.

Lisanne crawled onto her own seat, feeling drained but oddly energized. She felt like she could sleep for a week, or run a marathon.

She looked across to Daniel. He was leaning back with his eyes open, a faint smile illuminated by the moonlight that crept through the trees.

He looked over and picked up her hand, kissing each finger one by one.

"Thank you," he whispered.

He laid her hand back in her lap, then touched the locket around her neck and smiled.

Rolling down the car's window, he pulled out a smoke.

Lisanne almost told him that her mom would be mad if he smoked in her car, but decided that one cigarette was pretty low down on her list of sins, particularly considering they'd just fucked on the passenger seat.

She drove home with the windows open.

CHAPTER 17

As before, Daniel woke up with his girl in his arms.

He knew he was pushing his luck spending another night with her, but he hadn't been able to bring himself to let her go.

It had been some evening, what with dancing so hot and heavy that his balls were aching by the time they'd gone to chill out by the pool. Then that ape with the dirty mouth had insulted his girl. His knuckles stung slightly as he remembered that the fucker had gone down with one punch. Pussy. And then the surprising and unexpected car sex that Lisanne had initiated.

He could definitely have gone for round two when they'd arrived back, but he'd been happy to settle for just sleeping together.

Sighing, he glanced at the Mickey Mouse clock and eased himself out of bed. Lisanne was sleeping soundly. She was wearing his gray t-shirt, but he could still see the locket's chain. He'd had that in his pocket ever since the day after the beach, and he'd been waiting for the right moment to give it to her. He rubbed his chest, surprised by the ache he felt when he thought about it.

Shaking his head, he pulled on his pants and scooped up his t-shirt, heading for Harry's room. It was only when he'd closed her door that he remembered he'd left his socks and sneakers with Lisanne.

To hell with it—he'd get them later.

He opened the door and slipped inside, only to meet Harry's curious face.

"Did you just get back from the party?"

Daniel smiled. "Yeah, great party."

He dropped his jeans again and stretched out on the cot, falling into a light sleep.

Twenty minutes, later he woke up with a start.

Monica was standing over him with a cup of coffee in her hand.

He nearly tipped the cot over as he struggled to sit up.

"Sorry!" she said, obviously trying not to laugh. "I need all hands on deck this morning, so I thought I'd better wake you boys."

Harry was sitting up, scowling at his mom.

"Mom! It's only 7 AM!"

"I know, honey, but we've got a lot to do." She passed Daniel the coffee. "Three sugars," she said, with a wink."

"Thanks," he mumbled.

"Breakfast in 10 minutes," she said, too cheerfully. "If you're not there, you'll have to wait until lunchtime. Happy Thanksgiving!"

Harry lay back, but Daniel was wide awake. Jeez, that had been close. Thank fuck he'd woken up when he had. If Monica had found him with Lisanne, Thanksgiving would have more closely resembled the Valentine's Day Massacre.

At least Monica could report back to Ernie that all bodies were present and correct.

He drank down the coffee and wandered off to the shower, absentmindedly jerking off. As he'd told Harry, it was part of the routine.

He decided against shaving: twice in two days was bordering on fanatical. He ambled back to the room, where Harry was still apparently unconscious. He rooted through his bag, but no t-shirt had miraculously leapt out, washed itself, and scurried back in, neatly folded. He swore to himself softly and decided to see if yesterday's t-shirt would pass the sniff test.

"Problem, Daniel?"

Ernie realized too late that he was speaking to Daniel's back.

He tapped him on the shoulder, and cringed as the younger

man jumped.

"Fuck!" Daniel said loudly, waking Harry with a start.

"Sorry," said Ernie, looking slightly sheepish. "Just wondering if everything's okay in here. Have you lost something?"

"Yeah," said Daniel, irritated that Lisanne's father had been creeping around like some weirdo stalker and scared the shit out of him. "Baby d … Lis stole my t-shirt to sleep in. I was just checking out the alternatives."

He shrugged. He didn't care whether or not Ernie knew that Lisanne wore his clothes.

"Oh, I see. Right, well … fine. Breakfast is ready. Harry—up, now."

Harry finally hauled his skinny ass out of bed, and Daniel sat back to check his phone messages.

There was one from Zef.

> * How's life in Hicksville, you sad fucker?
> Happy Thanksgiving. *

And three from Cori.

> * Where are you?
> Answer your damn messages *

He hadn't felt the need to contact her, especially since she told him he was selling out by dating Lisanne.

> * Zef says you out of town but won't say where.
> Are you ok? *

And most recently:

> * text me, asshole! *

He tapped out a short reply:

* I'm fine. Happy TG *

And pressed 'send' before he regretted acting like a pussy.

Monica interrupted him by tossing a shirt onto his bed.

"Here, wear this today—you don't want to frighten my mother. And tell my daughter to do some darn laundry."

She disappeared before he could say anything.

The shirt was soft, brushed cotton, very white. It smelled of clean linen and for a moment Daniel was taken back two years, to a time when his parents were still alive. His mother yelling at him to put his clothes in the hamper … the way she used to stand in the kitchen while she was ironing … the way she'd sing when she was happy.

He pulled on the shirt with mixed feelings. And it was obviously too big to be Harry's.

Daniel shrugged. Clothes were clothes.

He headed downstairs and made his way to the kitchen. Alluring aromas were already drifting through the house and his stomach rumbled appreciatively.

"Oh my," said Monica, "you do look handsome. Pancakes okay for you?"

"Um, yeah, thanks," said Daniel, his cheeks tinged with a faint pink.

Monica glanced over her shoulder and smiled. He really was a very good looking boy. Ernie's button down shirt suited him. Pity about that ridiculous ring in his eyebrow. Thank goodness his *other* piercings were covered up—however many of them he had.

Daniel focused on eating the pancakes Monica placed in front of him, and wondered what the day would bring.

Lisanne had said her family made a big deal out of Thanksgiving, so he was apprehensive about how he'd fit in— meeting new people like that was something he generally avoided.

He felt his phone vibrate in his pocket. He guessed it was from Cori so he didn't bother to look at it.

He was relieved when Lisanne wandered into the room, looking soft and sleepy, despite having showered. She looked cute in her pale yellow sweater and sensible skirt. He smiled to see that she was wearing the locket.

"Hey, baby doll," he grinned at her. "Sleep well?"

"Uh-huh. Nice shirt!"

"Thanks. Your mom took pity on me—after you stole my t-shirt."

"Oh! I didn't think you'd mind."

"I don't," he said, quietly. "It fucking turns me on to think of you wearing it."

Lisanne smiled happily, glancing at her mom, who was beating more pancake mix with unnecessary violence.

"Good!" and she leaned down to kiss him.

He circled his hands around her waist and returned her kiss enthusiastically.

"Did you finish your breakfast?" she said, fingering the collar of his shirt.

"Yeah, why?"

"Dad says could you help him in the living room? He's shifting the table around to make more room—he could use a hand."

"Sure," he said helpfully, and kissed her hair before heading for the living room.

Soon, the sound of heavy furniture being moved reached the kitchen. Lisanne heard a thud and Daniel cursed loudly. She held back a giggle as her mom's eyebrows shot up.

"Goodness!" Monica said. "That was colorful."

Lisanne sighed. "I know. He's trying to keep it down."

"Hmm, well. I hope he tries harder in front of the rest of the family!"

"Don't bet on it," Lisanne muttered to herself, as she stood at the sink and started preparing vegetables.

After a while she ran out of potatoes to peel.

"What's next, Mom?"

"Could you start taking the picnic chairs through and then

you can set the table? Thanks, honey."

Lisanne carried in four of the folded up picnic chairs, while Daniel and her father fought with a trestle table. Then she returned to the kitchen for the next four.

Daniel's eyes widened slightly and Lisanne could see that he was counting the number of seats. A look of panic crossed his face.

"Lis?" he said. "How many people are coming today?"

"There'll be 15 of us around the table, and the kids can go outside on the patio," Ernie answered for her.

Lisanne saw the blood draining from Daniel's face.

"I gotta ...I can't ... I gotta go..."

He was nearly at the front door when Lisanne caught up with him.

She grabbed his arm and pulled him to face her.

"I can't," he gasped, rubbing his hands over his face. "It's too many people. I can't do it, Lis. Fuck, I can't do it."

"Ssh," she said, stroking his cheek, and trying to quell her own panic at his obvious distress.

"I've gotta go. I've gotta get out of here. I'm sorry, Lis. I can't. I can't."

"Just ... just come and sit down for a minute. Come on. Come with me."

She tugged his arm and for a moment she thought he'd refuse and make a run for it, but with dragging steps he followed her upstairs.

Even though her father had expressly forbidden her from having Daniel alone in her room, she drew him inside.

He paced the small area, grabbing fistfuls of his hair and breathing heavily.

"Daniel, it'll be fine," Lisanne said, trying to sound confident.

In truth, his growing panic was infecting her so badly, her bones rattled.

"It won't be fine!" he gasped. "It'll be a fucking nightmare. I can't, Lis. Please, just let me go."

The desperation in his voice made her heart stutter.

"Daniel, just … just sit with me. Come here … come and sit down."

Gently, she led him toward her bed and forced him to sit. He bent forward and rested his forearms on his knees, his breathing too fast.

Lisanne sat next to him and rubbed his back, trying to let her touch calm him. She didn't know what to say that would help him. She felt wretched. She should have realized how hard this would be. *So selfish.* The words throbbed through her, but they didn't make one cent's worth of difference.

There was a knock at the door, followed immediately by Ernie's entrance.

"Fucking great," muttered Daniel, knowing that the newest diktat decreed he wasn't supposed to be alone in his girlfriend's room.

He stood up and wiped his hands over his eyes.

Lisanne was devastated to see his fingers were wet with tears.

"Lisanne," said Ernie, "if you could wait downstairs, I'd like to have a word with Daniel."

"But, Dad…"

"Now, please, Lisanne."

There was no arguing with her father when he had that tone in his voice.

As she closed the door, Daniel seemed so miserable, her heart ached.

Daniel stared at Lisanne's father, fully expecting to be kicked out and told not to come back.

"Sit, please, Daniel," Ernie said.

"We weren't doing anything," said Daniel, angrily.

"I know. Please, just sit for a moment and hear what I have to say."

It had been two years since Daniel had had to endure a parental lecture—and this man was *not* his father. He felt angry and resentful as he sat on the edge of Lisanne's bed.

"Why are you here, Daniel?"

"We were just talking. That's all!"

"No, I mean, why did you agree to come home with Lisanne for Thanksgiving?"

Okay, so not the opening he'd expected.

Daniel shrugged. "She invited me."

"Is that the only reason?"

"Why do you care?" Daniel said rudely, already anxious, and irritated further by the interrogation.

"I care because she's my daughter," said Ernie, evenly.

Daniel twitched a shoulder.

"I wanted to be with her."

"So why are you thinking of leaving?"

Daniel's eyes flicked toward Ernie.

"You heard?"

"Yes."

"So you know why."

"I want to hear it from you."

Daniel's hands automatically reached for his cigarettes to relieve the stress, then realized that he wasn't going to be allowed to smoke. At least Ernie didn't look mad.

"It's hard," he muttered, his hands stabbing the air to express the futility of the situation. "I can only concentrate on one person at a time. You don't know what it's like when the conversation goes around the table and everyone laughs, and you're the sad fucker who has no clue what's going on. Or someone asks a question, and everyone's staring, waiting for you to answer. I'll look like a fucking idiot."

He stood up and started pacing.

Ernie waited patiently for him to calm down enough to look at him.

"Son, if that's the worst that can happen, then I'm really not seeing the problem."

Daniel stared at him.

"I just don't *do* this shit!" he shouted, frustrated that he couldn't make Ernie understand. "It's really *tiring*. Even being with people I know, I have to watch all the time to see what they're saying, I have to guess half of it. People get bent out of shape because they're being all nice and shit, and I just smile and nod because I haven't got what they've said. And with new people, it's so much fucking harder. I just..." his words petered out. "And because I can't stand people looking at me the way you're looking at me now—like I'm some puppy that's been whipped."

Ernie grimaced, acknowledging the truth of what Daniel was saying. He *had* been pitying him.

Daniel took a deep breath. "And I'm here because … Lisanne makes me feel like I'm not alone.

Ernie's face was a confused mixture of pride in his daughter, and concern that the two of them were even closer than he'd realized.

"Look, Daniel, I won't pretend that I know what you've been through in the last few years, but you've done well: you've stayed in school, you're going to college—you're moving your life forward. And we've all done or said foolish things in public, but in the grand scheme of things, a meal with our family isn't a big deal."

"It's *every* fucking time," snarled Daniel. "They'll all wonder what the fuck she's doing with me."

He faced the wall, resting his weight on his hands, and leaned his forehead against it. Without warning, he slammed his head hard.

Ernie leapt up and grabbed his arm.

"Hey! That won't help. Sit down, Daniel. Come on."

Daniel shook him off. "I've gotta get out of here."

Ernie tried again. "Just sit for a minute—if you still want to go, I won't stop you."

Daniel eyed him warily.

"My dad and Grandma Olsen already know. Harry knows and has obviously taken quite a liking to you. Lisanne's mother and I know, of course. We'll all help you. You're a guest in our home, Daniel, and that matters to me. I'm not happy about … some aspects of my daughter's relationship with you, but I can see how much she cares for you. And I can see you care for her, as well."

He paused, examining Daniel's face.

"Look, I know we haven't gotten off to the best start and I've said and done some things that I'm not very proud of—and my wife is giving me hell for it—but I'd like you to stay, too. Lisanne wants you to be with her, with her family at Thanksgiving. Will you do it for her?"

Daniel took a deep breath and nodded slowly.

"Good man," said Ernie. "Come and join the family— Lisanne will be out there building up a head of steam if I know my daughter."

Daniel attempted a smile and Ernie winked at him.

He followed Ernie out of the room, and saw Lisanne's anxious face peering up from the bottom of the stairs.

"Daniel is going to stay," replied Ernie to Lisanne's unspoken question.

Considerately, he left them alone together.

Daniel stared at Lisanne's face, full of love and concern, and felt like shit for making her look so sad.

"Are you okay?"

He nodded slowly.

"Yeah."

She laid her head against his chest and his arms circled her small shoulders. They stood together in silence for a long, peaceful minute.

A knock at the front door had Lisanne tugging on Daniel's arm.

"Let's go into the backyard—you can have a cigarette."

He smiled crookedly.

"I thought you hated smoking."

"I do, but right now you need to relax more than you need me bitching at you—although I can multitask—I am a woman."

He smiled softly. "Yeah, you are," and leaned down to kiss her. "Come on, woman—I need a smoke."

They sat on the porch, while Daniel sucked hard on his

cigarette, clinging to it with the fervent desperation of a condemned man. But it couldn't save him from Lisanne's aunt who came hurrying out, intrigued to meet Lisanne's first ever boyfriend.

It would be fair to say that subtlety didn't run in the Olsen side of Lisanne's family.

"Oh my goodness!" shrieked Aunt Jean. "Is this him?"

Lisanne tapped Daniel's arm and he looked over his shoulder. He stood up, tossing the stub into an empty flowerpot.

"Hi Aunty Jean," said Lisanne, doing her best to fake a sincere smile, "this is Daniel. Daniel, my Aunty Jean—Mom's older sister."

Daniel held out his hand but Jean enveloped him in a bone cracking hug.

"Oh Lisanne! Less of the 'older'! Everyone says I look years younger than Monica. But, my! However did a girl as plain as you land such a handsome boy?"

Lisanne shriveled and Daniel looked at her quizzically, not having heard the unpleasant remark.

Jean was followed by her eldest daughter Ashley who, thankfully, had inherited calm genes from her father. She greeted Daniel more formally and smiled, then yelled at two kids of seven and nine who came barreling onto the porch.

"And those two monsters are Ryan and Morgan. Don't let them pester you to play football with them. They think every guy they see wants to."

Daniel smiled. "I don't mind. I like kids."

Ashley raised her eyebrows and looked at Lisanne. "Hang onto this one, honey, he's a keeper—if he means what he says."

Daniel laughed at Lisanne's blush.

Ashley was right about her boys. They ambushed Daniel immediately, and soon he was throwing balls for them to run after and catch.

Ashley's two eldest girls, Kelly and Lacey, made their appearance. They were only a few years younger than Lisanne and determined to be bored with, and superior to, everything they saw. Lisanne didn't have much in common with them—she wore her heart on her sleeve and always had done.

But their eyes brightened when they saw Daniel.

"No way!" hissed Kelly. "No way he's your date, Lisanne. He's like, hot!"

"That's Daniel," Lisanne said, coolly. "My boyfriend. We go to school together."

Kelly raised her perfectly plucked eyebrows at Lisanne's tone, then rudely proceeded to whisper to her sister.

Lisanne ignored them—something she'd been doing for years.

Three more boys ran out into the yard—her Uncle Malcolm's kids, Kellan, Marty and Joseph. They headed straight for the football action. Harry arrived on the scene, muttering about it being a dumb game, but he joined in anyway.

Ernie followed, looking relaxed, and sat down on the porch with a beer in his hand. Behind him was a tall, bearded man—his younger brother Malcolm—similarly accessorized.

"Think I'll go play some ball," said Malcolm, after watching for a while.

He ambled down the steps into the yard and joined in, which evened out the numbers and upped the ante as far as the older kids were concerned.

Ernie watched the impromptu game with a smile.

"He's got a good arm," he said, gesturing in Daniel's direction.

"He was his school's quarterback," Lisanne said, proudly.

"Really?" said Ernie, sounding impressed. "But he didn't try out for the college team?"

Lisanne rolled her eyes at her father, even though a few weeks ago she'd asked exactly the same question.

"Dad, you really want me to answer that?"

Ernie looked embarrassed. "Of course. Right."

To Lisanne's surprise, Daniel dropped out of the game after just a few more minutes, unmoved by the shouts of disappointment that he couldn't hear. He sat on the porch with her, looking rattled.

"What's the matter?" she said, quietly.

Daniel jerked his head at Uncle Malcolm.

"I can't read him."

"What?"

"I can't lip read him, Lis. He's got a fucking beard. I can't see his mouth for all the fucking fur!"

"Oh," she said, helplessly. "Oh, okay. Do you want me to say something to him?"

Daniel shook his head with an irritated gesture.

"Well, let's go see if Mom needs any help."

He stood up immediately and pulled Lisanne to her feet.

In the kitchen, Monica was looking harassed as her own mother followed her around, offering the kind of unwanted advice that could be classified as criticism, at every step.

"Those potatoes will boil dry like that, Monica. Did you remember to salt them? The turkey won't be ready in time unless you turn up the heat—you don't want it to be soggy and half raw like it was last year."

Monica fumed silently.

"You really don't deal with people well, do you, Mon?"

"That's because you're so critical!"

"Critical? Me? No I'm not critical. I could be and I could constantly tell you what you should do with your life, but you're lucky I'm not like my friends with their children—I let you live your own life." She took a breath. "And I really think you should turn the heat up on the stove."

"It's all *fine*, Mom," Monica snapped.

"Well, someone got up on the wrong side of the bed this morning, didn't they?" She turned her attention to Daniel. "I do like a man in an ironed shirt. Now why don't you take out that silly ring you've got in your eyebrow? Here, I'll do it for you."

"Grandma!" said Lisanne, sharply. "He's fine—leave him alone."

Daniel smirked and leaned down to whisper in Lisanne's ear. "Should I show her my other rings?"

She dragged him out of the kitchen, knowing full well he'd be prepared to do exactly that if challenged.

Pops was sitting in the TV den watching the news.

"Happy Thanksgiving. You two hiding out already?" he said.

"Something like that," said Lisanne, with a sigh.

"Huh, me, too," said the old man, then glanced over at Daniel. "Bet you're wondering why you signed up for this, aren't you, son?"

Daniel smiled, collapsing onto a sofa and pulling Lisanne to his lap. "Nope, not really," he said.

Pops laughed. "Good for you."

Lisanne snuggled into him, surprised that she didn't feel embarrassed to show Daniel affection in front of Pops.

Lunch was loud and chaotic. The under 12s ate outside, running in and out with plates of food, leaving a trail of crumbs behind them. Ernie and Malcolm were becoming increasingly convivial as the beer continued to flow. Lisanne snagged a couple of cans for Daniel and shielded him as much as she could from Grandma Olsen and Aunt Jean.

Grandma Olsen had entertained the table with a thorough, if highly imaginative description of Daniel's tattoos, ending in a request that he take off his shirt to show everyone. Monica vetoed that suggestion and began an interrogation of her own about how much wine her mother had drunk. Harry snickered until Monica sent him to refresh the water jugs.

Kelly and Lacey had begun a coordinated campaign of flirtation with Daniel, who remained patient and stoic in the face of their increasingly lubricious display.

Then Ashley noticed Lisanne's locket.

"That's pretty, Lis. Where'd you get that from?"

Lisanne's hand automatically rose to her throat as half the table stared at her.

"It was a Thanksgiving gift from Daniel."

"Wow!" said Kelly. "Is it real gold?"

Lisanne looked at Daniel for confirmation, and he nodded.

"That's very sweet of you, Daniel," said Monica, sounding

rather severe, "but a boy at college shouldn't be spending his money on expensive jewelry like that."

Daniel looked annoyed but didn't say anything.

Then Grandma Olsen stuck in her two pennies worth. "In my day, a young man wouldn't waste his money unless he was serious about a girl."

Lisanne winced.

"You shouldn't have accepted such an expensive gift, Lisanne," said Ernie, frowning at his daughter.

Daniel reached his limit. "I didn't spend anything," he said, quietly but firmly. "It was my mom's."

There was a lull in the conversation and all eyes were fixed on Daniel. Kelly and Lacey almost swooned.

Lisanne took Daniel's hand. "Cigarette break?"

He nodded stiffly and followed her outside.

"Still glad you came?" she asked, anxiously.

He ran his hands through his hair before smiling at her and lighting a cigarette.

"I might need some more awesome car sex to make up for it."

"Maybe you should get a car."

"Nah. Sirona would be jealous. You know what females are like."

"Finally, something Sirona and I have in common," smiled Lisanne. "Other than you, of course."

Then she heard her name being called.

"Ugh, I have to go," she sighed. "It's a family tradition. You stay here and finish your smoke. I'll be back in a minute."

Lisanne left him sitting outside as she ventured back to the living room.

"Where's Daniel?" whispered her mom.

"Halfway to Texas if he's got any sense," snapped Lisanne.

Monica looked embarrassed. "Yes, that must have been quite an ordeal. I hope you explained to him about grandma."

"Not just that—you and Dad getting on his case as well."

"If only you'd told us about the necklace, honey, we

wouldn't have said anything."

"I was going to tell you, Mom. I just wanted to have it myself for a while, okay?"

Her mom didn't seem to know what to do with that answer.

"Well, grandma and Pops have been asking for your party piece," she said. "Better get it over and done with."

Ever since she'd been a little girl, Lisanne had sung for her family. It had become a Thanksgiving tradition. It was always the same, the *Skye Boat Song*, to celebrate, as Pops insisted, their Scottish roots.

Kelly and Lacey acted bored, and were sitting huddled together looking for all the world like they just needed a cauldron to complete the picture.

Grandma was sitting up expectantly, a little lopsided due to the industrial quantities of wine that had disappeared down her throat over the last two hours.

Aunty Jean was already looking emotional, even though she wasn't a Maclaine, and Ashley was sitting calmly, with an encouraging expression.

Lisanne stood next to her father, who proudly put his arm around her waist.

> *Speed bonny boat, like a bird on a wing*
> *Onward! the sailors cry.*
> *Carry the lad that's born to be King*
> *Over the sea to Skye.*

"Oh, it's so lovely," barked Grandma Olsen, loudly.

> *Loud the winds howl, loud the waves roar,*
> *Thunderclaps rend the air;*
> *Baffled, our foes stand by the shore,*
> *Follow they will not dare.*

Lisanne was unaware that Daniel was standing nearby, watching her intently.

> *Though the waves leap, soft shall ye sleep,*
> *Ocean's a royal bed.*
> *Rocked in the deep, Flora will keep*
> *Watch by your weary head.*

"Have you ever heard anything so lovely, Daniel?" asked Ashley, meaning to be kind.

"No," he said, tightly.

"You must be so proud of her."

He nodded, but didn't speak. Ashley looked at him oddly, but didn't say anything more.

After she'd finished singing, Lisanne couldn't help noticing that Daniel was unnaturally quiet. He seemed more like the distant, arrogant guy she'd first met, and nothing like the playful, adorable boyfriend she'd fallen in love with.

He deflected all attempts at conversation, and wouldn't say anything to her except that he was 'fine'. In the end, he'd disappeared up to Harry's room and re-emerged wearing his oil stained t-shirt, saying he had work to do on Sirona before they headed back in the morning. She watched him crouched down next to his bike, quiet, absorbed, alone.

"Just leave him be," said Pops. "It's been a lot for him to take in the last few days. I love your mom and dad, but they drive me crazy sometimes—and they're my family. It's even harder for your young man, what with having lost his own parents. I'm pretty certain he's done his share of biting back the truth this holiday. Let him have his time alone—he'll be fine."

Lisanne wasn't so sure. Up until that moment, she'd felt like it was the two of them against everyone, against the world. Suddenly, she was on the outside. It was a cold place to be.

It was well into the evening when everyone finally started to leave. Daniel avoided that drama fest by taking Sirona 'for a test drive'. When he returned, over an hour later, it was just the Maclaines and Pops left. Grandma Olsen was spreading her affection between her children, and now it was Jean's turn. The house was considerably quieter.

Lisanne realized that Daniel must have retrieved the bottle of Jack from her mom's car, although she hadn't seen him do it. She could smell the whiskey on his breath when he kissed her goodnight.

Checking they weren't being watched, she ran her hands over his tight butt and tucked them into the back pockets of his jeans.

"See you later," she whispered.

Daniel shook his head and gave her a small smile. "Not tonight, baby doll. We've got a long ride tomorrow and I'm kinda wasted."

"But..."

"Sleep well, baby," he said, and kissed her forehead before disappearing into Harry's room.

Lisanne felt like crying.

CHAPTER 18

They'd been back at school for two weeks and Lisanne had hardly seen Daniel. She definitely didn't consider a handful of texts a reasonable substitute. When she *had* seen him he'd been jumpy and short-tempered. Worse still, they hadn't had sex even once, and although a couple of their make out sessions had got pretty heated, he'd always pulled back with an excuse that he had to be somewhere else.

Lisanne was upset and confused.

"I think he's getting bored of me, Kirsty. He won't talk about it and I don't know what to do," she confided one evening.

"You need to spend some quality time with him, Lis. From what you've said about Thanksgiving, it was kind of heavy. You guys just need to relax, talk."

Lisanne rolled her eyes in frustration.

"I know! But he hardly comes near me, and when he does, it's almost always with other people around."

"So, don't ask him, tell him. Plan a date—go out to dinner. *Talk* to him. But if it's any consolation, Vin says he's being weird with everyone."

"What do you mean?"

"Well, you know before Thanksgiving, the guys had all planned to go see that football thing after New Years? Yeah, well, he cancelled on that with no explanation, and you know what a big deal that was supposed to be."

Lisanne bit her lip, wondering if she dared voice what was really on her mind.

"Um, you don't think … do you think he's seeing someone else?"

Kirsty looked at her seriously. "What makes you say that?"

"Well, a couple of times he's gotten texts and he won't say who they're from, and he got all annoyed and defensive when I asked him. And one of his friends from Economics wanted to know where he was because he'd cut class. When I asked him, he flat out lied to me, and said he hadn't cut any classes."

Kirsty wrinkled her nose in sympathy. "Did Roy or any of the guys say anything? Maybe he's got shit going on at home?"

Lisanne shook her head. "Roy *said* he didn't know anything, but…"

"But what?"

"He mentioned that Daniel does this sometimes when he's 'stressed'."

Lisanne used air quotes to express what she thought of that comment.

"Maybe he is … I mean, living with his brother … and hasn't he got a big Math paper due or something?"

"I don't know. Maybe."

"Well," Kirsty said, slowly, "I wouldn't normally suggest this, but in the circumstances…"

"What?"

"Get hold of his cell phone. Check his texts and emails. If something's going on…"

"I can't do that!"

"Lis, if he won't talk to you, he's not giving you much choice." Kirsty shrugged. "That's the way I see it."

Lisanne decided to give Daniel one more chance to talk to her—and if that didn't work … ugh, she hated the thought of spying on him.

Kirsty easily agreed to make herself absent on Friday evening. Lisanne had intended on telling Daniel the good news during their Business class that morning—but he was a no-show without even a text to explain his whereabouts. She didn't know whether to be pissed or worried. She settled for both and texted him immediately.

> * L: where are you? Are you ok?
> I'm worried. LA xx*

There was no reply even though she checked her phone continually during Professor Walden's lecture.

Finally, half way through lunch break, he replied.

> * D: I'm ok. *

"That's it?" said Kirsty, annoyed on Lisanne's behalf. "'I'm okay'? You totally have to text him back."

"And say what?" Lisanne sighed, trying to ignore Shawna's smug expression.

"Tell him he's meeting you at the dorm, and to bring takeout. Then seduce him, and make him tell you everything. Use your feminine wiles."

Lisanne snorted. "Yes, because I have so many of those."

"We can work on that, girlfriend. Emergency shopping expedition."

"What?"

"Don't worry—I have Victoria's Secret on speed dial."

Lisanne didn't think she wasn't joking. And when she found herself buying ridiculously expensive lingerie two hours later, she felt like she'd fallen down some weird damn rabbit hole in an alternate universe.

She texted Daniel immediately she got home.

> * L: Dinner, my place 6:30. Bring Chinese :) *

But his answer wasn't what she expected.

> * D: Busy tonight. Sorry. *
> * L: pouting—doing what? *
> * D: meeting old friend—don't be mad *

* L: why would I be mad? *
* D: old girlfriend *

"What?!" she screamed, her phone blinking at her innocently.

* L: now I'm mad *
* D: no need. Do something tomorrow? *
* L: what do I do with my new
Vic Secret panties and bra? *
* D: you are killing me! *
* L: shame to waste them.
Maybe I'll go out with K&V & guys tonight? *
* D: don't joke, baby doll. Make it up to you tomorrow.
Promise. *
* L: still pouting *
* D: (: *

Despite Daniel's promise, Lisanne was fed up, and she didn't feel like staying in by herself. It was only two weeks before Christmas and one week before the end of the semester, and everywhere—except her dorm room—there was a party atmosphere in the air.

Well, screw him. He was off seeing one of his (many) exes, she was damned if she was staying in on a Friday night, all pining and pathetic.

She called Kirsty who told her where to meet them and to help herself to anything in her closet. Lisanne decided to do exactly that. Maybe Daniel wasn't the only guy who'd think she was hot. Her heart sank at the thought, but she was determined to put on a brave face and party on—if people still did that.

By the time she was on her third cocktail, Lisanne realized they were far more alcoholic and less fruity than she'd realized. When her phone vibrated with a message, she nearly dropped it.

* D: at your room. Where are you? Are you ok? *

He really had a nerve. Dumping her for some other girl and then expecting her to wait in for him! She shoved her phone back in her bag and ignored it when another message came in, and then another.

Kirsty threw her a curious look.

"He can wait," she said, and threw back another drink.

"Atta girl!" shouted Isaac, and swallowed his fifth tequila.

Two hours later, with her head swimming, Lisanne was remembering why she didn't drink. Kirsty had put her in a taxi with a fierce message to the driver to make sure her friend got safely through the front door of the dorm rooms.

Lisanne staggered out of the cab, cursing the high heels that were causing her to wobble and overbalance. Then she saw Daniel's bike parked in its usual place and her stomach lurched unpleasantly.

He was still here?

Apprehension sobered her as she slowly trudged up the stairs to her room. She was sure seeing Daniel was going to mean a fight.

He was hunched on the floor outside her door, the worried expression clearing as soon as he saw her.

"Baby doll! Fuck, you scared the shit out of me! Are you okay?"

"I'm fine, Daniel, thank you," she slurred, her words therefore lacking the dignity with which she'd hoped to imbue them.

"Why didn't you reply to my texts? I was imagining all kinds of shit."

He blinked, studying her face and taking in her swaying body for the first time.

"Are you drunk?"

"I might be. Why shouldn't I? You dumped me on a Friday night to see an *old girlfriend*."

His face tightened perceptibly.

"What the fuck does that mean?"

"You're smart, Daniel. You work it out."

She fumbled trying to get her key to fit in the lock that for some bizarre reason had shrunk and kept sliding around. He took the key out of her hand, and opened the door for her.

Even though she hadn't invited him, he walked in behind her and quietly poured her a glass of water.

"Drink this. You'll feel better."

She ignored the proffered glass.

"Why are you here? Are you checking up on me?"

His face was immediately angry. "I wanted to see you. I guess the feeling isn't mutual."

"If you wanted to see me, maybe you shouldn't have gone out with another girl."

"She's an old friend, that's all. Don't be so fucking paranoid."

"Fuck you!" she screamed, ripping off her t-shirt and skimpy skirt, revealing a set of pretty underwear in deep jade green. "I did all this for *you*, but you were too busy seeing an old *girlfriend*."

And she burst into tears, furious that liquor and anger had robbed her of coherence.

She threw herself onto the bed, crying out her frustration.

Without speaking, Daniel sat down next to her and stroked her hair. Suddenly, she sat up and pressed herself against his chest and tried to kiss him.

He pulled away from her and held her arms firmly.

"I'm not going to fuck you when you're drunk, Lis."

"How noble!" she spat, tearing her arms free.

He scrubbed his hands over his face.

"Do you want me to go?"

"Yes!" She hesitated, "No."

Some indefinable emotion flitted across his face.

"Come on, baby doll, let's get you into bed."

He pulled a t-shirt out of the chest of drawers, raising an ironic eyebrow when he recognized it as one of his own. He helped her into it, and unhooked her bra with one hand, slipping the shoulder straps through the sleeve holes and sliding it off in a smooth, practiced move.

Lisanne wondered fleetingly if he had a lot of experience undressing drunken girls. Probably, her unhappy heart told her.

She lay back on her bed, and found that the room was spinning. Was that supposed to happen?

"My head hurts," she mumbled, but he couldn't hear her and then she passed out.

In the darkest hour before dawn, Lisanne woke up.

Her head was pounding and her mouth was as dry as Death Valley. From the foul taste, it was quite possible something had died there, too. She sat up slowly and saw Daniel lying on his side next to her, sound asleep. She stood up carefully, staggering slightly and headed for the bathrooms. Then she saw his phone blinking in the dark, and Kirsty's words came back to her.

Before she thought through what she was doing, she swept it up and hurried out of the door. The bathroom was just down the hall and empty at that time of night—day—whatever it was. Stumbling and feeling sick, Lisanne slumped down into one of the cubicles and held Daniel's phone in her trembling hands.

The new text was the first one she saw. It was from someone called 'Cori'. And when she scrolled through, she saw several more messages from her. The rest were from Zef and Vin, a couple from Harry—which annoyed her as neither of them had seen fit to mention that they'd stayed in touch—and the rest were from her.

Zef's messages were surprisingly prosaic: all about bills that needed paying to avoid utilities being cut off. That must be worrying him but was something else that he'd never mentioned. Vin's were about arranging dates to meet up, most of which Daniel seemed to have cancelled.

So she opened Cori's messages, and her world shattered.

* C: You should tell her *
* C: When are you going to tell her? *
* C: This is a mistake. We both know it. Miss you *

He'd only sent one reply to the three messages, but it was

more than enough.

> * D: she doesn't need to know.
> I want this. You know why *

Her hands shook as her finger hovered over the latest message—the one that had arrived while they'd slept. If she opened it, it would be obvious she'd been snooping. She just wasn't sure she cared anymore.

> * C: You sure know how to
> show a girl a good time!! :) xx *

Lisanne turned and threw up into the toilet bowl. She felt sick and shivery. How long? That was the thought that shuddered through her brain. How long had Daniel been cheating on her?

She looked at the messages again. He'd sent a text to 'Cori' the day they'd got back from her parents—before she'd even finished unpacking, before she'd had a chance to show Kirsty the locket he'd given her.

> * D: I need to see you tonight, 7. Usual place. *

By the time she'd stopped throwing up and felt brave enough to go back to her room, she was chilled to the bone and her head throbbed unforgivingly. But it was her chest that hurt the most. Her heart ached with his loss, even though he was still sleeping in her bed.

He was curled up on his side just as she'd left him, his right arm stretched out as if he were reaching for her. His golden skin seemed silvery in the morning light and his tattoos had dissolved into shades of gray. His long lashes fanned his cheeks and his lips were parted in a small pout as his chest lifted in deep, even breaths. In sleep he looked so innocent, and it was hard for Lisanne to believe the evidence of the text messages she'd read.

She'd so badly wanted to believe in him. Her heart tore a little more as she stared at him sleeping peacefully, caught out in a lie.

His eyelids fluttered and opened, and she saw the exact moment consciousness returned.

"Hey, baby doll," he said, sounding groggy. "Are you okay? Bet you've got a killer headache," and he smiled at her crookedly.

"I want you to go," she said.

He frowned and rubbed his eyes. "Say that again, baby?"

She stepped nearer to him and tossed his phone onto the bed.

"I want you to go."

She enunciated each word clearly and carefully.

Confused, he stared first at the phone, then at her.

"What?"

"Go!" she hissed at him. "Go! Get out!"

Shock passed over his face and his eyes flickered back to his phone.

"Baby doll…"

"Don't call me that! You don't get to call me that! Get out, Daniel! Just go!"

"Lis, please, baby. It's not what you think."

She turned her back on him, then changed her mind. She walked over to the bed in two long strides and slapped his face hard.

He must have seen the blow coming but he didn't even try to stop her.

He stared at her for a moment as his cheek was stained red, then swung out of the bed and pulled on his jeans and t-shirt. He didn't even wait to fasten the buckles on his boots before he slammed the door behind him.

Lisanne collapsed onto the bed, tears choking her. Outside her window, she heard Sirona roar into life.

Several hours later, Kirsty found her, still curled up under her duvet, her eyes red, and all cried out.

"Oh, honey. I'm so sorry," she said.

Kirsty's kindness brought on a fresh bout of tears.

The last week of the semester was horrible.

Despite the Christmas decorations, the cards, gifts and last minute holiday shopping, Lisanne felt empty. Everywhere on campus reminded her of him: the lecture halls, the quad, the library, the cafeteria—even the fitness center because he'd talked so often about working-out there. The only saving grace was that nobody had seen Daniel. He seemed to have dropped off the face of the earth. Lisanne tried very hard not to care, but she was lying to herself.

Kirsty encouraged her to come out and enjoy the seasonal festivities, but Lisanne didn't have it in her. Even her final gig of the year with *32° North* seemed featureless, and she knew her singing was below par.

Roy said he hadn't seen Daniel but Lisanne suspected he was lying, and JP hadn't been able to meet her eyes. Only Mike acknowledged that he'd seen him, and reading between the lines, Lisanne suspected that Daniel had been drunk, or stoned, or both.

On Friday morning, the last day before the Christmas break, they received their grade for the business studies assignment. Professor Walden had awarded Lisanne and Daniel's paper 'A', with the word 'excellent!' scrawled across the top. Lisanne stared at the paper but Daniel wasn't there, and it seemed meaningless.

After the final class of the day and the year, Lisanne went to her room to pack. The last time she'd had to do that, she'd been heading for home, excited because Daniel was making the journey with her. Now, a few short weeks later, well, she didn't feel like celebrating.

Kirsty walked in looking flushed and happy. She was spending Christmas with her parents and then flying out to Aspen to spend New Years skiing with Vin and his family.

"Hey, roomie," she said. "How are you?"

Lisanne shrugged. "Okay, I guess."

Kirsty looked at her sympathetically. "It'll get better—I

promise. Oh, hey, you got mail."

Lisanne glanced without interest at the envelope Kirsty had dropped onto her bed. Then her eyes took in the scrawled handwriting and her stomach lurched. She'd seen it enough times as she'd studied in the library.

"What's the matter?" said Kirsty, her blue eyes concerned.

"It's from Daniel."

She held the letter as if it might explode, or hiss at her, or burn her fingers—maybe hurt her heart even more than he already had.

"Do you want me to open it?"

Lisanne shook her head. She sat on her bed, leaning against the headboard, and tore the envelope, pulling out a single sheet of lined paper. She wasn't sure what to expect: an apology, an attempt to rationalize his cheating, perhaps? But she was wrong, in every possible way.

Hey, Baby Doll,

I know you're going to be mad at me, so I won't even go there, but I can't do this anymore.

Everything has changed since I met you. I thought I knew who I was, what I was, but being with you, I've learned about the kind of man I want to be.

The last three weeks have been so hard and I've hated lying to you, but I thought you might try to stop me if you knew what I was doing. I know you read Cori's texts and if it helps any, she tried to talk me out of it. But I guess I can be pretty stubborn, too.

You didn't give me a chance to explain that night, and I'm not sure I could have done it right, which is why I'm writing you now.

I went to see Dr. Pappas when I got back from your folks, and I decided I'm going to get the implant. He can't tell me if it'll work, but the docs are going to try. I don't have anything to lose but if I can hear you sing, if I can hear your voice, that'll be enough.

This isn't on you, please don't think that. I've tried to live without my music and I can't do it. It slays me to see you up there, singing your heart out, and not to hear it. Pappas says there's a good chance, so what the hell? I'll be almost bionic the next time you see me. Ha ha. Yeah, I'll have a chunk of metal in my head, but I'll still be me—and I hope you'll still want me.

I'm sorry I've hurt you. I hated not telling you, but you can talk me into anything and I knew you'd try to stop me. I need to do this, baby.

I'm sorry.

I love you.

Daniel x

Wordlessly, she passed the letter to Kirsty who read it quickly, her eyes widening with each line.

"Lis, I don't understand. What's he done? What's this implant he's talking about?"

Lisanne took a deep breath.

"It's called a cochlear implant. It's … um … I'm not sure. Sort of a hearing aid that's put inside the ear. It's quite a big operation and…"

But the tears had started and her words got stuck as she tried to force them past her tongue.

Kirsty sat on the bed next to her and hugged her tightly, taking care not to crease the precious letter.

When Lisanne's sobs had eased, Kirsty gently pushed her away so she could see her face.

"I still don't understand, honey," she said, dabbing at Lisanne's eyes with a tissue. "Is Daniel ill?"

Lisanne shook her head. "He's deaf."

Kirsty's face was blank. "Who's deaf?"

"Daniel! He's deaf. That's why I got so mad with you when you kept saying he was being rude. He can't hear you—he can't hear anything. He lip reads. He's been deaf for nearly two years now."

Kirsty was clearly flabbergasted.

"I can't believe it! I mean … I had no clue! How could I not know? How could anyone not know? He hid it so well."

"*I knew*," said Lisanne, softly. "It was during our first study session in the library—the fire alarm went off—he didn't react. Just … nothing. And then he told me the whole story."

"Wow! I mean, wow! That's just … so this operation? He'll be able to hear again?"

"Maybe. No one can tell until afterward. I have to find him," Lisanne choked out. "I have to stop him. He mustn't do this."

"Why not?" said Kirsty, trying—and failing—to understand. "It's a good thing, isn't it, if it might work?"

"I don't know," moaned Lisanne. "He always said he didn't want a piece of metal in his head—that he didn't need to be *fixed*. This is all my fault! Will you drive me to his house, Kirsty? I need to talk to him."

"Of course I will."

"Thank you," Lisanne gasped.

But once they were mobile, it wasn't as easy finding Daniel's house as she'd thought.

For one thing, it had been months since she'd been there, and for another, he lived on the other side of town. It didn't help that they took a wrong turn, finding themselves navigating through rows of identically dull, suburban streets.

Eventually, using Kirsty's GPS and Lisanne's memory, they found the right address. But the house was dark and quiet.

She that there was no point knocking, so Lisanne tried the door. Locked.

"He could be in there," said Lisanne, anxiously scanning the unlit windows. "He could be in his room. Let's see if the back door is open."

They made their way around to the backyard, Kirsty staring with distaste at the rubbish heaped against the fence.

But the back of the house was equally dark, silent and locked against them. Just to be certain, Lisanne sent Daniel a text saying that she was outside. There was no response.

"What do you want to do?" asked Kirsty.

Car headlights strafed beams of light across the street, and there was the distinctive sound of metal grinding on metal.

"That's my fucking car!" shouted Kirsty, running out to the front.

The rear bumper was hanging off, and one tail light had been shattered, the glass crunching under Zef's boots as he staggered toward them. His own vehicle was abandoned at a crazy angle, half on and half off the sidewalk.

"Well, fuck me," he sneered, "you've got a fucking nerve turning up here."

"You trashed my car, you fucking asshole!" yelled Kirsty.

"Who's your friend?" jeered Zef, "she's got balls … and great tits."

"Shut up, Zef! Where's Daniel? I need to speak to him."

"You're asking me? That's fucking funny."

Lisanne pushed her finger into Zef's chest. "Where is he?!"

He straightened up and stared down at her.

For the first time Lisanne realized how dangerously angry Zef really was. And drunk. Very drunk.

"Do you care?" he said, his voice a low growl. "Do you? Because *my little brother* is in hospital having a fucking hole drilled in his skull, because *you* made him feel like he wasn't good enough. Bitch."

Lisanne gasped and her hand flew to her mouth.

Zef tossed his empty beer can at Kirsty's car and crashed through the door of his house, cursing loudly.

Kirsty tugged on her arm. "Come on, let's go."

Lisanne shook her head. "I have to find him, Kirsty."

"But we don't know which hospital he's in. God knows how many there are in the city limits. And I don't think his charmless brother is going to tell us."

But Lisanne was determined. "Then I'll just call every hospital until I find him."

They drove back to the dorm room, all thoughts of packing or leaving aborted. Each of them fired up their laptops and made a list of hospitals to call, dividing the task between them.

Their plan was to pretend to be Daniel's cousin and then play it by ear, fingers firmly crossed behind their backs.

They'd crossed off two hospitals each, and Kirsty was on her third call when she suddenly gesticulated wildly at Lisanne.

"Yeah, my cousin, that's right. His brother, um, Zef, gave me this number, but he forgot to say … oh, I see. No, that's fine. Thank you."

She hung up and stared at Lisanne. "He's in surgery now," she whispered, her voice strangled.

"Oh God! I'm too late."

The list of numbers fluttered from Lisanne's fingers, and as the tears trickled down her face, her lungs desperately tried to pull in gulping breaths.

She wanted to go to him—she had to go to him. She stood up abruptly.

"I need to call a cab!"

Kirsty grabbed her hands. "I'll drive you. Don't worry about that. But you should call your parents. They'd want to know."

"But…"

"Call your Mom."

She picked up Lisanne's phone and handed it to her.

It rang twice before her mother answered.

"Hi, honey! This is a nice surprise. How are…"

"Mommy!" Lisanne gulped out the word between sobs.

Immediately her mother heard the distress in her voice.

"Lisanne! What's happened? Are you all right?"

Lisanne shook her head, unable to speak.

"Lisanne! Lisanne!"

"Mommy, it's Daniel," she gasped.

Her mother's voice became cautious.

"What about Daniel?"

"He's … he's…"

"What? Has he hurt you?"

Lisanne could hear her father's anxious voice in the background.

"Daniel's in hospital."

There was a long pause.

"What happened? Is he all right?"

"He's…"

But the tears were falling too fast for her to speak coherently. She sobbed into the phone, clutching it tightly as if the small piece of plastic held a solution.

"Lisanne, sweetheart, take a deep breath. Try to tell me— what's happened to Daniel?"

Struggling to control her tears, Lisanne pulled in some shuddering breaths.

"Mommy, he's gone to have surgery. He's having a cochlear implant … they have to cut into his skull … they have to…"

The words choked in her throat.

Her mother's confused voice was quiet at the other end.

"I thought … you said he didn't want anything to do with those implants. I thought he'd decided…"

"He had!" wept Lisanne. "He hated them! He didn't want to have anything to do with them! He said they were ugly and unnatural and he couldn't imagine why anyone would voluntarily ask to have a piece of metal shoved into their heads! He said *that*—it's all my fault!"

"I don't understand—why did he change his mind?"

"He … he said he wanted to hear me sing!" she cried.

The phone was silent.

"Oh, my poor darling," said her mother, and Lisanne wasn't sure if she was talking about Daniel or herself. "We'll be there in three hours. Hold on until then. Daddy and I will be there."

Kirsty put off all plans of leaving and insisted on driving her to the hospital. Lisanne was so grateful her friend was there. At first they couldn't find anyone to tell them anything, but then Kirsty used the lawyer voice that her father had taught her, and they were finally able to talk to someone.

The nurse was an older woman with a sympathetic yet calm, professional air.

"Yes, I can confirm that Daniel Colton is being treated here," she said. "Are you relatives of his?"

"Yes," said Kirsty.

"No," said Lisanne, at the same time.

"She's his girlfriend," Kirsty admitted, quietly.

The nurse took in Lisanne's puffy, red-rimmed eyes and haunted expression.

"I see. I can only relay confidential information to his family."

"I'm his cousin," said Kirsty.

The nurse smiled. "Well, I'm glad to see Daniel has some … family who will be able to take care of him during his recovery. I've met his brother…"

Her smile fell away and she frowned.

"Is he all right? Daniel, can I see him?"

"I'm sorry, no. He's still in surgery. They've only just taken him in. This sort of procedure takes two to three hours."

She examined their worried faces.

"It's quite a standard operation these days and he's a fit young man. We would normally expect someone to stay in hospital for between one and three days, but it varies from individual to individual. You're welcome to stay in the waiting room."

"Thank you," whispered Lisanne.

The waiting room was relentlessly cheerful, the pale yellow walls covered with posters and children's drawings, but the chairs were comfortable and there was a water cooler in the corner of the room.

"You should go now, Kirsty," said Lisanne. "Your parents are expecting you."

"I'm not leaving you by yourself."

"My parents will be here in a couple of hours—I'll be fine."

"Then I'll wait for them to get here," said Kirsty, firmly.

Lisanne didn't have the energy to argue.

Slow minutes dragged by as they waited, Lisanne's eyes glued to the door. Kirsty brought her coffee, and held her hand. They didn't speak.

Two long, slow, anxious hours later, the nurse returned.

"He's out of surgery and the doctor says it went well. He'll be in recovery for about an hour."

"Can I see him?"

"Not yet. When we've moved him to his unit."

Lisanne thanked her again, wiping tears from her eyes.

"See," said Kirsty, "he's going to be fine."

Lisanne nodded, but couldn't share Kirsty's optimism. That he'd put himself through this for her sake—it seemed so wrong.

They heard a noise out in the corridor and Lisanne recognized her parents' voices. She was already on her feet when her mother swept into the room.

She hugged her tightly and whispered soothingly into her hair. Lisanne finally looked up to see her father talking quietly to Kirsty.

"Have you seen him yet?" said Monica.

"No. He's in recovery and I can't see him until he's moved. Soon, I hope."

"Have you been able to find out anything else?"

Lisanne shook her head. "No, but I saw his brother. He blames me—he says it's my fault. Mom, I thought he was breaking up with me. He's been so secretive—now I know why,

I just feel so horrible. I *never* wanted him to do this. Why did he do it?"

Her question set off a fresh wave of tears.

"Daniel made his own decision, darling. The doctors obviously thought it was a good idea or they would never have gone ahead with it."

Kirsty came over to give her a hug. "Will you be okay if I go now? My mom is going crazy that I'll be driving after dark." She rolled her eyes. "I told her they've invented headlights, but, well, you know."

"No, that's fine. Thank you for staying. I really appreciate it."

"Of course. Where else was I going to be? Text me when you've got some news?"

Kirsty left after one more quick hug and Lisanne sat down with her mom.

"Where's Dad gone?"

"He went to find a doctor," said Monica, with a fond smile. "He's gone into 'dad' mode. You know how he gets."

Lisanne forced out a weak smile. Right now, dad-mode was exactly what she wanted.

He returned a few minutes later with a tall, thin man in a surgeon's blue scrubs.

"Good evening. I'm Dr. Palmer, Daniel's surgeon. I understand you have a few questions. I normally only speak to family members unless otherwise authorized, but I understand that Daniel doesn't have parents ... so, in the circumstances…"

"Could you tell us about the procedure—I'm afraid this is all new to us," said Ernie. "Daniel didn't tell us … my daughter is his girlfriend; she's a music major," he finished quietly, as if offering an explanation.

A look of understanding mixed with pity passed over the doctor's face.

"Well, simply put, I have inserted the internal parts of the cochlear implant underneath the skin. The receiver—which we call a stimulator—sits in the bone just behind the ear." The doctor gestured to his own head. "The electrode array is inserted directly into the cochlea."

"So when he wakes up he'll be able to hear?"

"No, not yet. I've only fitted the internal parts of the device which includes a small magnet under the skin toward the back of the head. A CI isn't a hearing aid: it bypasses the damaged hair cells in the cochlea and directly stimulates the auditory nerve. We'll have to wait between three and six weeks after surgery, to allow any swelling or tenderness around the implant site to subside. Only then can the external parts of the device be fitted. That includes the processor and transmitter."

"But, he told my daughter that hearing aids didn't help him?"

"No, an external device by itself wouldn't offer the level of amplification Daniel needs. And we still can't tell how successful this operation will be. Typically, it has good results, but nothing is guaranteed," he re-emphasized.

"But he might be able to hear?" said Lisanne, desperate to understand.

The doctor sighed.

"There is no pre-operative test to determine how much a patient will be able to hear. I wish there were. The range of hearing varies from near normal ability to understand speech, to no benefit at all, and everything in between. I would hope that Daniel will be able to have some immediate benefits but improvements will continue for about three to nine months after the initial tuning sessions, sometimes for several years. He may even be able to use a telephone; however, I should warn you that not all people who have implants are able to do so. He'll be able to watch TV more easily, although he may not hear well enough to enjoy music, for example."

"He … he won't be able to listen to music?" asked Lisanne, sounding distraught.

The doctor looked at her cautiously.

"Some people who've had this procedure enjoy the sound of certain instruments, the piano or guitar, for example, and certain voices, but a band or an orchestra—that is a far more complex range of sounds to be processed. We'll just have to wait and see."

"What about side effects?" said Monica. "My daughter mentioned that there's a possibility of injury to the facial nerve?"

"It can happen during surgery, very rarely, but I'm happy to tell you that this is not the case for Daniel."

Finally some good news, thought Lisanne.

"I would expect Daniel to experience some dizziness or attacks of vertigo, so he won't be able to drive his car for a while."

"He doesn't have a car, he has a motorcycle—a Harley Davidson," said Lisanne, unable to stop herself from adding the detail that was pointless to everyone except Daniel.

"No, he mustn't ride that," said the doctor shuddering, and muttering something under his breath about 'donor-cycles' which made Monica look faint.

"Daniel may experience some taste disturbance, but as the surgery went well, I think that's unlikely. There may be some numbness around his ear..."

"Can ... can it be damaged, the implant?" asked Lisanne.

"It's made from titanium—even harder than Daniel's skull."

He saw the expression on her face, and cleared his throat.

"Sorry—doctor's joke. Until recently we advised against contact sports, for example, but with adequate protection, he should be fine. He mustn't get the external devices wet, of course, so he'll have to remove those for showering or swimming."

"When can he come home?"

"Recovery rates vary, but I'd hope he'll be feeling well within 12 to 24 hours. Usually we'd expect a patient to go home the next day but I understand Daniel won't have anyone to look after him..."

When he didn't receive a response to that, the doctor plowed on.

"In which case we will encourage him to stay in a second night to aid his recovery. He'll be given an appointment to have the stitches out in a week, and he'll be back at school after New Years. That's why he pushed for surgery before Christmas—he's a very determined young man. He was lucky to get a slot so quickly—most wait months, but then again most people don't want their holidays spoiled. Well, if you don't have any more questions...?"

Lisanne raised her hand. "Um, I was wondering, why has he only had one implant? I mean, he's deaf in both ears."

"Well," said the doctor, rubbing his eyes tiredly. "Two reasons: we need to be sure that Daniel will benefit from a unilateral implant and by how much; secondly, this is a fairly recent procedure. The first commercial CI implant took place in the mid 1970s. We've only reached our present level of development fairly recently. My belief is that great strides will be made in the next ten to twenty years. Anything else?"

They all shook their heads wordlessly, stunned by the influx of new information.

The doctor gave them a professional smile and left them alone.

"Well," said Monica, rather shakily. "That all sounds … very positive."

She looked at her husband worriedly. Lisanne closed her eyes, trying to pull back more tears. They didn't help anyone.

A commotion outside was punctuated by the door to the waiting room being thrown open.

"How fucking cozy is this?" hissed Zef, staring wrathfully from Lisanne to her parents.

"Excuse me!" barked Ernie, in his best teacher voice.

"No, I won't fucking excuse you," Zef spat back. "This is all *her* fault," and he pointed at Lisanne.

The nurse came bustling in. "If you can't keep your voice down, I'll have to ask you to leave."

"Not without seeing my brother!" he shouted.

"Sir, lower your voice and I'll take you to him. You and his girlfriend."

"How come she gets to see him? She's not family."

The nurse ignored him, and walked out of the door. Lisanne followed hurriedly, casting nervous glances at Zef. At least he seemed to have sobered up.

"We've just moved him from recovery—he's in here."

She opened another door and showed them inside.

Daniel was lying pale and too still against the white hospital sheets.

His eyebrow ring had been removed, along with his nipple rings, and his tattoos stood out starkly against his skin. But the most obvious difference was the thick bandage wrapped around his head, with heavy padding by his left ear.

Lisanne could also see that he'd shaved off most of his hair, leaving just a short buzz-cut showing on the crown of his head, above the bandages.

Zef glanced at his brother, his face contorting, but he refused to look at Lisanne.

She swallowed back tears as the nurse fussed around him, checking Daniel's blood pressure, noting the results on his chart.

"The surgery went well," she said, cheerfully. "He'll be waking up soon. He'll be groggy and he'll have a headache, but we can control that with painkillers."

"I should fucking hope so," snarled Zef.

The nurse's smile lost some of its brilliance.

"Yes, well. If he needs anything as he starts to wake up, just press the button here."

As soon as the nurse left, Zef turned and stared at Lisanne, his face dark with anger.

"This is your fault. He was happy before he met you. Now look at him!"

"I ... I didn't ask him to do this," whispered Lisanne, feeling sick to her core. "I wouldn't. I..."

"You should have stayed away from him," said Zef, bitterly. "I told him you were dangerous."

"I love him," she mumbled.

"Is that right?" sneered Zef. "Is that why you wanted to change him? Now he's got a chunk of metal stuck in his head. He'd never have done that by himself. I hope you're fuckin' pleased with yourself."

He stormed out of the room, too filled with fury to look at his little brother's girlfriend any longer.

CHAPTER 19

Daniel's eyes flickered and gradually opened. He took in the overly bright room and squinted up at the electric lights.

He felt a pressure on his hand and he turned to look, then immediately regretted moving. *Fuck, that hurt.* A face came into focus, hovering above him. Serious, gray eyes and straight brown hair.

"Hey, baby doll!" he croaked, wondering why he felt like he'd been on an all-night bender.

And then he remembered: hospital—anesthetic—operation. It explained the reason his head felt like it had been stuffed with cotton balls.

He licked his dry lips as his eyelids drifted down slowly.

She tapped his hand, and he opened his eyes again.

She was holding up a cup of water. Baby Doll always knew what he needed.

He tried to nod, but his head was too heavy. He felt the bed moving under him, and he caught the faint scent of her perfume as she leaned down toward him.

He was thirsty, but the damned beaker only let him have a few sips. He tried to hold it but he had no strength in his hands, and they flopped back onto the bed.

He closed his eyes again and felt her fingers squeeze his hand.

She was here. His Baby Doll was here.

The relief that Lisanne felt when Daniel opened his eyes and spoke to her was without measure. He was the same: he was Daniel, and he was going to be all right.

She sat on the hard, plastic hospital seat and took his hand in hers. It was dry and a little cool. She pulled the blanket further up his chest, and stood up to place a gentle kiss on his cheek.

She had to tell him … explain how she felt … but it was the words of a song that said it for her. Roy had mentioned once that the Crowded House song *Fall At Your Feet* had been a favorite of Daniel's.

She sat down again and began to sing softly.

> *I'm really close tonight*
> *And I feel like you're moving inside me*
> *Lying in the dark…*

His chest continued to rise and fall slowly.

> *I think that I'm beginning to know him*
> *Let it go*
> *I'll be there when you call.*

She ran her fingers across the back of his hand.

> *And whenever I fall at your feet*
> *Won't you let your tears rain down on me?*
> *Whenever I touch your slow turning pain…*

And she touched his cheek.

> *You're hiding from me now*
> *There's something in the way that you're talking*
> *The words don't sound right*
> *But I hear them all moving inside you*
> *Know*
> *I'll be waiting when you call.*

"You are so stubborn," she said, her voice soft with hidden tears. "You hold back so much of yourself. You don't share your problems with me; you won't let me in. But you make me laugh and you've shown me who I want to be, too. You're so strong and so gentle all at the same time. You're so full of life, and I hate seeing you lying here like this, and I hate thinking it was because of me. You're beautiful inside and out, Daniel Colton, and I love you."

363

Then she rested her head on his bed and let the tears fall.

The nurse made her go after that, but she left Daniel's room feeling calm. Her parents saw the change in her immediately.

"How is he?" asked Monica, reaching for her daughter.

"He's going to be okay. I think he's going to be okay. He was thirsty. That's a good sign, right?"

"Well, the doctor seemed like he knew what he was talking about," said Ernie, with authority. "There's no reason why Daniel shouldn't make a full recovery."

"Your father and I have checked into a motel for tonight," said Monica, reaching out for Lisanne's hand. "Harry's staying with the Milfords. Anyway, it's too late to drive home and this way, we can bring you to see Daniel in the morning."

Lisanne hugged her parents, grateful to have them look after her, grateful to have them in her life, grateful to have them in Daniel's life—for however long he'd let them.

During the ride back to the dorm she texted the good news to Kirsty. There was no immediate reply—she was probably still driving.

Her thoughts turned to Zef and the ugly things he'd said. Clearly he blamed Lisanne for Daniel's decision and in all honesty, she couldn't help but agree with him.

Daniel had been vocal in his rejection of the implant at the start of the semester. He'd gotten mad with Dr. Pappas during his consultation, but he'd also admitted that seeing her sing at the club had hurt. The guilt she felt unfurled, curling around her.

So she slept badly, waking often, haunted by Zef's angry eyes, and Daniel's wounded ones.

Feeling tired and anxious, Lisanne reluctantly spent the morning shopping with her mom, while her dad took a tour of the city. They'd been told to let Daniel rest and not to visit until 2 PM. Consequently, she'd had four hours to build up the dread of bumping into Zef again. As they arrived at the hospital, Lisanne grit her teeth as her parents waited in the lounge.

Daniel was sitting up in bed, looking far more alert than the previous day. His head was still swathed in a bandage, and his beautiful face was grumpy as he gazed out of the window.

When he saw her walking through the door, his astonished smile was radiant.

"Baby doll!"

"Hi." She managed a small smile in return then hesitated, trying to work out what to say. "You cut your hair."

"Seemed like a good idea."

They stared at each other.

"What are you doing here? I thought you'd be home with your folks by now."

She rolled her eyes. "After that letter you sent me?"

He looked away, embarrassed.

She sat down on the bed to hold his hand, and he looked up at her.

"I wish you'd told me."

He frowned. "You'd have stopped me."

"You should have talked to me."

"Yeah. Not so good at that."

"I loved what you wrote," she said, shyly. "Did you mean it?"

He looked at her quickly, then looked away. "Yeah."

The silence between them was uncomfortable, a little awkward, but not unpleasant.

"So, how are you?"

"Apart from feeling like someone sawed my head off and reattached it the wrong way around? Yeah, pretty good." He shrugged. "Headache."

"Um," said Lisanne, awkwardly, "my parents are here. They'd like to see you—can they come in?"

He looked at her blankly. "Here? At the hospital?"

Lisanne nodded.

"Why are your parents here?"

"I … I called them. I was … upset. They wanted to come and make sure you were okay."

Daniel was puzzled. "Why?"

She rolled her eyes in frustration. "Because they care about you, dummy!"

He still looked doubtful.

"So can they? Come in?"

"I guess."

Muttering under her breath about the obtuseness of men in general and Daniel in particular, Lisanne brought her mom and dad from the lounge.

Daniel looked tense as they entered, and utterly baffled as Monica swept him up into a hug that made him wince.

"Careful, Mom!" Lisanne warned her.

"Oh, sorry, sorry!" she said to the side of Daniel's head—which meant he couldn't understand her anyway.

"Now then, Mon," said Ernie, and he held out his hand to Daniel. "How are you doing, son? You gave Lisanne quite a scare."

Daniel's eyes flicked back to Lisanne. "I did?"

"Yes, you idiot!" she yelled, shocking her parents.

Daniel grinned at her. "You're cute when you're angry."

"She gets that from her mother," said Ernie.

The men folk shared a moment as the women stared in disbelief.

"Yes, well, I'll go get us some coffee," said Ernie, completely over the whole male bonding moment.

"Three sugars for Daniel," called Monica.

"He takes it black," yelled Lisanne.

Ernie stalked away muttering into his teeth.

"Baby doll, will you walk with me? I'm sick of this damn room."

"Are you allowed to?"

"Yeah, but I have to have someone go with me in case I get dizzy or shit."

Daniel pulled back the bed sheets before Lisanne could agree or not. She blushed automatically, a Pavlovian response to his nakedness. Except that he wasn't.

"Pajama pants?" she said, raising her eyebrows.

"Sure! You expecting something else, baby?" he teased. "I

wanted to get them for hospital. Maybe I should have worn one of those gowns—with my ass hanging out."

"What do you usually wear, Daniel?" said Monica, with a maternally inquisitive air.

Daniel grinned at her. "Nothing."

"Oh!" said Monica, her face matching her daughter's.

Lisanne didn't think it was time to confirm that Daniel was telling the truth.

He lurched to one side as he stood up, and had to clutch the bed rail.

"Fuck," he said, as his free hand flew to his head.

"Are you okay?" Lisanne gasped.

"Whoa, vertigo. That was weird. Nah, I'm good."

Warily, he released the bed rail and caught his balance, before taking a cautious step.

"Okay?" said Lisanne again, biting her lip.

"Yeah, I got it," said Daniel.

"Lisanne, take his arm, just to be on the safe side," Monica ordered. "Oh, and Daniel, I think you should wear something on your top half." She tossed him a t-shirt that he'd abandoned on the bed. "I'll wait here."

Daniel smirked but complied, and Lisanne's eyes travelled hungrily over his body as he pulled the shirt on.

She felt slightly guilty, ogling him when he was sick.

She linked her arm through Daniel's, happy to have the excuse of touching his warm smooth skin. A tingle shivered through her and Daniel gave her an odd look.

He stumbled slightly, and she put her arm around his waist, letting her hand rest over his right hip.

They set off down the corridor, walking slowly,

"I missed you, baby doll," he said softly, watching her face carefully.

"Me, too. Ass."

"Ass?"

"Among other things."

"Are you mad?"

"Daniel Colton, you haven't even seen mad yet. Just you wait until you're better."

"Okay," he said, happily.

"We got an 'A' on our Business assignment."

He smiled. "Told you, baby doll." Then he stopped as a thought occurred to him. "Were you here, last night?"

"Yes, of course."

"Oh. I thought I'd dreamed you."

"You … you dream about me?"

He answered by pulling her into his chest.

"Always," he breathed onto her lips, before kissing her completely.

"I don't fucking believe this!"

Lisanne broke away from Daniel as she heard Zef's angry voice behind them. Daniel, of course, hadn't, and he smiled at his brother.

"Hey, man!"

His smile faltered as his eyes took in Zef's glare of hate, burning its way toward Lisanne, and her tension—almost fear.

"What's going on?"

"Nothing, little brother," said Zef, forcing a smile. "Brought you some shit."

He waved some motorcycle magazines in Daniel's face.

"Thanks, man. We're just getting some coffee. You want in?"

"Nah, I'm good. Just dropping these off. Got some business to take care of. Catch you later … when you're alone."

He said the last part so only Lisanne knew what he'd said, then shoved the magazines into her hands before loping off down the corridor. Daniel watched him, looking worried.

He turned to Lisanne.

"Has he said something to you?"

"Um, well…"

"Lis, please? I hate people talking *about* me and not *to* me."

Lisanne sighed. But she was saved answering when her dad reappeared carrying four coffees in paper cups.

They made their way back to his room, Daniel walking

slowly and carefully. He looked tired now, as if the short conversation and shorter walk had utterly worn him out. Lisanne was so used to his limitless energy as he bounded around, that this listlessness worried her. His balance worsened, making it necessary for Lisanne to carry the coffee, while her dad helped Daniel back into his bed.

He frowned and leaned back carefully, his hands on his head.

Monica threw a look laced with significance at her daughter. "I think we've tired Daniel out—we should go now. You can come back later on."

Lisanne nodded, then tapped Daniel's hand.

"We're going now."

He gave her a weak smile. "Sorry," he said, quietly.

She kissed his cheek, and laid her hand on his chest over his heart. And she was wearing the locket he'd given her—she knew he'd understand.

The mood as they left the hospital was somber. They'd arrived with such high hopes and now Lisanne was feeling not only deflated, but concerned, too.

"Honey, would you like us to stay one more night?" asked Monica, sensing her daughter's anxiety. "Then we could drive Daniel to his house when he's released. Harry will be fine with the Milfords for another night. We can all travel home together."

"Thanks, Mom," said Lisanne, quietly.

Her dad gave her a hug.

"He'll be fine. It's still less than 24 hours since his operation. Give him time."

While Ernie called the motel to reserve their room for another night, Lisanne and her mom waited at the entrance. Monica tried to persuade her that worrying wouldn't help.

"Daniel needs you to be positive right now. I can't imagine what he's been going through—and without any real family support from what I can see," she added, frowning. "Despite what has been going on between you two."

"I … I thought he was going to break up with me. Mom, I was so horrible to him. I feel so bad. And now this…"

She passed her mother the letter Daniel had written, and watched her face as Monica read it through. When she'd finished, she hugged her daughter tightly.

"Daniel is a very special young man," she said. "I'm glad he's found my very special daughter."

Lisanne managed a small smile, mostly to reassure her mom.

When they returned to the hospital several hours later, Monica and Ernie decided to wait in the lounge again, giving their daughter a chance to see Daniel alone. But as she entered his room, he'd only had a chance to smile and say hi, before she was overtaken by a young doctor, tailed by a bevy of medical students.

"Mr. Colton, I'm Dr. Mendez, I'll be taking a look at your wound."

"Where's the other guy—Palmer?" said Daniel, sounding defensive.

The doctor turned and looked at Lisanne when he answered. "*Doctor* Palmer has instructed me to supervise your recovery period."

"Well, you can start by looking at Daniel when you speak to him," snapped Lisanne, "as he's just had a cochlear implant and he still needs to lip read you because he's *still deaf*."

The doctor looked irritated and flustered, but turned to repeat the information to Daniel. Lisanne noticed that several of the students were holding back grins.

"Are you family?" he said to Lisanne, trying to reassert his authority.

She crossed her arms. "Yes."

The doctor sniffed and looked disgruntled, then directed his attention to Daniel's wound. The students stood in a semicircle around him, dutifully taking notes.

"This patient presented with idiopathic sensorineural hearing loss from the age of 14, and chose this elective procedure after losing hearing below 110 decibels, at the age of..."

"Fuck!" yelped Daniel, as the doctor knocked his ear while pulling off the bandage.

Lisanne took a step closer, ready to act as a bodyguard, should it be needed.

The doctor probed the wound, more carefully this time, but Daniel still winced. Lisanne's face lost some of its color when she saw the jagged six inch incision snaking upwards from behind his left ear, sewn together with small, precise stitches. Either side of the wound, his head had been completely shaved. She could see now why he'd opted for the buzz cut.

The skin looked pink and angry to Lisanne, but the doctor seemed pleased.

"Yes, that's healing up nicely. No sign of infection. Any tenderness?"

Lisanne sighed and stood in front of Daniel. "He wants to know if there's any tenderness?"

"Of course there's fucking tenderness! Are you sure this guy's a doctor?"

This time the medical students chuckled quietly and the doctor flushed with anger.

Lisanne giggled. Daniel winked at her, and a slow smile stretched across his face.

"Lis, can you check to see if my brain is hanging out? I'm not sure this guy would recognize it."

She slapped his arm.

"Stop it!"

He just grinned. "Take a souvenir picture for me, baby doll?"

Lisanne grabbed his phone and took a couple of shots of the grisly sight. She couldn't wait for it all to be a dim and distant memory.

"Any numbness? Can you feel that?"

The doctor touched the tip of Daniel's ear.

"Huh, no, nothing. That'll be a cheap piercing." He raised his eyebrows at Lisanne, who tried to look cross.

"Any loss of taste?"

"I've been eating hospital food all day—how the hell am I supposed to know?"

Lisanne snickered.

371

"So, doc, can I get out of here?"

The doctor walked around to face Daniel again, obviously annoyed.

"Let me see how your balance is, Mr. Colton."

Daniel swung out of the bed smoothly, but wobbled as he stood up, another attack of vertigo sweeping over him.

"And walking?"

Daniel grit his teeth and made it across the room, swaying slightly.

"Hmm, Dr. Palmer has recommended one more night in hospital, Mr. Colton," said the doctor, ignoring Daniel's curse, "and I concur. We'll see how you are in the morning. I'll send in a nurse to dress your wound. You'll need to keep the gauze strips for another week."

The doctor swept back out of the room, his head held high, the flock of students lagging behind.

Lisanne heard one of the students whisper, "He was cute! He can be my patient any day."

She threw an angry look but it bounced futilely off of the girl's back.

Daniel was oblivious and sitting back on the bed, looking mutinous.

"Hey," she said, stroking his cheek. "It's only one more night. You were expecting that, right?"

"Easy for you to say," he said, sulkily. "Seeing you is the only good part of the whole fucking day."

She smiled happily. "Kirsty says 'hi' and Harry said something that I didn't understand: *he's practicing*. Does that mean anything to you?"

Daniel smirked. "Guy talk. Don't worry about it."

"Ugh, I don't think I want to know."

"Did you tell Kirsty?"

Lisanne sighed as the shutters came down, and Daniel's expression resorted to the careful blankness that she found so frustrating.

"She drove me here—I had to tell her."

"Has she … told anyone else?"

"I don't know. Vin maybe. I could ask her…"

He lifted his hand to his head then dropped it again. "Yeah, I don't want anyone else to know…"

"Okay."

He rubbed his forehead tentatively.

"Have you got a headache? Sorry—dumb question."

He lay back, wincing as his head touched the pillow.

"It's weird—talking feels sort of uncomfortable. It feels like the vibrations from my voice are moving the implant. I don't know. I know that's not possible. It's freakin' bizarre to think I have a chunk of metal in my head."

Then he opened his eyes again and smiled up at Lisanne.

"You know what's good for curing headaches?"

"What?" she said, wary of the wicked gleam in his eye.

"Hey, come here."

He held out his hand and pulled her down until she was sitting on the bed next to him, smiling the sexy smile that always got Lisanne hot and bothered.

"Sex," he said.

"Excuse me?"

"Sex is great for headaches. Just sayin'."

"Daniel! We can't … I'm not … I can't even believe you're suggesting it! You've just had surgery! No. Definitely not."

He kissed her neck and licked the base of her jaw.

She moaned softly.

"I've missed you, baby doll," he whispered. "Feel what you do to me."

He moved her hand down, and she felt him becoming hard beneath the hospital sheet.

She gasped and glanced toward the door, but she didn't move her hand away either.

He shifted his hips upwards.

"Lis…" His voice was almost pleading.

Keeping her eyes on the door, she slipped her hand underneath the sheet.

She glanced quickly at Daniel. He was watching her intently, his lips slightly parted. He was hot and hard under the sheet and she ran her fingers along his length, seeing his eyes darken with need and lust. She grasped him firmly and a soft noise broke from his lips. She moved her hand more quickly, feeling his body responding.

And then her mother knocked on the door. Lisanne jerked her hand away so quickly, Daniel gagged and nearly swallowed his tongue.

"Is everything okay in here?" said Monica, staring anxiously at Daniel's flushed face.

Then she looked at her daughter, who seemed to be finding the floor of extreme interest.

"Daniel has a headache," Lisanne stammered.

There was an appalled silence.

"I see," said her mother, tightly. "Well … we should be going now, Lisanne. We'll give you a ride back to campus. You feel well, Daniel."

Lisanne raised her eyes to Daniel, who seemed to be having trouble forming words.

"Yeah, yeah," he gasped.

"Um, I'll see you tomorrow."

"Uh huh."

Monica grabbed her daughter's arm and marched her out of the room.

Daniel wished to hell and back that Monica had waited just another two minutes before deciding to check on them, and interrupting what was proving to be a very enjoyable hospital visit. Two goddamn minutes! That woman could win a gold medal at cockblocking.

It had felt so good to have Lis's hands on him. He hadn't been sure he'd see her again after she'd slapped him that night—he'd really thought it was all over for them. She wasn't the first woman who'd hit him and he knew it didn't usually mean anything good. He'd just held onto the hope that Lisanne would relent once she knew the truth—once she'd read his letter.

It had been hell not touching her after Thanksgiving, but somehow it had felt wrong when he knew what he was keeping from her.

Seeing her again at the hospital, it had been a relief. More than that—it had given him some peace. But now his frustration was at an all time high. Sighing, he shuffled into the private bathroom to finish the job in hand, then cleaned himself up.

While he was there he brushed his teeth, even though it hurt to open his mouth fully. Everything in his head ached and he wondered if he could have more painkillers yet. He'd have given his left nut for a smoke—or some weed.

The bathroom door opened a fraction and he saw Zef peering cautiously around the door.

"Hey, man. Thought you might be on the can. You okay?"

"Yeah, but I've got to stay another night. Balance is all shot to hell."

Zef frowned. "Bummer. Can you ride Sirona like that?"

"No, not till the doc says so. Could be a week or so."

"How you gonna get around, man?"

Daniel shrugged. "Walk. Take the bus. Maybe you could give me a ride?" he said, looking at Zef hopefully.

"Well, yeah, but I'm pretty busy."

"With what?"

"Don't ask."

"Come on, Zef. You said you'd talk to me after Thanksgiving, but I've hardly seen you."

"That's because *you* were planning to get that junk shoved in your skull."

Daniel felt angry. Not this *again*. "Don't start."

"All because of some piece of skirt! What is going on with you?"

"Don't talk about her like that!" Daniel's voice held a quiet warning.

"You want to talk, so let's talk!" Zef said, angrily. "You always said you never wanted the operation, then you meet this chick and suddenly you're having surgery on your head. Explain it to me."

Daniel took a deep breath, trying to order the words that he'd thought a thousand times.

"If this works, I'll hear music again. It's about the music. Lis—she just ... I see what music means to her." He shrugged. "She reminds me of me ... how I used to be."

Zef sighed, and his shoulders dropped as his aggressive stance relaxed.

"Yeah, I get that. I just hated the way you snuck off and did it. I mean, fuck. I'm your *brother* and you told that bitch but you didn't tell me."

"If you call her that again, we're going to have a serious fucking problem." Daniel paused. "And I didn't tell *anyone*. It was *my* decision—no one else's."

Zef shook his head. "Whatever. Just tell me that Medicaid covers *everything*. We're not going to get landed with any big hospital bills or shit."

A bitter expression crossed Daniel's face. "No. It's covered."

"Good." Zef stared at his brother. "Look, I've got to get going. I brought you some smokes and a little something extra." He winked. "See you at home tomorrow."

After Zef left, Daniel dragged himself back to bed. Despite bitching like crazy about having to stay in for another night, he was secretly relieved. Everything at the hospital was in order, everything was calm. He didn't have to worry about who the hell was in his house, or what shit his brother was getting into. If his Baby Doll could have been there, it would have been damn near perfect—except for feeling like he'd lost a fight against a bad-tempered rhino, and now had a hangover that could have felled a Canadian hockey team.

He climbed wearily onto his bed, pulling Zef's gift toward him: the plastic bag contained two packs of Camel, a lighter, blunt wrappers, and a small cube wrapped in tin foil. Daniel sniffed it—resin dope. It explained the blunt wrappers. Jeez, he was tempted.

He hadn't told Zef, but he'd tried to give up smoking before the operation—an additional reason that Lisanne had found him jittery and with a short fuse. It wasn't the best timing, what with feeling so fucking stressed, but he figured he'd feel shit enough in hospital without being desperate for a smoke, as well. Trouble was, three weeks hadn't been long enough to break a three year, 20 a day habit.

He checked the window by his bed. Typical hospital arrangement—it would only open a few inches. Not enough room to lean out and have a smoke. Or take a fucking dive. Sighing, he dropped the bag on the floor where it was out of sight, and lay back carefully. His head hurt like a bitch and he could only lie comfortably with his face turned to the right.

He knew he wasn't the world's most patient person, in fact he'd go so far as to admit he was an impatient son of a bitch— which meant that the next few days of sitting around were going to be a pain in the butt. And it would be well into January before the audiologist first attempted to tune in the processor and transmitter, followed by more weeks of waiting to see how much—or if—he'd be able to hear.

He hated the thought of having to deal with a hearing device, batteries, and all of that again. He remembered when he'd first worn hearing aids to high school. His real friends had treated him pretty much the same, but there was all the usual name-calling: 'soundproof', 'earwax', 'cyborg', 'Dan Deaf'—short conversations with fuckwits that Daniel had ended with his fists. Conversations that had driven his parents crazy because of all the times they'd been called in to speak to the Principal about another fight he'd gotten into.

But worse than the fights had been the pitying glances. Girls who'd flirted with him and thought he was hot, now looked like they felt sorry for him and wanted to bake him cookies instead of making out behind the gym. He never wanted to see that sort of pity on Lisanne's face. He couldn't help worrying how she'd react the first time he wore his new hearing processor. He knew from experience that it was one thing to know that someone was deaf, but a whole other thing entirely to see the physical manifestation of that *disability*. Would she look at him differently? Would he start to see the sideways glances? Would he read regret in her face? Regret for getting involved with someone like him.

And while he was still concerned to maintain his privacy at college, he didn't care so much anymore about the negative comments from people he didn't know. They could all just fuck right off.

His thoughts turned to Zef. He'd never seen him wound so tight. Whatever was going on was serious.

He rubbed his forehead again. It was the only part of his head that didn't hurt.

A nurse came in with more Tylenol and looked like she wanted to stay and chat, but Daniel was feeling drained and his eyes were closing.

He slept fitfully, dreaming that Lisanne's disappointed eyes were turning away from him.

By morning, Daniel was desperate to leave. His headache had lessened, and he'd practiced walking across the room, testing his balance and fighting off sudden attacks of vertigo. He was left kicking his heels until the doctor made his rounds again. Daniel was just thinking of heading the hell out, when the same guy as the day before wafted in.

"Good morning, Mr. Colton," said the doctor, trying to sound severe.

"Yeah, can I get out of here now?"

Dr. Mendez checked the wound again, declaring himself satisfied—but wouldn't sign off because of the fact that Daniel was still lurching as he walked across the room.

"I think one more night just to be sure, Mr. Colton."

"Not going to happen, doc. Things to do, places to be."

"That would not be sensible."

"Come on, give me a break. You want me out of here just as much as I want to go."

The doctor finally cracked a smile.

"Will you have someone to look after you for a couple of days until you're back on your feet?"

"Sure. My brother is ... home."

"Fine," said the doctor, resigned. "I'll get the pharmacy to send up a pack of gauze so you can have your brother dress your wound. You'll need to return in five days to have the stitches removed."

Daniel nodded.

"And I'll have an orderly bring a wheelchair to take you down."

"Fuck that! I'm not going to be wheeled out of here!"

"I thought you might say that," sighed the doctor, "but if you fall over on your way out of the hospital, it'll be my ass that gets sued. And wait until your taxi is at the curb."

Daniel looked like he was about to argue.

"Just take the damn chair," snapped the doctor. "Please."

Daniel smiled then cautiously pulled on a black beanie, making sure it covered the gauze as well as both ears.

"Fair enough."

It turned out that the porter was a football fan, and soon forgot that he was supposed to be wheeling Daniel *in* the chair as they walked along. Instead they talked about the new Falcons signing who could bench press 225 pounds 24 reps, and run a forty yard dash in 4.43 seconds.

Daniel was so focused on the conversation that he almost missed Lisanne and her parents, as they made their way through the crowded entrance.

He felt someone grab his elbow, nearly tipping him over. When he'd caught his balance he glanced up to see Lisanne's worried face.

The porter hurried away, looking guilty.

"Hey, baby doll" said Daniel, with a grin. "I got sprung."

"Are you sure? You look kind of wobbly."

He winked at her, and she sighed.

"Fine. Mom and Dad are here—we can give you a ride."

"'S'okay, I can get a cab."

"Shut up and get in the damn car, Daniel."

He grinned. "Feisty, baby doll. I like it."

She pulled his arm again, more gently this time, and placed it around her waist, where Daniel was more than happy to have it.

Monica hugged him and kissed his cheek, which made Daniel duck his head in embarrassment. He was much more comfortable with Ernie's brisk handshake.

He climbed into the back of their station wagon, trying to ignore the annoying feeling of vertigo every time he leaned forward. That shit could make you nauseous. He gave Ernie the zip code for the GPS, and sat back in the car, feeling Lisanne's warm hand in his. He wished he could kiss his girl properly, but he knew she wouldn't want that in front of her parents. He sighed. It was three weeks until the start of the next semester—three weeks before he'd see Lisanne again.

He felt her fingers tighten on his hand and he smiled at her, before leaning back and letting the streets drift past him, a silent parade of shops, offices, people, cars.

When they reached Daniel's house, Monica turned worried eyes toward her husband. There seemed to be a party going on at the Colton home. Cars and motorbikes lined the road and loud music blared out. One guy was urinating by the side of the house, and two more were sitting on the front steps, sharing a bottle of tequila.

Daniel kept his face neutral, but he could make a pretty good guess what Lisanne's parents must be thinking.

"We can't leave him here!" hissed Monica.

Ernie nodded, his face angry.

"Daniel…" Lisanne began.

"Hey, don't worry, baby doll," he said, kissing her cheek lightly. "It doesn't bother me—I can't hear any of it, so no problem."

Lisanne hated hearing him laugh it off like that.

He leaned forward to open the door, pausing until the head rush passed.

"Hey," she tapped his hand, "do you have any food in the

house at all?"

"Sure. I stocked up on Pop Tarts. I'm kidding! Yeah, I bought food, no problem."

"Is … is Zef home?"

Daniel shrugged. "Don't know. Baby doll, don't worry about me. I'm fine. Text me when you get home? Thanks for the ride Monica, Mr. Maclaine."

"Mom!" said Lisanne, urgently. "Dad?"

Her parents looked at each other, a silent agreement passing between them.

Monica turned around so Daniel could see her face.

"Why don't you come and stay with us while you recuperate. You'd be more than welcome."

Daniel glanced at Lisanne in surprise.

"Um, that's really nice of you, Monica, but…"

"You can't stay here!" said Lisanne, desperately. "Who'll look after you?"

Daniel started to shake his head, then winced.

"I'll be fine, Lis. I wasn't expecting anything—this is what I'm used to. And I have to be back at the hospital in five days for them to take the stitches out."

"But…"

"I should stay near the hospital where the surgery was done, Lis. Just in case."

Which was the winning argument.

Lisanne bit her lip. "But you'll come after that? Mom, Dad, he can come for Christmas, right?"

"Of course," said Monica, looking to her husband for confirmation.

"You'll be very welcome," said Ernie.

Daniel still looked surprised as he turned to Lisanne. "I just gotta get through the next week, baby doll." Then he looked at Monica. "Is it okay if I let you know?"

"Yes, of course. Be well, Daniel. But … you know you can call if you need anything?"

He gave a wide, genuine smile. "Thanks, Monica."

Moving slowly, he climbed out of the car and made his way up to the front door, turned carefully and waved.

CHAPTER 20

Daniel made his way past the men sitting outside his house, who glanced at him with slight curiosity, then pushed his way through to the hall. It was jammed full of strangers—and even more trashed than usual. He hadn't thought that was possible, without actually torching the place.

The living room was full of gyrating bodies dancing, drinking and snorting fuck knows what. His eyes narrowed on a woman who was shooting up in the corner. Nobody noticed, or if they did, nobody cared. Fuck, he had to admit that things had gotten a lot worse recently.

For the first time he felt disgusted with what his home had become. He could put up with people drinking, smoking weed and snorting coke—hell, he'd done all of those things and often. Well, not so much since he'd started college—or rather, since he'd started seeing Lisanne—but he didn't count it as anything too serious. If people wanted to party, that was their choice. But this—this was different. He thought back to what Detective Dickwad had told him—that Zef was dealing meth. As far as Daniel knew, that shit could be smoked, snorted, injected or just plain swallowed. Maybe Dickwad was right, and this had all been going on under Daniel's nose, so to speak. Maybe Daniel had closed his eyes to all of this for too damn long. He tried to push the thought away but it was like a virus, working through his body, spreading its insidious poison.

As he trudged up the stairs, the whole scene happening in the rooms below made him wonder if he didn't need a better lock on his bedroom door. Or maybe just reinforced steel plate.

He wished again he could afford to move out, then felt guilty for thinking about leaving Zef. His brother was all the family he had left.

Instead, he sent him a text letting him know that he was home.

His head was pounding and the skin on the left side felt tight and sore. All he wanted to do was lie down in his own damn bed and rest. Tired as he was, his brain was twisting with thoughts and ideas, trapped in the eddies and whirlpools of his consciousness. He'd learned that you can run from everything but your own sweet self.

He tried to focus.

When had Zef changed his business pattern? Daniel searched backward through his memories: when, when had things started to accelerate toward the bad?

He sat up suddenly and had to clutch his stomach, as a brief wave of nausea rushed through him.

Fuck, he'd been so blind!

He lowered himself down carefully, and knelt on the dusty floorboards, pulling out a box from under his bed. It was filled with financial documents, many from his parents' time: their Wills, along with health insurance, college fees, bank statements, bills, credit card statements—and details of his college trust fund. He'd gone through it all when he'd decided to have the CI operation. He'd needed to confirm that Medicaid covered it, as it turned out—at least until he was 21. But now, he couldn't find the trust fund documents. He searched through the papers but they'd vanished. Frustrated and starting to see double, he went through each document for a third time. Still nothing.

Daniel sat back on his heels and tried to look at all the possibilities, but everything was pointing in one obvious direction—he'd just been too self-absorbed and preoccupied to see it before.

Fact one: his brother had dropped out of college when their parents had been killed. He always said it was because studying wasn't for him and he'd rather be out in the 'real' world, but now

Daniel wasn't so sure. Zef was a bright guy—before he'd gotten into 'retail', he'd been as interested in engines as Daniel, and had been studying mechanical engineering.

Fact two: Zef had always insisted that their parents' life insurance had paid off the mortgage on the house, with money left over for living expenses for a few years. Daniel had been 17 and away at school, so it hadn't occurred to him to challenge it—but what if Zef had exaggerated the amount of money as a way of protecting his little brother from an uglier truth?

Fact three: Zef had totally lost his shit when Daniel had gotten the $1000 speeding fine—the fine Daniel had said he'd pay for out of his college trust fund. He'd even hit him—something Zef had never done before.

Fact four: the paperwork about his trust fund had mysteriously gone missing.

Fact five: only one person besides himself knew where he kept those documents—and had a key to his room.

Which, as far as Daniel could see, added up to one, clear, indisputable fact number six: they were both neck deep in shit.

A cold, sick feeling swept through him—one which had nothing to do with his recent operation.

He picked up his phone to text Zef again.

* D: need see you. am at home. *

He stood up slowly and hunted through his cabinet for the food that he'd bought before going into hospital—crackers that he'd stashed along with a bag of apples. He stared at the food items that were supposed to constitute his eating plan for the next two days. What a moron: he'd bought two items that were going to require some serious jaw action—and consequently hurt the most to eat right now. Idiot. Hungry and depressed, Daniel continued to rifle through the cabinet, hoping that something more palatable might emerge from the depths. Finally, he unearthed two packets of instant soup at the back. They were only six months out of date, so consequently nothing he was

385

going to worry about.

He left the room briefly to fill his kettle from the faucet in the bathroom. When he returned, Zef was sitting on his bed, looking tired and slightly strung out.

"Hey, bro. They let you go."

"Nah, had to dig a tunnel."

Zef gave the ghost of a smile. "Let's see it then."

Daniel pulled off his beanie and showed Zef the line of gauze and tape.

"Whoa, impressive. Makes you look like a double hard bastard."

"Thanks, I think."

"Just sayin', man. When do you get hooked up to the sound system?"

"Not till after the holidays."

"Think it'll work?"

"Maybe. No one knows for sure."

"Bummer."

Daniel nodded, then winced.

"So, you said you needed to see me. What's up?"

Daniel stared at his brother without blinking. "How much do you owe?"

"What?"

"I'm not a fucking idiot, Zef. All that shit downstairs, this isn't you. Or it didn't use to be. Is all the money gone—what Mom and Dad left?"

The silence stretched out between them until Zef exhaled in one long, sour breath.

"Yeah, it's all gone."

Daniel closed his eyes, having seen the words that confirmed everything he'd been dreading.

"Did … how much … did they really leave what you said— or was that a lie, too?"

Zef looked down. "No, they left us in pretty good shape. I was the one who fucked up."

"Were you going to tell me?"

Zef pulled a face. "I was hoping I wouldn't have to. I'd planned to wait until the end of the school year. I kept thinking I'd be able to make the money back, but I just got in deeper. I'm sorry, bro."

Daniel rubbed the side of his head carefully. "How much have you borrowed?"

"It's not like that."

"What's it like?"

"I owe some favors to some people you don't say 'no' to, okay."

Daniel's temper exploded, sending a pulse of pain through his skull.

"Okay? Are you fucking kidding me? This is so far from 'okay' I don't even know what fucking planet you're on!"

Zef's fierce expression softened as he saw his brother's physical and mental pain. "Look, I made some bad business decisions, but the house is safe. I wouldn't risk that. You'll always have a home here, bro."

"You call this a home? Full of strangers shooting up? I have to lock my bedroom door—I have to lock the fucking bathroom door to stop it getting trashed. I can't bring any friends back here. I mean, have you even *looked* at this place lately?"

"I knew this would fucking happen," sneered Zef. "As soon as you got your little middle-income bitch of a girlfriend, and started visiting her place in the burbs, pretending you're ... whatever the fuck you think you are now—too good for your own home ... *college boy*."

Daniel clenched his fists, and Zef saw a moment flash across his brother's face when Daniel thought about hitting him—about beating the crap out of him.

"Don't, Zef. Just ... don't. Can't you see what's going on here? You are so fucking close to getting your ass thrown in jail. The cops *know* you're dealing. Hell, I get stopped at school every other day by some fucker trying to score. The cops could take you down any moment, but they're waiting for you to fuck up big time or something. You think they'll stop at you –when they

387

finally get a search warrant for this place? I'm just as likely to go down as you are. You even *care* about that?"

"Yeah, because you're so fucking snow-white! I've seen you totally wasted, man, don't pretend I haven't."

"I don't fucking deal!" shouted Daniel.

Zef was silent. "No, you don't: you just live off the proceeds of it."

Daniel's expression was stricken as he stared at the stranger with a familiar face.

Zef stood up and brushed past him. Without facing Daniel he said, "I'm so fucking sorry, brother."

The door closed and Daniel slumped down onto his bed. So many feelings swept through him, that he didn't know which one to deal with first. Anger was the dominant emotion, but there was also fear and disappointment, along with a strong sense of betrayal. He'd trusted Zef.

Daniel's progressive and rapid deafness had isolated him in so many ways. At a time when his school friends were worrying about zits and wet dreams, sounds were becoming misty, and jokes lost in waves of words where he could no longer distinguish consonant from vowel. Even when he'd gone to the special school, he'd been largely alone, refusing to see himself as part of the deaf community.

When he'd gotten the news that his parents had died, it had been Zef who'd driven through the night to tell him, brother to brother. Through it all, through every dark moment, Zef's large presence had offered humor at the blackest times, and strength at Daniel's weakest.

But at that moment, sitting in the bedroom of his family home with his brother mere feet and inches away, Daniel's sense of loneliness had never been greater.

Right now, he had one good thing in his life.

As if thinking about her had conjured her, Daniel's phone vibrated in his pocket. He smiled when he saw the message.

* L: we're home. mom & dad fought 3 hours solid.

I have headache—how's yours?
wish I could help with pain relief ;) LA xx *
* D: me too, you have no idea. offer still open?
could come up Friday after check-up. *
* L: YES!—shouting—you safe to ride? LA xx*
* D: will take bus. *
* L: can't wait! LA xx *
* D: :) x *

Now he had things to do, decisions to make. But not yet. Tomorrow was soon enough.

Over the next few days, Daniel's strength began to return. His headache withered and gave up, although the wound was still tender, and trying to dress it himself was a bitch—'fiasco' was an equally apt word. He refused to ask Zef for help. The spells of dizziness decreased, too, although they were still debilitating when they happened.

Occasionally, he'd forget to be careful—which was a good sign in some ways—but then he'd whack his ear or his head and spend the next five minutes cursing loudly, colorfully and imaginatively.

Zef had stayed out of his way, and Daniel spent most of the time sitting in his room reading, only heading out on foot to forage for food, careful how much money he spent. His bank account was already on the critical list—he didn't want it to expire during the holidays. He had plans for increasing its health as soon as possible.

Which meant that the first visit he made as soon as he was able, was to the auto repair shop where he'd worked over the previous two summers.

The workshop area was dark and every piece of woodwork was slick where oily hands had touched it. But Salvatore Coredo had an enviable reputation as a restorer of classic cars. Motorcycles were a profitable sideline.

"Dan! What you doing here? You finally get religion and decided to make me a happy man? The offer on your Harley is

389

still open."

Daniel smiled at the familiar banter. Ever since Sal had set eyes on Sirona, battered as she'd been, he'd coveted her. And every time he saw Daniel, he tried to talk him into selling.

"Maybe, Sal, but I'm looking for work. Can you give me some hours?"

"Thought you were going to school? You drop out already?"

Daniel scowled and Salvatore laughed.

He'd known Daniel for two years and had helped him rebuild Sirona—he knew exactly which buttons to press.

"No, I'm still studying. I just need a job."

"Could give you some hours on Christmas Day—you interested?"

"Very fucking funny, Sal."

"Watch the mouth, Dan." He paused, seeing the tiredness that clung to Daniel. "Sure I can give you 10, maybe 20 hours a week. Start after the holidays."

Daniel felt relieved. It wasn't easy getting part-time work with so many students looking for jobs, and being deaf—well, you could treble the level of difficulty. Which was probably a conservative estimate.

If he was careful with the money from this job, he could rent a room somewhere and have just enough to live off, too. Getting an affordable room on campus was out of the question, and he'd have to get a loan to pay for his next year's college fees.

"So, how much would you give me for Sirona?"

Salvatore gaped at him then looked serious. "You need money that bad, kid?"

Daniel shrugged, unwilling to go into the details with Sal.

"Well, now let me see. I could maybe go up to $2,750."

Daniel shook his head, trying not to wince, both at the pain in his head, and the pain of selling his beloved Harley. "I want $3,000. You know she's worth it."

Salvatore grinned. "I'll think about it, Dan. We'll talk again when you start work—after the holidays."

After the holidays—that seemed like an impossibly long time in the future.

Daniel nodded and they shook hands on the almost-deal.

He was looking forward to seeing Lisanne—although he couldn't with all honesty say he was looking forward to seeing her parents, but they'd been kind to invite him. He was just glad they had no idea of all the things he was planning to do to their daughter during his visit. He licked his lips at the thought.

He was about to text her the good news that he'd got a job when he remembered that he hadn't shared his financial problems with her. That was a conversation to have face to face, if at all. No, she didn't need to hear all the shit he had going down.

He bought the local paper and scoured it for rooms that were within his limited price range, but the two that he subsequently visited were shitholes that should have been condemned, and would have been little better than staying at home.

On Friday, he took the bus to the hospital with mixed feelings, completely separate from the fact that he hated not being able to ride Sirona. That was one thing he intended to sort out with the doc pretty damn quick. He needed his independence back, especially if he was apartment hunting.

The outpatients' clinic was busy, full of people like him— people who'd had the CI operation. Some were children who weren't old enough to understand what was happening, but most were adults in their sixties and seventies. Only one person was anywhere near Daniel's age—a woman in her late twenties. She was also the only other person who hadn't brought someone along for support.

She smiled when she saw Daniel. He nodded and sat down in the far side of the room, not interested in starting a conversation. But she had other ideas, and came to sit opposite him.

S: Hello. Do you sign?
D: Yes.

S: I'm S.A.M.A.N.T.H.A.

She spelled out her name and Daniel did the same, one letter at a time.

D: D.A.N.I.E.L.
S: Are you having the CI?
D: Had it. Last week.
S: Me, too! Six weeks ago. How's it going?

Daniel shrugged. "Okay."

S: Do you lip read?
D: Yes.
S: You don't talk much, do you?

Daniel just looked at her.

S: Come on! We're the only ones here who aren't preschoolers or retired. Are you getting your processor and transmitter today?
D: No. Stitches out.
S: Since you asked, I got tuned in a month ago. It's … weird. I could only hear beeping from the system. I knew that there were sounds, but I couldn't distinguish between them. The audiologist said that's normal. To be honest, I'm a bit freaked out.

She paused.

S: You here by yourself, too?

Daniel smirked and glanced around him.

S: Why?

Daniel shrugged.

S: You don't want to tell me. That's cool. Can I ask you something? I hardly know you, but ... I don't have anyone else to ask.

Daniel was curious but wary. He wasn't big on gratuitous sharing of emotions with complete strangers—or even with people he knew well.

D: You can ask.
S: Seriously ... why did you decide to have this? You lip read—you can blend.
D: Why did you?

She sighed.

S: I had a baby last year. I wanted to hear her laugh.

She smiled.

S: That simple. What's your story?

Daniel hesitated. They'd strayed into personal territory in less than five minutes.

D: Why do you want to know?
S: What if this doesn't work? Will I care? How much will I care? I managed okay before. Do you feel like that?
D: I've got nothing left to lose.

Which was the truth. He hadn't thought about it that way until he'd met Lisanne.

S: Do you feel weird about having a chunk of metal in your head? I know I do.
D: As long as it works. I'll let you know.
S: I'd like that.

Daniel glanced at her. That wasn't what he'd meant.

S: Do you think your hands will get lonely?
D: What?
S: I like signing. It's so expressive. I've been doing it since I was a kid. I think I'd miss it if I stopped completely.

Daniel had nothing to say to that. To him signing was a tool, something he'd had to learn, but he didn't consider it a complete alternative to speech. From his lack of reaction, Samantha took the hint and changed the subject.

S: There are some other things I've noticed about the CI: it's easier for me to understand men—that's just because of frequencies. It's driving my girlfriend nuts—she actually accused me of hitting on her husband! I've known her 10 years. Can you believe it?

Daniel didn't say so, but frankly yes, he could believe it. But there was one question he wanted to ask her, now she'd started the conversation.

D: Can you listen to music?
S: Not really. It's pretty meaningless at the moment. I'm hoping it will improve.

She studied his face.

S: You miss music.

Daniel shifted uncomfortably on his seat but finally looked up at her.
"Yeah, I do."
Samantha smiled sympathetically.

S: I don't really remember sounds—I was only three when I

lost my hearing. I'll have to relearn everything.

She paused, seeing the tension in his expression.

S: Do you have plans for the holidays?
D: My girlfriend's place.
S: That explains the backpack. Does she go to school?
D: Yes.
S: You, too?
D: Yes.
S: What are you studying?
D: Economics and business, with math.
S: Wow! That must be a pretty full timetable. What does your girlfriend study?

Daniel could pretty much have predicted the look on Samantha's face when he told her.

D: Music.

Samantha's response was utterly predictable. Yeah, that was the look he'd expected: pity mixed with sympathy. He was getting pretty damn tired of that.

A light blinked on the wall and everyone turned to look at the name that flashed up—'Miss S. Wilson'.

S: That's me.

Samantha scrabbled in her handbag, then passed him a piece of paper with her phone number scribbled on it. She smiled at his expression.

S: I'm not hitting on you! Although you are cute. I'd just like to know how it works out for you. It would be good to stay in touch, swap notes. Take care, Daniel.

Throwing him a smile, she disappeared down one of the

corridors and Daniel was left alone. For a moment he thought about tossing the piece of paper, but in the end he shoved it in his pocket and forgot about it.

When Daniel's name came up, he loped off down the same corridor as Samantha. He was relieved to see that it was Dr. Palmer waiting in the consulting room.

"Good morning, Mr. Colton. How are you? Any problems?"

"Hey, doc. No, all good."

"Any nausea? Dizziness?"

"Bit. It's wearing off, I think."

"Good. Tenderness when you have the dressings changed?"

"Bit. Specially if I pull my ear by mistake."

"You've been changing your own dressings?"

"Well, yeah."

Dr. Palmer frowned. "Right. I'll take a look."

He prodded and probed. It hurt, but was bearable. He walked around to face Daniel.

"That's all looking fine. Nothing to worry about. I'll take those stitches out now. It'll be a little uncomfortable."

Five minutes later, Daniel felt as if the doctor had been trying to open his skull with a crowbar. But it was a relief to have the stitches out.

Dr. Palmer moved back to speak to Daniel.

"There's some tenderness, but no more than I'd expect. It'll have settled down nicely in a couple of weeks and we'll be ready to fit the transmitter and processor. Do you have any questions?"

"Can I ride my motorcycle?"

Dr. Palmer frowned. "No, too early for that, especially if you're still experiencing some dizziness. Ask me again after your fitting, Mr. Colton."

It was the answer Daniel had been expecting, but it was still galling.

"Okay. See you next year, doc. Thanks and all that."

"Happy holidays," said the doctor quietly, as he watched Daniel leave the room.

Daniel was glad he'd arrived at the bus station early. Along with airports and train stations, they made him nervous. If there was a platform change or gate change announced over the public address system, he couldn't hear it. He'd missed a couple of connections on previous journeys because there'd been a last minute change and he hadn't known. He kept an eye on the Atlanta bus, checking and rechecking the signboards until it was time for departure.

Daniel took a seat at the back and closed his eyes. He wouldn't have admitted it to the devil himself, but he was glad not to be riding Sirona all the way up to Lisanne's place.

The bus was pretty full with people traveling for the holidays, brightly colored parcels stuffed into bags, but nobody bothered him in his corner. He was aware how unapproachable he looked, being tall and broad shouldered, with a week's worth of stubble, his piercing, his beanie pulled down low, heavy boots and his black leather jacket. He didn't need a sign telling people to stay the hell away.

After an hour of dozing, he sat up straighter and rubbed his eyes. He pulled a battered copy of E. F. Schumacher's *Small is Beautiful* out of his backpack and tried to concentrate on the pages. He couldn't wait to see his girl, even better to feel her body wrapped around him. He knew her parents would be hawkeyed, watching and waiting for him to put a finger—or tongue—out of place, but Daniel felt confident he'd find a way. Hell, yes.

The book fell to his lap and his eyes drifted to the landscape flashing past the bus window: trees, fields, orchards, houses, another small town, more trees. But instead of seeing the Georgia countryside, he was thinking about how much his life had changed.

Starting college was a big deal for most people but for Daniel, it had been a leap into the unknown. Against all the advice his high school had given him, he'd been determined to keep his hearing loss a private matter. He'd had to work harder and longer and concentrate more than other students; he'd had to fight—literally—against the expectations formed by his relationship to Zef; and he'd met Lisanne. He'd had every intention of keeping himself to himself, but now he found he had a girlfriend—serious, maybe—and he was on his way to spend the holidays with her family again.

And then there was the huge, potentially life changing decision he'd made to get the CI.

He wasn't even sure how to feel about that, but once he'd seen Lisanne singing, seen her passion for music pouring out of her, his reasons for not having the implant had been scoured away.

And he had no regrets.

He thought again about what it meant to have a girlfriend, or rather, what it meant to him to have Lisanne in his life. He liked sex—a lot—and ever since he'd lost his virginity at the age of 15, he'd worshipped the god of one night stands, relentlessly pursuing short-term gratification. It had begun as self-protection from the pain of rejection, but it had become a self perpetuating habit.

It was different with Lisanne. So different that Daniel had to admit he was pretty much in uncharted territory. She had stripped away his defenses one by one, leaving him vulnerable and exposed. It was unnerving, but at the same time he didn't feel so alone. She'd rejected isolation as a solution to his deafness, and had led him back toward the world. But the problem remained—it was a world full of hearing people, where deafness was routinely the butt of jokes. It was daunting, especially because he had no way of explaining to her what she was asking of him.

And yet, the operation had been another step into that world. Daniel was all too aware that the CI was a piece of technology that could help, but it was just a tool—he'd still be deaf. He wondered if Lisanne really understood that. If he was honest with himself, he was waiting for the moment when she'd be tired of having a boyfriend with *a disability*. Christ, the weight of that fucking word.

He also felt a responsibility toward her, having been the first man she'd ever slept with. Hell, as far as he could tell, he was the first guy she'd ever kissed. But as her confidence grew, the sex just kept on getting better. She was trusting him to help her explore further. He was looking forward to more of that.

Daniel scratched at his beard. Probably time to shave it off—his Baby Doll had sensitive skin.

He felt his phone vibrate, alerting him that a text had dropped in.

* L: I'm at the bus station.
Can't wait to see you. LA xx *

He smiled at her message.

He'd meant everything he'd written in the letter, and it scared him. The way he felt about her … relying on other people made you weak. Zef proved that.

But when he climbed off the bus and saw her anxious face transported by a huge grin, his doubts were pushed into a distant place and locked away.

"Baby doll," he said, dropping his backpack onto the floor and pulling her toward him.

"You grew a beard!" she squeaked.

"Don't you like it?"

"Um…"

He leaned down to kiss her and she wrapped her arms tightly around his neck. Her lips were soft and warm on his, her tongue hot and eager.

Daniel lost himself in the kiss, forgetting he was standing on the forecourt of a concrete bus station. It was his cock that reminded him, as his hips automatically tried to grind into her.

He pushed her back gently and felt her slight resistance. He blew out a long breath and raised his eyebrows.

"I like the way you think, baby doll, but we should get out of here first." He touched her cheek that was looking a little pink from their kiss, "And I'll shave."

Lisanne gave an embarrassed laugh.

"I can't seem to behave properly around you!"

"Just as long as you behave improperly, you'll have no complaints from me," he whispered into her hair.

She sighed happily. "Mom and Dad are at a school thing, and Harry's with his friends."

Daniel got the hint.

"Drive fast, baby, because I don't think I can wait for you much longer."

He bent to pick up his backpack, and experienced a brief wave of dizziness that made him stumble.

"Daniel!"

"Don't freak, baby, I'm good," he said, standing up more slowly this time.

Lisanne made sure her arm was firmly around his waist as they walked toward the car, and felt reassured by his solid presence.

It took half an hour to get to Lisanne's home. Daniel spent most of the drive with his left hand resting on her thigh. It was enough to make Lisanne grip the steering wheel until her knuckles were white. A part of her had never believed that he'd really come.

They were both relieved when the journey was finally over.

Lisanne turned off the engine, and tension crackled in the air, sparks that would ignite at any moment.

She turned her head to look at him, meeting his eyes.

"So, everyone's out."

"Yes."

"How long?"

"A couple of hours. Maybe."

"Let's go."

She opened the front door, and without speaking, led him up the stairs, hand in hand, to her bedroom.

Daniel let his backpack fall onto the carpet, and kissed Lisanne hungrily.

She started to respond, her hands pushing up under his

leather jacket, but then pulled back. Daniel stared at her in confusion.

"Would you … your stubble … everyone will know."

He smiled in understanding. "I'll shave."

Her relief was obvious. "Sorry, I just…"

"Not a problem, baby doll."

"Daniel…"

"What is it?"

"The operation…"

He stiffened.

"What about it?"

She chewed her lip and tugged nervously on the sleeve of her coat.

"Can I see—can I see your scar?"

He didn't move but didn't stop her when she gently pulled off his beanie.

"Oh," she whispered, running her eyes over the line of gauze and tape that snaked up his skull.

Daniel turned his face away from her. Was *this* the moment when reality would be too much?

But instead her soft hands pulled his mouth toward hers and she kissed him slowly, lovingly.

"I like your hair short—it suits you. You look like a Marine or something."

He snorted, because yeah, the Marines recruited so many deaf people.

"Or something. I don't think they allow piercings in the Marines."

He pulled his shaving kit out of his bag and tugged his t-shirt over his head, smiling to himself as her eyes followed the material's route up his body. He headed for the bathroom.

When he looked into the mirror, he saw Lisanne standing behind him.

"Let me do it."

"What?"

"I want to shave you."

He stared at her.

"Don't you trust me?"

"I just don't want to look like I've gotten into a fight—anymore than I already do."

"Hey," she said, slapping his arm. "I have a very steady hand."

"Mmm," he said, nuzzling her neck, "I like your hands."

She pushed his shoulder to make him look at her.

"So you'll let me?"

He sighed theatrically. "Fine, but I've already got one six inch cut, baby doll, so be careful, okay?"

He settled himself on the stool she placed in front of the mirror, and watched her root around pulling out his shaving foam and razor.

The bathroom began to fill with the same tension that they'd experienced in the car. Daniel's arousal, begun in the driveway, and increased in the bedroom, was now becoming really fucking uncomfortable. He shifted on the stool as his eyes were on a level with Lisanne's breasts.

She shook the can then pressed the nozzle, watching the foam bloom onto the palm of her hand. She spread it across each cheek, his chin, the patch of skin above his full lips, and down over his throat.

He stared up at her, his hazel eyes wide and trusting.

Picking up his razor, she stepped nearer so she was standing between his legs. She rested her left hand on his shoulder and he stretched his neck upwards.

Lisanne leaned forward and tilted Daniel's head to the side. Moving with precision, she placed the razor at the base of his sideburn, less than an inch from the incision behind his ear, and with slow, careful strokes, he felt her draw the razor down his left cheek. A long, smooth sliver of skin was revealed. His bare chest rose and fell evenly and his eyes followed hers. When she moved to his upper lip, he pulled it down; when she moved to his right side, he tilted his head for her.

She rinsed off the razor in the sink and her eyes traced the path of a drop of water that rolled down his chest, glistening for a moment before disappearing into the waistband of his jeans.

With great focus, she moved carefully, shaving him cleanly, finishing with an upwards stroke from his throat to his chin.

She wiped a final swirl of foam from his right cheek and gently patted his face with a towel.

"All done," she said, her voice husky.

He took the razor from her hand and lay it carefully at the side of the wash basin, watching as the water ran down the plughole.

He glanced at himself in the mirror and ran his fingers over his smooth face. "Nice job." He turned and looked into her eyes for several seconds before he spoke again. "Can I take you to bed now?"

"I started taking the pill."

Her abrupt announcement halted him. "You did?"

"Yes."

"Okay." He wasn't sure what she wanted him to do with that piece of information.

"So you don't have to, you know … you don't have to use a condom."

He stared and her face reddened.

"I thought it was what you wanted!" she snapped at him.

He blinked in surprise, as much at the anger on her face as the actual words.

"No, I didn't mean … baby doll, I wasn't … I mean, that's great. I know I'm clean because I get tested regularly—and I had to have blood work done before the op. You just surprised me—I've never gone unwrapped before."

"Oh, okay." Lisanne nodded. She looked up at him boldly. "I want you to make love to me, Daniel."

Once again, her words made him pause and he suddenly felt uncertain. He knew sex. He knew fucking. He knew how to make a woman come so hard she saw stars, the galaxy, and the whole damn Milky Way. But making love? Was that what it was? Was that why it was different with her?

He licked his lips as her hand rose to take his, leading him back to her bedroom.

He watched the roll and sway of her hips as he walked behind her, and his cock wept with happiness.

"Put the chair against the door," she said, "just in case."

Daniel lifted her desk chair and wedged it under the door handle, then pulled off his boots and socks.

"You don't usually wear a belt with your jeans," she said, suddenly.

He shrugged. "Stops my pants falling down."

"You haven't been eating, have you?"

"You really want to have this conversation now, baby doll, because I just want to put my dick inside you, where it's been fucking begging to be for the last half hour, and then feel you tighten around it when you come, yelling my name."

"Oh."

"Yeah."

Daniel laid down on her bed, grinning up at her. "Want to make out?"

"I want to do a lot more than that," she said, confidently.

Lisanne scrambled up the bed until she was straddling his thighs. She leaned down and kissed his chest, tugging gently on first one, then the other nipple ring.

Daniel breathed deeply, feeling waves of desire flame through him. She had no idea how fucking sexy she looked doing that, taking control. His arms lay at his sides as she continued to taste every inch of bare skin that she could find.

When she cupped him over his jeans, he groaned.

She slipped her hand inside and her mouth dropped open with surprise.

"You're not wearing any underwear."

He grinned. "Didn't get around to doing any laundry."

Her hand squeezed around him and he sighed with the overture of gratification.

"Fuck, that feels good, baby doll."

She unbuckled his belt and popped the button on his jeans

before yanking down the zipper.

Daniel yelped.

"Oh, sorry," she gasped.

"Fuck, Lis, I've been damaged enough this week. Be careful with my dick—he needs some loving."

"Oh, poor little thing," she smirked. "Do you want me to kiss it better?"

Daniel's intention to deny that his 'thing' was 'little' died in his throat as she pulled his cock free and started to place small, sweet kisses all over it.

She sucked the end tentatively, her serious eyes peering up at him.

She released him long enough to ask, "Is this okay?"

"Yup," he managed to cough out, as coherence exited the building.

She smiled and went back to inexpertly licking, sucking, and generally working out what movements got the best reactions. It was sort of like a science experiment but with pornographic surround sound, as Daniel moaned, groaned, and gasped.

When he felt his balls and stomach tighten, he pushed her shoulders.

"Lis…"

"Yes?" she said, bemused as he bucked beneath her.

"I'm going to come, baby doll, if you keep doing that."

She frowned. "Isn't that the point?"

He managed to smile at her confused expression as he propped himself on his elbows to see her face better.

"Well, yeah, but then it'll be over too quick. Gotta pace myself."

"Is that what you do—pace yourself—with me?"

She looked slightly hurt.

Daniel tried to explain, while his dick cursed him. "It depends. Sometimes I just want to fuck, hard and fast, right?"

She swallowed and felt her insides tighten in response.

"But sometimes," he continued, "sometimes I want to make it last—like right now. I want to touch you, I want to taste you, I want to see your face when you come, I want you screaming because you don't want it to stop—and because you do. I want to make it good for you, baby, real good."

He looked down at his cock, that was almost purple with urgency.

"And *then* I'm going to fuck you hard and fast. How does that sound?"

"Um, okay."

He grinned at her. "Good. Come here."

While she crawled back up the bed, he shoved his unhappy and painfully rigid dick back in his jeans, then unfastened the buttons on her shirt one by one.

"I know it's dumb," she said, quietly, "but I feel sort of nervous. You know, because we haven't done *this* for a while."

"Tell me about it. I've got fucking blue balls, and your hymen has probably grown back by now."

"What?" said Lisanne, looking panicked.

Daniel chuckled. "Kidding! Jeez!"

"I knew that," she muttered.

He pulled open her shirt and saw the brilliant jade green Victoria's Secret bra that he'd caught a glimpse of when she'd been drunk. The night she'd slapped him and thrown him out of her room. It looked sensational against her pale skin. He might even have groaned out loud: he didn't know.

He buried his face in her breasts while she ran her hands over the bunched muscles of his biceps, following the swirling lines of his tattoos.

"I've missed this," she sighed, even though Daniel couldn't hear her.

With one hand, he unhooked her bra and slid it from her small shoulders.

Her nipples were already standing proud, but using his tongue and teeth, he teased them into tight little fists.

"Mmm, strawberry," he said to himself.

Lisanne flushed, the heat traveling from the centre of her body to every furthest inch.

She rolled onto her back and Daniel tugged off her jeans. She shivered slightly and he looked up.

"Okay?"

"Y-yes!"

Smiling, he worked her panties down until they were tangled around her ankles.

He eased a couple of fingers inside her and watched with pleasure as she stretched out her body and shuddered softly.

"Have you made yourself come without me, baby doll?"

She mumbled something but Daniel couldn't read what she'd said.

"Say again, baby."

"Um, yes. Once," she muttered.

"Way to go, Lis," he said, trying not to laugh at her mortified expression. "Did it feel good?"

"It was okay. It's better when you do it."

Daniel grinned—he wasn't going to argue with that. "Do you like it when I do this?"

Lisanne gasped.

"Or this?"

Her hips bucked off the bed.

"Or this?"

She screamed out and clutched the sheets with stiff fingers.

Smiling to himself, Daniel couldn't resist licking her. Damn, she tasted good. He wondered if he could make her come again with just his mouth.

Five minutes later, he had his answer.

Lisanne was a sweaty mess, lying flat on her back, utterly open and exposed, glowing from a second, stunning orgasm. Daniel was happy his girl was satisfied, but the granite in his pants was giving him some serious grief. He kicked off his jeans, with a feeling of relief, and she opened one eye.

"I can't move," she gasped.

"You don't have to, baby," he said. "I'll do all the work. Just … enjoy the ride!" He reached for his jacket and the packet of condoms, before he remembered that she'd said they weren't necessary. He hesitated for a moment. He'd done a lot of shit with a lot of women, but he'd never gone bare before. He was more than happy for Lisanne to be his first. The thought made him smile.

Gently, he rolled her onto her right hip and lay down behind her so they were spooning. He pushed up her knees with his own, wrapped one arm underneath her, pulling her tightly into him, then rubbed his straining tip against her, feeling her warmth and wetness.

He pushed into her faster than he'd meant to, but she didn't stop him. Feeling her skin to skin, her satiny walls clenching all around him, Daniel almost came on the spot.

"Fuck, that feels so … baby doll…"

As it was, he was having trouble holding on. She pushed her ass back against him, and he was a lost man. He pounded into her hard and exploded in a rush of heat, pulsing into her, emptying himself into her.

Fuck, that was intense. He was almost embarrassed that he'd come so quickly—that hadn't happened in a long time.

He pulled out and saw with fascination that his cum was running down the back of her thigh. Goddamn it but that was sexy.

Lisanne squirmed in his arms until she was facing him.

"Hi," she said, shyly.

He kissed her soft lips. "You are so fucking amazing, you know that, right?"

She giggled. "So are you. I've missed having, um, orgasms with you."

"You sure have a way with words, baby doll."

She pretended to pout, and he laughed.

"I've missed all of this," she said, lifting her hand to stroke his cheek.

"Me, too," he sighed, planting a soft kiss on the tip of her nose.

"Ugh!" she sat up suddenly.

"What's the matter?"

Daniel's eyes darted to the window. Maybe she'd heard her parents coming back?

"I'm ... oh God, this is so embarrassing!"

Daniel stared at her with worried eyes. As Lisanne started to get out of bed, he laid a restraining hand on her arm.

"What is it, Lis? You're freaking me out here."

"Oh, God. Just ... nothing. Wait here."

"Lis!"

"Oh for God's sake, Daniel! I'm *dripping*, okay? I'll be back in a minute."

She heard Daniel's loud laughter all the way to the bathroom.

Muttering inaudibly, Lisanne cleaned herself up. Nobody had mentioned *that* side effect of taking the pill. She suddenly wished they'd used condoms. It had felt amazing, not having any barrier between them but even so, condoms were so much *less messy*.

She wondered if she had time for a shower and decided it was an absolute necessity. Then a thought occurred to her— maybe they could have a shower together. Kirsty had given a rather too vivid description of when she and Vin had done exactly that in his private bathroom at the frat house. Lisanne thought it sounded rather dangerous, what with all the slipping and sliding around on tiles, but now she had the chance, Lisanne found she rather wanted to try it for herself.

She wrapped a bath towel under her arms and brought a spare one for Daniel.

He wasn't lying on the bed anymore, but leaning out of her window, giving Lisanne a very fine view of his very fine ass. She hoped he wasn't smoking: her dad had a nose like a bloodhound when it came to things like that.

But he wasn't smoking and now Lisanne thought about it, she hadn't seen him have a cigarette since she'd picked him up at the bus station.

But before she had a chance to ask him about it, he turned around and jumped when he saw her.

"Fuck, Lis! You nearly gave me a heart attack—I thought your folks had come back early."

She smiled smugly, glad that he was the one on the wrong foot for a change. Her eyes traveled up and down his body. He'd definitely lost weight but otherwise there was nothing to suggest he'd been through an invasive surgery—nothing except the gauze on the side of his head.

"I'm going to have a shower. Do you want to have one with me?"

Daniel's eyes lit up but then he frowned.

"Yeah, but I have to keep this dry," he said, pointing to his ear.

"Okay, I'll be gentle with you," she said.

He raised his eyebrows, then chased her into the bathroom.

CHAPTER 21

Lisanne made a mental note to put shower sex at the top of her list of favorite things to do with—and to—Daniel. Whether it had been the steam, his slick soapy hands, hot water, and hotter sex, the combination had been an alchemist's dream, creating a wonderful golden, molten moment.

She glowed, and Daniel looked very pleased with himself. Unfortunately and perhaps inevitably, his dressing had been completely soaked.

Lisanne was shocked again when she saw the long scar and shaved skin, although his hair was beginning to grow back, creating a soft, peachy fuzz.

Hiding how she felt as she looked at the ugly scar, guilty by association, she still insisted that they couldn't risk going back to bed. Either Harry or her parents would be home soon.

"Five more minutes," begged Daniel, pressing her naked body up against the bedroom door.

"No!" she said, insistently. "Put your damn pants back on. Anyway, we need to fix your head."

"Many women have tried," he said, solemnly.

"Hardy ha ha! Now get dressed."

It didn't take Daniel long: one pair of pants, one t-shirt, and he was done. Lisanne's reassembly took a little longer and she wanted to blow-dry her hair, thus avoiding anyone asking why she had soaking wet hair just after her boyfriend had arrived to visit.

Daniel lay back on her bed watching her, a small smile on his face.

"What?" she said, once she'd finished.

He shrugged. "This—I like it."

"What, watching me dry my hair?"

He smiled, although his eyes looked a little sad.

"Yeah, but not just that. All of it: you, me, spending time, nowhere special to be, no pressure, you know. No roommate."

"I know what you mean. But Kirsty's not so bad. You two get along now, don't you?"

"Yeah, she's okay I guess. I just meant ... ah fuck it. I don't know what I'm talking about."

"We could maybe go to your place sometimes?"

Daniel shook his head. "No, baby doll. I wouldn't do that to you. Besides, I'm moving out. I'm going to get a room somewhere. I've seen a couple of places…"

"But ... what about Zef? Isn't it your house, too?"

"It's not really working out anymore—things have gotten kind of intense. I just need to find my own place. Hey, I forgot to tell you, I got a job."

Lisanne's face fell. "What about school? What about your degree?"

"I'll only be doing 15 or 20 hours a week, that's all. It means I'll have to work weekends, but I'll still go to school. I might have to drop one class—I'll try it first."

"I'll never see you!"

He stood up and wrapped his arms around her shoulders. "We'll work it out—if you want to."

"Of course I want to! Why wouldn't I?" She kissed him quickly. "Idiot."

He smiled down at her.

"I don't know, Lis, I come all this way, and you abuse my body the second I walk through the door, and now you're name-calling?"

She pinched his ass, making him jump.

"Get used to it—you're mine for the holidays."

Five minutes later, Lisanne's parents found them sitting innocently at the kitchen table while Lisanne taped pieces of gauze to Daniel's head.

"Hello, Daniel," said Monica, warmly. "How are you, dear? Oh, you look so much better than last week," and she kissed him on the cheek, making him duck his head and grin.

He stood up to shake hands with Lisanne's father, which earned him an angry reproach from Lisanne as her fingers skittered over his wound, causing him to wince.

"Sit still," she said, swatting his back to make her point.

"Lisanne!" hissed her mother.

"Well, he can't hear me, Mom, so I have to," said Lisanne, petulantly. "It's the only way I can make him pay attention." She pulled on Daniel's arm so he looked at her. "My mom thinks I'm being too rough with you."

Daniel laughed. "Yeah, you're pretty scary."

"See, Mom," said Lisanne. "He's fine."

"Well, still … may I offer you a drink, Daniel? Some iced tea or a coffee perhaps?"

But Ernie had already reached into the refrigerator and pulled a can of beer from a six-pack. "Or one of these?"

"Yeah, great. Thanks, Mr. Maclaine."

"I'll have a beer, too, Dad," said Lisanne.

"You certainly won't!" snapped her mother.

"Why not? Daniel is only a few months older than me!"

"Lisanne!" said her, mother in a warning voice.

Lisanne pouted, and Daniel winked at her.

"Honestly! I think you like Daniel more than me!"

Ernie rolled his eyes. He taught hormonal teenagers for a living. Having them at home, as well—that was wearing, to say the least.

"I'm going to watch some TV," he announced to no one in particular. "There's a Bruce Willis film on in a minute."

Monica shook her head.

"I don't know what plans you two have this evening, but I'm beat. I can order pizza if you're hungry."

Daniel looked worriedly at Lisanne, who was nodding happily.

413

"Um, Lis," he said, quietly, "I don't have any money on me. I'll, ah, have to go to the ATM tomorrow to pay for it."

Monica laid a hand on his shoulder.

"Nonsense," she said. "You're here as our guest. We won't hear of it."

Harry interrupted them by slouching in through the back door and slamming it behind him.

"Hey, Dan! Whoa, wicked scar! That's awesome. It must really hurt."

Lisanne pushed her brother, but he shoved her back, making her stumble.

"For goodness sake!" yelled Monica. "Can you two at least pretend you're housebroken!"

"Sorry, Mom," said Harry, cheerfully. "She started it."

Daniel had only caught part of the conversation, but he guessed the rest.

"How you doin', man," he said to Harry. "You want to see where they took my brain out?"

"Yeah!" said Harry, peering at Daniel's half covered scar. "They really took your brain out?"

"Sure," said Daniel, "but I think they put it back the wrong way around."

"I can't tell the difference," said Lisanne.

Daniel grinned as Monica gave her a hard stare.

"Lisanne, finish up with Daniel's dressing and tell me what pizza you both want."

Harry wandered away after extracting a promise from Daniel that they'd hit the arcade at least once during the holidays, and Lisanne placed the last piece of tape on Daniel's wound.

He pulled his beanie back on, covering her work.

"Are you going to wear that inside as well?"

He nodded. "Yeah, so?"

"I just think it looks weird wearing a hat indoors."

"As opposed to a six inch fucking hole in my head," he snapped.

Lisanne bit her tongue as an angry reply surged forward. For once, she took the hint from his irritated expression. It was obviously a sensitive subject in more ways than one.

"Sorry," she said, softly. "Sorry."

She placed a gentle kiss on his short hair as he rested his head against her body, and let his arms wrap around her waist.

Monica suddenly felt like an outsider in her own kitchen, as she witnessed their private moment. She was proud of her daughter for dealing with Daniel's disability with pragmatism and directness, but at the same time she was terrified by the depth of feeling she saw between the two of them. He was Lisanne's first boyfriend, the first boy she'd ever shown the slightest bit of interest in, and it was obvious to Monica that her daughter was head over heels in love. Daniel was less demonstrative in his affections but his actions spoke louder than his few words. Monica was in awe that he'd elected to have a surgical procedure because he wanted to hear Lisanne sing.

And the physical nature of their relationship, that was a concern, too. Especially since Monica had cleaned Lisanne's room after their Thanksgiving visit and found a number of used condoms in the wastebasket. *That* particular fact of life she'd omitted to mention to her husband.

She'd tried to have 'the talk' with Lisanne but, stubborn as ever, her daughter had insisted that she knew what she was doing and that it was none of her mother's business. It had been a short conversation.

"Why don't you two go on through to the TV room and I'll order the pizza. Hawaiian, honey? And what would Daniel like?"

Lisanne ran through the menu from memory and Daniel settled on the Meat Feast, winking at Lisanne as he did so.

Monica didn't miss the look on her daughter's face as Daniel made his choice, but she very much wished she had.

Lisanne led him into the TV room to await the arrival of the food.

"Dad, can we have the subtitles on, please?"

"Oh, right," said Ernie. "Of course."

For ten minutes, they watched Bruce take down a helicopter

with a car and generally save everyone from the bad guys, when the doorbell rang. As Monica got up to answer it, Harry looked at Daniel.

"How do you answer your door?" he said, suddenly curious.

"He stands up and opens it, moron," muttered Lisanne.

"No, really," persisted Harry.

Daniel had missed Harry's question, but he'd seen Lisanne's reaction.

"What, baby?" he said, frowning. He really hated it when people answered for him.

She sighed.

"Harry wants to know how you answer the door," she said, scowling at her brother.

Daniel stiffened slightly but replied easily. "My dad fixed up a light linked to the bell. Someone rang the doorbell and the light would flash in the living room."

He didn't bother to mention that it had been broken over a year ago.

"What if you were in the kitchen, or in your bedroom?"

Daniel lifted one shoulder. "Someone else would have to answer."

"But what if there wasn't someone around?"

"Harry," said his dad, "that's enough."

Daniel flicked his eyes to Ernie before replying. "If friends are visiting, they text me first. Otherwise I'd hope they'd leave a note."

Harry looked down.

"It's okay," Daniel said, quietly. "You're wondering how it works—I get that."

"Yeah," said Harry, sounding subdued. "Sorry."

Daniel shrugged. "I can still kick your ass at Ridge Racer."

Harry raised his eyebrows. "You think?"

"Sure. Bring it on."

Lisanne smiled to herself and rubbed Daniel's thigh softly. He lifted her hand to his mouth and kissed it. Lisanne found herself suddenly breathless, then she remembered where they were and that her dad was watching them out of the corner of his eye.

Monica returned carrying the pizzas, and everyone dug in. Lisanne was just chewing on a slice of her Hawaiian, and smacking Daniel's hands away when he tried to steal pieces of pineapple, when her phone buzzed in her pocket.

She glanced at the text but didn't comment.

"Who was that?" said Monica. "One of your college friends?"

"No," said Lisanne, shaking her head and hoping her mom would take the hint.

"Who was it then?"

"Mom!"

"Well, I'm just asking. It's not a state secret, is it?"

Daniel winked at Lisanne, amused by her scowl.

"It was Rodney."

Her answer wiped the smile from Daniel's face. "Who's he?"

Lisanne threw an irritated look at her mom, and Monica had the grace to look slightly abashed.

"A friend from high school."

Daniel continued to look at her.

"He was in the orchestra, okay."

"Yeah, and he had a crush on Lis for like forever!" snickered Harry. "He was always asking her out."

His mother gave him a look and Harry suddenly found his ham and mushroom pizza of great interest.

"Well, tell Rodney we said 'hi', and that I hope Reverend Dubois has gotten over his strep throat."

"Okay," Lisanne said, quietly.

Daniel was silent, apparently lost in thought, and ate his pizza without asking anything further.

She saw him wince as he chewed.

"Are you okay?" She touched his arm so he'd look at her. "Are you okay?" she repeated.

He gave her a lopsided smile. "Yeah, I'm good."

"Does it hurt?"

"Only when I laugh."

"I'm serious!"

"I'm fine, Lis. I've just been living on instant soup for a few days. This is giving my jaw a work out—that's all."

Monica looked appalled and glanced at her husband. He gave a slight shake of his head and carried on watching the film.

"Didn't ... didn't Zef help you at all?"

Daniel frowned and said quietly, "Drop it, Lis."

"But he should have helped you!"

Daniel didn't reply, but picked up his beer and took a long drink.

Lisanne's phone beeped again but she ignored it.

"You got another message, Lis," said Harry, helpfully.

Lisanne was about ready to strangle her little brother, and from the innocent look on his face, he knew it, too.

Daniel looked at her quizzically, so she pulled out her phone and checked the message.

"It's from Rodney," she said, answering his unspoken question. "He wants to meet up tonight. I'll tell him I'm busy."

"You should see your friends, Lis," said Daniel.

His look was challenging and Lisanne felt like screaming with irritation. If Daniel wanted a pissing contest with Rodney, well, who was she to stop his fun? Although she wasn't sure how much fun it would be for Rodney. But she did want to see him.

"Fine! Fine! I'll tell him we'll be there in an hour."

Daniel raised his eyebrows then took another sip of beer.

Lisanne sent the text, and stomped upstairs to change, leaving Daniel with her parents. As far as she was concerned that was his punishment for ... when she thought about it she wasn't exactly sure why she was mad at him. She just knew she was.

She decided to channel her inner Kirsty and resurrect the denim miniskirt that had led to some very steamy car sex with Daniel. Well, to be fair, all the sex she'd had with Daniel was steamy. That boy just exuded heat. No wonder all the girls at college wanted him. She sighed. He'd written in his letter that he loved her but he'd never said it to her face—he'd never even come *close* to saying it.

The precious letter was kept between the pages of her favorite violin score, Jules Massenet's *Meditation*. She unfolded it thoughtfully and read it again. Yes, there it was in black and white—*I love you*. So why couldn't he say it out loud?

She sighed, tucking the letter away carefully. When she was old and grey and wrinkled and sagging, she'd pull it out and say to herself, 'I, too, was once adored'—because it sure looked like she wasn't going to hear it anytime soon.

She ransacked her makeup bag, glad that the contents had increased in both quality and quantity under Kirsty's vocal encouragement, but when she looked at the overall effect five minutes later, she suspected she might have overdone it—just a little.

Although she felt a slight sense of unease, she also felt irritated and rebellious. So she found her tightest t-shirt and pulled on the same pumps that she'd worn to her cousin's wedding, and Sonia Brandt's eventful party, even though she knew they were little short of foot coffins.

Daniel's backpack had been removed to the guest room, and when Lisanne came downstairs, the only change he'd made was to throw a plaid shirt over his t-shirt—unbuttoned, of course.

His eyes widened with surprise when he saw her but he was also smart enough not to say anything. Her mom, on the other hand, saw no need to hold back.

"You're not going out dressed like that!"

"What's wrong with it, Mom?" snapped Lisanne, her eyes blazing.

"You look … you look…"

"What do I look like?" she spat out, her hands on her hips.

"I think you should put something over that t-shirt," said her mom, backtracking several long steps. "You'll catch your death."

"It's fifty nine degrees outside!"

"At least take a jacket—so you can cover up."

"Don't tell me what to wear! I'm nearly 19, Mom!"

Ernie slid further down in his chair as Monica sucked in a

deep breath, and opened her mouth as a preliminary to blasting her daughter.

But Daniel's reaction was faster. He wrapped his arm around Lisanne's shoulders, and steered her out of the room. "Come on, baby doll. You can have my shirt if you get cold," and he gently walked her away.

As soon as they were out of the living room, she shrugged off his arm and stamped out of the house.

Daniel watched her thoughtfully before climbing into Monica's car without speaking, and Lisanne started the engine. But then Daniel switched on the inside light, and she turned to look at him.

"What's the matter?"

"Nothing," she snarled.

"Lis, for fuck's sake! What is it?!"

"Why wouldn't you touch me after Thanksgiving?"

He frowned, wishing he knew what the hell had turned her into a rabid ball crusher during the last sixty minutes, although he could make an educated guess.

"Well?"

"It didn't feel right."

"What does that mean?"

"Because I hadn't told you about this." He gestured toward his head.

"What difference does that make?" she yelled.

He didn't understand her anger, but then the meaning of her words sank in. She didn't care. *She really didn't care that he was deaf.* Daniel couldn't help but grin at her—which drove Lisanne into a complete rage.

"Why are you smiling!" she shrieked.

He leaned over and pulled her into his arms and kissed her hard. She resisted for a fraction of a second, then scrambled onto his lap and began to grind against his jeans.

They were both lost in the moment when Lisanne heard her phone beep with yet another message. It brought her to her senses, and she remembered that they were still sitting in her mom's car, with the interior light showcasing their every move—on her parent's drive.

She clambered inelegantly from Daniel's knee, too intent on pulling her phone out of her purse to see that he had to adjust himself.

"Rodney wants to meet at a coffee shop instead," she said, shortly.

She was rather relieved. She knew that Reverend Dubois and his wife would be shocked by Daniel—his tattoos, his pierced eyebrow, and certainly by his swearing, which he almost never managed to curb entirely, no matter how hard he tried.

"Don't want to be late for Rodney," Daniel said, snidely.

"You don't have to come," she snapped.

Daniel stared at her in disbelief.

Consequently, the drive to the coffee shop continued in stony silence although, to be fair, Daniel couldn't have seen anything Lisanne said anyway, firstly, because it was dark inside the car, and secondly, because with only seeing her profile it was virtually impossible to read what she was saying. He didn't have to worry—Lisanne was berating herself for agreeing to meet Rodney and therefore getting them all into what she was sure to be a highly uncomfortable confrontation.

She parked outside the coffee shop and hoped to speak to Daniel before they entered. But he was already holding open the café door by the time she'd picked up her purse and climbed out of the car. All she had time to say was, "Be nice!"

He raised his eyebrows and suppressed a smirk. Almost.

Rodney was sitting at a table near the back, staring moodily into a cup of foaming cappuccino. He was nice looking in a blond, preppy sort of way—he looked safe. It was the opposite of how people looked at Daniel.

Rodney started to smile when he saw Lisanne and then his eyes bugged out as he swept his gaze up and down her, taking in the micro mini, heels, and heavy makeup. When he saw Daniel, his mouth dropped open in a silent pop.

Lisanne hugged him tightly—because Rodney was her friend,

her one true friend from high school—and also because she hoped it would make Daniel insanely jealous. She couldn't help questioning the wisdom of making her highly volatile boyfriend even more incendiary, but she couldn't seem to stop herself either.

"Look at you! College must agree with you, hot stuff!" said Rodney, kissing her cheek.

Lisanne fully expected to see Daniel scowling when she turned around to introduce him, so she was bewildered to find a broad smile on his face.

"Um, Rodney, this is my boyfriend Daniel Colton. Daniel, this is my friend from high school, Rodney Dubois."

The two men shook hands, and then Daniel headed to the counter to order a latte for Lisanne and his usual black coffee.

"So," said Rodney, slowly, "*that's* your boyfriend."

"Yes," said Lisanne kindly, but firmly.

"He's different."

Rodney's voice was amused but without judgment.

Lisanne smiled. He was so right.

"And *you* look different, too. My mom would have a heart attack if she saw you now."

Rodney's voice took on a wistful tone that made Lisanne regret dressing so skimpily. She hoped it didn't look like she was rubbing his face in the fact that she now had a boyfriend—and it wasn't him.

Daniel returned and slouched down in his chair, angling it so he could face both of them at the same time.

Rodney turned his gaze to Daniel.

"Are you studying music, too?"

Lisanne winced but Daniel kept his gaze neutral.

"No, economics with business, and math as a minor."

"Oh," said Rodney, clearly surprised. "I thought..." he glanced to Lisanne for help.

"What about you?" said Daniel, steering the conversation away from himself. "Lisanne hasn't said ... You were in the school orchestra together?"

"Yeah, I played the cello—but nothing like Lisanne." He smiled at her fondly, "She was out of everyone's league."

They both stared at her and she felt her face heat up.

"I've been going to theological college to train to be a pastor, like my father."

Daniel raised his eyebrows. "Can't be easy for you."

Lisanne frowned. It wasn't like Daniel to make assumptions like that, but when she looked at him, she saw something like sympathy in his eyes. She was puzzled.

Rodney sighed. "I used to think it was…"

Lisanne stared. "But you've wanted this like forever!"

"Things change," he said.

"Yeah," said Daniel, nodding slowly in agreement. "They do."

Some sort of unspoken communication passed between them, and Lisanne felt very much on the outside.

They were interrupted by a girl who asked them for the time—presumably as a pretext, because she made no attempt to restrain her open ogling of Daniel. Lisanne sighed. She was getting used to it, although it still pissed her the hell off. She rested her hand on Daniel's thigh in a clear, territorial display.

Daniel smiled down at her and Rodney looked amused.

They chatted amiably and Lisanne was surprised—and if she was honest, slightly annoyed—that the guys seemed to be getting along so well. She just wouldn't have figured it. Wasn't Rodney supposed to be pining for her? Wasn't Daniel usually jealous of any guy who talked to her? It was very confusing.

She was even more surprised when Rodney suggested they go on to a club where the bouncers were a little lax on IDs. And even more surprised when Daniel said it was fine by him.

"Um, I don't think Mom and Dad would…"

"Come on, Lis," said Daniel, nuzzling her hair. "No disrespect to your folks, but I don't think I can handle the rest of the evening watching Bruce Willis films with your dad, while he tries not to leap out of his chair every time I touch you."

Rodney chuckled knowingly and Lisanne threw him a dirty look.

"Come on, baby doll," whispered Daniel persuasively, using the sexy smile that he knew she couldn't resist.

Lisanne tried once more. "Do you think you should, after … you know?"

Daniel frowned and pulled away from her, his eyes flicking up to Rodney, who looked puzzled.

Lisanne capitulated. "Okay, fine. But please don't drink. I hate being the only sober person, and I have to drive."

Daniel still looked irritated and agreed curtly. Rodney just shrugged and nodded.

"I'm driving, too," he said.

As they walked out onto the street, Lisanne shivered slightly. Daniel looked down at her and without speaking, pulled off his shirt and handed it to her.

She couldn't help smiling to herself as she slipped it on and tied it in a knot at the front.

Rodney was staring at the tattoos he could see winding their way down Daniel's arms.

"Nice ink," he said.

Daniel hadn't seen him speak so he didn't answer. Rodney frowned but chose not to comment.

The club was one that Lisanne hadn't heard of before—although clubbing had never really been her thing—and was surprised that Rodney seemed to know about it. The two bouncers were well muscled men, clean cut, and identically dressed in white t-shirts and tight jeans.

Rodney turned to Daniel.

"I should have said but I didn't think you'd say yes."

Daniel smirked. "I don't give a shit."

Rodney blinked then gave a small smile. "No, you don't, do you."

"Just so long as the only hands I feel on my ass belong to baby doll."

Lisanne was puzzled, her eyes toggling between the two of

them. What on earth were they talking about? She didn't know what was going on. It must be a guy thing. How irritating was that?

Stopping at an ATM so Daniel could withdraw some money, then paid the club's cover charge, and Lisanne walked in with Daniel's arm draped casually across her shoulders. It was almost darker inside than on the nighttime street. Lisanne peered into the gloom, wondering if there would be anyone she recognized.

She could feel the music vibrating through the soles of her shoes and relaxed slightly, knowing Daniel could feel it, too. She understood now why he felt comfortable in clubs—if they didn't have live bands—he wasn't at a disadvantage.

Rodney pointed his chin toward the bar and they all followed—it was the only part of the club where there was a chance of speaking and being heard. The irony was not lost on Lisanne.

She asked for a bottle of water and both of the guys had beers. She frowned but didn't say anything. Daniel took a long drink and then leaned down to speak into her ear. She felt his cool lips and warm breath on her skin, causing a tremor to run through her.

"Want to dance, baby doll?"

She nodded and he pulled her out onto the dance floor. Rodney watched from the bar, his face holding a slight smile, although his eyes were filled with longing.

Lisanne felt bad for leaving him by himself, but it had been his idea to go to the club after all. Then she felt Daniel pull her into his chest and she stopped thinking about anybody else.

She loved how at ease he was with his body, feeling the rhythm, perhaps hearing the music in his mind. It was hard to say—he so rarely talked about things like that—personal things. The only time he'd truly opened up had been in his letter. It was frustrating.

She felt his hands on her hips, pulling her closer. So she let her fingers drift up his chest, brushing over his nipple rings, and tightened her hands firmly behind his neck. He grinned down

425

then suddenly dipped her low to the floor, making her squeal. She caught a flash of Rodney's grinning face at the bar as Daniel stood her upright, and kissed the bare skin beneath her throat.

They seemed to be getting quite a bit of attention with people staring at them. Lisanne felt herself moving to Icona Pop's pumping vibe, *I Love It*. At first, she felt rather self-conscious but Daniel didn't seem to notice or, if he did, it didn't concern him. Plus, everyone around her seemed to be heading to the dance floor to let loose for that tune, and the DJ pumped up the bass.

Twenty minutes later, and Lisanne was out of breath. She tapped on Daniel's shoulder and signaled a timeout with her hands. As they walked back toward the bar, a man stopped them and said something to Daniel. She couldn't hear what it was, but Daniel shook his head and hooked a finger into the pocket of her denim skirt. The man held up his hands and backed away. It occurred to Lisanne that there were very few women in the club. Looking around the room, she glimpsed two men kissing openly, and she nudged Daniel. He glanced over then smiled at her, totally unfazed.

Rodney looked challengingly at Lisanne.

"There aren't many girls in here," she said, slowly. "I think this is a gay club."

"Yes," said Rodney, "it is."

"Did you know?" she said, wide-eyed.

Rodney nodded so she turned to Daniel, who was watching her with amusement.

"Did you?"

Daniel grinned at her.

"Baby doll, the look on your face. You're so cute!"

Lisanne stared in confusion. "Why are we in a gay club?"

Daniel looked at Rodney. "Do you want to tell her or should I?"

"What?" said Lisanne. "Tell me what?"

Rodney grimaced, then looked up at Lisanne. "I'm gay."

Lisanne stared.

"No, you're not."

Now it was Rodney's turn to stare.

Lisanne had heard what he'd said, but the words seemed to take forever to make sense.

"But … what…? When…? I mean … are you sure?"

Rodney looked dumbfounded by her question. "Well, yeah. I'm sure."

"Since when?!"

"Well, always, I guess."

She turned her accusing gaze to Daniel. "How the hell did you know?"

He shrugged.

Dumb. Dumber. Dumbest. Lisanne flushed with anger and embarrassment.

"Well why didn't you tell me?" she yelped at Rodney.

"It's not so easy. We've been friends like forever. I thought you'd figure it out. Eventually." He sighed. "But you never did and … your parents are friends with mine and Dad's a preacher…"

Lisanne felt hurt. "So you can tell my boyfriend that you've known for all of two hours, but you can't tell me? We've been friends since kindergarten!"

"I didn't have to tell him, Lis, he just knew. I didn't know how to tell you. I hoped … you know … you're not mad?"

"Yes! I'm so mad at you! I'm mad you didn't tell me. I'm not mad you're, you know, gay, for goodness sake! We're *friends*, Rodney."

He looked relieved. "Thanks, Lis."

"Do your parents know?"

He shook his head. "I'm waiting until after Christmas for *that* conversation … and that I won't be going back to theological college."

Lisanne shook her head, sadly.

"It'll break Dad's heart," said Rodney bitterly, and Lisanne didn't know if he meant because he was gay or because he no longer wanted to train to be a man of the cloth. She was tired and feeling emotional, and still kind of pissed at Daniel because he'd guessed in a few minutes what had been under her nose for years.

She'd always thought that Rodney liked her *that* way. It was beyond embarrassing. But what Rodney had to face—that was way harder. She gave herself a mental kick—this wasn't about her.

"Well, fine. I suppose you want to go shopping with me now."

Rodney rolled his eyes and pretended to sigh. "That is so cliché!"

Lisanne gave him a big hug and kissed him on the cheek. "Serves you right for not telling me."

Rodney gave her a squeeze and looked at Daniel. "Look after my girl."

Daniel smiled. "It's a full-time job." He looked at Lisanne's tired face. "Do you want to go home now, baby doll?"

She nodded and looked at Rodney. "Are you going home, too?"

"No. Think I'll stay for a while," he said. "Maybe we could catch up again before New Years?"

"Sure, I'd like that. Take care, Rodney."

She slipped her hand around Daniel's waist and they strolled out of the club.

They hadn't walked more than half a dozen paces before Lisanne heard someone calling her name.

"Hey, Maclaine! Mouse Girl!"

She turned with a horrified expression.

Grayson Woods.

And associates.

"Your faggoty fucking friend broke my goddamn nose!" he growled.

Lisanne looked up, realizing that Grayson's nose had indeed been remodeled.

Daniel glanced around him and his lips tightened into a thin line.

"Get back to the car, Lis," he said, quietly.

"No!" she gasped. "I'm not leaving you!"

His gaze was strained and deadly serious. "Go now, Lis!"

He was still staring at her, his eyes burning with intensity—when Grayson hit him, catching the left side of Daniel's face.

Suddenly he was on the floor, holding the side of his head, and Grayson Woods was standing over him with a cruel smile twisting his lips.

"I'm going to fuck you up," he snarled, aiming a kick at Daniel's unprotected ribs.

Lisanne screamed as one of Grayson's friends aimed a second kick. Daniel was still holding his head, using his hands to cover the left side. He coughed and gasped, as the second blow caught him low in the stomach. Lisanne ran forward but Grayson batted her away.

Lisanne screamed again, and the bouncers from the club looked up and started toward them. Before Lisanne could react, there was an old-fashioned melee going on at her feet. More men ran out from the club, and soon it was Grayson's friends who were getting a beat down, curses filling the air and fists flying. The fight broke apart, and Grayson fled, sprinting down the street, his friends trailing behind him.

Lisanne was on her knees next to Daniel. He looked dazed and she realized blood was seeping through his beanie.

She pulled it off and saw the gauze was soaked red. Her heart shuddered and she felt sick.

One of the club guys pushed her out of the way.

"I'm a nurse, let me look." He checked Daniel over quickly, running his hands along his body to see if anything seemed to be broken.

Daniel sat up shakily and the nurse only needed to glance at the dressing, before giving Lisanne a significant look.

"Okay," said the nurse, "let's get him off the street."

Hooking Daniel's arms around their shoulders, two burly men half dragged, half carried Daniel back into the club. Rodney came running over, his face pale and shocked.

"What happened?"

"Grayson Woods," gasped Lisanne, her hands trembling from fear and adrenalin.

"Fucker!" hissed Rodney.

Rodney saw the blood-soaked dressing on Daniel's head and looked confused, but the nurse was thoughtful. "I think we should get him to hospital," he said, calmly. "Just to get him checked over."

Lisanne rubbed Daniel's arm, and he looked up at her, his eyes slowly focusing.

"They're going to call an ambulance."

He shook his head slowly. "No. No more hospitals, baby doll."

"Daniel…!"

"Please, Lis," he said, sounding dazed.

"You're bleeding all over the place!" she cried.

He gave her a lopsided smile. "Yeah."

"Take him into the office," said the nurse. "They keep a first aid kit in there."

Rodney and one of the other men helped Daniel to stand, and led him into a room a short distance from the main entrance, lowering him into a seat.

The man who'd identified himself as a nurse gently pulled off Daniel's dressing.

"Has he had a procedure?"

Lisanne nodded. "Yes. A cochlear implant—a week ago."

The nurse glanced up at Lisanne's worried tone.

"Okay, that doesn't look too bad." He stood in front of Daniel and spoke slowly and clearly. "Where you had stitches, one has pulled apart slightly. There's no bleeding from your ear that I can see. Breathe deeply for me."

Daniel pulled in several deep breaths, letting them out slowly. Lisanne could see it caused him some pain but the nurse looked pleased.

He stood in front of Daniel and gave another instruction.

"Can you tell me where you are?"

"Shit-poke, Iowa." Lisanne nudged his arm and Daniel sighed. "Well, I guess it must be Georgia then."

"Can you repeat the months of the year in reverse order?"

"Give me a fucking break," said Daniel.

"He's only trying to help," snapped Lisanne.

"December, November, October, September…" Daniel intoned, obediently.

"Okay, that'll do. Let's take a look at your ribs."

Wincing, Daniel pulled up his t-shirt and Lisanne's hand flew to her mouth. Several large bruises were billowing out across Daniel's smooth skin.

The nurse ran his hands over Daniel's chest and stomach. "Nice nipple rings. Ahem. There doesn't appear to be anything broken, but I still think you should have an x-ray to check if your ribs are cracked."

"Fuck that," said Daniel, tiredly. "They wouldn't do anything even if they were—except tape them up. I can do that myself."

The nurse shook his head but smiled.

"Okay, Mr. Oh So Stubborn. Last test. See if you can touch my finger and then touch the tip of your nose."

Daniel dropped his t-shirt down and straightened up. Lisanne winced in sympathy. She was glad that he didn't have any trouble following the nurse's instructions.

"Sure I can't persuade you of the benefits of a quick trip to the emergency room?" said the nurse.

Daniel shook his head and cursed again.

"No, I'm good."

"Honey, you're more than good," sighed one of the other men. "Vernon, next time *I* want to play nurse with the hot guy."

The nurse smiled and Lisanne wanted to sink through the floor—even guys were ogling her boyfriend now. At least they weren't hitting on him—yet.

"He's pigheaded, that's for sure," said the nurse. "Hard headed, too. I'll just put some butterfly strips over his wound. I suggest you wait here for 10 minutes and if there's any dizziness, call an ambulance, no matter what he says."

Lisanne nodded.

When the nurse was done, he tried one last time to persuade Daniel to go to hospital, and also to persuade Lisanne to call the police. Daniel wouldn't allow either, and eventually the nurse left them alone with Rodney.

"Are you going to tell me what's going on?" asked Rodney. "What's this implant you were talking about?"

Lisanne turned to face him.

"Daniel's deaf. He had surgery a week ago and they placed what's called a cochlear implant just behind his ear, under the skin. Eventually it'll help him to hear. We hope."

Rodney stared at Daniel. "He's … you're *deaf*? Completely deaf?"

Daniel met his gaze evenly. "And you thought you were the only one who was different."

Rodney's breath caught in his throat, and the two men stared at each other.

"Wow, I … I don't know what to say. I'm sorry, man."

Daniel stretched slowly, feeling his ribs as he did so. "Yeah, I get that a lot."

Rodney gave a rueful smile. "Yeah, right." He shook his head. "I didn't even guess."

"That's the general idea."

"But how?"

"Daniel lip reads." Lisanne answered for him.

Rodney looked out of his depth. "But why do you hide it?"

Daniel gave him a disbelieving look. "*You're* asking *me* that?!"

Rodney stared, then laughed out loud and shook his head. "Most guys try and act cool about it—except for the Neanderthals like Grayson Woods—but even the ones who pretend they aren't that bothered make jokes about keeping their backs to the wall. You don't."

Daniel shrugged, but Lisanne saw a small ripple of pain run through him.

"Well, hell, man, I've been called every crappy name under the sun—know every dumb joke about being deaf: 'How does a deaf person know if someone is screaming or yawning?' Funny, huh. Got into a lot of fights. I don't give a shit who you fuck as long as it's not baby doll because that's *my* job."

Rodney smiled and raised his eyebrows at Lisanne, who was trying to cool down her flushed cheeks. *Such a dirty mouth!*

"So," Rodney asked at last, "why did that asshat hit you?"

"Daniel broke his nose at Sonia Brandt's Thanksgiving pool party."

Rodney snorted. "Seriously? A lot of people have been wanting to do that for years. The guy's a bullying bastard. But why did you hit him in the first place? At the party—which no one invited me to, by the way."

"You were away, remember?"

"Whatever—tell me about Grayson."

"He was … rude to me," Lisanne said, simply.

Rodney looked at Daniel with renewed respect. "And you broke his nose?"

"With one punch," Lisanne said, a touch of pride tinting her words.

Rodney shook his head. "Well, Woods knows how to hold a grudge, so you'd better watch your back while you're in town."

"Rodney! If you think I'm going to give him the chance to do this again—or to someone else … my Dad plays golf with his dad. Once he sees…"

"Lis," said Daniel, patiently, "I broke the guy's nose—he could have landed my ass in jail. I think you should just leave it."

Lisanne was furious that the omerta of guy on guy fights seemed to be alive and kicking. She started to protest but Daniel looked so tired and battered, she bit down on her lip to stop the words flooding out.

"Do you want to go home?"

"Yeah, baby doll. I don't think I can take any more 'fun' tonight."

Rodney looked sympathetic then glanced at Lisanne. "Poor, Lis. All dressed up and no one to have 'fun' with."

"We did *that* before we came out," she said, coolly.

433

Rodney looked surprised. "Whoa! Way to go, Lis. You *have* changed."

Lisanne wondered whether he was right. She still felt like the old Lisanne Maclaine but people did seem to treat her differently. Was it just the outside that had changed? Some more makeup and shorter skirts? Or had she changed on the inside? Had college and Daniel and living away from home, had these things changed her?

She was still pondering the question as Daniel struggled to his feet.

"Fuck. I feel like I've been run over by a truck."

"What are you guys doing tomorrow?" Rodney said, hopefully.

"Fuck all," replied Daniel. "Merry Christmas."

"We'll catch up before New Years," said Lisanne. "Text me?"

"Sure," said Rodney, then waited until Daniel was looking down. "By the way, tell your boyfriend I like his nipple rings. They're … inspiring."

They left Rodney grinning to himself as he headed back into the club.

One of the bouncers walked with them to Lisanne's car, winked at Daniel, blew him a kiss and then smiled cockily at Lisanne.

She sighed and started driving home.

Why had she ever thought her life was boring?

CHAPTER 22

Daniel woke up wondering why the hell he had an elephant sitting on his chest.

He moved slowly and pushed down the sheet to stare at the large, purple bruises that discolored his ribs and hip.

He touched his head and winced slightly, but it didn't feel too bad. He hoped that the implant hadn't been damaged—there was nothing rattling, so far as he could tell. The doc had said it was made of titanium, but he was still supposed to be careful. Getting that bastard's fist in his face was probably pushing the whole 'careful' game plan.

He swung his legs out of bed and waited for the usual dizziness and nausea, but there was nothing. That was a relief.

Pulling on his jeans, he then rifled through his backpack. Daniel quickly realized he was down to his last clean t-shirt. And damn it, his beanie was stiff with dried blood. He pulled a face— he'd better get Lisanne to show him how their washing machine worked. He glanced at his phone, noting that it was already after ten. He was surprised no one had woken him up.

Scraping his hand over his stubble, he wondered if Lis would get on his case about that, too. After the mood she'd been in yesterday, he thought it highly likely. He'd better shave. Jeez, when had he gotten so pussy-whipped?

As he shuffled toward the bathroom, Monica was walking in the opposite direction.

"Oh my goodness! What happened?"

He grinned at her. "Rough night out," and left her gaping in the hallway.

The shower helped him loosen up a lot and he spent some time letting the steam do its work on his sore, bruised muscles. He turned and relished the feeling as the water cascaded over his back, and he lazily jacked off.

Ambling down to the kitchen to see if there way anything that looked like breakfast, he realized that letting Monica see him bare chested had been a mistake.

Harry was hunched over a bowl of cereal, and his parents were sitting with their arms crossed.

"Daniel, take a seat, please," said Ernie, in full teacher mode. "I want to know what happened last night. Monica says you're badly bruised. Have you been in a fight?"

Daniel leaned against the doorpost, ignoring the first request, and oozing insolence.

"A misunderstanding. It's cool."

Ernie inflated with annoyance.

"I won't have you involving my daughter in … whatever happened."

Daniel's hackles were well and truly raised.

"I wouldn't let *anything* happen to Lisanne."

"Clearly something did happen. Now, you're a guest in our house, so please have the courtesy to explain yourself—so I don't have to worry about her."

If Ernie hadn't added those last few words, Daniel would have turned on his heel and walked out. He took a deep breath, acknowledging that they both had Lisanne's best interests at heart.

"We were jumped by a guy Lis knew from high school and a couple of his buddies. Someone else broke it up—end of story."

Ernie gaped at him. "It was someone Lisanne knew? Who?"

"We were never introduced," Daniel answered, evasively.

At that moment, Lisanne walked into the kitchen looking tense, clearly having heard the last part of Daniel's statement. He felt her touch his arm and he smiled down at her.

"Who was it, Lisanne?" barked Ernie.

She jumped slightly, and Daniel frowned.

"Grayson Woods."

Harry's head snapped up and there was a sudden silence around the table.

"Barry Woods' son?"

"Yes."

"And he just … decided to hit Daniel? For no reason?"

Lisanne bit her lip and looked up at her boyfriend.

"We, um, we bumped into him at Sonia's party at Thanksgiving."

"And…?"

"Dad, you know what a bully Grayson is."

"Lisanne, I want to know what happened. I play golf with Barry Woods every week, for goodness sake!"

"Yeah?" said Daniel, looking furious. "Well, tell him his son is a dirty mouthed fucker who got everything he deserved—when I broke his nose."

He stormed from the room and was out of the front door and halfway down the road before Lisanne caught up to him, slightly out of breath.

She grabbed his hand to slow him down.

"Hey," she said, softly. "Hey, it's okay. They just worry."

Daniel's anger was still surging through him. On one level he understood Ernie's reaction—the asshole was the son of his buddy, one of the good ole boys—but on another level, Daniel was infuriated that it was always assumed that *he* was the one at fault. Always the outsider. He was honest enough to know that he brought a lot of that on himself, but fuck, was it any wonder?

He stopped walking long enough to let Lisanne pull him into a hug, while he stood there stiffly, his nostrils flaring as he breathed hard.

Her soft hands held his face and he looked down into her eyes. She kissed his lips and he relaxed a fraction.

"Come on. Let's go back. Dad didn't mean it like that."

Daniel took a deep breath.

"Just … just give me a moment, okay. Fuck, I could use a smoke."

"Well, go ahead. I don't mind. Much."

Daniel gave her a crooked smile.

"Don't tempt me."

"Why not?"

"Because I gave up, baby doll."

She stared at him in disbelief. "When did you do that?"

"After Thanksgiving—a couple of weeks before the op. I didn't think jonesing for a smoke while I was in the hospital would be the best idea."

He shrugged, trying to make it sound insignificant, because she looked upset that she hadn't noticed during all of those weeks.

"Oh," she said, quietly. "That explains why you were so cranky." She looked up at him. "And I'm sorry I was such a grouch last night. Time of the month," she mumbled, embarrassed.

Daniel smiled at her and raised his eyebrows. "Yeah, I know."

The pink in Lisanne's cheeks deepened. "How do you know?"

"I can count the number of days in a month, baby doll. Besides, you were being such a bitch, it was pretty fucking obvious."

He smiled when she smacked his arm harmlessly.

"It's horrible timing though," she said. "You being here for the holidays and we won't be able to, you know…"

"It doesn't bother me that you got your period." He grinned at Lisanne's shocked expression and shrugged. "I'll always want you." He'd never been bothered by shit like that. Hell, wasn't that what shower sex was invented for?

"Um, I don't think so," she said, her face scarlet.

I hear you, he signed at her, and she gave a nervous laugh.

"Elephant shoes," she whispered back, which made him smile.

Daniel was disappointed but not surprised that she'd vetoed sex for the rest of the week. He also suspected that given time, she might change her mind. At least he hoped so.

She tugged on his hand again. "Are you ready to go back now?"

Daniel breathed out slowly. "Yeah, I guess."

"How are your ribs today?"

"Okay." He'd had worse playing football.

They walked back hand in hand and found Harry sitting on the doorstep, waiting for them.

"Did you really break Grayson's nose?"

"Yeah."

"Cool! Everybody hates him."

Daniel's answering smile dropped away when Monica suddenly appeared. "Please don't encourage him, Daniel," she said, severely. "We don't condone violence in this house, *whatever the reason.*"

Daniel tensed up again and Lisanne glared at her mother.

"In the kitchen, please," she snapped. "We're going to clear this up now. Your father is all for calling the police after I described the mess Daniel was in when I saw him this morning. But as we know there was more to this than you're telling us, I think my husband deserves to know the full story, don't you?"

Daniel fumed silently. This was turning out to be one fucked up Christmas Eve. He had the option of leaving, but he didn't want to put Lisanne in the position of having to choose— especially when he wasn't sure that she'd choose him.

He followed Monica into the kitchen and stared stonily at a red-faced Ernie.

Monica waved at a couple of chairs and, reluctantly, Daniel and Lisanne sat.

"Lisanne, please tell us exactly what happened at Sonia's party. What led up to last night's … events?"

Lisanne sighed. "Basically, Grayson was rude to me. Daniel told him to shut up. He didn't, so Daniel hit him … and broke his nose."

"What did he say to her?" gasped Monica.

Daniel's eyes slid over to Lisanne's mom, but he didn't reply.

"Lisanne?" her mother said.

"Mom, it's really embarrassing. I don't want to repeat it."

"I am *this close* to calling the police!" roared Ernie. "You will tell us what he said!"

"Fine!" shouted Lisanne. "He said, 'Who knew you could be such a hot piece of ass'. Daniel told him to shut up and then…" her voice trembled, "and then he said, 'Looks like that uptight bitch finally opened her legs for someone'. That's when Daniel hit him."

Tears glinted in her eyes and Daniel put his arm around her, his face stern.

Monica had her hand over her mouth, her eyes tight, her expression horrified.

Ernie took in his wife's devastated expression, Lisanne's humiliation and Daniel's still present anger and resentment. He stood up slowly, as everyone turned their eyes to him. Taking a deep breath, he held out his hand toward Daniel.

"Thank you," he said.

Daniel stared back then nodded his head. He shifted his chair back so he could stand and lean across the table to shake hands with Lisanne's father.

"Well," said Monica. "Well."

Lisanne was feeling very emotional, too.

"I think we need a drink after that!" Monica wheezed.

Daniel hoped that she'd be offering him a beer or, better still, Ernie would be breaking out the bottle of Jack that he hadn't seen since Thanksgiving, but instead Monica put the kettle on. Daniel declined a drink, and went outside to get some air and let his boiling temper cool.

Lisanne grabbed herself an iced tea from the refrigerator and went out into the backyard with Daniel.

He sank gracefully onto the grass and sat cross-legged as he pulled out a pack of gum—he'd much rather have had a smoke.

Lisanne nudged his elbow and he smiled at her.

"By the way, how did you know Rodney was gay?" Lisanne said, almost crossly. "I've known him for years and I never knew. You met him for 30 seconds and knew straightaway. I don't get it!"

Daniel gave her an amused smile. "He was checking out my package in the coffee shop."

Lisanne choked on her iced tea. "What?! He was hugging me! I thought he was checking *me* out?!"

"He was, baby doll, but he was probably thinking 'not that skirt with those shoes'."

"What was wrong with my shoes?"

Daniel rolled his eyes. "It's a metaphor."

"I like those shoes," Lisanne muttered to herself.

Daniel laid back on the grass and let his eyelids drift down. "I know you're looking at me, baby doll." He felt her hand on his stomach and opened his eyes.

"You're so beautiful," she said.

He blinked in surprise. "Yeah, you too, baby."

"No, I mean it. You're beautiful inside and out."

Daniel frowned, feeling deeply uncomfortable. "What's on the schedule for today?" he said, deflecting quickly. "Can we go somewhere? I don't think I can take any more mom and dad time—although I need to do some laundry."

She pulled teasingly on the waistband of his jeans.

"Are you going commando again?"

Daniel raised his eyebrows. "Why don't we go to your room so you can find out?"

Lisanne laughed. "Don't you ever stop?"

"Do you want me to?"

"No, not really."

He grinned at her. "Okay."

"Anyway, I already put your laundry in."

He looked at her, surprised and pleased. "I didn't expect you to do that, but thanks."

She smiled shyly. "Well, don't get used to it. It's only because you're a guest."

He winked at her.

"We can head out for a few hours if you need to do any

shopping or anything. We do gifts in the morning," she hesitated. "Not that I'm expecting…"

He silenced her with a kiss, and she didn't notice when her iced tea spilled onto the grass.

They spent the rest of the day taking it easy, having long quiet coffees and strolls by themselves. The town was full of people doing last minute shopping but Daniel felt like he was in a bubble of happiness, embracing just him and Lisanne. It was a good place to be.

Harry had willingly loaned Daniel a beanie to wear, and then headed straight for his friend's house. It was clear he couldn't wait to tell everyone that Grayson Woods had been taken down.

Daniel was still amazed that Ernie had shaken his hand and thanked him. It was something of a head spin after the way the day had started.

Not only that, he appreciated the peace and order of Lisanne's home. Yeah, her parents could be kind of suffocating, but he thought again about getting a place of his own where he and Lis could be alone together. He was determined to find somewhere, even if it meant he'd be living off ramen noodles for the next few years.

He made a decision to head back for a couple of days before New Years and check things out. They hadn't discussed how long he'd be staying at Lisanne's during the holidays, but he had a feeling she wouldn't be pleased if he told her he was leaving early. Even so, finding somewhere of their own was a priority.

It was with a feeling of shock that he realized he'd thought of it as 'their' place. He wasn't expecting Lisanne to move in, of course. But even as he rejected the idea, another part of him said yes, that was exactly what he wanted. He tested the idea out in his mind. Not this year, of course. She had her room on campus, but next year maybe? He had a pretty good idea what Monica and Ernie would think of that, but Lisanne didn't always do as they said.

The more he thought about it the more he liked the idea of them living together, sharing their worlds. It was exhilarating and fucking scary all at the same time. Would she do it? Would she put up with him? Living with his punk ass? He took a deep breath and she looked at him quizzically.

"Are you okay? Do your ribs hurt?"

Fuck, he couldn't get enough of the way she looked at him when she thought he was hurting.

"No, I'm good, baby doll. Just thinking about how cute you're going to look in your Christmas present."

She smiled delightedly and her skin flushed a pretty shade of pink. "You bought me something to wear?"

"Yeah."

"We have a family tradition where we all sit around the tree in the morning and share gifts."

"That could be interesting," said Daniel, raising his eyebrows.

"Why?" said Lisanne, suspiciously.

"Let's just say it's something I want you to wear for me," and he winked at her.

"Oh."

"Yeah."

Lisanne thought for a moment. "I think maybe you should give it to me before the whole tree thing."

Daniel smiled. "I intend to."

"But we're not having sex, because, you know…"

"Sure I can't persuade you?"

"Um, no!" she said, wrinkling her nose. "That's totally gross!"

He looked at her seriously. "Nothing is gross with you, baby doll. I always want you."

She looked up hesitatingly. "You do?"

"Always," he whispered, and it wasn't clear to either of them what he meant by that.

They stared at each other until Daniel placed a soft kiss on her lips, then pulled away with a peaceful smile.

They arrived back just as Monica and Ernie were leaving for the evening carol service at their local church.

"Harry is home," said Monica, sending a clear message with flashing warning lights, adorned with baubles.

"Sure, Mom," said Lisanne, rolling her eyes.

Daniel grinned. "Have a great evening, Monica, Mr. Maclaine."

"I think you can call me 'Ernie', son," said Lisanne's dad, smiling at Daniel's stunned expression.

"Wow!" said Lisanne, as the door closed behind her parents. "You should hit Grayson Woods more often!"

"Just give me the fucking chance," snarled Daniel, instantly losing his good mood. "Mother fucker."

"Hey, it's Christmas! Good will to all men."

"Not that bastard."

No fucking way!

"If I let you kiss me, will you be in a better mood?"

Daniel raised his eyebrows. "If you *let* me? Are you saying you that you'd stop me if I did this?" and he held her hips, running his tongue up Lisanne's neck and nipping her earlobe.

"I might *let* you do that," Lisanne agreed, breathlessly.

"Aw, hell! Are you guys gonna make out all night? I live here, too," said Harry, misery and distaste etched on his face.

Daniel's eyes swiveled toward the pile of food that Harry was carrying, and lit up. "Hold that thought, baby doll, I'm fucking starving."

It was the best Christmas Eve Daniel had had for two years. Sure, it would have been improved if he could have persuaded Lisanne to get naked, but having her cuddle up to him while they watched TV, that was pretty good, too. And the refrigerator was groaning at the seams in a way that made his eyes bulge. Lisanne had certainly made good on her promise that Monica would feed him up.

Then there was an extended make out session in Lisanne's bedroom, interrupted only when her parents arrived back from church.

Daniel headed to the guest room and stopped when he opened the door. All his laundry had been dried and left neatly folded on the bed. Monica must have done it because he'd completely forgotten about it while he was out with Lisanne.

His chest felt warm in a way that was almost unrecognizable. Having someone look after him like that—it had been a while.

He sat on the bed, staring at the clothes, and rubbed his forehead tiredly. It was probably just as well baby doll didn't want to fuck—his body was aching from the beating he'd taken and his head was throbbing. The last 24 hours had been intense. But there was something about the way Lisanne's family came together—it was kind of corny how protective Monica and Ernie were, but Daniel could see it made them all strong, too. And baby doll was so strong. Each time he thought she'd pull away, she'd surprised the hell out of him.

Her whole family had surprised him. Their petty rules were irritating, and the double standards were laughable, but they were a family and they cared.

Daniel pulled out his phone and sent Zef a message for the first time since they'd argued.

*** Merry xmas, fucker.
Take it easy. D ***

He wandered into the bathroom to brush his teeth and enjoy a long piss. When he strolled back into his room, he glanced at the phone, but there was no reply.

Whatever the fuck Zef had done—and the stupid bastard had done pretty much everything—he was family. If that still meant something.

Daniel pulled off his clothes and climbed wearily into bed, enjoying the feel of the clean sheets on his bare skin.

He slept uneasily, waking often when he rolled onto a part of his body that hurt, and dreaming about Zef, standing alone in a forest made of pylons. His eyes had been sewn shut.

Daniel woke up with his heart hammering, and Lisanne standing over him looking almost afraid.

"Are you okay?" she gasped.

"Crap, sorry. Bad dream." He rubbed his hands over his eyes then sat up, quickly rebooting his brain. "Hey, merry Christmas! Or maybe this is a good dream—a sexy woman bringing me coffee in bed on Christmas morning. Yeah, must be a dream—my life is never this good. I might just have to touch you to see if you're real."

He ran his hand under Lisanne's sleep shirt and she nearly spilled his coffee.

"Stop that!" she hissed.

"Yeah, you're real. Baby doll likes to shout at me. It kinda turns me on." He lifted his sheet and looked down at his morning wood. "Yep, definitely turns me on."

"You're so bad!" she snorted, while he grinned up at her.

Lisanne managed to put his coffee down safely before he pulled her toward him for a Christmas kiss.

"I haven't brushed my teeth!" she moaned.

"Neither have I, baby," and he sucked the skin on her neck, just below her ear.

This time her moan meant something different, but only Lisanne heard it.

She pushed away from him, far too aroused for her own good. "Stop that! I'm not supposed to be in here, remember? And anyway, your bruises look awful. Do they hurt?"

"I thought you liked me looking hard, Lis," he snickered.

"You know, sometimes you're such a *boy*."

"Told you before, baby doll. I'm all man."

His hard kiss punctuated the point.

"Hey, I got your present."

He rolled over to reach under the bed—knowing full well that he was giving her a glimpse of his bare ass—and pulled out her gift.

"Wrapped it myself," he said proudly, displaying the butchered paper and wonky bow as if it were straight from Tiffany's.

She picked up the tiny package and fought with the Scotch tape until the paper was shredded and Lisanne was almost crying with frustration. Finally, she extracted a scrap of silver material. Her face reddened as she realized it was the smallest thong she'd ever seen—a minute triangle at the front was the most substantial part of it. She looked closer. Yes, she had seen it correctly—a tiny triangle of silver material printed with an image of mistletoe.

"Wear it for me today," he said huskily, and whenever you want, I can kiss you under the mistletoe.

He watched Lisanne swallow and nod wordlessly.

Her head turned when she heard a knock at Daniel's door. She stuffed the thong into her fist as Monica leaned inside.

"I was just taking Daniel a coffee," Lisanne muttered, her face still fiery.

Daniel suspected that Monica was trying not to laugh as she nodded solemnly. "So I see. Merry Christmas, Daniel. Breakfast in 20 minutes."

"I'll be there," he said, cheerfully.

Lisanne followed her mother out of the room. "Merry Christmas!"

He grinned to himself.

After he'd showered and rid himself of the morning log that most definitely *hadn't* disappeared during Lisanne's visit in her cute little sleep shirt, he knocked on Harry's door and poked his head inside.

"Hey, man. Merry Christmas," and Daniel tossed a magazine shaped parcel onto Harry's bed. "Don't open it when your parents are around."

He closed the door, smiling to himself at the stunned look on Harry's face. The kid would definitely get some use out of a Christmas edition of *Swank*. Daniel had spent a pleasant half hour deciding what to get Harry for Christmas. At the last minute, he'd included a copy of *Playboy*, too. You had to respect the classics.

He wandered into the kitchen and found Monica and Ernie in a tight clinch.

"Merry Christmas, folks," he said loudly, grinning as they

leapt apart.

Monica looked flustered but Ernie just told him to help himself to fresh fruit and cereal. Daniel didn't need to be asked twice. The food in the Maclaine household was awesome—it was amazing none of them were the size of buffalo.

By the time he'd finished, neither Lisanne nor Harry had put in an appearance. He hoped it was because they were both individually making the most of their Christmas presents. No, better put that shit out of his mind because if he started thinking about baby doll in that thong, he'd be walking with three legs.

Instead, he offered to help Monica peel some potatoes but after he nearly removed several layers of skin with a potato peeler—which caused an extremely vocal response that made her wince—she set him to work on the simpler and considerably less dangerous task of setting the table.

The rest of the Maclaines surfaced once most of the work was done. Obviously they were dodging whatever jobs Monica had to offer. Daniel didn't care. This is was his first real Christmas for two years—and he was enjoying it.

He pulled Lisanne into a tight hug, not caring that her family was watching. She squirmed slightly but hugged him back quickly, then threw a warning look.

"We'll do presents now," said Monica brightly, and they all trooped into the living room.

Daniel only had two further presents to add to the small piles under the tree: a Lewis Grizzard book for Ernie, and a Ray LaMontagne CD for Monica.

Monica in particular was effusive with her thanks.

"Oh, I just love Ray! He makes me want to dance around the kitchen while I'm making dinner. Thank you, Daniel, that was thoughtful," and she gave him a big hug and kiss, while he was immobile, still digesting the news that Monica had some moves.

Ernie grunted his thanks but looked pleased nonetheless.

Monica looked at Lisanne. "What did Daniel get you, darling?"

Daniel answered for her. "Lis and Harry have already been

given theirs."

Wisely, the senior Maclaines didn't ask for further details.

Lisanne took his hand and squeezed it gently. "I love my present," she whispered.

He winked at her. "Are you…?"

She nodded, and Daniel immediately regretted asking, as his cock begged to join the party.

"Um, I got this for you. I don't know if you'll like it."

She handed him a package that had to be a book. He pulled it open and frowned, not recognizing the title or the author.

"It's an autobiography of Evelyn Glennie. She's a world-class percussionist—and she's deaf, too," Lisanne said.

Daniel felt everyone staring at him.

"Thanks, baby doll," he said quietly, as he kissed her hair.

Monica and Ernie passed him a flat package and Daniel pulled it open, filled with curiosity. Probably not *Swank*. He couldn't help a broad grin escaping when he saw the title.

"Seriously? A subscription to *American Iron*? That's awesome! Thank you!"

He flipped through the motorcycle magazine happily.

Harry was given new games for his Xbox and Lisanne was delighted with a high-tech Smartphone.

"Wow! Thanks, Mom! Thanks, Dad!"

Lunch was something else—a real southern special with country ham, collard greens, snaps, potatoes seasoned with smoked ham hocks, tomato pudding, baked sweet potatoes and cranberry sauce, followed by pumpkin pie, and a three layer yellow cake with an icing made from chocolate and crushed orange slices.

Daniel was stuffed to the point of being comatose, and Lisanne lay against him on the sofa, groaning and holding her stomach.

"I've eaten too much," she moaned, forgetting that Daniel couldn't read her lips from that angle.

But he recognized her general demeanor and massaged her stomach gently.

They spent the rest of the day watching TV until Monica reminded them that as she'd cooked, it was up to the rest of them to clean up. Grumbling, Lisanne washed while Daniel dried and Harry put things away.

Daniel paused with the dish towel in one hand when his phone buzzed.

Lisanne nudged him and he looked up. "Zef?"

He shook his head. "No. A friend."

"Who?"

"Cori." He raised his eyebrows, knowing that Lisanne had read all Cori's texts on his cell phone.

Lisanne's lips tightened. "What does she want?"

Daniel looked at her, incredulously. "To tell me merry Christmas. Do you want to see it?"

Lisanne really, really did want to see the message but she wouldn't give him the satisfaction of letting him know that.

"No. Fine. Whatever," she said, disdainfully.

Daniel felt irritated but he understood. He'd shared something important with Cori and left Lisanne in the dark. She was bound to feel anxious about another woman. Hell, if the situation had been reversed, he'd want to take the guy's head off.

He swallowed his annoyance. "Baby doll, she's a *friend*, that's all. You can meet her if you like—you'll see. She's more like a sister."

"But you *slept* with her," hissed Lisanne.

Daniel's patience was fracturing fast. "For fuck's sake, that was when I was a kid. My dick hasn't been anywhere near her in nearly three years!"

From the corner of his eye, he saw Harry slip out of the kitchen. He didn't blame him—he felt very much like doing the same.

"Are you going to see her again?"

"Well, yeah!"

"Fine, then!" she snapped back. "Go to her! See if I care!"

Daniel gave up before his temper snapped completely, and walked out of the room.

He headed upstairs and started shoving clothes into his backpack before he remembered that he wouldn't be able to catch a bus home until the following morning.

Frustrated, he picked up his phone and sent a short message back to Cori and another to Zef. He still hadn't heard from his brother, and it bothered him.

When his door opened, he looked up and saw a tearful Lisanne standing there.

"Sorry," she whispered.

He gave a small smile. "No harm, no foul."

Her gaze fell to his backpack and her lip trembled. "Are you leaving?"

He nodded slowly. "Yeah, I should head back to C-port in the morning."

"Are you mad at me?"

"Kinda," he said, honestly, "but that's not why I'm going. I need to get busy finding somewhere to live."

She looked like she didn't believe him. "I'm really sorry I was such a bitch just now."

He rubbed his forehead. "Yeah, you were but don't worry about it."

"It's just … you told Cori about the surgery and you didn't tell me. I just…" She couldn't finish, afraid to say that she thought she was losing him.

"Hey, come here."

She sat down next to him and he wrapped an arm around her, holding her in silence until they were both somewhere near the place of peace they'd reached—before her jealous outburst.

She pulled away gently so she could look at him. "Do you really have to go? Stay one more day? Please?"

Daniel shook his head. "No, you need to have some time with your folks and I've got things to do."

"But we'll be together to see in the New Year?"

"Sure, baby doll. Where else would I want to be?"

She smiled gratefully. "Do you want to come back here?"

He pulled a face. "Maybe. See how it goes."

451

His words did little to reassure her.

They sat at opposite ends of his bed talking quietly, until Monica tapped on the door and hinted that it was time Lisanne headed to her own room.

The mood the following morning lacked the easy atmosphere of the previous day. Lisanne looked despondent as she pushed some cereal around her bowl, and Daniel felt her tension.

Monica and Ernie seemed surprised that he was going so soon, and Harry shot his sister angry looks, blaming her that he and Daniel hadn't gotten their day at the arcade.

Daniel was glad Lisanne hadn't mentioned that he was looking for an apartment—he didn't need an inquisition on his motives.

Lisanne drove him to the bus station, and they spent their last few minutes with their bodies pressed together, possessed of a desperate need to touch that surprised them both.

Finally, the bus's departure was announced and Daniel made his way to the back seat, his chest feeling oddly constricted as he waved goodbye to Lisanne, who looked very young and very small as she raised one hand.

As the bus departed into the city traffic, Lisanne let the tears fall. She felt certain it was her fault that he'd left early, and cursed her hormones for yelling at him for no reason.

When the pointlessness of staring after the vanished bus occurred to her, she dragged herself back to the car and sent him a text.

* L: Miss you already.
Can't wait for New Years. LA xx *

But the only reply she got was a winking smiley.

CHAPTER 23

Lisanne was miserable, but there was one person who appeared to be having a worse Christmas.

Rodney sent a text as she was driving home, begging her to meet him.

She pulled up outside the same coffee shop they'd patronized two happier, less complicated days earlier.

Rodney was already waiting, his face tense.

"Thank God you're here," he said, sweeping her into a tight hug. "Where's Daniel?"

Lisanne bit her lip. "He had to get back."

Rodney looked surprised.

"How come?"

"Well, he *said* it was because he had to find a place to live…"

"And you don't think that was true?"

Lisanne shrugged. "We had a stupid, horrible fight—it was all my fault. I was such a bitch. I wouldn't blame him if he wanted to get away from me."

Rodney squeezed her hand. "No way. The guy's nuts about you."

Lisanne looked up hopefully. "You think?"

"Jeez," said Rodney, "don't you *talk* to each other?"

"Oh, that's rich, coming from you, *Mr. I've been gay for years and never told my best friend!*"

"Touché," grimaced Rodney.

"Anyway, how'd it go with your folks?"

"Oh, just great," said Rodney, his voice heavy with sarcasm. "Mom burst into tears and Dad started praying. And that was when I told them I was dropping out of college."

"Ouch!"

"Yeah, and then I told them I was gay." Rodney took a shaky breath. "Mom just cried some more and Dad didn't know what to say. I had to get out."

Lisanne put her hand over his, strongly aware that Rodney's problems outweighed hers considerably. He looked wretched. He was putting on a good show, but she could sense the pain he was trying so hard to hide.

"You know," she said, slowly, "you could transfer to my college, couldn't you? We're only one semester in—you could catch up. There's always room in general ed classes—until you decide what to do."

She could see that her words had thrown him a lifeline.

"You think? Hell, yes! You and me in the city? Well, you, me and Daniel. That would be amazing."

He looked at her gratefully.

"Really? You think it could work?"

"Why not? It's a good school. Your mom and dad will be happy you're still getting your degree. And you won't be alone—you'll be with me. And they know I'm a good girl."

She emphasized the last two words and finally managed to pull a small smile from Rodney.

She was glad one of them was feeling more positive.

When he went to order more coffee, Lisanne checked her phone again, but there was nothing from Daniel.

Rodney caught her as he walked back—he was definitely looking lighter and more relaxed.

"Still no word from Daniel?"

"Nothing."

He shrugged. "It's a man thing. Wait till he's nearly home then give him a call ... um ... text him." He looked at her sympathetically. "He's a pretty great guy. I mean, the way he was with me. When I saw him I thought he was, you know, so alpha male, that there was no way he'd let a gay guy hang out with him. But he was totally cool about it. And I'm serious—he's crazy about you."

Lisanne sighed. "Sometimes I think so, but he's so hard to read. He never *tells* me anything. I don't know, like he thinks he's protecting me or something."

"Maybe he is. You said his home life isn't the best."

"You have no idea," she said, miserably.

"Tell me about it," said Rodney, with feeling.

The friends shared a look, and Rodney reached across the table to hold her hand. "You'll work it out."

But by that evening, Lisanne still hadn't heard from Daniel. Her emotions had been playing hopscotch, leaping from irritation to anger, from concern to doubt, and winding up with full-scale paranoia. Maybe the bus had crashed off of the road? Maybe the pretty blonde who'd got on the bus before him was currently enjoying Daniel's considerable charms—maybe he'd charmed the pants off her—literally?

She threw her phone onto the bedside table and went to sleep, pissed and miserable.

By morning there was still no news, and Lisanne began to be really worried.

Monica tried to calm her down.

"You know what men are like, darling. Half the time your father forgets to take his cell phone with him and when he does, it's almost never charged up or even turned on."

Lisanne shook her head. "Daniel *always* has his cell phone on him—it's not like he can use an ordinary phone—he *has* to text."

Monica frowned.

"Harry said you two had a fight. Maybe he just needs some space?"

Lisanne let her head drop into her hands. She was worried that her mom was right. How much space did he need? So much that he was breaking up with her?

But Rodney had a different idea.

"Look," he said, on the phone later that morning, "why don't we go down there and shake his tree. If you're that worried, I'll drive you there. God knows I need to get away from my parents. I really appreciate them praying for me, but it's driving me a little crazy, too. God made me gay—they'll just have to get over it."

"Really, you'd drive me? Because Mom would never let me take her car and getting around by bus is a real pain."

"Sure, why not. We'll need somewhere to stay though."

Lisanne chewed her thumb nail, what was left of it after the last 24 hours.

"We could stay in my dorm room—I know how I can sneak you in. Kirsty won't be there … what do you think?"

Rodney laughed. "A pajama party? Oh my God, that sounds so gay! I must be making up for lost time. Yes, let's do it."

Monica and Ernie were less enthused when she told them the plan.

"For goodness sake, Lisanne! You can't go chasing after Daniel like that."

"I'm not chasing after him, Mom," Lisanne lied. "I'm just … worried about him. And Rodney wants to check out my college so … it all fits in."

Ernie frowned, but then surprised Monica by agreeing with Lisanne.

"We won't get any peace in this house with her all wound up, and Rodney's a steady, sensible boy."

Obviously Ernie hadn't gotten the memo, but Lisanne wasn't going to argue with her dad when he was on her side.

"Thank you, Daddy!" she sang, and ran upstairs to pack her bags.

Two hours later they were on the road.

"I've prepared a play list of road trip songs," said Rodney, pleased with himself. "I didn't think I'd get the chance to use it so soon."

Soon the sounds of Ultra Nate's *Free* were pumping through the car, and Lisanne felt her spirits lift, if ever so slightly.

She raised her eyebrows. "I remember this one."

Rodney grinned. "You could call it my anthem."

Lisanne smiled.

"Ready?" said Rodney. "Rooooad triiiiiip!" and hit the accelerator.

By early evening they were cruising through the Savannah suburbs.

"Do you mind if we go to Daniel's place first?" Lisanne asked anxiously.

"Course not, Lis. This is what we're here for. Besides, I want to see this famous den of iniquity."

"That's not funny, Rodney—it's his home."

Rodney winced. "Sorry."

As they drove up the street to Daniel's house, it was eerily quiet. On her first visit, Lisanne had seen cars and bikes lining the road, and people spilling out onto the sidewalk. But there was nothing. No one.

When she saw the house, her mouth fell open.

"Holy crap," breathed Rodney, his voice filled with shocked awe.

The front door was hanging from its hinges, and there was hardly a single pane of glass that hadn't been smashed. Bottles and beer cans littered the front yard, and a bonfire of something that smelled really bad was still smoldering at the side of the house.

Whoever had done this—and it must have been more than one person—was long gone.

Lisanne felt sick and scrambled out of the car.

"Wait!" hissed Rodney.

He climbed out, locked the car and had his finger hovering over 911 on his speed dial.

Lisanne was too keyed up to let him go first, and ran up the steps.

"Hey," called Rodney. "Look!"

Walking toward them, as if every footstep was pulled to the earth by its own unique gravity, was Daniel. He looked tired, dirty and unshaven, but he was alive and in one piece.

Lisanne ran forward, throwing herself at him, locking her arms around his neck. He stood stock still, then slowly let his head sink down to her shoulder.

Neither of them spoke.

Rodney leaned against the car and let them have their moment. Whatever had happened to Daniel, he'd clearly been through hell.

After a minute, Lisanne loosened her grip and stepped back so she could see his face.

"Are you okay? What happened? Where have you been? I've been going crazy!"

His eyes were glazed with tiredness and he seemed confused. Lisanne was immediately worried that he'd injured his head and she turned his cheek gently to inspect the wound. She couldn't see anything obvious, except that he was clearly in need of a hot shower and some food—probably a long sleep, too.

He looked at her as if he didn't understand her question, but as his eyes tracked across to his home, some of the fire she loved to see flared in his eyes.

"Fucking meth heads," he said, tiredly.

"What?!" gasped Lisanne, her eyes meeting Rodney's shocked face. "Druggies did this?"

Daniel nodded slowly. "Yeah, after the police bust the place wide open." He looked at the wrecked building, and anger rippled across his face. "I'd better take a look."

If anything, the inside was worse. All the soft furnishings had been slashed open, carpets ripped up—even some of the floorboards. Every closet, cupboard and cabinet had been emptied, the contents carelessly strewn around. In what was left of the kitchen, the refrigerator was lying on its side, a carton of sour milk puddled on the floor. The back door had been left open and a few leaves had blown inside. At least it hadn't rained.

Cautiously, Lisanne picked a route up the stairs that avoided some of the potential hazards of torn carpeting and suspicious stains. The same destruction had made its way to the second story. At Daniel's room, they all paused. The door had been smashed open by something heavy, causing the lock to disintegrate. His once tidy room had been torn apart, the sheets pulled from the bed, the mattress slashed to pieces. All the books had had the covers ripped off and had been tossed to the floor. The rug was shoved to one side and even the little loft space above his bed had been violated. Clothes had been pulled from the closet, dumped onto the floor, and walked over.

"It looks like there's been a riot here," whispered Rodney.

Lisanne didn't know what to say. The police had done a very thorough job of searching the place—and then it had been trashed by people who were looking for something, anything to sell for their next fix.

"Come on, let's get out of here," said Rodney. "We'll get some food and go back to your place, Lis, then decide what to do. Okay?"

Lisanne nodded. Any plan that involved getting the hell away sounded good to her.

"Wait for me outside," said Daniel, quietly.

Back in the fresh air, Lisanne felt a loosening of the claustrophobia that had choked her inside the devastated house, but her head had started to throb and she felt nauseous.

A few minutes later, Daniel followed them out. He was carrying a plastic bag with some of his clothes but very little else.

"They took my guitar," he said in a hollow voice. "And I checked the garage—Sirona's gone. Fuck. The place has been left wide open—everything's gone."

"Who's Sirona?" whispered Rodney.

"His Harley."

Daniel bent down and picked up a half-full bottle of vodka that was lying at his feet.

Lisanne was about to tell him not to drink it when he shoved some sheets of newspaper into the neck and pulled out his lighter.

Flames licked up the paper and Daniel aimed the missile at his home.

"No!" shouted Lisanne, and jogged his arm so he missed his target, and it smashed onto the bonfire, exploding harmlessly.

Rodney looked shocked and completely out of his depth.

"What are you doing?" yelled Lisanne, pulling Daniel around to face her.

"Torching the shithole," he replied in a dull monotone.

"I think we'd better get him out of here," Rodney said, in a hushed voice.

Lisanne led Daniel to the back of Rodney's car and pushed him inside. She slid in next to him, holding his hand, staring anxiously at his face. He leaned back against the seat and closed his eyes.

Keeping her voice quiet out of some sort of atavistic belief that it would calm the wounded in spirit, Lisanne gave Rodney directions to the dorm rooms. They stopped briefly to pick up food, but Daniel didn't speak again.

Once they arrived, she told Rodney to wait by the fire exit with Daniel, until she could let them in without being seen.

The dorms were quiet and seemingly deserted, but from somewhere, music floated through the empty corridors—happy, upbeat music—the kind you listened to when you hadn't a care in the world. Lisanne tried to work out where the music was coming from and which rooms might be occupied, but everywhere appeared empty.

She opened the fire exit and motioned Rodney to enter. He pulled a zombie-like Daniel behind him.

Once in her room, Daniel slumped onto her bed and Rodney gazed around him.

"Not bad. Could do with a private bathroom though."

"Yeah, they're putting that in all the girls' dorm rooms for next year. If it wasn't a requirement for out-of-towners to live on campus for the first year, I think they'd have a lot of empty rooms."

She looked at Daniel. "Are you hungry?" She walked toward him and tapped his arm. "Are you hungry?"

He shook his head. "Tired."

"You should sleep. Do you want to get a shower first? There's hardly anyone around—I could wait outside, make sure no one walks in on you."

"Yeah, I guess."

Lisanne poked her head around the door and escorted him to the women's showers. Her eyes drifted down his body as he undressed, and she saw that his bruises had turned yellow and were beginning to fade. That was something. But he looked so tired.

His shower was brief, probably because he'd have fallen asleep if he'd stayed any longer. He dried himself with Lisanne's towel and pulled on his jeans. He grimaced at the grubby t-shirt and walked back to her room barefoot and bare chested.

Rodney had made inroads on the food, but she saw him trying not to stare as they walked back in. Lisanne threw him a look, and his eyes dropped to his egg roll.

Daniel seemed marginally more awake and accepted some of the food, but his eyelids were drooping. Lisanne knew he needed to sleep but she *had* to ask.

"What happened?"

Daniel sighed and pushed his food away. Lisanne immediately felt guilty.

"I got back from your place. I hadn't got any money for a cab so I'd walked from the bridge. I'd just pulled out my door key when the cops showed up. I got arrested and spent two days in a police cell before I got bail."

Lisanne gasped. "What were you arrested for? You hadn't even been there!"

His head dropped. "Zef's going down. They wouldn't even give him bail. It's a felony—intent to distribute." His voice was hollow as he recited the bare facts. "He could get up to 10 years."

He rubbed his head, tiredly.

"Why didn't you call me?"

Daniel shook his head. "I needed my phone call for the lawyer. I thought about asking her to get a message to you…"

"But…?"

"You don't need to be involved in anymore of my shit, Lis."

She groaned with frustration. That was *so* like him! By trying

461

to protect her, he'd scared the shit out of her.

"What about your guitar?" she said, in as calm a tone as she could muster. "What about Sirona? Will you report them stolen?"

"No point. They'll be long gone."

"You can claim on the insurance," Rodney added helpfully.

Daniel just stared at him, and Rodney's cheeks flushed.

"So that's it?" said Lisanne. "They took everything?"

"Yeah, laptop, CDs—fuck even most of my clothes."

"What about your schoolwork?"

He tapped his hip pocket. "Got that backed up on a flash drive. And my music."

Rodney frowned but didn't offer any more asinine advice.

"Baby doll, I know you've got more questions, but I really need to sleep now," he said, staring longingly at Lisanne's bed. "Can we talk in the morning?"

"Of course," she said softly, moving the boxes of food so he could lie down.

He caught her hand and pulled her toward him.

"I'm so fucking happy you're here," he whispered. "It makes it hurt less."

He leaned his head against her waist then stood up slowly. Giving her a small smile, he dropped his jeans and slid down between the sheets and rolled onto his side.

Lisanne bent down to kiss him, but he was already asleep.

Rodney motioned something, hissing in a stage whisper, and Lisanne raised her eyebrows. "He can't hear you."

"Oh, God, sorry. I keep forgetting. Jeez, all this makes my problems seem pretty damn pathetic."

"I know what you mean."

"I had no idea this thing with his brother was so serious. Sounds like he'll do time."

"Yes, I think so. Maybe it's for the best."

"At least he spoke up for Daniel."

Lisanne's reply was bitter. "That was the least he could do."

Rodney chewed slowly. "What will Daniel do now?"

"I don't know. Find somewhere to live. Try and go to school. He's got a job lined up at an auto repair shop. I hope he doesn't drop out because of all this. He's really smart. He helps me with my math and everything."

Rodney choked on his chow mein. "What?! I tried to do that for years and didn't get anywhere. He must be good."

"He's great," she said, sadly.

"Hot, too," added Rodney.

Lisanne laughed a little. "Yeah, hot, too."

"You know, except for the windows, it wouldn't be too hard to fix up his place enough to make it livable. Your dad isn't too bad at all that stuff. Do you think he'd help? We've got ten days."

Lisanne suddenly felt energized. "God, I could kiss you!" she said, leaping to her feet. "I'm sure Mom and Dad would want to help. And Harry." Then her face fell. "But the windows are still a problem. There's no way Daniel would be able to pay for that and I can't ask my parents…"

"We'll figure something out. Look, phone your folks—tell them Daniel's okay and we'll sleep on it. Well, you go sleep with your fabulous, hot, *naked* boyfriend and I'll tuck myself into this lonely little single all by my lonesome, and dream of tight butts and lickable biceps."

"Oh my God," said Lisanne, "you sound just like Kirsty. It must be that bed."

She phoned her parents and although they were shocked by what she told them, they promised to be there by lunchtime the following day.

For the first time in several days, Lisanne allowed herself to hope as she curled up next to Daniel.

He slept for 14 hours, solidly. He'd been so still, Lisanne had even prodded him to make sure he was breathing. He'd sighed softly, which reassured her.

"He probably didn't sleep much in the cop shop," said Rodney. "I know I wouldn't want to." He shuddered.

"No, I guess not." She chewed her lip for a moment then

stood up. "I'm going to put some laundry in for him—not that he has much left in the way of clothes."

"What was he saying about his guitar? I didn't get that."

Lisanne sighed. "He was a musician. Like me. He started losing his hearing when he was 14. And he wrote the most amazing music. I sing four of his songs in the band. It's horrible, what's happened to him."

"Thank God he found you," said Rodney, too quietly for Lisanne to hear.

Lisanne went to load Daniel's laundry while Rodney stayed in the room. He was surprised when she stomped back, her face furious.

"What's up now?"

"I found this!" she said, tossing a piece of paper onto Kirsty's bed.

Rodney picked it up. "Huh. A woman's phone number. Lis, he must get given things like this all the time."

"But why did he keep it?" she seethed.

"He has been rather preoccupied," said Rodney, raising his eyebrows. "But if you're that worried about it you can ask him when he wakes up."

Lisanne huffed but didn't argue. She stomped back out of the room and came back 40 minutes later with Daniel's clean clothes.

"Still no sign of life," said Rodney, affably. "But I think you'd better wake him up so we can meet your folks at his place."

Lisanne stroked Daniel's cheek and watched his eyelids flutter open.

"Hey, baby doll," he said, his voice hoarse. "I was dreaming about you."

Behind her, she heard Rodney's theatrical sigh.

"Nice dream?"

"Fucking amazing," he said, with a smile. "If it had been anyone else but you who woke up me, I'd have been pissed."

He sat up and rubbed his eyes. "Oh, hey, Rodney. Forgot

you were there, man."

"It happens a lot," Rodney replied, waspishly.

Daniel grinned.

"Better put some clothes on," Lisanne reminded him, and tossed him his clean jeans and t-shirt.

"Fuck, you are an amazing woman," said Daniel, gratefully.

Rodney averted his eyes while Daniel swung out of bed and pulled on his jeans, tucking his semi inside.

"We're really going to have to get you some underwear," commented Lisanne.

"Spoilsport," Rodney muttered to himself.

"Is there any of that Chinese left?" asked Daniel as he stretched, dragging on his t-shirt.

"Some. Or we could go out for breakfast."

"I'll take whatever's left," said Daniel, eyeing the food hungrily.

He started eating with a vengeance while Lisanne explained to him about her parents coming to help. He stopped with the chopsticks half way to his mouth.

"They're coming here?"

"Of course," said Lisanne. "They want to help."

"Why?" Daniel was genuinely puzzled.

"Because they *care* about you, you dope!"

"Oh," said Daniel, still unsure. "Okay, thanks."

"Um, there's something else," said Lisanne, fingering the note she'd found in Daniel's jeans. "What's this?"

He frowned and then his face cleared. "Oh yeah. Some chick I met at the hearing clinic. She'd just had the CI. Wanted to swap notes." He rolled his eyes.

Rodney winked at Lisanne, a relieved smile on his face.

Daniel carried on eating.

"You never said why they arrested you."

Rodney groaned audibly as Daniel sighed, and dropped the chopsticks.

"I had nearly an ounce of dope in my room. They were trying to say it was possession with intent to distribute, but my lawyer bargained it down to personal use. That's a misdemeanor—incarceration for up to a year."

He looked at Lisanne and shrugged, which fired both her anxiety and irritation.

"Why did you have the drugs, Daniel? I mean, I've never seen you … not with me…"

He gave her a small smile. "Zef brought it to hospital—sort of a 'get well soon and get your lazy ass out of here' present. I shoved it under my bed and forgot about it." He shrugged. "Zef told the cops the same thing, so my lawyer says I could get off."

His casual tone pushed Lisanne over the edge of her carefully sewn together composure.

"What the hell, Daniel? We're supposed to be together, and you keep all of this from me? Zef gave it to you while you were *in hospital!* That was two weeks ago! And you never mentioned it! What does that say about our relationship?"

She stormed out of the room, slamming the door behind her.

Rodney turned his gaze on Daniel, who looked equally furious.

"I'm protecting her from all this shit!" Daniel spat out.

"She doesn't want to be protected—she wants to *help* you."

"She can't."

"She can help if you share how you're feeling. Jeez, Daniel!"

"All the shit she's been through because of me. I don't even know why she's still here."

Rodney sighed in exasperation. "Because she loves you, you asshole!"

Daniel's eyes widened slightly and he sat back silently.

"And I think you love her."

Daniel nodded slowly. "She's everything."

"Then *tell* her. Jeez, you two … I don't know which one of you is worse. Damn it, I've been *out* for precisely two days and you've got me doing a Dr. Phil or Ricki Lake or something. Give me a break!" He twitched his shoulders in an impatient gesture.

Daniel grinned. "Ricki Lake?"

"So? My grandparents are from Baltimore—I like *Hairspray.*

Just do something to make her feel special—so that she knows you care. It doesn't have to be anything expensive…"

"Thank fuck for that because in case you hadn't noticed, I'm broke," Daniel said, bitterly. But at the same time an idea came to him. Maybe.

"Look, we should go," said Rodney, glancing at his watch. "I'll meet you outside—give you and Lis a few minutes to yourselves."

Rodney opened the door as Lisanne stamped back inside, nearly taking him out as she barreled past him.

"Good luck," Rodney breathed, although neither Daniel or Lisanne could hear him.

Lisanne ricocheted around the room, collecting her jacket and purse, feeling like she wanted to whack Daniel around the head with it—on his good side, of course.

He sat patiently, waiting for her to look at him.

Finally, she whirled around. "I'm *so* mad at you!"

"Yeah, I got the memo," he said, dryly.

"This isn't a laughing matter!" she yelled.

"I'm not laughing, baby doll," he said, holding back a smile. "I'm sorry, okay."

"No! No it's definitely not okay! You never tell me anything! I have to find out everything by accident. That's not the basis for a relationship, Daniel."

His chest squeezed unpleasantly.

"Lis, please. I'll try, okay. I just … it … I haven't had anyone to tell this shit to in a while."

His hazel eyes begged her to understand and she didn't have it in her heart to punish him anymore. He'd said he'd try. She couldn't ask for more.

"Okay, but we're in this together, Daniel. Just *tell* me. If it affects you, it affects me. Get that through your thick skull!" and she tapped him lightly on his head.

"Working on it, baby doll," he said, seriously.

She sat on his knee and he nuzzled her neck. She was in his arms and there was nowhere else she wanted to be.

They were interrupted by her phone ringing and Rodney's irate voice telling them to stop *making* out and to *get* out.

Throughout the whole drive Rodney complained grumpily about being the only person not currently getting any action. Lisanne ignored him and Daniel, sitting in the backseat, looked like he'd fallen asleep again.

They arrived just as the Maclaines' car was turning into the road.

It was like an extreme version of shows on the DIY network.

That first day, Daniel was astonished by how much they got done. Ernie had called ahead to have a dumpster delivered, along with industrial amounts of white paint, brushes and rollers. He'd also arranged for a glazier to come and fit new glass in the seven broken windows. And then he handed out tasks to everyone.

Daniel worked harder and longer and took fewer breaks than anyone else, galvanized to see his childhood home re-emerge from the rubble. He even managed to retrieve some photographs of his parents that weren't too badly damaged.

Halfway through the afternoon, two men had driven past in a beaten up VW van to buy coke, but Ernie saw them off by threatening to call the police.

"That'll happen for a while," he said, thoughtfully, "but the message will soon get around … providing it stays that way."

He gave Daniel a hard stare.

"It will," snapped Daniel. "I don't want that shit anywhere near me or … I don't want it around."

Ernie nodded and went back to work.

On the fourth day, after most of the clearing out had been done and small structural repairs completed, they started the painting. Harry turned out to have a good eye for staining woodwork without the lines bleeding, so he was put in charge of door frames and window sills. Everyone else was hands-on painting the walls and ceilings.

Ernie even rented a sander, and showed Daniel how to use it on hardwood floors. Some of Pop's skills with tools had rubbed off on Ernie.

Daniel was worried about how much it was all costing, but Ernie simply said he hoped someone would do the same it if was his kids who needed a helping hand. That was the end of the discussion—at least as far as Ernie was concerned.

The biggest problem was furniture. Monica and Lisanne were given the job of haunting the thrift shops to see what they could find.

"Nothing girly, please, baby doll," begged Daniel.

Lisanne snickered quietly. "You'll love whatever I get," and kissed him quickly so he couldn't reply.

They were pretty successful, securing sofas, chairs, a kitchen table and two double beds with decent mattresses.

Each night Rodney and Daniel stayed at the house, camping out and washing in cold water, until the oil tank could be refilled. Both of them were wearing five day old stubble.

Lisanne had wanted to stay, too, but had been outvoted by her parents and even by Daniel, who was worried in case any of Zef's customers came back.

But Ernie seemed to have been right about the word getting around, and no one bothered them again.

On New Year's Eve, there was one more piece of good news.

Daniel was scrubbing out the downstairs shower room that hadn't been used for two years, except for storing liquor, when his cell vibrated in his pocket.

As he read the message his face lit up, and his shout of happiness could be heard all over the house.

Lisanne came running over. "What is it?"

"They've found Sirona! Some asshat tried to sell her to Sal, the guy from the auto shop who's given me a job. He recognized her and called the bastard on it. I can pick her up today."

Monica drove him over to collect his beloved Harley and he rode her home, grinning from ear to ear, wearing a helmet that Sal had given him, with another stashed in the saddlebags as a spare for his girl.

Rodney leaned over to whisper loudly. "Your boyfriend

looks *hot* in leather."

"I know," Lisanne said, smugly.

That evening, they celebrated the house's rebirth, Sirona's return, and New Year's Eve with Mexican takeout, beer and large quantities of ice cream. Daniel and Rodney celebrated by taking turns in a shower that pumped out hot water.

The house still looked a bit empty and the furniture was shabby if functional, but it was a home again. Or trying to be.

Harry and Lisanne were fighting over the last of the Rocky Road when Daniel stood up, shifting awkwardly from foot to foot.

"Yeah, so it's New Year's Eve and tomorrow, shit, well, it's a new year. So, um, I just wanted to, you know, thank you all for everything you've done. It's been like having family, that's how it feels, to me, I mean. And Rodney, man, you came through and I know you've been going through your own shit, so if you need a place to stay … this is home, okay. Monica, Ernie, you guys have been fucking awesome. Um, sorry. But you have. You, too, Harry. You've worked hard, man." His eyes turned to Lisanne, who was holding her hand to her mouth, her eyes bright with tears. "Baby doll, you … I … just … thank you. I mean, thank you for everything. Fuck, I…"

She stood up and walked over to him, looking into his eyes. "I know."

There was a silence, so full of emotion that it had to be broken.

"Here's to new beginnings," said Rodney, holding up his beer.

"Hear! Hear!" agreed Monica, softly.

Lisanne pulled Daniel down onto the sofa with her and held him, until his embarrassment had faded.

"I loved what you said," she whispered.

"I sounded like a fucking moron," he groaned. "I had it all planned out what I wanted to say and then, ah, fuck."

"No, it was perfect."

He raised an eyebrow at her. "Perfect, huh?"

Lisanne kissed him on the nose. "Except for all the cursing."

He grinned at her.

At midnight, they sang *Auld Lang Syne*, and Daniel wrapped his arms around Lisanne's waist, pulling her against his chest, feeling the vibrations of the song echo through her small rib cage.

Rodney's words came back to him, *Just do something to make her feel special, so that she knows you care*. He suddenly knew what he wanted to do.

Several things changed that New Year. After a long night of talking it over with Daniel, Rodney had decided to transfer to the same college, and he was hopeful his parents would support that decision. Daniel had offered him a place to live as a thank you for everything he'd done. Rodney accepted gratefully, but insisted on paying rent money—which Daniel refused, until Lisanne took him to one side and told him that she wasn't going to appreciate him working 20 hours a week on top of studying, when Rodney's contribution meant he'd only have to work eight. With Rodney and Lisanne ganging up on him, Daniel had lost that argument.

The following day, the Maclaines went home, full of promises to visit again soon. Harry reminded Daniel that they still had to plan an arcade date.

Rodney was leaving, too, but only to collect his things before moving in, ready for the new semester.

Daniel and Lisanne were alone together for the first time in well over a week. Before Rodney and the Maclaines were at the end of the road, they were pulling off each other's clothes and wouldn't even have made it to the bedroom, if Daniel hadn't picked her up and carried her in bodily.

Lisanne was a hot and sweaty puddle, her flesh still quivering from soft aftershocks following a very much needed orgasm, when Daniel rolled onto his side and ran a finger down her cheek.

"Better?"

"Yes," she sighed. "Much better."

He grinned.

"Good," then his smile faded and he looked uncertain.

It wasn't a look she associated with Daniel—it worried her.

"What's wrong?"

"So, um, I have my first tuning session on Thursday."

"Okay," she said, carefully.

"They'll fix me up with the transmitter and processor…" He took a deep breath. "I was wondering … do you want to go with me? I mean, you don't have to … if it's too weird…"

"Oh," she said, swallowing with difficulty. "Oh! Yes, of course I'll go with you."

"You will?"

"Yes, idiot!"

"Okay."

"Okay!"

He pulled her onto his chest and she lay there listening to the steady, even beat of his strong silent heart.

CHAPTER 24

Daniel was jittery. He wondered if it had been a mistake asking Lisanne to come with him to the clinic. But there was no backing out now. Where he was reluctant and dragging his weary ass, she was eager and almost fucking skipping along.

Even some very hot wake-up sex hadn't put him in a better mood, and that shit was just wrong. Wake-up sex put *everyone* in a good mood, didn't it?

He tried to ignore Lisanne's high spirits, but every time he looked away, she tugged his arm to make him look at puppies or balloons, or who knew what crappy happy shit. And he *really* wanted a smoke.

They walked past a guy who was pulling a cigarette from a new packet, and Daniel seriously thought about mugging him for his Marlboro's—a brand he hated.

He stopped abruptly outside the entrance to the hospital, and Lisanne almost crashed into him.

"Just … give me a minute, baby doll," he grit out, trying to calm his breathing.

She reached up and held his face, cupping his cheeks with gentle fingers. "It's going to be fine," she said, placing a soft kiss on his lips. "It's going to be good."

He gave a staccato nod, took a deep breath, and opened the door.

Lisanne walked through, then turned to look at him. She held out her hand and he took it, grateful for the contact.

He was checked in at reception, and they were pointed toward the waiting room. He *hated* waiting rooms. He hated waiting, period.

They'd been sitting for less than a minute and his leg was bouncing up and down so hard that he could feel the vibrations in his teeth.

Lisanne rested her hand on his knee, soothing him.

"It'll be fine," she said again, chanting out the words as if they were a talisman against every evil.

He didn't feel fucking fine. He felt sick to his stomach. What if, after all this shit, what if it didn't work? He'd read the statistics, he'd read every online blog and account that he'd been able to find. He knew the implants didn't work well for everyone, a minority perhaps, but the way his damn luck was going, he'd be that minority.

He leaned forward, resting his forearms on his knees, and let his head hang down.

Please let this fucking work.

Lisanne tapped his arm gently and he looked up.

A woman was standing in front of him smiling. Oh yeah, what was her name?

"Samantha. How are you?"

S: Good, thanks. You?
D: Okay.
S: I was hoping you'd get in touch.
D: Been busy.
S: So I see! Is this your girlfriend?
D: Yes. L-I-S-A-N-N-E.

"Lis, this is Samantha. She's had the CI, too."

"Oh, hi," said Lisanne, scanning Samantha quickly, then she remembered to make the correct sign.

S: She's the musician?
D: Yes.
S: Are you here for your tuning session?

"Yeah, first one."

S: You look a bit nervous. That's why I came over. But it'll be worth it. I promise.

"Yeah, I hope so."
Daniel's name flashed up.
"That's me."

D: Take care. Bye.
S: Bye.

Lisanne waved awkwardly, smiling nervously at the attractive older woman.

"What did she say?"

Daniel was clearly distracted, but his thoughts weren't running in Samantha's direction.

"What? Oh, yeah, she said it would be worth it."

His mouth tightened into a flat line.

Lisanne held his hand as she walked into the consulting room with him.

Dr. Palmer was there, which reassured them both.

"Hey, doc," croaked Daniel, his throat inexplicably dry. "Um, Lis, this is Dr. Palmer. Doc, this is my girlfriend, Lisanne Maclaine."

"Miss Maclaine, a pleasure to meet you again."

Daniel frowned. *Again?*

"Hello," Lisanne said shyly, shaking his hand.

"And this is my colleague Dr. Devallis—she's your audiologist, and will oversee the tuning today. I just wanted to check that you hadn't had any problems with the implant."

"Yeah, it's okay," said Daniel. "I can feel it when I swallow which is a bit weird."

"He got into a fight," said Lisanne, suddenly.

Daniel gave her an annoyed look, and she looked a little disconcerted.

"A fight?" Dr. Palmer echoed, his eyes flicking between Daniel and Lisanne. "Was there any damage to your head?"

"No," said Daniel.

"Yes," said Lisanne.

"For fuck's sake!" Daniel growled, irritated beyond belief. "The bastard stamped on my ribs—my head is fine!"

"He hit you on the left side of your head and one of the stitches split open," Lisanne said in a defiant tone, crossing her arms over her chest.

"Well, I'll just have a quick look," said Dr. Palmer. "When did this happen?"

"The night before Christmas Eve," said Lisanne, softly.

Daniel tore off his beanie and stuffed it in his pocket. The doctor probed the wound but Daniel didn't move a muscle.

"Well, it seems to be fine," Dr. Palmer said, at last. "But I really can't recommend getting into fights."

"Believe me, doc," said Daniel, dryly, "it's not my idea of fun."

"Hmm, well. Do try and protect your head. Are you still riding your motorcycle?"

"Hell, yes!"

The doctor sighed. "And what about football?"

Daniel frowned. "What about it?"

"Ah…?" Dr. Palmer looked at his notes. "I thought you played football—quarterback, wasn't it?"

"Was, doc, *was*."

Dr. Palmer met Daniel's gaze. "You don't play anymore?"

Daniel shifted uncomfortably in his chair while everyone stared at him. He felt Lisanne's small fingers on his hand.

"I played at high school—a special school. I didn't try out for the college team."

"Mr. Colton, we have anti discrimination laws these days," said the doctor, patiently. "Besides, there are some excellent helmets out there that would protect your implant, and…"

Daniel interrupted him, tetchily. "I know all that, doc. Give me a fucking break."

Lisanne swatted his arm.

"Sorry," Daniel mumbled.

"Well," said Dr. Devallis, raising her eyebrows, "I'm going to talk to you about the external pieces of the device that you'll need. It's been charged up overnight, so it's ready to go."

"I'll leave you to it," said Dr. Palmer, shaking hands with Daniel and Lisanne. "Let my office know if you have any problems."

"Yeah, thanks, doc."

Dr. Palmer left the room, and the audiologist smiled at them. She pulled open the square box that was lying on the desk in front of her.

Inside was a round piece of plastic the size and shape of a quarter, attached by a five inch wire to something that could be mistaken for a cool, new iPod—maybe.

"Okay, first things first."

She spoke slowly and clearly, showing Lisanne as well as to Daniel.

"This is where the power cell goes. It's a rechargeable battery—most people charge it up while they're sleeping. This part here," she tapped the plastic body, "this is the processor and just above it is the built-in TeleCoil. The hook part here, that's called the Microphone Auxiliary Earhook. The main microphone is up here on the top. Now, to the parts you really need to know. This is the LED status light and just below is the volume control."

"What's that switch?" said Lisanne.

"That's the program switch. You use it to change between different environments—for general use, when it's very noisy and so on. And this piece contains the transmitter and magnet."

Daniel looked at Lisanne's face. She seemed completely absorbed in what she was being told."

"Ready to try it?" said Dr. Devallis.

Daniel swallowed and nodded.

The doctor placed the unit behind Daniel's left ear and clipped the magnet at the side of his head. Lisanne was fascinated to see it staying in place.

"A second magnet was placed under the skin during surgery," explained Dr. Devallis.

"Oh, right. Of course," Lisanne stuttered.

Daniel's eyes flicked across to her.

"Okay, here we go."

The doctor turned to her computer screen then looked back to Daniel.

"We'll stimulate each electrode along the array, one at a time. That way we can find the lowest level of current needed for you to just barely hear a sound—that's the sound threshold. Then we find the upper level of stimulation by raising the current to find a level that is comfortably loud. Then it's a case of balancing the level of current across all electrodes. Daniel, you'll hear a series of beeps now."

She pressed some keys on her computer.

"Fuck!" said Daniel, his hand automatically flying up to his ear, his hazel eyes open wide.

"You're doing fine," said the doctor, soothingly.

Daniel glanced up at Lisanne, and saw her brush away tears. She gave him a thumbs up and a big, hopeful smile.

The doctor pressed another key and Daniel blinked. It was the weirdest feeling. It wasn't sound as he remembered it—but it *was sound.*

"This will take a little time to get right," said the doctor. "Just bear with us. Your aural rehabilitation won't be instant—as I'm sure you're tired of people telling you. Okay, I'm mapping the process for you. Imagine an electric organ keyboard: each electrode will play a particular 'note'. There'll be a lot of fine-tuning involved."

Dr. Devallis spent the next 40 minutes trying out different levels of sound. Finally, she deliberately turned away from Daniel.

"Can you hear what I'm saying?"

She waited and Daniel frowned. Then she turned to face him and repeated the words.

"Can you hear what I'm saying?"

Daniel stared at her.

"Um, there's something. It's like … fuck, I don't know … ducks quacking maybe?"

The doctor nodded and smiled. "Good, we're getting there." She made some more adjustments. "The sound will seem odd until you get used to it. Most people describe it as 'mechanical' or 'synthetic'. But don't worry—that perception will change over time. Okay, let's try and broaden the range."

Daniel glanced at Lisanne, who looked like she was holding her breath.

"Breathe, baby doll! I don't want you passing out—even if we are in a hospital."

She rolled her eyes but he saw her take a deep breath. Having her there was immense. He'd have run the fuck out by now like some pussy, if she hadn't been there.

Dr. Devallis smiled. "How does this sound?" and she pressed some more keys on her computer.

Daniel concentrated. "It's sort of … muffled … like I'm underwater or something…"

"Okay, that's good. You're doing fine. As your brain adjusts and learns a complete sound picture, it will begin to sound more natural. It'll be tiring at first, but it'll get easier."

For another hour, she tested a range of sounds until Daniel looked exhausted. Lisanne had to stop him from rubbing his head.

"You've done really well for a first day," said Dr. Devallis, at last. "You have an appointment scheduled for tomorrow afternoon—we'll do some more work then. Okay?"

Daniel nodded tiredly.

"I want you to practice wearing the processor and transmitter for an hour this evening. Don't try too much—no TV or radio—just talking, okay?"

Daniel nodded again, feeling like he wanted to rip the fucking thing from his head. His scalp felt raw where the transmitter was attached, and his head was aching.

He couldn't get out of the hospital fast enough. He felt Lisanne pulling on his sleeve.

"Daniel?"

"I just need … let's get the fuck out, Lis. I just…"

Her fingers wrapped around his hand and they walked back to Sirona without speaking. Daniel passed her the helmet and pulled on his own.

He was trying to process how it all felt and he needed silence. The fucking irony.

The morning had felt unreal. He couldn't explain the sensation as the implant was stimulated—the sound didn't fit with any of his memories. He knew it was too early to be disappointed, but the overwhelming feeling was there anyway. He couldn't get past the idea that he had a chunk of metal in his head. He'd almost been able to ignore it after the operation, but feeling it working, it freaked him out. And the way it felt having the transmitter stuck on his head. A shudder went through him.

Instinctively, he knew he needed something familiar, and he headed for the diner, driving faster than was legally permitted. Lisanne's hands tightened around his waist and he didn't know if it was from fear, but he slowed fractionally.

He'd just pulled off his helmet when his stomach sank to his boots. Fuckin' luck that *she* was here. What were that chances?

Daniel felt Lisanne lace her fingers through his.

"Are you okay?" she said, anxiously scanning his face.

"I think we should go somewhere else."

"Why?"

He pulled a face. "Cori's here. That's her car."

"Why don't you want us to meet?" she said, tightly. "You said you'd introduce us."

Her expression was challenging and Daniel immediately felt his hackles rising.

"Because I can't take any more fucking drama right now, Lis, and you look like you want to start yanking her hair."

Lisanne snorted. She was hardly the violent type, although…

"I promise I'll be on my best behavior with your *ex-girlfriend*," she said, drawing a cross over her heart. Then she felt guilty seeing how stressed he was. "Hey, don't worry! Honestly, I won't start anything."

He closed his eyes and shook his head slowly.

Lisanne stood on tiptoe and kissed him lightly. "*Honestly.*"

He gave her a tight smile and made sure his beanie was firmly in place. They walked to the diner together and he opened the door for her.

Cori had already seen them and was sitting with her arms folded, and silent, which was never a good combination in Daniel's experience.

He took a deep breath and walked forward.

C: Hi, stranger!
D: Hi. This is L.I.S.A.N.N.E.

"Lis, this is Cori."

Lisanne used the only sign language she knew. *Hello.*

C: Can you sign?
D: No. She just knows 'hello'.
C: She's cute. Not your usual type.
D: Don't start.
C: Who me?

Daniel raised his eyebrows then turned to Lisanne, who was looking lost.

"She thinks you're cute."

"Oh!" Lisanne blushed. "That's nice of her to say that, because she's gorgeous."

C: 'Gorgeous'?! I like her.

"She likes you," he said, to Lisanne.

The two women smiled cautiously at each other, and Daniel rubbed his head.

481

"Can you lip read?" Lisanne asked Cori.

Daniel watched the reply. "She can but she says it's tiring. She prefers to sign."

"Oh, okay."

Lisanne saw him rubbing his head again and she caught his hand. "Does it hurt?"

"Headache," he said, shortly.

C: From the CI?
D: Yes.
C: How does it feel?
D: Weird. I don't know. Bit sore.
C: Can you hear?
D: Not much. They say it'll get better.
C: So you'll be one of them now?

"Fuck off," Daniel said, without much heat.

Lisanne looked shocked.

"She's being a pain in the ass," he said, jerking his head at Cori who simply smiled back beatifically.

"What did she say?"

"Leave it, Lis."

"No! What did she say? Was it about me?"

"Fuck. She said, 'Are you one of them now?' Okay?"

Lisanne frowned. "What does she mean?"

Daniel rubbed his eyes. "She thinks I'll be part of the hearing world now and I won't want anything to do with … other deaf people. She doesn't get that I'll still be deaf—that this," he pointed to his head, "is just another tool. But it's not like being a hearing person." He looked at Lisanne. "I'm not sure you get that either. This is for life, Lis. I'll never be like you."

Lisanne's eyes filled with tears as his voice began to rise.

"I know," she whispered.

Cori kicked him under the table.

C: You're being an asshole. You've made her cry.

Daniel stood up abruptly and walked out, leaving Cori and Lisanne staring at each other. Cori reached across the table and touched the back of Lisanne's hand, smiling sadly.

Lisanne swallowed and felt her lips twitch upwards. It was the best either of them could manage.

Daniel was sitting on the curb, his head in his hands. When he felt someone rub his arm, he didn't need to look up to know it was Lisanne.

She touched his cheek and he leaned into her. She ran her finger along his lips and he kissed it gently.

"Fuck, sorry," he said.

"Me, too. I've ordered for you—lots of grease. Come on, come back. Please."

He stood up slowly, feeling drained. A lot of grease sounded good, he just didn't know if he could handle Cori and Lisanne firing questions at him. It was enough to give a man indigestion *before* he ate.

They walked back into the diner and Cori smirked at him.

C: She handles you well.
D: What part of 'fuck off' didn't you get the first time?
C: Seriously, I like her. She'll be good for you.
D: Patronizing much?
C: Suck it up.

Lisanne's phone beeped and she pulled it out of her pocket.

"Oh, it's from Kirsty. She's posted some pictures from Aspen."

She passed her phone to Daniel and he flipped through various snowy scenes.

C: Can I join in or is this a couples thing?

"Cori wants to know what we're looking at."

"Kirsty is my roommate. She's skiing in Aspen with her boyfriend, Vin."

483

D: Lis's irritating roommate and her boyfriend Vin. They're skiing in Aspen.
C: Lucky them! And I'm stuck here looking at your ugly face.
D: Even I'm getting bored of saying 'fuck off'.

Lisanne handed the phone over to Cori.

C: Hey, he's cute!

Daniel rolled his eyes.

"What?" said Lisanne.

"Please don't make me fucking say it," grumbled Daniel.

"Come on, what did she say?"

He groaned. "She thinks Vin is 'cute'." He used air quotes to show how deeply uncomfortable he was, talking about another guy like that.

Cori giggled and Lisanne couldn't help smiling.

"He's not my type," said Lisanne.

Cori laughed and pointed at Daniel.

"Yes, *he's* my type," said Lisanne, nodding.

Daniel stared at them both. "Hey! I'm right here!"

He was relieved when Maggie arrived with the food.

"Where've you been, handsome? I've missed your sweet face," and she leaned down to pinch his cheek. "I hope you're keeping him in order, girls," she said.

"Fuckin' hell," sighed Daniel.

"Less of the cussing, Danny Colton!" said Maggie, severely.

Lisanne held back a giggle, still slightly intimidated by the waitress.

They ate their food in silence, Daniel refusing to translate while there was a meal in front of him.

Afterward, they had an awkward three-way conversation where Daniel told Cori about Zef and the house, and that Rodney would be moving in.

C: Is he cute as well?
D: Not your type.
C: What's that supposed to mean?
D: He's gay.
C: You swinging both ways now? Don't bother saying 'fuck off' again.

"Oh, tell her we're going to have a party when Rodney's moved in."

"What? No way!"

"Fine, I'll tell her." Lisanne spoke slowly and clearly, and watched the furrowed concentration on Cori's face.

It was clear she found lip reading much more difficult than Daniel. It made Lisanne wonder how tiring it was for him. He'd always made it look so effortless that she realized she'd taken it for granted. But seeing Cori struggle, she was forced to re-evaluate her thoughts.

C: Cool! Party! You weren't going to invite me, were you, you bastard!
D: Can't imagine why I wouldn't.
C: Fuck off!

He grinned at her.

Over the next three days, Daniel had two more tuning appointments. Each time, Lisanne went with him, and each time there were small improvements, but Daniel's frustration was clear.

He couldn't distinguish between men's or women's voices, and couldn't tell who was speaking. He found some of the sounds 'ugly', although he couldn't explain what he meant by that.

Lisanne thought she understood—being a musician, and being so attuned to the quality of sound, some combinations just didn't seem right. But she kept that thought to herself.

485

Jane Harvey-Berrick

Daniel knew that his hold on his temper was tenuous and tried not to take out his constant anger on Lisanne, but it was hard.

He was almost relieved when Rodney returned, and the intensity of being with his girlfriend 24/7 was diluted.

One good thing had come out of their time together—the sex had been awesome. She had fewer and fewer inhibitions and had surprised him several times by taking the initiative. But they fought, too. Fuck, they fought!

He admitted to himself that he drove her crazy with not talking about how he was feeling, but come on! It just wasn't a guy thing to talk every other fucking second about how he was *feeling* all the time. Sometimes he needed to just *be*. Lisanne didn't seem to understand that, and accused him of shutting her out.

On the plus side, the make up sex was always fucking fantastic.

Baby doll was feisty. He liked that. He liked that *a lot*.

Lisanne, on the other hand, found their fights exhausting. She admitted as much to Kirsty when she got back from Aspen.

"I mean, he sent me this heart wrenching letter but he can never actually say the words to my face. He's so closed off—I never know what he's thinking and we end up fighting. Again."

"But he is talking to you," said Kirsty encouragingly, as she continued unpacking her impressively large suitcase. "It sounds like he's trying."

Lisanne sighed. "Yes, I know he is. And then I get mad at myself for getting mad at him. He's done all this for me and I end up yelling at him. I'm such a bitch."

Kirsty stopped unpacking and looked at her, a half smile tugging at her lips.

"Oh, believe me, babe, that is so far from the truth. Besides, you said he asked you to go to those clinic appointments with him?"

"Yes, I nearly died when he asked me. He usually keeps all that stuff to himself. You know, about being deaf."

Kirsty rolled her eyes. "Yes, I do remember an epic shit fit

486

when you told me. So the clinic thing, it's a really big deal for him?"

Lisanne nodded. "Yes, I think he knows he has to start sharing this stuff if we're going to really be together."

"Wow!"

"I know."

"And, you're like, practically living with him!"

Lisanne shook her head. "No, I was just staying for a few days until classes started."

"Your parents must have freaked out about that."

"Well, not really—maybe a bit. They gave me the whole lecture about 'needing to spend time apart' and 'enjoying my freedom'. I mean, I think they've accepted that we're sleeping together—I think—they just don't want me moving in with him. I'll save that bombshell for next year."

Kirsty gaped at her. "Really? You think?"

Lisanne nodded slowly. "Yeah, I think definitely maybe."

"Wow!"

"I know!"

They both dissolved into giggles and Lisanne was glad to have some quality girl time.

They ordered pizza and Kirsty told her all about Aspen which, of course, was 'awesome' and 'amazing'. Lisanne was slightly shocked to hear that Vin's parents had been totally cool with them sharing a room.

Truthfully, she was a little jealous that her parents weren't as open-minded. But then she felt mean for thinking like that, especially when they'd been so wonderful with helping Daniel fix up his house—they'd treated him like family. It hadn't been a smooth ride, but they'd done such a lot for him. Daniel had said as much on New Year's Eve. Lisanne loved her mom and dad and she couldn't imagine being without her parents, even if they were overprotective sometimes. Daniel had lost his...

"Hey, where'd you go just now? Missing Daniel already?"

Lisanne grinned at her friend. "Yes, but I'm not missing the fighting."

"Not even make up sex?"

"Definitely missing that!"

Kirsty winked at her.

"So, what's he going to do now?"

"What do you mean?"

"Well, is it still a big secret, you know, that he's deaf?"

Lisanne frowned. "I don't think anything has changed. He's still super private. It'll be bad enough when people found out that Zef got arrested."

Kirsty nodded. "God, I can't imagine what Daniel's going through. I'm so glad he's got you, Lis." She saw her friend's disbelieving face. "No, I mean it. I know I haven't been his greatest fan but, well … I admit it. I was wrong."

"Thanks, Kir. That means a lot to me."

"But…"

"Uh-oh."

"No, it's just, I had to tell Vin."

Lisanne sighed. "We figured you would. I don't think Daniel minds that much—he and Vin were getting along."

"If it's any consolation, Vin was seriously impressed. Well, shocked as hell at first. He kept on like he couldn't believe it. Anyway, I finally convinced him and told him about the hospital and everything. He won't say anything but I think he was going to text Daniel." She shook her head. "Frankly, I think it's inevitable that people will find out. I mean, you said he covers it up with a beanie—is he going to wear it all summer?"

"Some guys do," said Lisanne, defensively.

"To the beach?"

"He can't wear the processor when he's swimming anyway."

"You know what I'm saying."

Lisanne nodded. "Yeah, I do."

Suddenly their door was flung open and Shawna marched in.

"Ooooh! You're back!" she squealed, going from zero to supersonic in less than a second.

She launched herself at Kirsty, chattering away about her Christmas and New Years. Finally, she acknowledged that

Lisanne was in the room.

"Oh, hey," she said, coolly.

Lisanne just smiled and carried on texting Daniel.

"By the way," said Shawna, "I just passed Daniel Colton."

Lisanne's head snapped up as Shawna continued squawking.

"Ohmigod, have you seen him? He cut his hair! I told him ages ago that buzz cuts were the sexiest thing ever—he must have heard me!"

Kirsty shook her head in disbelief.

"Shawna, are you completely deluded? He's so into Lisanne it's not even true!"

Shawna laughed. She actually laughed and Lisanne wanted to shove her vacuous face into the nearest trashcan.

"Oh sure!" she said, still smiling. "See you tomorrow!" and she sauntered out.

"Sorry about that," muttered Kirsty.

Lisanne forced a laugh. "I don't care."

"Yeah, that's why you looked like you were about to snatch her bald-headed." She paused as Lisanne grinned at her. "So, is Daniel coming over, because I thought we were having some girl time?"

"It's news to me," said Lisanne, "but he's nothing if unpredictable."

Her phone beeped with a text and she smiled to see that Daniel was waiting downstairs for her.

"Young love," sighed Kirsty, and Lisanne threw a pillow at her.

Lisanne hurried out of the room and accidentally caught up with Shawna. Lisanne was filled with a sudden urge to tell that bitch that Daniel was off the market—permanently. Or just hit her. But Lisanne didn't want to make things difficult between Kirsty and Shawna, particularly as they were on the same course.

"Shawna?"

"What do you want, nerd?"

Shawna's unprovoked bitchiness was a mistake.

"Daniel is *my* boyfriend."

489

"Yeah? Well, it looks like a pity parade to me."

Lisanne took a step forward, her fury boiling over. "He will *never* want your saggy ass. He will *never* touch your fake boobs. He wouldn't be seen dead with a girl who dresses like a drag queen channeling Joan Rivers."

Shawna gaped at her.

"Stay away from me. Stay away from Daniel. Or…"

"Or what?" hissed Shawna.

"Or I'll beat the shit out of you."

Lisanne was proud that her voice didn't tremble once. She folded her arms across her chest and stared coldly.

"Are you threatening me?" Shawna said, her voice disbelieving.

"Yes."

Shawna gasped and was going to say something, but when she saw Lisanne's small hands curl tightly into fists, she stomped off down the corridor, throwing hateful glances over her shoulder.

Lisanne took a deep breath, and went to look for Daniel.

He was leaning against the wall beside the fire door, his face filled with tension. Lisanne immediately forgot about the verbal bitch-slap with Shawna.

"What's up? Are you okay?"

He didn't speak but pulled her into a tight hug, burying his face in her hair. She felt his breath on her neck as he breathed deeply several times. After nearly a minute of standing, holding her, while she stroked his back, he let her go.

"Sorry," he mumbled. "I just…"

"It's okay. You want to come in?"

"Is Kirsty there?"

"Yes, but she won't mind."

He shook his head. "No, I won't stay. I just wanted to see you."

"Daniel, you saw me less than two hours ago. What's happened?"

"I got a call from the prison. Zef wants to see me. I have to be there tomorrow at twelve."

"Oh. Are you going to go?"

His face tightened perceptibly. "Of course I'm going to fucking go—he's my brother."

Lisanne kept her face still, trying to hide her irritation.

"Yeah, so, I won't be able to meet you for lunch."

She didn't ask why he hadn't simply texted her—she knew the reason.

"Do you want me to come with you?"

He smiled briefly then frowned. "No, I'm good. But I could meet you after school. Rodney's making Thai."

He rolled his eyes and Lisanne chuckled.

"Hmm, Rodney's experimental cooking! And you want me to suffer along with you?"

"Yeah, that's one reason!"

His eyes darkened, and told her what reason number two might be.

"Mmm, I could definitely eat some Thai," she teased him.

He pulled her toward him, hungrily. "Yeah, I could eat some … Thai, as well."

He kissed her deeply and when she kissed him back, pushing her hands into the back pockets of his jeans, a moan rumbled up from his throat.

"Fuck, baby doll, I just can't get enough of you."

He left, with his kiss seared onto her lips, and her knees weak.

That boy!

The next day was unseasonably warm, and when Daniel parked Sirona, he gratefully took off his leather jacket. He was still anxious about leaving her in unfamiliar places, but he figured the well protected county jail was probably safer than most places.

There was a low watchtower outside the gates, and thick barbed wire spiraled along the concrete walls. The jail itself squatted behind its protective barrier, flat and unassuming, despite who and what it contained.

Daniel took a deep breath and headed toward the visitor entrance. Right now he really wanted a smoke and was very tempted to open one of the packets of Camel he'd brought for his brother. He decided against it, having been smoke-free for well over a month. Lis would kill him if he blew it now. Besides, he couldn't afford his 20 a day habit anymore.

He gave his name to the guards on duty at the security checkpoint, and was asked to remove his boots and jacket, and empty his keys and wallet into a plastic bin. A sign informed him that he had two chances to make it past the metal detector or he would be denied entry. He walked through the machine and it immediately started beeping.

A guard told him to check his pockets and stood over him while he did so. Daniel was about to try and make it through again when he remembered the implant. Feeling like an idiot, he explained the problem. The guard looked skeptical until Daniel pulled off his beanie and showed the guy his scar. He also had his tuning appointment letter in his wallet.

The guard read it carefully then returned it to Daniel's wallet.

"Next time tell us before you try and go through the metal detector, son."

Daniel was relieved—the guy could have been an asshole, but considering he worked in a jail, he was pretty damn nice about it.

He was told to wait in a room with a number of other visitors. He felt awkward standing with a group of women, most of whom seemed to have small children. One woman was crying, tears running down her cheeks, and snot pooling beneath her nose. Daniel looked away.

After a ten minute wait where the woman continued to sob pathetically, they were escorted through a number of gates to another holding pen. A large poster declared:

WEAPONS OF ANY KIND ARE NOT PERMITTED.

AVOID LOUD, EXCESSIVELY EMOTIONAL, OR DISRUPTIVE BEHAVIOR.

PLEASE BE CONSIDERATE OF OTHER VISITORS.

SPEAKING TO OTHER OFFENDERS OR VISITORS IS NOT PERMITTED.

HANDHOLDING IS PERMITTED ONLY IF HANDS REMAIN IN PLAIN VIEW.

A BRIEF HUG IS PERMITTED AT THE BEGINNING AND CONCLUSION OF VISITS.

AN OFFENDER MAY HAVE CONTACT WITH HIS CHILDREN.

IF YOUR VISIT BECOMES EMOTIONAL, STAFF WILL ASSIST AS NEEDED.

Daniel kept a close watch on the door. He hadn't worn the processor because of needing his helmet. He'd tried it once and his skull had felt bruised and tender, almost raw where the magnets met.

He saw a guard come in and call, "Next."

He raised his hand and the guard checked down his list.

"Go through the door to your right. Make sure it closes completely behind you. When the buzzer sounds, go through the next door. Once inside, go directly to Table 12. Any questions?"

"Um, yeah."

"What is it?"

"I'm, um, I'm deaf."

"Excuse me?"

Was this guy fucking laughing at him?

493

"I'm deaf. I can't hear the buzzer."

"Do you want this visit, kid, because I've had just about enough…"

Daniel tore off his beanie and turned to show the guy his scar. "I'm fucking deaf, okay! I can't hear any damn buzzer!"

He turned back and pulled the beanie firmly down his head.

The guard looked irritated. "Fine, I'll have someone escort you."

A few minutes later, an enormous woman in guard uniform walked toward him. "You the deaf kid?"

Daniel felt his muscles tense but he tried to keep his face neutral.

"Yeah."

"Huh. You don't look deaf. This way."

He followed her through one door and down a short corridor. After a pause, she pushed open a second door.

"Have a nice visit."

Daniel looked around and found a small table branded with the number 12. There were already several visitors sitting with prisoners. One man was holding a child of about two on his knee and blowing bubbles onto her stomach. Daniel could see that she was laughing.

His stomach clenched and he quickly swallowed the rising nausea.

A door at the far end of the room opened and he saw Zef. Daniel had expected him to be handcuffed and was relieved that he wasn't. In fact, if it hadn't been for the prison overalls, they could have been meeting in some cheap diner.

"Hey, little bro. How you doing?"

Daniel stood up and they hugged quickly.

"Thanks for coming, man. Shit, it's good to see you."

"Yeah, you, too. You look good."

The weird thing was, it was true. Zef looked relaxed and clear-eyed, not strung out or high. Daniel realized it had been a long time since he'd seen his brother like that.

Zef laughed lightly. "It's all the clean living," and he raised his eyebrows.

"So, how is it? In here?"

Zef's shoulders slumped, infinitesimally. "Well, it sucks, but nothing I can't handle. 'If you can't do the time, don't do the crime', right?"

"Yeah, I guess. Hey, I brought you smokes."

"Fuckin' lifesaver. Thanks, Dan."

Daniel nodded.

Zef lit a cigarette and breathed in appreciatively. "You not having one?"

"Nah, man. I quit."

"Seriously?"

"Yep. Over a month now."

Zef blew out a slow lungful of smoke and sighed. "That little girlfriend of yours must be a good influence, or something."

Daniel frowned and Zef spread out his hands in a gesture of capitulation.

"I don't mean anything. It's cool. It's great you've got someone." He paused. "How's the hearing thing?"

"Okay. Weird but getting better. I can hear some sounds, but it's still kinda muddy. They say it'll take up to a year before it's fully functioning."

"That long?"

"Could be sooner. No one can say for sure."

"Have you worn it to school?"

"Once. It was pretty shitty. It sounded loud in the hallways but I couldn't pick out one sound from the others—it was garbage, so that was a bit crap."

Zef nodded slowly. "No regrets then?"

Daniel paused. "No, I just wish…"

"What?"

"I thought … I thought I'd be able to hear music. You know, maybe be able to … I tried but it's just a bunch of fucking noise."

Zef's face was sympathetic.

"Shit, I'm sorry, man. I know that was a big thing for you."

Daniel shrugged. "Yeah. Whatever." He looked directly at his brother. "So, are you going to tell me why I'm here? Why you were dealing fucking *meth*."

Zef gave a wistful smile. "I wasn't sure you'd come."

Daniel rubbed his hand across his jaw. "You're my brother."

"I wish I'd been a better one."

They shared a look.

"I mean it, Dan. I've been a shitty brother. I wasn't there for you. All the shit that went down—you tried to get me to stop and I was too fucking blind to see it. But you know what? I'm not sorry the cops caught up with me because I don't think I'd have got out alive otherwise. I was into some pretty heavy scenes that I haven't even told you about. I just kept getting pulled in deeper." He gestured with his hands. "Here, well, in prison, I get a chance to clean up my act. I might only get five years."

Daniel took a sharp intake of breath.

"Hey, don't sweat it, little brother. This place is a picnic compared to where I was headed. Besides, I can study. Might get my degree before you. And the state prison has got a pretty good mechanics shop." He sighed. "So, um, how's the house?"

"I was going to torch it."

Zef's eyes bugged out. "Sweet baby Jesus! You didn't, did you?"

"Lis stopped me."

"Well, thank fuck for that!"

"Yeah, turned out okay. Her folks helped me fix it up. I had some photos on my phone, but I wasn't allowed to bring it in. Maybe I could print some out for you?"

They both knew that Daniel was really asking if Zef wanted him to visit again.

"Sure, that'd be cool."

The guard approached, signaling the end of the visit.

They shook hands, and Zef pulled his brother in for a hug. "I'm so fucking sorry," he whispered, knowing that Daniel couldn't hear him.

The guard loomed closer and Zef pulled away.

"Look, one more thing. Just … don't trust Roy, okay?"

"What the fuck? Zef?"

But Zef was already being led away.

Daniel didn't go back to school after visiting Zef. He didn't go home either. Instead, he drove to the coast and found a patch of beach where he could stare out at the ocean, watching the waves curl onto the pale sand.

It had been a kick in the guts seeing Zef in jail. He was glad his brother wanted to use the time he'd have to serve to clean up his act, but fuck—five years. That meant Zef would be nearly 30 by the time he got out. It seemed a lifetime away to Daniel.

He'd lost his parents and now his brother had gone, too. And what was that shit about Roy? Why hadn't Zef told him outright what was going on?

His phone vibrated and when he pulled it out, there was a text photo that Lisanne had taken of herself, pulling a silly face.

* L: see what you don't have to keep on missing?
Hope it went ok. LA xx *
* D: pick you up 40 mins? *
* L: Got a ride with R. be at your place.
R has a date!!! LA xx *
* D: ?!*?!!&! *
* L: I know! Later. LA xx *

Daniel smiled to himself. Baby Doll could always make him smile. And Rodney had a date. The guy moved fast.

He drove back slowly, thinking about all the meanings of the word 'home': what his home had been, what it was now, what it could be or would be, even what it *should* be. Mostly, he thought about Lisanne waiting for him.

It was nearly 7 PM when he arrived back, and Rodney's car was still parked outside. Daniel was disappointed. He'd been looking forward to having Lisanne to himself. Rodney was okay—living with him was easier than Daniel had thought and although he wasn't the tidiest person, it was nothing after living with Zef and his asshole customers for two years. At least he didn't feel the need to lock his bedroom door anymore—not that he had anything worth stealing. He patted Sirona's saddle — except her.

He locked her securely in the garage and headed inside. His nostrils were immediately assailed by the heady scent of strong aftershave.

Rodney wafted past looking excited, a bright smile on his face.

"Fuck, man! You smell like a whore's bedroom!"

"I know," said Rodney, winking at him. "Don't wait up!"

Shaking his head, Daniel went to look for Lisanne. She was in the kitchen unpacking food from a shopping bag. He wrapped his arms around her waist and kissed her neck.

She twisted around and rested her head against his chest. When she looked up, her eyes were soft and concerned.

"How did it go today?"

He grimaced. "Okay. As okay as it could be, I guess."

"Do you want to talk about it?"

"Not really."

"But will you? Maybe later?"

He sighed. "Yeah, later. Maybe."

She rolled her eyes. "Are you hungry?"

"Starving."

She laughed lightly. "You're always starving. Okay, I'll make something—Rodney's Thai extravaganza has been put on hold. Oh, hey, did you wear your CI today?" He shook his head and she pursed her lips. "You know Dr. Devallis said you had to practice *every day*. Go put it on while I get dinner."

"Baby d…"

"No, I mean it, Daniel. Go put it on. Now."

Grumbling and muttering to himself about how bossy she was, he headed for his bedroom and fished the device out of its box. He checked the battery and hooked it over his ear, then attached the magnet.

He still felt self-conscious about wearing it, so he pulled his beanie back on, then ran downstairs. He stopped halfway, aware that he could hear himself running. The shock travelled up his body and lodged somewhere in his chest.

He saw Lisanne's anxious face peering up at him.

"Are you okay?"

"Yeah, fuck. I ... I could hear myself ... on the stairs. It just freaked me out a bit. 'S'okay, I'm good."

Her face lit up. "It's getting better, isn't it? You can hear more with it?"

"I don't know if it's hearing more or ... like my brain is working out what the different sounds are. It's hard to explain."

He walked down the stairs and jumped the last two steps, landing with a thud. A huge smile spread over his face.

"I definitely heard that!"

Lisanne's face crumpled and Daniel was immediately uneasy. "What's the matter, baby doll? What's wrong?"

She shook her head and scrubbed at the tears that were threatening to fall.

"I'm just ... happy!" she said. "You heard that. You really heard it!"

He swept her up into a tight hug and his mouth slammed down on hers. She responded immediately, and her tongue dove into his mouth, twisting and twining with his.

He felt himself growing hard as his body pressed against her.

"Bed!" she gasped.

Daniel picked her up and felt her legs wrap around his waist. He turned and carried her up the stairs slowly, refusing to lose contact with her mouth. They crashed into his bedroom and fell sideways onto the bed.

Lisanne grabbed at his t-shirt and tugged it roughly over his head, dragging the beanie with it.

Daniel's hand moved to the device, ready to yank it off.

"Leave it on," Lisanne breathed. She pulled back slightly so he could see her face. "Leave it on."

He looked at her doubtfully, but then she pushed him down and straddled his thighs, running her tongue up the centre of his body. He stretched his arms above him and held onto the headboard, his biceps bunching, making his tattoos ripple so that Lisanne wanted to lick those, too.

Daniel felt his cock hot and heavy in his jeans and he breathed deeply, enjoying the feeling of her warm body moving over his. He sat up suddenly and caught her before she fell backward.

He pulled her toward him by her shirt, unfastening one button at a time, before slipping the sleeves down her arms.

"Fuck, I love your tits," he said, and pushed his face between them, feeling their softness and fullness.

She moaned and he looked up. He wasn't sure if he'd heard something or maybe it was the damn device and its phantom sounds.

She opened her eyes, and they were filled with dark, sexy humor.

"Maybe you'd rather have dinner?"

"Yeah, I would," he said. "I'm going to eat *you*."

He could see Lisanne's whole body heat up and his heart started to hammer. His cock punched at the zipper on his jeans, demanding to be freed. He lifted her away from him and dropped her onto the bed before yanking off his boots and getting rid of his socks. He kept his eyes on her face as his jeans joined the rest of his clothes on the floor.

His cock leapt free, hard and proud, and aiming straight at Lisanne.

She licked her lips and his cock waved at her, impatiently.

Daniel crawled slowly up the bed, his whole body dangerous and predatory.

"Are you wet, baby doll? Are you soaking for me?"

She nodded, her eyes wide and full of longing.

He peeled her jeans down her legs and used his teeth to tug her panties to her thighs.

She kicked them free and he knelt between her legs, pushing her knees up and wide apart.

"You look so beautiful, all wet for me, baby doll. Do you

know how much I want you?" He glanced down at his cock, showing the truth of his words. Her small hand wrapped around his length and he had to take a deep breath to stop himself from slamming into her and pumping hard.

He grinned as he forced her to let go, blinking as she flicked his tip as she conceded the contest.

"Bad ass!" he murmured against her stomach.

He felt her shiver, as he kissed his way up each thigh, before burying his face deep inside her. Fuck, he loved to do this to her, fucking her with his tongue and his fingers. He knew she still didn't get why he liked doing it, but she enjoyed it too much to stop him.

Her orgasm came quickly, the stress and tension of the first day back at school relieved, as her body pulsed around him.

Her eyes fluttered open, and she leaned up on her elbows as he pumped himself three or four times. It was such a fucking turn on to know that she liked to watch as he pleasured himself.

"You still want me, Lis?"

"I'll always want you," she said, echoing the words he said to her so often.

Her face was so serious, so full of love, that Daniel felt that same sharp pain in his chest. His breath caught in his throat.

"Make love to me, Daniel," she said, watching his face carefully.

She lifted her feet and wrapped her legs around his waist, pulling him closer. Unable to resist any longer, Daniel pushed inside her, a low groan swelling out of him as her warm, wet body enclosed him completely.

She tightened her legs until her heels were digging into his ass, gripping him tightly.

Daniel shuddered, feeling another notch of control slip away. He took their combined weight on his forearms as her body lifted off the bed with each vigorous thrust.

He felt the flutter of another orgasm begin to build inside her, the movement sending him into a frenzy as he lost the battle to control his body.

Sounds vibrated through her so strongly, he could feel them in his own chest. He was confused, could he feel them or could he hear them? His brain was too deluged with sensation to analyze what he felt.

Her hands scrabbled at his shoulders, her short nails digging into his skin. Sweat broke out on his forehead and on his back, and he felt the tensing in his balls and stomach that told him he had about five seconds before he came.

"I'm close," he gasped in a strangled voice. "Lis? Lis?"

Lisanne gripped tighter, her face contorted and she screamed. "Daniel!"

His orgasm erupted from him, jets of heat passing from his body into hers, his heart hammering, breath squeezed from his lungs.

He collapsed onto the bed, momentarily crushing her.

He felt Lisanne push his shoulder gently and he pulled out of her, his brain a chaos of confusion. He lay on this back, his arm thrown over his face.

He couldn't catch his breath, he couldn't think. He was gasping, drowning.

Lisanne's soft hands pulled at his arm. He resisted, afraid to look at her. She pulled again and this time he let her.

Her warm hands were on his face and her fingers were sweeping gently across his cheeks.

He opened his eyes and saw her, so full of love, concerned now.

"Daniel! Why are you crying? Daniel! Talk to me!"

He struggled to sit up, his beautiful face torn with emotion.

"I heard you."

"What do you mean?"

He rubbed his eyes, surprised to find them wet with tears.

"I heard you. You … you called my name."

Lisanne stared at him, then understanding warmed her eyes.

"Of course. I always call your name. I love you, Daniel."

He choked back the fear as he looked into her soul, and for the first time he believed her.

"I heard you," he said again, those three small words expressing a world of wonder.

"I know," she said with a soft smile.

"Baby doll ... I ... I love you."

CHAPTER 25

Lisanne was in a fury.

How dare he! How absolutely fucking dare he!

Daniel had come to her dorm room with a torn t-shirt and bruised knuckles to *inform* her, no less, that he'd told Roy to stay away from her. Consequently, Roy had quit the band—and they had a gig in less than a week but no lead guitarist.

When she asked him what had happened, he'd simply said that 'Roy had it coming'. That was it. *He had it coming?* What the hell did that mean? Like that was supposed to explain everything! And obviously the whole 'telling' situation had involved fists rather than words. She was slightly awestruck that Daniel had taken on a mountain of a man like Roy, who had at least forty pounds and a couple of inches on him—not that she was going to admit that. Not even for one second.

She'd yelled at him, called him on his macho bullshit, told him he was an asshole, and then kicked him out.

It was a shame—they'd been getting along so well lately.

Ever since Daniel had said the words, had admitted that he loved her, their relationship had changed. It was more intense, it was more relaxed. It was more adventurous, it was less strained. He was playful and loving, and every day they discovered something new about each other.

He'd talked about his parents, telling her stories from when he was a kid. He'd opened up about how he felt a little more, although there was still so much he kept back. He'd even admitted some of his fears about how well the implant would work. She tried to reassure him and pointed out the small improvements that had already happened.

She smiled to herself as she thought about that amazing, special moment—when he'd heard her call out his name as they made love. It had been huge for both of them.

He was embarrassed that he'd cried but she loved it, because it told her everything that she needed to know, and everything that he found so hard to say.

And then, two weeks later, after yet another tuning session at the hospital, came the miracle moment.

The scene was so perfect in her mind, so ordinary in location, but she kept it like a jewel—a special memory that she took out when she needed to smile.

She was standing in Daniel's kitchen, washing dishes, while he leaned against the counter next to her and dried. It was an uncomplicated, everyday piece of drudgery. Not that she minded—she loved those quiet domestic moments when it was just the two of them.

And she'd started to sing—one of Daniel's songs—her favorite song. It seemed to describe her relationship with him perfectly.

> *When I hear that song*
> *Feeling every note*
> *It's a special kind of place*
> *Singing words we wrote.*
> *Sounds fade away*
> *Every mile signed*
> *But first thing in the morning*
> *You're always on my mind.*

And then at her side, she'd heard his soft voice singing along with her.

> *Wish I was that man*
> *Touching every void*
> *It's a special kind of place*
> *Music we enjoyed.*

Her voice shuddered into silence, and she stared at Daniel as he continued by himself.

Words that don't last
And feelings not always kind
But last thing every night
You're always on my mind.

She dropped the plate she'd been washing, making the suds leap into the air, and turned her eyes toward him, throat cracking.

"You … you could hear me! You heard what I was singing!"

He nodded, his face serious.

"You didn't say anything! How long? How long have you been able to…?"

"I thought once before … maybe … and then today … after the tuning session … I wanted to be sure, baby doll."

They held each other for so long, the simple act meaning so much.

"I always liked that song," he said, quietly.

It gave them hope. Daniel still found that listening to recorded music was impossible, a fact that frustrated him inordinately, but he could hear Lisanne, and his most basic wish was fulfilled.

In some ways it made things easier, but in others, it was harder for him.

Rodney, in particular, was prone to forgetting that Daniel was deaf. He'd turn away during conversations, or cover up his mouth, or talk while eating—all things that made it impossible for Daniel to understand him. He bore it with more stoicism than Lisanne, who would flare up at the slightest infraction.

She could tell when Daniel didn't understand, when he was getting left out of the conversation. He couldn't hear children at all, their high pitch inaudible to him. He had a similar reaction to Shawna's continual shrieking, but that was no loss. He couldn't hear whispers and he still relied on lip reading. But Lisanne could see that the balance was beginning to shift.

He was stubborn and independent and she loved him more than breathing—and he drove her completely crazy.

He still refused to let any more of his classmates know that he was deaf, and he sat in lectures with his beanie pulled down low. Some days he said he couldn't wait to rip the device from his head, but other days he seemed to tolerate it better.

He was still ill at ease with the knowledge that his skull contained a piece of titanium, but they were working through his issues together. She'd asked him if he thought it was worth it. He'd nodded but not really answered her. Lisanne was disappointed inside, but she hadn't pushed him. She was learning, too.

She tolerated his moods, and he put up with her monthly sulks. She was also beginning to spot the signs that told her when he needed to be by himself. She sighed, thinking how alone he'd been for the last four years in one way or another. He was doing better now—going out more, taking more chances at being social. Vin had been working on getting Daniel to try out for the college football team, even to the extent of looking online for specialist helmets. Daniel hadn't agreed so far, but Lisanne was hopeful. And sharing the house with Rodney had been good for Daniel, too. Even so—and Lisanne scrunched up her face—when Daniel hit overload, he still clammed up.

But if he thought for one damn second that he could control her life by fighting with Roy, he had another thing coming.

Lisanne had worked up quite a head of steam before she decided to go to the auto repair shop where he was working, and confront him. She grabbed her jacket—and stopped.

Lying on the bed, hidden under her coat, was an envelope, her name written in Daniel's spidery scrawl.

Lisanne's heart squeezed painfully. The last time he'd written her, it had been about his operation.

She pulled out a single sheet of paper and began to read.

Baby Doll,

You asked me if it was worth it, having the CI. I know you feel like you pushed me into it, but that's not true.

Meeting you was the best thing that ever happened to me.

Getting the CI so I could hear you was the next best thing.

So, was it worth it?

It's worth it because:

    * I can hear you sing

    * I can hear you talk

    * I can hear you laugh

    * I can hear the wind in the trees and the sound of the ocean

    * I can hear my music

    * It makes me want to discover the world with you.

And when we make love, I can hear you call my name.

I love you, so much.

    Daniel x

She sat down on the bed, holding the letter in her hands. How did he do that? How did he utterly floor her with just a few words—words that he couldn't even say out loud?

She realized he must have brought it with him to give to her before they'd had their fight. God, he was infuriating! A beautiful, brilliant, complex man—really damned annoying—and she loved him.

She loved that he'd thought about her question instead of dismissing it. She loved that he'd written down what he couldn't say out loud. And she loved that he'd left it behind for her to find, even though they'd been yelling at each other.

Lisanne pulled on her jacket and made the trek across town to the auto repair shop. The bus ride gave her a good 40 minutes to decide what she wanted to say to him, but as she walked toward the faded entrance, she still had no clue how she was going to start.

Daniel was leaning over the hood of a V6 Mustang, doing something manly and macho with a torque wrench, his very fine ass on display, despite the work overalls.

The V6 Mustang was bright yellow, not a color Lisanne liked on cars, but he'd been working on it for a couple of days, saying he needed the overtime. Lisanne suspected it was more because the car was 'a classic' and Daniel couldn't resist a sexy piece of automobile. To Lisanne, now she'd seen it, it still looked like a box on wheels, but she was amused by the reverence with which Daniel talked about the car. It was a 'she', of course, although Lisanne managed not to be too jealous, despite *her awesome lines* and *her great body*.

She pulled herself up to sit on a low wall, her legs dangling, enjoying the view. She was quite content waiting for him to finish whatever he was doing, and not wishing to break his concentration. Besides, it had been a while since she'd had the opportunity for some undisturbed ogling.

The overalls showed off his slim waist and narrow hips, and with the sleeves rolled up, his strong forearms were also on display. He had a smear of oil across one cheek but his hands were encased in thin, plastic gloves.

She was surprised how much of a turn on she found it, watching him waist-deep in the car's engine. She remembered Kirsty's words from the very first time they'd seen him—*That boy is fine*. The words seemed even more true to her today, knowing how beautiful he was on the inside, too.

Her contented reminiscing was interrupted by a middle-aged woman in an expensive pantsuit climbing out of a taxi. She threw some money at the driver and stalked across to the auto shop, her cell phone clutched in one hand, a takeout coffee in the other.

Lisanne could see the woman running her eyes up and down Daniel's ass and broad shoulders in a blatant display of eye fuckery before she coughed loudly and deliberately, clearly expecting some response from him.

Lisanne knew he didn't wear the CI when he was working, finding it too distracting. As the woman approached Daniel, she tapped her phone impatiently with her long glossy fingernails and huffed.

"Some people have no damn manners!" she snapped. "Hey, you! Hey, you're working on my car so I pay your damn salary!"

Lisanne saw red. She marched up to the woman, her small hands clenched into fists.

"You're the one with no manners," said Lisanne, in a cold, clear voice.

"What? Who asked you? Mind your own damn business!" The woman's face was incredulous as she took in Lisanne's plain t-shirt and discount store jeans.

Lisanne felt her face heat up but she stood her ground.

"He *is* my business—and he's not being rude—he's deaf. Yes, that's right." She crossed her arms. "Don't assume everyone is like you!"

The woman was speechless, staring at Lisanne angrily ,but also with doubt written all over her face.

Lisanne walked to Daniel's side and he looked up in surprise.

"Hey, baby doll! What are you doing here?"

She gave him a small smile, and glanced over his shoulder. "You have a customer."

Daniel turned around.

"May I help you, ma'am?"

It amused Lisanne to hear Daniel being so ultra polite, when normally he couldn't complete a sentence without uttering some sort of cuss word.

Her eyes narrowed when she saw the customer's raptor like smile.

"I'm sorry to interrupt you," the woman said, faking sincerity perfectly, "but that's my car y'all are working on. I was told I could pick it up this afternoon, but if you need more time...?"

Daniel let loose his most irresistible smile, and Lisanne suspected he knew exactly what he was doing. When he winked at her, she was certain, and grinned back.

"No, ma'am, she's good to go. She was idling high because of the idle air control," he said, authoritatively, "and the 2005 model is known for front end noise and rattles, but she'll be fine now."

He turned back to drop the hood.

"Thank you, young man," the woman purred to his back. She raised her eyebrows then tapped him on the shoulder.

Daniel turned around. "Yes, ma'am?"

"Thank you," she said again. "I can see you really know what you're doing."

Her tone was suggestive as her eyes flicked up and down his body.

"Sure, no problem," said Daniel, as if he hadn't noticed. "The office will have your invoice for you."

Then he peeled off the plastic gloves and walked over to Lisanne, grinning.

The woman flounced off to pay her bill, and Lisanne gave an internal fist pump.

Daniel gently smoothed her hair away from her throat and nuzzled the soft skin.

"Are you still mad at me?"

"Being cute doesn't make you any less annoying!"

"Yeah? But what if I'm hot?" and he pulled her close to his body, gripping her hips firmly and running his teeth down the side of her neck.

"Still annoying," she breathed out, in a whisper that was more like a moan.

She gathered her scattered wits and pushed him away. No matter how many times he kissed her, she always had the same reaction—complete mental paralysis, and damp panties.

She was pleased that he wasn't immune to her charms either, and his overalls couldn't disguise that he was growing hard.

He groaned as she pushed him away, a look of disappointment painted across his lovely lips.

"I got your letter," she said.

511

His eyes slid away from her and he shoved his hands in his pockets. "Yeah?"

She lifted her hand to his cheek. "I loved it. Thank you."

His answering smile was shy and it made the breath catch in her throat.

"Okay," he said, quietly.

"I'm still mad at you about Roy!" she said, putting her hands on her hips.

Daniel scowled.

"What did he do that was so bad?"

His only response was to grimace

"I mean, you've left us without our lead guitarist six days before the gig! What the hell were you thinking? If this is just about you being jealous…"

But she didn't get to finish her rant.

"Yeah, I'm jealous!" he yelled, making her jump. "I'm jealous that he was up there playing with you and I'm not. I'm jealous that he's second-rate and can still play better than I can now. I'm jealous that he gets to hear you sing—really sing—and I don't. So, yeah! You could say I'm fucking jealous!"

He looked so angry and hurt, and Lisanne was mortified that she'd made him feel like that, but she needed to have this out with him.

"So who's next?"

"What do you mean?" he said, still breathing hard.

"Who are you going to fight next? Mike? Carlos? JP? You said you wanted me to have music for both of us—but perhaps that doesn't apply anymore."

Daniel looked furious, then a look of resignation passed over his face.

"Baby doll, fuck, look … yeah, I'll be jealous whoever you play with … but Roy … I couldn't let him hang with you anymore."

"But why?"

He rubbed a hand across his forehead.

"I had an idea about Roy, but … when I saw Zef, he told me

not to trust him—not to trust Roy. I didn't know what he meant, so I asked around…"

"And?"

"And he's up to his neck in shit, Lis. The heavy stuff. Like Zef was. It's just a matter of time and I don't want you anywhere near him when that happens. Okay?"

Lisanne found it hard to believe—Roy seemed like such a sweet guy. He'd always been kind to her, although there was that time he'd let her make her own way home late at night after having promised her a ride.

She sighed. "Why didn't you tell me? Why did you have to go charging in on your crusade? You could have gotten hurt—again."

Daniel shook his head. "I just wanted…"

"To protect me. I know. Please, Daniel. Please. You *have* to talk to me about these things."

"I don't want that shit touching you, baby doll," he said mulishly, warning Lisanne that they'd reached an impasse.

"Okay," she said, "but you still owe me a lead guitarist."

He gave a small smile. "Already done."

"What?"

"JP's a pretty good guitarist and he'd been getting bored letting Roy do all the good stuff. You don't need Roy. You'll be fine."

"Any other arrangements you've made in my life that you'd like to tell me about?" she snapped.

The annoying man just grinned at her. "Can't think of any, but if I do, I'll try to remember and let you know."

Yep, very annoying.

Lisanne glared at him but found she couldn't keep it up with him looking at her like that, all hot and disheveled, all sexy and shameless.

"Are you done here?"

"Why? Baby doll want to play?"

"Oh yes," she said, nodding her head. "She really, really does."

Daniel was right about JP. He'd relished the chance of stepping out of Roy's shadow, and had been very happy to work with Lisanne on a new song she wanted to try. She'd kept it a secret from Daniel—it was going to be a special surprise.

"Sit still, damn it!" Kirsty scolded. "These curling irons are super hot! I don't want to burn you—or me."

Lisanne was being primped again. She still found it borderline torturous but she couldn't deny Kirsty her pleasure either, and she had to admit she was pretty awesome at turning an average face and figure into something that would stand out on a stage—even if it was in a dive on the music circuit to nowhere.

Lisanne had been colored, curled, painted and powdered and finally poured into a fabulous gold sheath dress that clung in all the right places, and made her boobs look impressive.

"Ta dah!" sang Kirsty. "You look knockout, honey! Daniel will probably want to kidnap you so no other guys can see the hotness that is you."

Lisanne wasn't sure about that, but she appreciated Kirsty's encouragement. And she definitely didn't think it would do any harm for Daniel to see her all dressed up for a change. He didn't seem to mind that she lived in jeans and t-shirts but he was a guy after all, and what guy didn't like to see their woman in skirts and heels?

There was a knock on the door and Rodney's voice boomed through the panel.

"Your pumpkin awaits, mademoiselle!"

Kirsty grinned and pulled open the door. Rodney and Kirsty had hit it off immediately and she'd even tried to persuade him to major in fashion. Rodney was still thinking about it but said he didn't want to 'live the stereotype'. He was undecided, if only in what he wanted to study—because he'd been dating Ryan, a second year Mech Eng student, for three weeks, and had been happily exploring the local gay scene.

Rodney stopped and applauded when he saw Lisanne.

"Outstanding! God, you're so amazing, Kirsty!"

"Hey, what about me?" wailed Lisanne. "Person about to go on stage needing encouragement here!"

"You, too, Cinderella," said Rodney, pulling her into a warm hug. "I'm so proud of you," he whispered. "Now, let's get this show on the road!"

"Wait!" yelled Kirsty, and took a photo of Lisanne looking rather startled.

As they approached the club, Lisanne wished very hard that Daniel was in the car with her, holding her hand, but he'd gotten a ride with Vin and was going to meet her inside. Sirona might be sexy (as Daniel insisted), but she had her limitations when it came to mass transportation.

Her phone beeped in her purse.

> * D: you look SO HOT!
> You make me want to be very bad man. x *

"Kirsty, did you send that photo of me to Daniel?"

Kirsty grinned at her. "Guilty as charged. What did he say?"

"Nothing really," mumbled Lisanne.

"Oh my God! I bet he did! What did he say?" and she snatched the phone from Lisanne.

"Hey!"

Kirsty giggled hysterically.

"Share! Share!" chanted Rodney.

"Kirsty!" hissed Lisanne.

"He says she looks hot," said Kirsty.

"That's a given," agreed Rodney.

"And that the way she looks makes him want to be *a very bad man!*"

"Oh, yes, please!" gulped Rodney with a melodramatic sigh, fanning his face.

Lisanne slunk down in the car, beyond embarrassed, while her so-called friends made a number of suggestions about how she could take Daniel up on his offer. She wanted to crawl through the floor of the car—or take notes.

Quietly, she texted him back.

> * L: I'm freaking out. Wish you were here. LA xx *
> * D: You will be awesome
> and now I know what I'm talking about. X *
> * L: Hope so! LA xx*

It was Saturday night and the club was jammed. People were lined up along the block to get in. As they walked past them to the staff entrance, Lisanne started to feel nauseous. *Breathe, Lis. Breathe*, she told herself.

They knocked on the door and were let in by two supervisors that Lisanne had never seen before. She felt a slight pang for Roy's reassuring bulk, then chastised herself for being so dumb.

Daniel was waiting in the dressing room with Mike, JP and Carlos. They were drinking beer and whiskey chasers—without the beer—and all four of them looked nervous.

Daniel's face lit up as he saw her, and her body flamed as his eyes drifted down her legs and settled somewhere around her chest, before realizing he'd been busted ogling his girlfriend. His sexy smile was inflammatory and he prowled over to her, cupping his hands over her ass.

"Am I allowed to kiss you?" he said, hungrily licking her neck.

"No!" said Lisanne. "Well, not my lips. Kirsty spent forever doing my makeup."

Daniel pouted. "Baby doll, you look so fucking kissable—how is that fair?"

Lisanne realized he was slightly drunk and she frowned at him.

"What?" he said, smirking at her, and running his tongue along his teeth.

She shook her head, knowing that she wouldn't be able to be stern—he was too damn cute.

"I want to take you home and undress you *slowly*," he said.

Lisanne shivered and broke out into a cold sweat. He was doing a great job of taking her mind off of the gig, and the four hundred people crammed into the club.

She realized he was wearing his beanie—which meant he was wearing his CI. Although the scars had faded into a faint, pink line, and his hair had grown out, he still wore the beanie to cover up the device.

"Are you turned on?" she said, then immediately regretted her choice of words.

Daniel raised his eyebrows. "That's a bit fucking forward, Ms Maclaine, but seeing as you ask…" and he pushed his hips into her.

Yep, no doubt. He was turned on.

"I meant your … you know," she hissed, swatting his ass.

He smiled ruefully and shook his head. "No, I might try it later but I don't think I'll get anything—too much background noise—too many different sounds," and he grimaced.

She rested her head against his chest until JP gave a discreet cough.

She looked up and smiled at Daniel. "I'll see you out front?"

"I'll be there, baby doll. Ready to punch any fucker who lays so much as an eyeball on you."

He winked at her and left her with the rest of the band members. Lisanne hoped he was joking, but she wasn't sure.

They ran through the set they were going to sing, and she sang some scales to warm up her voice. Then the emcee announced them…

"Playing live tonight, a hot, happening local band, let's hear it for *32 Degrees North*!"

Lisanne took a deep breath, offered up a quick prayer, and walked out onto the stage with her head held high.

Mike, Carlos and JP ripped out the opening bars of *Mercy* and Lisanne began to move, her eyes scanning the crowd until she found the face she was looking for.

He was standing with Vin, Kirsty, Rodney and Ryan, a huge

smile on his face.

Lisanne opened her mouth and began to sing.

She felt the music surge through her, making her strong and powerful. She was where she was meant to be—making music—sharing music with everyone there. Her voice soared, filling the dingy room, lifting the rafters and pouring into every corner.

Rodney's mouth dropped open, awe and wonder in every aspect of his expression.

The band worked through Imagine Dragon's *Radioactive*, were all over Gloriana's *Wild at Heart*, played Lisanne's two favorites of Daniel's songs, *On My Mind* and *Total Recall*, and totally nailed *Black Sheep* and *Man Like That*. All Lisanne needed was Gin Wigmore's tattoos.

Then came the moment Lisanne was most looking forward to, and most dreading.

"Thank you, guys! You're great!" yelled JP, the newly appointed spokesperson for the band. "We're going to try a new number tonight," he said, strapping on his acoustic guitar, "specially chosen by our amazing singer *Lisanne Maclaine!*"

She saw Daniel touching his ear and she knew, *she knew* that he'd be able to hear her.

> *I'm really close tonight.*
> *I feel like he's moving inside me.*
> *Lying in the dark*
> *I think that I'm beginning to know him.*
> *Let it go*
> *I'll be there when you call.*

Lisanne's amplified voice soared over the soft sounds of the acoustic guitar—a pure, clear note of love. Daniel's face had frozen, gazing up at her. Did he understand? Did he understand what she was trying to say to him?

> *And whenever I fall at your feet*
> *Won't you let your tears rain down on me*
> *Whenever I touch your slow turning pain.*

His eyes seemed glassy, but he hadn't moved.

> *Don't hide it from me now.*

> *There's something in the way*
> *that you're talking.*
> *Words don't sound right*
> *I hear them all moving inside you.*
> *You know*
> *I'll be waiting when you call.*

Lisanne poured every ounce of emotion, of respect and admiration and love into the song—everything she felt for the man standing in front of her.

> *The finger of blame has turned upon itself*
> *And I am more than willing to offer myself*
> *Do you want my presence or need my help?*
> *Who knows where that might lead.*
> *I fall.*
> *I fall at your feet.*
> *Fall at your feet.*

The crowd burst into applause, screaming and shouting their approval, feeling everything that Lisanne had shown them.

Daniel nodded his head, a blinding smile accentuating the tears in his eyes.

He raised his hands and sent the message that meant so much to both of them. The soundless words that expressed the road they had traveled together.

I hear you, he said with his hands. *I hear you.*

EPILOGUE – ONE YEAR LATER

Daniel was standing in the kitchen, leaning against the sink, an amused look on his face.

"Aren't you shocked or anything?" Lisanne said, her eyes almost bugging out.

"At which part?" he said, trying not to laugh. "That Harry has a girlfriend or that your mom caught them making out?"

"You knew!" she said, accusingly.

"Sure. He texted me … for tips."

"Ugh!" said Lisanne, "I don't want to know!"

He laughed. "Fine. Change of subject. What do you think of the new song?"

His expression was tense, as Lisanne looked up at him.

Even after all this time, his beauty still took her breath away. His perfect cheekbones, his full lips, the sparkle of mischief in his hazel eyes. His hair was longer than when she first met him, but that was to help disguise the shaved area where the transmitter attached, as well as his CI. He still wore his beanie most of the time but occasionally, in the summer, he'd go without it.

It had been the talk of the college when word got around that Daniel Colton, *the* Daniel Colton, was deaf. A lot of people hadn't believed it, and Shawna had laughed out loud at the notion, until Kirsty had a quiet word with her.

To Lisanne's disgust, Shawna finally dropped her pursuit of Daniel after the revelation. Kirsty didn't see much of her course mate after that. Vin wasn't the only one who was relieved.

Daniel hadn't changed his mind about not wanting people to know, but when he'd made it onto the football team with Vin at the end of his first year, some PR person in the administration had decided it would be good for the college to be seen as supporting equal opportunities.

Daniel had been furious, throwing a shit fit of epic proportions, and threatened to kick some asses, change colleges, or drop out altogether. Lisanne had persuaded him to do none of those things, and to simply suck it up.

It had been one hell of a fight, followed by a whole weekend of make up sex. *That* was something that hadn't changed—they fought like crazy, and their passion for each other still blazed. Rodney had gotten used to turning his music up loud—a lot.

When Lisanne had moved in with Daniel at the beginning of her second college year, her parents had resigned themselves to the fact that their only daughter was living in sin. Although the fact that the son of a preacher shared the house had given them some peace of mind—until Reverend Dubois had informed them that his son was gay.

They hadn't had much to say after that.

Zef had been sent down for seven years, although it was possible he'd get out in five, and was currently residing in the State Prison.

He'd been charged with intent to supply and distribute, which was a felony offense. The police had timed their raid badly—from their point of view—finding Zef with less than 10 pounds of 'product'. The sentence was two to 15 years in prison for a meth possession conviction, so both brothers knew he'd been lucky—very lucky. If he'd had the usual amount of drugs stored at the house, it would have been a lot worse. Zef had also consistently refused to name his supplier, on the grounds that he was more scared of them than of the police. And although he didn't explain further, he didn't want the potential fallout of naming names to come back to bite his little brother—especially as he wasn't there to protect him anymore.

Daniel saw Zef once a month and although he'd asked

Lisanne to visit with him, so far she'd refused. He was confident that he'd break her down eventually.

His own case had been dropped due to Zef's insistence that the resin dope was his, and the fact that Daniel had continued to deny knowing about anything.

Roy had disappeared, but Zef had heard on the prison grapevine that he'd gotten into some shit in Virginia. Nobody seemed to know the details and cared less, except perhaps Lisanne, who still had a soft spot for the man mountain.

They saw Cori occasionally, although now she was in DC at Gallaudet, it was only during vacations. It had taken a while, but she'd accepted Daniel's choice in the end. She'd also made the decision to work on her own communication with hearing people, and was attending a speech therapy class. But she still felt that ASL was her first language.

The implant seemed to have settled to a reasonable level. On the down side, Daniel still couldn't use a telephone, but he sometimes watched TV without the subtitles, although he found it tiring. When he'd started the CI tuning sessions, Dr. Devallis had insisted that Daniel shouldn't use TV subtitles, on the grounds that this would help train him to use his device properly. Lisanne reminded Daniel of that fact constantly. Sometimes he did as she suggested. But only sometimes. On the plus side, he'd been to an ordinary movie for the first time in four years. True, it was a shoot 'em up sort of film with minimal dialog, but it had made him happy.

It had made Kirsty happy, too, because Vin had gone to the movie without her. This left Kirsty to enjoy a girly evening in with Lisanne and Rodney.

But the best thing, the absolute best thing, was that Daniel found he could hear well enough to play the guitar. His weekend work in the auto repair shop had earned him enough money to buy a decent instrument—not as good as the Martin that he'd lost, but good enough. He couldn't play in the band or listen to amplified music—there were too many complexities of sound for him to handle—but he could play for Lisanne. And he could write songs again.

This had been huge for both of them, and it gave them hope for the future. Maybe their life *could* be in music. *32° North* had developed a solid following locally. None of them dared suggest it could be more—that was too much like tempting fate—but individually, they hoped.

For Daniel most of all, neither the limitations of the past, nor fear of the future held him back.

"Yeah, it's a great song," Lisanne said, enthusiastically. "I love it! It'll fit in with the longer set we play really well." She glanced across at Daniel and couldn't help smiling when she saw the tattoo on the inside of his left wrist that had the letters 'LA' surrounded by stars. "And the lyrics in the second verse were just beaut … hey! I'm not going to talk to you if you're not interested."

"I am, baby doll," he said, as he gazed out of the window, "because that's…"

CRASH!

Daniel jumped as Lisanne knocked over her coffee mug, the dark liquid dripping across the table and onto the floor.

She was staring at him, open mouthed.

"What the fuck?"

"You were listening," she said.

"Yeah? So?"

"Daniel, you were listening! You weren't looking at me! You were *just* listening!"

He looked up slowly and gazed at her in wonder.

"You heard me!" she whispered.

He closed his eyes and blinked several times. When he looked at her again, his eyes were blazing.

"I heard you. Oh, God, I heard you." His head dropped to his chest and he blew out a shaky breath. "I love you, baby doll. So much."

THE END

NOTE FROM THE AUTHOR

The title of this book is taken from the well known phrase coined by Lady Caroline Lamb. She described her lover, the poet Lord Byron, with the words, 'Mad, bad and dangerous to know'.

The following lines are taken from Bryon's poem 'The Corsair', but I think they describe Daniel at the start of this story.

> *That man of loneliness and mystery,*
> *Scarce seen to smile, and seldom heard to sigh.*

**HARVEY
BERRICK**
PUBLISHING

Don't forget to look for bonus chapters **www.janeharveyberrick.com**

Coming Soon!

At Your Beck & Call

Hallen Jansen has it all. At 28, he has a flashy car, a great apartment, and a job he's good at and that he loves—as an escort—working at your beck and call.

His life is easy, with no emotions or attachments slowing him down—choosing to keep moving, always running from the past.

But when a new client awakens unfamiliar feelings, all bets are off. Can he convince a recently divorced woman twenty years older to trust men again—to trust him? Can Hallen trust himself not to screw things up?

Surrounded by people who choose to judge them, will they make their relationship a reality, or is it heartbreak for both?

Not all services are professional.

Dazzled

Miles Stevens is a jobbing actor in London when he stumbles into the role of a lifetime.

Hollywood claims him as one of their own and so begins his journey through the parties, premieres, agents and leading ladies—and everyone wants something from him. His best friend Clare is determined that they'll have to go through her to get it.

Will appeal to readers of 'Wallbanger' and 'Love Unscripted'.

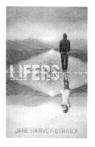

Lifers

After eight years in prison, twenty-four year old Jordan Kane is the man everyone loves to hate.

Forced to return to his hometown while on parole, Jordan soon learns that this small town hasn't changed since he was sent away. He is the local pariah, shunned by everyone, including his own parents. But their hatred of him doesn't even come close to the loathing he feels every time he looks in the mirror.

Working odd jobs for the preacher lady, Jordan bides his time before he can leave this backwards town. But can time or distance erase the pain of living?

Torrey Delaney is new in town, and certainly doesn't behave in a way the locals believe a preacher's daughter should. Her reputation for casual hook-ups and meaningless sex quickly spreads. And that's on top of her budding friendship with the hardened ex-con handyman—the good Reverend is less than thrilled with her estranged daughter's path.

As friendship forms, can two damaged people who are afraid to love take their relationship to the next level? Can Torrey live with Jordan's demons, and can Jordan break through Torrey's walls? With the disapproval of a small town weighing heavily on them, they struggle to find their place in the world. Can they battle the odds, or will their world be viciously shattered?

Is love a life sentence?

The Education of Sebastian

A friendship between the lost and lonely Caroline, and the unhappy Sebastian, leads to an illicit love that threatens them both.

"This book made my heart RACE. It was a captivating story of forbidden love. I'm still recovering from the huge cliffhanger ending and most definitely planning to go straight on to book #2." Aestas Bookblog

The Education of Caroline

Ten years after their first affair, Sebastian and Caroline meet again: this time in very different circumstances, against the background of the war in Afghanistan. Now a successful journalist, Caroline meets US Marine Sebastian Hunter—can old passions be rekindled?

The concluding story of 'The Education of Sebastian'.

"Ohhh I had so much anticipation going into this one!! After the brutal cliffhanger at the end of **book one** *that had my heart in knots and my heart in my throat I just NEEDED more!"* Aestas Bookblog

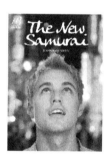

The New Samurai

Teaching in an inner city school in London is hard enough, but when Sam loses his job and his domineering girlfriend dumps him on Valentine's Day, he decides to start again somewhere new … in Japan. It's not long before his 'no women' rule is under attack.

Sexy and funny, this book will appeal to fans of 'One Day'.

Expo$ure

What would you do if you found out a really, really important secret? What would you do if people were prepared to kill to stop you revealing this secret? And what would you do if the secret was held by the US government?

A thriller that will appeal to readers of 'The Ghost'.

The Dark Detective: Venator

At 20 years old, Max Darke finds himself in sole charge of the Metropolitan Police Demon Division in London. It's not a job for the faint hearted and some days, work is Hell.

For fantasy readers.

40326461R00300

Made in the USA
Charleston, SC
31 March 2015